C000300595

Andy Livingstone was born on New Year's Day in 1968 and grew up with an enthusiastic passion for sport (particularly football) and reading. An asthmatic childhood meant that he spent more time participating in the latter than the former and an early childhood encounter with *The Hobbit* awakened a love of epic and heroic fantasy that has never let him go. He is a press officer and former journalist and lives in Lanarkshire, Scotland, with his wife, Valerie, and two teenage sons, Adam and Nathan. He also has four adult stepchildren, Martyn, Jonathon, Melissa and Nicolas, and four grand-bundles-of-energy: Joshua, Riah, Jayden and Ashton. He can be found on Twitter @markethaven and at his website, www.andylivingstone.com

Also by Andy Livingstone

The Seeds of Destiny
Hero Born

Hero Grown

ANDY LIVINGSTONE

Book Two of The Seeds of Destiny Trilogy

HARPER
Voyager

Harper*Voyager*
An imprint of HarperCollins*Publishers* Ltd
1 London Bridge Street
London SE1 9GF

www.harpervoyagerbooks.co.uk

This Paperback Original 2016

First published in Great Britain in ebook format by Harper*Voyager* 2016

A catalogue record for this book
is available from the British Library

ISBN: 978-0-00-816025-8

For Valerie

Prologue

'Peacetime has no need for heroes.'

The storyteller swept his arm towards the doorway far above, the evening light of a high-summer evening drifting in a soft haze into the village's meeting hall. Every face packed into the concentric circles of benches rising from his central stage to ground level high above turned to follow his gesture.

'Listen to the sound of peace. Hear the sounds of the insects, the birds, the children, the mill wheel turning and the river that drives it. Were this a short while ago, you would have the laughter of casual conversation, the clash of the smith and the shouts of workers and lowing of cattle in the fields.

'Nowhere are the sounds of war: the screams, the whispers of fear, the moans of terror, the shouts of hate, the silence of despair.

'The sound of peace is the sound of nature and children, of neighbours and daily life. The sound of war is death.

'But we have peace. So we need no heroes.'

His piercing gaze swept the benches, every pair of eyes feeling that they locked with his.

'Or do we?

'Do you know no ships are beaching on the nearest shore? Or that men are not marching this way already? Or that weapons are not, even now, drawn in eager hands in the very woods that skirt your homes? Or even at that door above you now?'

A nervous shifting shuffled around the hall. A smile of reassurance danced across his lips. 'They are not. But it is well to remember that they might.

'War rarely creeps into life. Not for the ordinary people. Kings and generals may see its approach from afar, or they may not, but for the folk of the first village, or town, or city, or trade convoy, or ship that is attacked, it begins in the blink of an eye, the strike of an arrow, the flash of a blade. In an instant, war has arrived.

'That village, or town, or ship may not have a hero. But war is a monster with an appetite that is as voracious as it is insatiable. It feeds and grows faster than you can imagine, and without our heroes, we will be devoured. But where are our heroes, if in peace we had not need of them? From where will they come to fight our cause, to breed hope and inspiration?

'We must always have heroes. But we see them only when life is at its worst.'

A long moment passed. With a smile, this time for himself, the storyteller reflected on the irony that, in peace, tales of war and blood were relished, while soldiers in the lull between horrors craved stories of simple peaceful life, of harvests and weddings and trips to the market.

2

He crouched, drawing their attention to him as if he pulled in their minds on a thousand cords.

'Last night, you heard how a hero was born. Now listen to how he grew.'

Chapter 1

A soft noise behind was all that it took for him to be on his feet and turn, knife in hand. He only hoped that it was not apparent that his feet took four small steps before he found his balance, nor that his fingers had fumbled in grasping the hilt, nor that his eyes were squinting to adjust from the glare of the view from the window to the shadow of his chambers.

The desert-dry voice, now familiar, started as she moved closer, a tray with a ewer of iced water and two fine goblets borne before her in place of an instrument of assassination.

'Your steadiness may waver, you may flounder for your weapon, and your eyes may be straining, but they are all better than when I first saw you here. Let us hope, however, that your dagger is sharper than your reactions, and your mind is sharper than both.'

'If they were half as sharp as your tongue, crone, I would be ruling the world.' He sank into his chair, slipping the blade back down the side of the cushion, but this time ensuring that the hilt protruded a little more than it had before.

She poured water for him and he took it in silence. She filled the other goblet for herself, and he let her do so. She could do so without rebuke on this occasion, he resolved. Just as he resolved every afternoon at this time.

She stared with him across the training fields to the dusty plains beyond, two pairs of eyes on the same scene but neither mind seeing it. 'You could.'

'What?' Though he knew.

'Rule again.'

'A man cannot win a duel without the right strategy to exploit his opponent, the right horse to bear him, the right armour to defend him and the right blade to strike the killing blow.'

Her voice was like the dry sandy wind that blew in from the desert. 'Your mind is your strategy, your desire will carry you, their blinding contempt will be your armour.'

'And the sword? This is no ordinary duel, it will be a fight like no other, and to the victor will come the Empire. It will need a blade the like of which we have never seen. What of it?'

'Fear not, child of fate.' Old fingers reached out and gently touched his arm. 'He is here.'

****

The ship cleared the headland, bringing their first glimpse of the city as they began to swing through the entrance of the harbour.

Brann glanced to his right, shorewards, and almost stopped rowing in astonishment. The harbour itself would have been classed a lake in his land, but even it was dwarfed by the city beyond. White buildings reflected the glaring

6

early morning sun over an area larger than he had ever seen covered by man's constructions, until his eyes wandered and saw the built-up scene replicated time and time again to the limits of his gaze. Scattered like carelessly discarded jewellery, occasional buildings had golden-clad roofs amongst the red of the majority, giving the same effect, as the ship moved their viewpoint, as the sun did when it dropped a thousand flashes on the surface of the sea.

He was jolted from his astonishment by Gerens's elbow. 'Just because you haven't seen the Jewel of the Empire before, it doesn't mean you can leave the rowing to us.'

Grakk turned slightly without missing a stroke to speak over his shoulder. 'If you can look and row, young untravelled boys, you should take the opportunity. There is no better view of the largest city in the world than from here, other than from the Royal Palace itself, and you are unlikely to be afforded the latter perspective.'

Cannick strode down the aisle, his boots loud on the wooden planks even above the sound of a galley in full rowing action, accompanied by a familiar warrior.

'Brann, to the Captain, after you've had a scrub. Galen will take your place for the last stretch, now that we are all free men and friends.'

Galen grinned through his shaggy beard. 'Well, we're all free men. Let's not get too hasty with the rest of it.'

As Cannick moved back up the aisle, Hakon managed to stretch a long leg and nudge Grakk in the back. 'Looks like you were wrong, oh infallible wise one. One of us seems likely to be treated to that other perspective you were talking about.'

Grakk responded by adroitly tripping Brann as he walked past. 'You still need to work on your awareness of potential danger, I see,' he observed pleasantly.

As the ship skimmed across the calm of the harbour towards long stone piers that stretched from the shore like tentacles reaching for any craft that came close, Brann washed for the first time since they had stopped to resupply the previous week. A large tub had been filled with fresh water near the stern and he quickly stripped and scrubbed himself, the practicalities of three months at sea having robbed him of his aversion both to public nudity and cold water, neither of which appeared to be an issue among Einarr's people in any case.

The Captain was leaning, his back to the door, over a sea of papers strewn across his table when Brann was shown into his cabin. He waved a hand at clothes laid on the bed without turning.

'You'll need those,' he said distantly, staring at a sheet of notes. As Brann moved across the room, however, he straightened and turned, running both hands up his face and through his hair. 'Apologies,' he sighed. 'If there's one thing I hate more than being polite on diplomatic missions to pompous arses, it's the studying you have to do beforehand.'

He got to the bed before Brann and stopped him, holding him at arm's length to observe him. 'You've grown,' he said. 'Up and across the way. It should help you swing a sword a bit more easily, but hopefully you have not outgrown these clothes. You're still undersized, though, so they probably will fit.'

Brann smiled. 'I would think most people are undersized compared with anyone from your land.'

The Captain's eyes narrowed with amusement. 'I also think most people would find you undersized. Not that they would think that a dwarf had stepped from the mines of

8

the fables, mind you, you're just not as tall as some.' He cocked his head to the side and stepped back to examine Brann from further back. 'No, definitely not a dwarf.' He frowned. 'I think.'

Brann laughed this time. 'I have missed our ego-boosting chats.'

Einarr grunted. 'Well, I haven't missed having a page. No offence intended, but I work better on my own. Too many years working for a living, I suppose. But now, as you'll have guessed, I have need of a page once more.'

Brann executed a courtly bow. A very poor courtly bow, he knew, but his experience of court etiquette was non-existent. 'At your service, my lord.'

The Captain sighed and sat on the bed. 'You don't have to be, you know. You are a free man now. I can't order you to do anything other than your duties as a member of the crew of the *Blue Dragon*. I'm asking if you'll do it.'

'Do I have a choice?'

'Truthfully?'

'Yes.'

'No.'

Brann grinned. 'Just as well I was going to say yes, then.'

He started to get changed into the page's clothing. While typical of anything that came out of Halveka in that the garments were practical and hard-wearing, still they were of a finer material and cut than he was accustomed to and the feel of them helped his head adjust to his more elevated role.

'So,' he grunted as he stretched to pull his shoulders into a tunic that seemed slightly tighter than the last time he had worn it, 'have you met these pompous arses before? Is that how you know what they are like?'

'Not these particular arses. My previous visits here were as the captain of a contracted ship or, in earlier years, fighting for whatever cause was looking to buy military might. The sort of person I was then didn't tend to be received in the same royal chambers as a diplomatic envoy. But I know their like. And I know this city, and this empire. You will recognise the truth of my description soon enough.'

Brann shrugged. 'They can be what they like. You make a page's role easy, whatever anyone is like: keep my mouth shut, do what I'm told and look respectful.'

The Captain nodded seriously as the slightest of jolts in the ship's motion told them that Cannick had manoeuvred it into its berth with his familiar skill. 'I pronounce your lessons in pagery to be complete.' He swept the papers into a trunk and fixed his clothes, buckling on a finely tooled sword. 'Right, let us introduce ourselves to Sagia.'

From the moment they stepped from the gangplank, Brann felt the alien nature of a culture far removed from anything he had known. Disorientated, as if he had entered a different world, he scarcely noticed Konall, Hakon and two imposing warriors joining them and Einarr motioning to Grakk to approach as Cannick started to organise the unloading of the cargo. He sucked in a deep breath to try to gather his thoughts and drag his attention back to his surroundings.

Einarr placed a hand on Grakk's shoulder. 'I know I owe you a debt already, for the part you played in saving my nephew if for nothing else, and I know you have earned as much time in the taverns as the rest of the crew, but as a native of a part of this empire you are the closest thing we have to expert local knowledge. I would value your presence if you would accompany us.'

Grakk bowed his head, the sun gleaming on the intricate tattoos covering his smooth scalp. 'It is in the nature of my people to gather knowledge and share it with those deemed worthy. Besides, I do not partake of intoxicating substances by choice, so it will be a diversion of interest. It may also prove useful in providing an extra member of your party who is aware of your young page's propensity for inadvertently finding himself in trouble.'

Einarr clapped him on the shoulder in acknowledgement and appreciation. 'Your last point is probably the most relevant.'

An official in a plain white robe was waiting for them where the pier met the dockside, a flat satchel hanging at his hip and a broad hat on his head. As they drew closer, Brann was able to see the way a broad length of cloth had been wound, more draped, around his body and over his shoulders to leave his arms free and to ensure that his body, while covered from head to foot, was loosely clad. Already his own clothing was feeling heavy and stifling and the very air, now bereft of the breeze of open water, was hot and hard to draw in, like the first gasping breath when he had opened his mother's bread oven and been hit by the blast. The unexpected memory of home stabbed through him and he stumbled.

Konall glanced at him in enquiry and Brann pointed to the ground. 'Slipped on a loose stone.' His voice was laboured as he felt the effort of breathing.

'No surprise there.' The tall boy appeared as unperturbed as ever, his manner oblivious to the heat despite the hair that was plastered to his face by the sweat that was creeping from every pore.

'Do you not feel the heat?' Brann was incredulous. 'Your land is even colder than mine.'

11

Konall looked at him in bemusement. 'Even our coldest areas have warm days. I have actually seen the sun before, you know. It is the same sun. This is just hotter, for longer. We cannot change it. You deal with it or place yourself at a disadvantage, like all in life.'

'I just don't know how anyone could function in this,' Brann grumbled. 'It's all right for you, your head is at a higher altitude where it's obviously cooler. Every movement is an effort down here.'

Konall snorted. 'Grow up.'

'I'd love to.'

'I didn't mean physically.'

They were interrupted by Einarr. 'You will get used to it in a day or so, unlikely as your head will be telling you that it could be. But enough of the weather chatter.' He turned, halting the group out of earshot of the waiting man. 'Grakk, the welcoming figure on the dock. What can you tell me?'

'We are honoured guests,' the tribesman said, his soft tone as even and measured as ever. 'He is a slave, hence the chain around his neck, though it is a more slender version and more golden than the normal heavy iron chains of the general slave population. Here, power is everything; the most precious commodity is knowledge and the most powerful men are those who use their knowledge with the greatest skill. Their obsession is records. Everything is recorded, all is preserved in paper and ink, and the guardians of this, those who gather, record, store, guard and, in some cases, advise on the records are the Scribes, the slaves prized above all others. They are recognised by their satchels, as much a symbol of their office as a practicality, carrying paper, ink and quill, for a Scribe must always be ready to record what must be recorded.'

Konall frowned. 'They place all this trust in a slave? Not in the loyalty of a free man?'

'It is safer in the hands of a slave, young lord. Where you live, the loyalty of a free man, once given, is unquestioned and any loss of trust in that is considered worse than death. Here, every free man lives in competition with every other. Even the purchase of a loaf is a contest to be won. Accordingly, words are to be used, twisted, broken, all in the strategy of outmanoeuvring and winning. Trust is naive and dull-witted. Slaves, however, are ruled by total obedience and cannot leave to serve another unless their master wills it, and so their words are as letters carved in stone and their ambition serves only to enhance their owner's standing or success.'

Konall was still unhappy. 'Regardless, they send a slave to meet the son of a Warlord of Halveka. The insult is clear.'

Grakk shook his head. 'That is what they do, young lord. Would you own a ship but travel here by swimming? They will greet Lord Einarr in the appropriate setting. The honour here is clear: a Scribe is the ultimate level of slave – in fact many consider themselves superior to any free men below the level of the nobility and certainly they have more influence in many ways. Note the second golden chain, the one carrying his satchel: it denotes that he has reached the highest tier of his class. What is more, the royal seal burnt into the leather of the satchel itself tells us that, in all probability, he is owned by a prince, and has his ear.'

Einarr had heard enough. 'Thank you, Grakk. Let us meet this influential slave.'

The tall Scribe swept his hat to his chest and greeted them with a long inclination of his head that revealed intricate tattoos on his shiny pate of a style similar to Grakk's and which drew the eye of everyone present. As he raised his head, his eyes fixed on Grakk, but his gaze, emotionless almost to the extent of haughtiness, smoothly settled on Einarr. His hat still pressed to his chest, he spoke in a voice as lacking in expression as his face.

'Lord Einarr of Yngvarrsharn, may I express the welcome of my master, of his brothers in rule and of the great city of Sagia that sits at the heart of ul-Taratac, the greatest empire the civilised world has witnessed or ever will. If it is your pleasure, I will direct you to your transport to the palace, which awaits just a few paces from this dock.'

'Thank you,' Einarr said. 'And your name is?'

'I am merely a conduit for my master's words. My name is not important.'

'It is to me. Hence my question.' The lord's voice was calm, but still managed to exude menace.

'Of course, noble sir. My master calls me Scribe.'

Konall's face went white and he stepped towards the slave, whose face had not flickered into a single expression all the while. Without taking his eyes from the man, Einarr shot out his arm and halted his cousin with a hand on his chest. His voice was soft, almost amiable. 'That is a most interesting fact about your master. But I did not ask what he chooses to call you. I asked your name. And, as a slave being asked a question by a free man, you are obliged to answer.'

Though his face remained frozen, a flush started to creep into the Scribe's cheeks. He turned his head slowly to look at Grakk. 'You could ask your own slave. He would be able to furnish the answer.'

Brann glanced at Grakk but the wiry tribesman was impassive.

14

'I have no slaves. He is a free man.' Before he could control himself, the Scribe's eyes widened in surprise before settling quickly back to his frozen mask. Einarr continued, his voice as reasonable as if he were discussing the sailing conditions for a pleasure cruise. 'Unlike you. And I asked *you*. Could I make it clearer, or do I have to interrupt my journey to the palace with a visit to the Guild of Slavers to enquire about the etiquette of a conversation between a free man and a slave? And the consequences of breaching the etiquette? I am curious as to your name. The one your mother bestowed upon you.'

The man hesitated a long moment, his head bowed and his jaw clenching and moving as he fought to maintain control. He lifted his eyes to meet Einarr's once more, and said coldly, 'Narut.'

Einarr smiled. 'Thank you, Narut. Now let us go find this transport of yours.'

He strode past the Scribe and the others followed. As Hakon passed, he clapped the Scribe heartily on the shoulder. 'Well done, Narut. I knew you could do it. Now we can all be friends.' Beaming, he patted the man's shoulder again with enthusiasm. 'I'm proud of you.'

By the time the startled Scribe had regained his composure, the group was waiting further up the dock. Einarr cocked his head to one side and raised his eyebrows. Brann stifled a giggle. 'Narut?' Einarr's tone was concerned.

'Of course, noble sir.' The man hurried to lead them to a wide boulevard leading directly away from the dockside where two wheel-less carriages sat, with large slaves waiting unmoving beside them.

Grakk moved beside Brann. 'Try not to look so confused, young fellow. They will interpret it as weakness. These

15

carriages have people for wheels. We enter, they lift and carry, they set down, we alight. It is how people of wealth and rank travel about this city.'

Brann frowned. 'Why don't they just walk? Can't they?'

'When people choose not to do something that they could do and most people must do, some interpret that as power.'

'I interpret it as stupidity. I'd rather walk.'

'You may be right, but there are many things done by people in all societies to impress each other that could be interpreted as such. On this occasion, however, walking when transport has been provided by the highest of the high would be deemed an insult. And also, to speak on equal terms with the rulers, Lord Einarr must act as they would expect a noble to act.'

Konall frowned. 'Insult or not, should we not be making all haste to reach the Emperor with our news? It is the reason we have travelled here, cousin, and to be carried by ambling slaves would not befit the urgency of our mission.'

Einarr wiped his sleeve across his glistening brow and laid a reassuring hand on the younger man's shoulder. 'We are seeking audience with the most powerful man alive, and I have seen kings kick their heels for a week or more while they await that privilege. The Emperor does not know the importance of our message, or we would not need to bring it. To be admitted to his court the day we arrive may, I can only guess, stem from his curiosity or may just be our good fortune but, whatever the reason, we must fret not at the pace of our final approach but be thankful for the day it is taking place.' He smiled. 'And, believe me, these slaves do not amble.'

He stopped his party. 'I'll take my cousin and my page with me.' He turned to the Scribe. 'Narut, will you be travelling with us?'

16

He coloured at the use of his name in front of the carriage bearers, but his tone was as haughty as ever. 'I shall lead the way afoot. A mere slave does not raise his station above that of other slaves.'

Hakon snorted. 'If he actually believes that, I'm a mermaid.'

'Good,' said Einarr. 'That leaves room for my local expert.' He looked over to Hakon and the two guards. 'You three can spread yourselves about the second one, but given the size of you, it's probably for the best.'

They approached what was effectively a wooden box – albeit an ornately crafted wooden box – filled with cushions and with long handles protruding fore and aft to enable it to be lifted. A slender pole at each corner supported a canopy that afforded them protection from the sun's glare if not from its heat, and a slave moved to open a door in the side. Einarr waved him away with a smile and instead stepped over the low side and seated himself facing forward. Konall took his place beside him, leaving the opposite space for the other two. The others were already lounging in the other carriage, grinning like small boys. Brann could understand Einarr's choice in the two warriors he had brought: Magnus, wiry and quick, and tall Torstein were as skilled with their weapons as any of the other Northmen, but both were also considered enough of thought to carry themselves appropriately in any company. And, no mean accomplishment, they were almost as relentless in their good cheer as Hakon, so while the news they bore was grim, the mood in the party was lifted. Typical of his people, Einarr was practical in his outlook, and it achieved nothing to look constantly at the world through eyes fogged by the gloom of foreboding.

At a nod from the Scribe, the slaves hoisted them aloft,

resting the handles on their broad shoulders. Smooth as the action was, Brann grabbed at the side, clearly uncomfortable and disconcerted.

Konall almost smiled. 'Try not to fall out. It would probably cost a slave his life.'

Brann wasn't amused. 'I wouldn't put it past you to push me, just for the entertainment.'

The tall boy pushed his sweat-soaked hair away from his brow as the slaves set off at a fast trot. 'Talking of entertainment, cousin, I couldn't help but notice you enjoying yourself baiting that Scribe.'

His elbow resting on the broad wooden rail at the side of the carriage, Einarr shrugged slightly. 'I hate pompous arseholes. He is just the first of many we will meet. Unfortunately, I am denied by diplomatic necessity the chance to bait the rest of them, so I take the chance when I can.'

'Some would call that bullying, cousin.'

'Given his attitude, others would call it a moral obligation.'

Konall looked thoughtful. 'I suppose he does repress his emotions, somewhat. To a ridiculous extent, in fact.'

Grakk coughed and Einarr looked across just in time to stop Brann's words with a stare. 'Anyway, what is more important is what Grakk can tell us.'

Grakk grew serious. 'You will see that the buildings here are several stories high and closely built, from the necessity of the area. The city started as a small port but the large and deep natural harbour attracted trade enough for it to grow quickly. With residential accommodation surrounding the original dock buildings and roadways wide to facilitate large amounts of traffic from warehouse to docks and docks to the great selling halls, there was little room to expand further inland, so once they had spread right across the harbour edge they built upwards instead. As we progress, we will enter more and more affluent areas, where the houses become bigger and with more space around them, and subsequently where the houses become villas and the space around becomes space within, for they are built to enclose central areas where nature is brought into the stone of the city.

'This is not a city planned for defence, such as in your land, Lord, nor is it,' he nodded at Brann, 'a random arrangement that has grown according to opportunity and fancy, as often is the case where you were born. This is a city planned by wealth, prosperity, trade and social standing. Everything here is meticulous: the colour of the buildings to reflect the heat of the sun, the width of each road for its purpose, the area where each class lives according to purpose and logical placement for that purpose. For example, bakers near to the grain-storage houses, tanners near the beast pens and leatherworkers near to them. They love thinking everything out, hence the prominence of the Scribes. Even their army is created and operated with pre-planned purpose in every aspect: every free man must learn a trade from their fifteenth winter to their twentieth, and then serve the following five years as soldiers. Those proving to have most military value are retained as leaders and the rest return to their trade unless they choose to remain as soldiers. Those leaders help to train those who come after. They are drilled to work as one, to fight in formation, to fight identically, with identical weapons, to operate on the battlefield according to commands and not individual thought.'

Konall was confused. 'Then they have no great warriors? No feats of valour and legend?'

Grakk smiled, 'They do not, young lord, although they do have the tournament field where young nobles can prove their skill. No, they do not have great warriors. But they do have an empire.'

Einarr nodded, thoughtfully. 'That's interesting, Grakk, many thanks. But now I must think on this, if you don't mind.'

Grakk looked at him. 'It is the prerogative of a lord that my minding is immaterial.'

Einarr's eyes narrowed in amusement. 'But it is good sense for a lord to mind whether you mind or not, if I would like to increase my chances of the fullest of information in the future.'

'Your logic is sound,' Grakk acknowledged. 'And I do not mind.'

Einarr nodded and they rode in silence, and Brann's eyes drank in a world that could never have been successfully described to him had he not beheld it at first hand. Strange as the trade area around the docks had seemed, still the mix of nationalities bustling around the streets had lent it a recognisable feel and diluted the air of unreality. Here, though, in the heart of pure Sagia, everything was of this land and nothing of his own. Overwhelmed by the unfamiliar, he seemed to be floating through a dream.

Einarr's voice cut so suddenly that he jumped, something that nearly amused Konall.

'Pardon me, Grakk, but you covered but one aspect of the two that I had in mind.'

'Of course, lord. You would know of the rulers. The court and the nobility. They are...'

The lord held up a hand. 'Thank you, but no. I have knowledge of their court workings more than enough from the papers and documents I had to endure on the voyage. I would know of your friend Narut. You and he would seem acquainted beyond just a similar penchant for scalp decoration.'

There was a long silence, which served not only to make real the tension that Einarr's words had created but also to let Brann realise that he had become accustomed to the awkward sensation of being carried shoulder-height in a box.

With hard eyes, Grakk said, 'I have those few who I would consider friends but he is not, nor ever has been, counted among them.'

'But you know him.' It was a statement, not a question.

Grakk nodded. 'I do.'

'And your time with him is not remembered fondly.'

'There was wrongdoing.'

'By you or by him?'

Grakk's piercing eyes gazed at the passing buildings, but appeared to see scenes distant in location and time. 'By both. But though he has position, he is a slave and I now am not. So I cannot bear animosity towards one whose life has led him to greater suffering than mine has.'

'That's very noble of you, but that is what fate decreed for him and I am less interested in prying into your personal differences and more in the nature of the man. If he has the ear of a member of the royal family, I would know what he is like and if he can be trusted.'

Grakk's head snapped to look right into the eyes of Einarr. 'Lord, if there is one thing you remember always when you are in this city, it is that few you will meet can be trusted.

21

I can only speak of the man I knew many years ago, but then he was arrogant, unfeeling and remorseless, and just as punctilious as a Sagian. He may have changed his nature, but I can imagine nothing in the Sagian way of life that would not encourage those traits rather than mollify them, which has in all likelihood been behind his rise to his current position. Be that as it may, his lack of emotion would ensure that he did nothing from a position of spite, anger or vengeance. Even when he did wrong, he always believed he was doing what was right. He is a man of obsessive duty, and probably more at home here than in the place of his birth, despite his slavery.'

A sound of disdain came from Einarr. 'Arrogant, unfeeling, remorseless and punctilious? He has indeed found his spiritual home.'

Konall looked at him appraisingly. 'You don't much like these people, do you?'

Einarr sighed. 'The ordinary people are fine, much like anywhere you will go. But my experience of anyone in authority here has not been good. I'm sure there will be exceptions, but I have not found them any time I have visited. And the higher the rank, the worse it tends to get.'

Brann groaned. 'And we are about to meet the highest rank there is.'

'It may be imminent.' Konall pointed over Brann's shoulder, and he turned to see a gateway taller and broader than he could have imagined possible, leaving the two pairs of stock-still guards looking as large as the toy warriors his grandfather had whittled for him what seemed like a lifetime ago. Intricate geometric shapes were carved with consummate care and skill into the stone that framed the opening, and just craning his head to squint at the lintel twice as high above them as the top of the *Blue Dragon*'s mast made Brann's head swim.

'Imminent may be a premature expression, young lord,' said Grakk. 'The castle, and the palace within, are what you might term extensive.'

Brann soon learnt how far the definition of the word 'extensive' could stretch. The massive wooden doors of the gate – bound for strength in metal unknown, for they were clad in more sheet gold than several *Blue Dragons* could carry – lay open, with the grim eyes and naked blades of the four guards enough to discourage entry by any but those already permitted. A tunnel, arched even higher than the gateway, stretched twice the length of their ship, testifying to the thickness of the walls. It is a mighty structure indeed, Brann mused, that you measure in terms of a ship. If the city had been built for trade, the citadel had quite obviously been built for war.

Grakk leant over to him. 'And this is just the beginning, young Brann.'

It was. They passed through four curtain walls in all, each one higher than the last. Einarr was appreciative. 'You would lose an entire army before you came face to face with a defender,' he murmured.

Opulence and pleasure were everywhere, too, however. Between each pair of walls, ornate gardens were a picture of nature with shrubbery, winding streams and carefully arranged rocks. The noise and bustle of the city streets soon seemed distant as the occasional figure could be glimpsed strolling or resting in the calm.

A foot nudged Brann's knee. 'Don't be misled by the look of it, mill boy,' Konall said. 'There is not a bush above knee height and the walls are high. This is a killing zone as much as the streets of our towns.'

Brann's eyes narrowed as he looked around with new perspective. 'Of course, there is no cover. And what bushes there are would impede movement, as would the streams. In a climate as dry as this, the shrubbery would also burn easily, I would think.' He looked up. 'And the battlements are on the inside of the walls as well as the outer side, so defenders on both walls are protected from below as they send down arrows, spears and anything else on the attackers from behind as well as in front. And,' he finished triumphantly, 'each inner wall is higher than the outer, so if a wall is taken, the height renders those on the outer one vulnerable to those on the inner one.' He beamed proudly.

Einarr turned a hard stare at him. 'I'm glad to see you are thinking again at last, rather than being lost in wonder. We may be here on a friendly visit, but never relax your guard.'

Made surly by his deflated ego, Brann stared to the side. 'It seems we cannot relax our guard anywhere these days,' he grumbled.

'Correct.' Einarr's tone was hard. 'Be made wary by the unfamiliar, not distracted.'

The instruction was hard to follow, though. As they passed through the fourth wall, which had already dumbfounded the senses with a height and thickness that surpassed the unimaginable dimensions of the three that had preceded it, the vista opened to reveal row upon row of villas that rivalled those of the most affluent area they had seen before entering the citadel. Beyond them, a massive keep rose like the bluffs of a great cliff, shining as white as the curtain walls, the houses and every other vertical surface they had passed.

Despite Einarr's warning still hanging in the air, the words were out of Brann before he knew they were coming. 'It's like a whole town within a city,' he gasped.

Einarr sighed, and Grakk nudged Brann in amusement. 'These buildings furthest from the keep are the servants' quarters, while the more affluent properties belong to nobles of the highest order who are permitted to have a second home close to the centre of power.' He seemed to particularly enjoy the boy's desperate attempts not to react.

The Scribe led them to a wide and intricately decorated wooden ramp that rose at a shallow gradient and doubled back on itself over and over until it reached a yawning doorway around two-thirds of the way up the front of the keep. A few levels above the door, the wall facing them dropped back to form a massive terrace the full width of the building.

'We have roads of this shape cut into our mountains,' mused Einarr. He looked at Grakk. 'I assume this will be for defence? They can burn it easily if they want to cut off this entrance. But what is the reason, when these lower doorways exist?' He indicated a series of wide entrances at ground level.

'The ground-level portals give access for the supplies and serving-slaves in peacetime,' Grakk explained. 'The lower levels are for storage and for the work of the slaves and have narrow passages that are easy to defend and hard to attack, and with lanterns rather than windows supplying light, while the doorways themselves have suspended above them slabs of stone, ready to be released were the keep requiring to be sealed. Furthermore, concreted bins above and behind the doorways hold rocks ready to be let pour into the alcoves of the doors to shore up the stone slabs.'

'And the levels upwards from this door that seem to be our destination?' said Einarr.

25

'The province of the Emperor's extended family and those they choose to accompany them. From that terrace upwards, they live a life like none other. There the corridors are wide, windows draw in light and air, and opulence serves both to enrich the lives of the ruling class to the extreme that they desire and to diminish the importance of those who visit. This is the heart of an empire, after all.'

Konall was unimpressed. 'Not so easy to defend, then.'

'They feel, young lord,' Grakk said with a grin, 'that if an enemy host has battled past four huge walls and the areas of massacre between, broken through to the lowest level of this keep while under attack from above and fought through several levels of narrow passages to reach this stage, they will be either too depleted in numbers and energy to resist the defenders or will be indomitable. Either way, one more stage of defence will not alter the outcome. And they like their opulent living.'

Brann looked at the tribesman, who had the appearance of a creature of the wilds but the words to rival a Scribe. 'How do you know this, Grakk? Have you visited here often?'

Grakk smiled. 'Never, young curious fellow. But there exists a place where all the knowledge of mankind is written and stored, and there I have been. Not recently, nor even as recently as long ago, but often.'

Any further questions were cut short by their arrival at the doorway, where a large platform afforded more than enough room for the bearers to lower their burdens onto broad boards that shone with the evidence of constant care. The eight slaves who had carried the party hardly seemed out of breath and, although impressed, Brann couldn't help wondering if such impressive strength could not be put to better use than carrying people around a city.

Grakk seemed to read his mind. 'It's a better fate than finding themselves in the mines, quarries or war galleys,' he said quietly. 'There is always someone in a worse position than you, and someone in a better. It is life.'

The Scribe was waiting at the doorway and, on their approach, he turned without a word and led them into a world that drew a gasp of astonishment even from Einarr.

Grakk grinned. 'The desired effect of the first impression has been achieved!' But even so, his face showed his own admiration for the sight that greeted them.

The doorway opened onto a hallway the size of a town square, and extending above what looked like three full storeys. Two statues, each the size of a two-storey house, depicted in smooth white stone a lightly armoured warrior on a rearing horse, caught in the moment of thrusting a lance the size of a young tree, and his foe, a six-headed monster with each of the snake-like necks coiled to strike forward with massively fanged mouths. A large smooth black rock formed the boss on the warrior's shield and gold gleamed on his helmet, bracers and greaves, sword hilt and the trappings of his steed, matched on the fangs and claws of the beast, while its many-faceted eyes were jewels of the deepest red.

'So the fables are true,' Grakk breathed. 'Sometimes words on parchment cannot do justice to the wonder of reality.'

Hakon clapped him jovially on the shoulder. 'The desired effect of the first impression indeed, oh wise one.'

Grakk still looked dazed. 'I have a feeling it will not be the last impression we will have.'

They paced the length of the hall between the looming might of the statues, their boots clacking against tiles of alternate squares of white and pale yellow and the noise echoing off walls of a shiny white stone that, Brann saw on closer inspection as they neared the far end of the room, was streaked with veins, much like the strong cheese made in the southern parts of his homeland, though far more impressive.

A stairway the width of the *Blue Dragon* (again, he was measuring in units of ships, Brann realised) took them a third of the height of the chamber before it split right and left, the two arms sweeping round on themselves and meeting close to the ceiling where a golden balustrade edged a broad balcony that encircled the room, murals stretching the length of each wall in myriad colours.

Closer examination of the murals proved impossible at the summit of their climb as the Scribe took them straight forward through a wide opening into a wider corridor, rising at a gentle angle. Closely spaced windows, tall and slender and high-set, cast beams of sunlight onto a row of alcoves in the inner wall, each bearing a statue a little taller than a man. As they passed, Brann saw that many of them were actually carved in the likeness of men or women, while others were animals or even small trees or ornate flowers. All were in the same white stone as the two in frozen conflict in the hallway, and all were crafted to the same impeccable standard, down to the last crease at the corner of an eye or insect on a leaf.

The passage stretched for what seemed an eternity before turning abruptly, repeating the pattern. Each turn, sometimes taking them into the interior, sometimes back to the outer walls of the building, revealed more artistic treasures: statues, murals, tapestries the length of a bowshot, ornate weapons and armour, stuffed exotic animals – many of which Brann and, from their expressions, several of the others, had never imagined as existing – and carvings etched into the white veined stone of every wall.

Einarr spoke, directing his words at the back of the Scribe's tattooed head. 'We must have climbed a fair part of the building by now, Narut.'

'The noble sir is correct,' the man said, his neck colouring at the use of his name. 'We shall in time reach the highest levels, where the royal residences are located, though we will not, of course, enter that area, but pass it by.'

'Of course not,' Einarr agreed.

'Immediately above the royal chambers are the rooms of state.'

'Thank you, Narut.' Einarr's voice was amiable. 'That is very helpful.'

'As the noble lord commands.'

The royal floor was evident both from the huge doors – gold plate beaten into similar geometric intricacy as the frame of the first gate they had encountered – and the ten fully armoured warriors, as impassive as the statues they had passed, lined in front of them. Only their eyes moved, every movement noted as the small party passed across in front of them until they left the open hallway before the entrance. Their watchfulness was matched every step across the chamber by Torstein and Magnus, warriors' instincts drifting their hands onto sword hilts and setting their shoulders with tension.

The Scribe's cold voice drifted back to them. 'We approach the Throne Room of the Empire.'

The passage abruptly angled upwards towards another hall, this one with the carvings on the doors cut directly into the dark wood and inlaid with silver, the contrast star-tling. One guard stood each side but the doors lay open and the soldiers didn't even twitch as the Scribe led them directly through.

The room was vast, the omnipresent white statues lining the left side in front of murals that populated the length of the wall, from floor to ceiling, with images of the tiniest detail and finished in gold leaf. A row of wide windows ran opposite, more like doorways as they stretched to the floor and appeared to give access to a series of balconies, and the ceiling bore from the near end to the far a map that seemed to show every stream and hillock of what Brann assumed was the Empire as it stood.

And the room lay empty.

They walked in at one end, facing in the distance a great throne of plain unadorned stone, with a simple white ceremonial canopy above it and two smaller replicas either side of it, their footsteps echoing in the silence. They stopped, forcing the Scribe to turn.

'Narut?' Einarr said. 'Why is there no one here?'

The Scribe looked as if only his professional pride prevented him from sighing in disdain. 'There are three throne rooms: the Throne Room of the Empire, where you now stand; the Throne Room of Sagia, which affords a more intimate setting; and the Throne Room of the Heavens, which we would now be approaching had you not halted our progress. I am surprised that your free man has not prepared you with this information. Now, if we may proceed...'

The last was too close to an instruction and too far from a request for Einarr's liking. He casually turned to Grakk. 'Indeed, Narut. Did you know of this, Grakk?'

The tribesman's face was solemn. 'I regret to say that I did not. My learnings have leant more towards the external

30

aspects than the internal.' Grakk nodded towards the outlook beyond the balconies where open dry land, cleared flat initially, turned to a scrubland of bushes and trees, all dry twisted wood and dry dark-green leaves, that stretched to the horizon.

Einarr raised his eyebrows at the sight. 'I have never seen this side of the city in the past. The seat of the most powerful man in the world is directly exposed to that outside world?'

Grakk nodded. 'The four great walls meet at the back wall of the keep, and that back wall does, as you say, face onto the ground beyond. However, the city fills the top of a bluff that is a long and gentle slope to the shore but which, on its landward side, drops sheer to the flat ground beyond. The rock of this feature raises the defences high above the reach of siege engines, ladders or towers and extends the range of the catapults of the defenders and is impenetrable to siege mining. It was a feat of magnificent and long-forgotten engineering skills merely to sink foundations into it. There are natural caverns beneath the citadel and city alike that were linked by tunnels cut in the time of the grandfather's grandfather of the current Emperor's grandfather's grandfather, but not one tunnel leads to the land beyond.

'Were an army to attempt to cross that desert, in their desperate state they would face the massed ranks of the Imperial Host on the cleared plain of the Tournament Grounds you see before you. That is why not only has no foe ever taken this citadel, but no foe has ever even attempted to do so.'

Einarr nodded. 'Indeed. I can understand why. And if I am to request the aid of the Emperor, it is comforting to know his people have such an eye for military matters other than merely weight of numbers. So Narut, if you would care to lead us to the Throne Room of the Heavens, I would be most grateful.'

The tall man's robes swirled as he whirled and stalked down the hall without further ado.

A wide opening in the left wall, slightly higher than a tall man but previously hidden by two statues of curious creatures that were men from the waist up but had the body and legs of huge cat-like beasts, became obvious as they drew closer. A broad and shallow stairway rose before them and turned right halfway up, blazing bright sunlight across their path as they started to climb. On reaching the second flight, the deep blue of the mid-afternoon sky filled the opening ahead.

They emerged on the rooftop of the keep. Exposed without mercy to the full force of the sun, the heat of the air struck as if they had walked into the brick wall of an oven and Brann's eyes stung from the harsh brightness. It took a wipe of his sleeve before he could take in the view but, when he did, it took away his breath more than even the searing heat had done just seconds before.

They had stepped out onto the precise centre of the roof area. Directly ahead of them, far ahead and almost at the edge of the roof, sat five thrones on a raised dais, one large, the rest uniformly smaller and all replicas of those in the room below. But, this time, they were occupied.

The Scribe led them into the space between them and the thrones. While it lay empty but for a line of warriors standing before the dais, to either side a throng, garbed in a multitude of colours that reminded Brann of the meadow of wild-flowers that sat behind his village, stood silently behind a further row of warriors. All in the crowd wore fine robes similar to those of the Scribe, some with long, loose sleeves and others that ended at the shoulders; on closer inspection, he saw that the lack of sleeves matched the presence of a slave chain around their necks. Some of the free men and women wore tall, slender, brimless hats; some had a soft fabric wound intricately around their heads and ending in a veil-like gauze that hung across their faces; some were bare-headed. All appeared to follow one fashion or another, with no style of clothing seeming to attach to one gender or the other, and every one of them exuded wealth.

The soldiers were identical to each other in garb. Over light, pale-coloured tunics, sleeveless vests formed of overlapping horizontal strips of shining metal encased their torsos, while identical metal strips hung loosely from their waists almost to their knees. Each rounded helmet, extending down their cheeks and over the back of their necks and with a grill across the mouth and nose to leave only the eyes clearly exposed, was topped by a plume of green bristles. Each held a tall shield that was rounded at the top and arched at the bottom and a stabbing spear roughly his own height, much like Brann's people had used to hunt boar but with a narrower head. A broad shortsword and a long slender knife were strapped at either hip. Short or tall, broad or narrow, each was clad the same as his neighbour. Behind the dais, a row of archers stood, their armour identical to the other soldiers and one arrow held ready should the occasion demand it.

'The statues!' Brann gasped. Despite the imaginative range of beasts, plants and people at leisure, and other than the giant statue in the first hallway, every stone soldier he had seen had been identical to those he saw before him in the flesh.

Exasperation filled Konall's sigh, but his voice was quiet. 'It has taken until now to see it? Did you not listen to your

33

friend the tribesman? They do not have warriors. They have soldiers. All are part of the whole, and must act as one. There is no scope for exploiting opportunities. That is their way. All is ordered. All is for the Empire.'

Grakk coughed pointedly behind them, and their conversation ceased.

The silence as they walked towards the thrones was overpowering, the oppressive atmosphere heightened when the first soldiers they passed moved to close off the rectangle behind them, with the crowd pressing in behind. Those to the sides were unmoving, so when Brann's attention was caught by a figure keeping pace with them, he was intrigued. Reminded of the first time he had clapped eyes on Konall what seemed a lifetime ago, he watched but, wary of alerting the person to their discovery, he let his gaze wander over the crowd in general. He caught sight briefly of someone around his height but with a slightness and grace of movement that indicated a woman beneath the dark-blue robes and matching veil.

Unable to watch more closely without staring, he returned his attention to the way ahead. Their steps quickened as, with their goal in sight, the dire memories of the events brought about by Loku in the North seemed to sweep over the group. Exposed to the watching crowd and staring at the line of thrones, the ground was taking an eternity of frustration to cover. Frustration, but also mounting excitement, as the opportunity to enlist the help of such power drew closer with each rapid step. The exotic alien sights that had met his eyes since he had stepped from the ship, and which had built to this crescendo, filled him with a burning and breathless anticipation. He may have had to endure horrors and terrors to reach this point, but there was no denying that his fate had brought him to an experience that he could never have imagined, were a whole tribe of storytellers to try to describe it to him. Here was he, an apprentice miller from a small village on what seemed like the other side of the world, walking into the court of the fabled Emperor of the mightiest Empire their world had ever seen. Forcing himself to breath, he dared to look at the ruler himself as they approached.

The man was more normal than he had expected. His clean-shaven face was coloured by the sun to a hue that matched the dark sand of the land they had spied from the windows and creased by smile lines that lent amusement to his eyes and cheeks. Black hair was cropped efficiently short and cut straight across his brow, just above calm brown eyes and, as his head turned, a circlet flashed golden as it caught the sunlight. Clad in robes of pale blue, edged in gold and with a heavy chain of thick links of gold, he sat as easily on his massive throne of stone as though it were filled with cushions.

The four who sat to either side were of such similar appearance to the Emperor that the family resemblance was unmistakable. Their white robes were also edged in gold, and while they lacked the chain and circlet, they exuded the same air of easy authority. A Scribe stood at the shoulder of each of the five and a portly man, lavishly dressed in blue and crimson, was demonstrably stating a case to the Emperor but, on their approach, a slight flick of the Emperor's fingers was all it took for the man to be ushered to one side. As their eyes followed the man's movement, Brann saw an elderly man, his beard long, wispy and white but his back straight and his dark eyes keen, sitting to the side of the dais.

Shock hit him like a hammer between the eyes. Standing beside the old man, one hand resting casually on the high back of the chair, was a man Brann had last seen leaping from a window to his escape, a man who had engineered a plan that had come close to wiping out the rulers of Einarr's people, a man who bore a scar the height of his left check given by Brann on their last meeting. Loku had somehow travelled to Sagia before them and, more astonishingly, he had inveigled his way into the court of the Emperor.

Einarr noticed the man a moment after Brann and, without a hint of recognition in his expression, immediately extended a hand back in Konall's direction, a clear sign to his young cousin to hold himself in check. Brann glanced anxiously at the tall boy, but years of training ensured that, while his face had drained deadly white and his jaw was clenched with the effort of containing his fighting rage, his step never faltered and he made not a sound.

Grakk moved close to Konall and spoke so quietly that even Brann, walking beside the boy, barely heard the words. 'Patience, young lord. This is to Lord Einarr's advantage: he can discuss the matters in the North with the Emperor and at the same time expose the man who is linked with them. And it saves us the time and effort of hunting down the dog for vengeance.'

They halted in front of the dais. The Scribe held his right hand in front of his heart before sweeping it forward towards the Emperor, turning his palm to face upwards. He held the pose until the Emperor nodded, then intoned, 'Heart and Head of ul-Taratac, Ruler of the Civilised World, His Majesty the Emperor Kalos, Fifth of that Name, may I present Lord Einarr Sigurrson, Heir to the Territories of Halveka and the Seat of Yngvarrsharn, his cousin Lord Konall Ragnarrson,

Heir to the Seat of Ravensrest, and their party.' He inclined his head to the Emperor and Einarr in turn, and walked smoothly around the end of the line of soldiers and behind the dais to appear behind the Emperor's right shoulder. The Scribe who had held that place moved quietly away and stood to one side.

Einarr, who had stopped a few paces ahead of the rest of the group, stood still, head bowed. He only lifted his eyes when the Emperor spoke, his voice warm and full of welcome.

'Lord Einarr, it is good to see you here. I have heard much about you.' He waved a hand in an arc above his head. 'Welcome to my Throne Room of the Heavens, where all are reminded of the vastness that is the one ceiling for all citizens of the Empire.'

Einarr was respectful. 'Your Imperial Majesty, I am grateful for your prompt granting of our request for an audience. My only sadness is that the purpose of my visit to your court is to bear grave tidings from the North.'

Inwardly, Brann smiled as glee coursed through him. Loku was to be revealed for what he was at the first opportunity. The man must feel desperate to flee, were an escape route possible. Which there wasn't. Which made it all the more enjoyable.

The Emperor smiled, his eyes creasing in friendship. 'Be not sad, Lord of the North. I know exactly why you are here. I like your directness, and feel I already like you also.

'Which makes me, in turn, sad. Sad that you should die.'

At the last word, the weapons of the soldiers around them snapped down, caging them in a box of spear points. Instinctively, the hands of Einarr, Konall and their two warriors dropped to their weapons, while the other three, unarmed, felt helplessness join the shock slamming against them. Spears plunged into the two Northern warriors from behind, Magnus dying instantly and Torstein suffering a further thrust to the chest before his gasping croaks of rage and swinging sword were stopped. Scattered shrieks from the gathered throng were surprisingly sparse, and there was none of the scrambling for safety that Brann would have expected from such a gathering of affluent citizenry, people whose self-regard generally equates with overwhelming self-preservation. Instead, an excited curiosity seemed to suffuse them.

'I find that I like you, Lord Einarr, so I would advise you and your young cousin to remove your hands from your weapons, otherwise you shall, indeed, share the fate of your two men. Had you listened properly, I said that you "should" die. I have yet to decide if you will.'

The battle-experience Einarr had gathered over the years had kept him focused. His eyes fixed on those of the Emperor, he eased back to beside Konall and rested a hand on the boy's right arm, gently easing it away from his sword hilt.

His voice remained calm and controlled. 'Can I ask your thinking, Emperor? Two good men have just bled out their lives over what I can only imagine is a misunderstanding.'

'There is no misunderstanding, Lord Einarr. I would invite you to walk with me. Your party may accompany you.'

He stood, the Scribe following his every pace as he moved towards the edge of the roof. Soldiers moved in around them and expertly and quickly divested them of weapons. They were allowed to walk to beside where the Emperor stood facing the view, kept by a row of gleaming metal several paces from his right side. Such had been Brann's fixation on the people until this moment that it was only now that he became aware that the rooftop was exactly that, and no more: a perfectly flat surface, unadorned with any protuberance and, most significantly, no wall around its edge. The sides dropped abruptly away to the ground far below, escalating the impression of height and over-whelming him with vulnerability. He was acutely aware of the hot wind that plucked at his tunic but felt like a gale, and of the grainy surface that now seemed as treacherous as an icy slope. Born in a country of hills and dales, he had never been one to be nervous while standing at the edge of a drop. Until now.

The Emperor was unperturbed. His voice was calm. 'The city you passed through, that lies below us, is the greatest in the world. The land you see stretching before you, as far as your eyes can see from this loftiest of viewpoints, is but a grain of sand to the expanse of my Empire. Your mind cannot comprehend the number of people who fall under my control, who rely on my will. This,' he touched the circlet nestling among his thick hair and which Brann now saw was wrought to resemble a twisted branch that almost met at the front, 'reminds me of the first olive tree our forebears planted here when they ceased to wander these lands and settled this spot.' Brann had no idea what an olive tree was, but the meaning was clear. The Emperor lifted the links of the heavy gold around his neck. 'And this reminds me of the fact that I may have been elevated to be the first of all in this Empire, but in doing so I am in thrall to the Empire, a slave in service to the survival and flour-ishing of ul-Taratac.'

He turned slowly to face them, still toying with the chain. His smile was genial, disarming. 'And in all this expanse of land, in all these teeming hordes of people near and far, do you not think that there will be some who will wish me ill, for whatever reason? Every day, there are attempts planned on my life, but few have made it as close as you did.'

Einarr's composure slipped at the implication, and his tone was aghast. 'An attempt on your life? On the contrary, Your Imperial Majesty, as well as the events in the North, I would tell you of a viper in your midst.' He pointed directly at Loku, who looked worryingly unconcerned. 'That man is the danger to you. That treacherous dog is one of the reasons we are here.'

The Emperor laughed. 'That treacherous dog, as you describe him, is the reason I stay alive. How do you think I avoid these many and ofttimes highly ingenious attempts to kill me? Because I know of them. And how do I know? Because this treacherous dog, or Taraloku-Bana, to afford him his real name, operates for me a wonderfully efficient and effective network that gathers information from every conceivable source. His people bring me the real news of my Empire and, when the situation warrants it, he will gather the information for me personally, as he did in this case. I have him to thank for knowing of the discord you and your family have sown in the North, to try to lure my millens northwards to restore the order necessary for trade, whereupon, claiming invasion, you would seek to weaken my forces. On finding that my man had discovered your purpose, you tried to kill him and instead came here to seek to kill me directly. It is not complicated.'

'Why in the name of all the gods would we want to do that?' Einarr was incredulous. 'What could we gain from it?'

The Emperor looked puzzled. 'Ah yes, of course. We Southerners are slow of thought. We could not see your purpose. We could not envisage that, were the Empire to be destabilised, even short-term chaos would open up trade routes to your people currently controlled, carefully and for the benefit of all, by Sagia. The more you profited, the more powerful you would become, and the more you could work to establish your trade in the South. And so on, and so on. You would never rise to rival the might of the Empire, but you would have become strong enough to hold an influential bargaining position when the Empire settled back to normality.' His hand fluttered on high, as if scattering thoughts to the wind. 'But of course, we Southerners could never have divined that. Our arrogance would have convinced us that nothing could affect the Empire.'

Einarr's eyes blazed with cold fury. 'Emperor, you have been duped.'

There was an angry growl and the spear points surged forward. Kalos raised a hand and they stopped in an instant, but still the tension hung heavy. The smile remained, as easy and warm as ever. 'Have a care, Lord Einarr. Speak like that to an Emperor and you risk your life being measured in seconds.'

'Are we not dead men regardless, Majesty?' This time the title was spat out.

'Not you, nor your cousin. To put to death such high-ranking nobles as yourselves would be as much an act of war as anything else. I would be forced to acknowledge the attempt on my life and would be expected to send my soldiers north as a result, thereby allowing your people to achieve their original objective.' He sighed. 'Much as I would relish your death, I must place the good of the Empire ahead of my personal enjoyment. Far better to hold you and your cousin here as our, shall we say, *guests* until your father confirms in writing what your plans had been, then you can be ransomed back with certain conditions attached. So you two can be taken below to your chambers. The others can travel down by quicker means.'

He waved a nonchalant hand at the roof's edge as he turned back towards his throne. Brann's knees almost buckled at the horror and he fought to prevent his stomach from heaving, determined not to disgrace his people in the face of such injustice. Levelled spears prompted a shouting Einarr and Konall in one direction and Brann, Hakon and Grakk on a very different path.

A scream rent the air, followed by horrified shouts from several directions. Every second spear switched in unison towards the sound, the remainder staying with their original orders. More anguish filled the air. Unperturbed by blood and potential execution, members of the watching crowd were apparently able to be shocked by other means.

'My purse!'

'My gems!'

'My Scribe's satchel!'

'My purse, too!'

Similar cries came from at least a dozen sources, and Brann saw the blue-clad figure he had earlier noticed moving through the throng slipping quietly towards the edge of the roof. She was spotted and shouts alerted all to her presence. A man of astounding obesity was closest to her, and she slipped, encouraging him to lumber towards her. When he was almost upon her, she spun, her hands a blur and her robes whirling as they unwound around her. She stopped, clad in a close-fitting black outfit, a well-filled bag attached to her waist and her hands filled with the full length of the strip of fabric that had formed the robes. She looped the strip around the fat man and ran backwards, the loose ends of the strip feeding through either hand. She reached the edge and without hesitation dropped from sight, the fabric still running through her hands, leaving Brann with a fleeting impression of dark hair tied back to hang to the nape of her neck and even darker eyes flashing with triumph. The fat Sagian fought in a panic to avoid the drop and used his considerable bulk to resist being pulled by the slight girl towards the edge.

Hakon was the only one who reacted to the commotion. Knocking one spear aside with his right hand, he threw himself past it and barged the soldier's unsuspecting neighbour in the back with his shoulder, his weight and strength combining to knock the man to the ground and his momentum carrying him clear of the guards. He raced the short distance to the point of the girl's exit, arriving a moment after she had dropped from sight.

The archers drew, but with the primary function of protecting the Emperor, they were stationed behind him to have a target area covering any who would come straight at him, and their view of Hakon was blocked by scores of people.

With the briefest of glances back, he shouted, 'I'll alert our crew,' and dropped over the edge, grabbing at the strips of cloth that had, a breath before, slowed the thief's descent. His large frame was, however, more of a challenge for the bulk of the fat man who had been used by the girl. His eyes wide and his face the same crimson as the sleeves of his robes, his feet scrabbled desperately at the treacherous purchase on the sand-strewn smooth stone of the roof, but it was a battle he was fast losing. As Hakon disappeared from sight, the man abruptly shot forward and was cast, like a boulder from a giant's sling, into the void beyond the edge of the roof.

As his howl receded with him, Brann had rushed to the side of the building, his terror of the emptiness beyond forgotten as he saw his friend disappear. On hands and knees, he craned his neck to see the girl thief on one of the balconies of the Throne Room below them, black rope in hand, astonishment written clear on her face as she didn't know whether to look first at the fat man in billowing robes, screaming and grasping at air, who was plummeting past her, or the large Northerner who had landed beside her. The disappearance of the former and the continuing presence of the latter, who grinned cheerfully, clapped her on the back and pointed helpfully at the rope, returned her attention to the task at hand and, with the quick hands of the skilled thief she had already proved to be, the rope was looped around the balustrade and secured to itself with a metal hook at one end. Before it had even finished uncoiling, she was already sliding down it, swinging inwards as she neared its end to land on a similar balcony two floors below the one they had started from. She was followed closely, but rather less gracefully, by her new companion and, as soon as Hakon landed, a practised snap of her wrist set the rope to snaking above her until the hook flicked free and the line dropped. She was already using a hook at the other end to secure the rope to that balustrade and, in seconds, the pair of escapees was five balconies below the rooftop.

The girl repeated her trick with the rope and, as she gathered it in, Hakon leant into view and waved happily, with all the demeanour of a farm lad leaving for a weekly trip to market. The pair disappeared from view, and Brann realised that the whole episode had probably taken less than a minute. Soldiers, who had received orders and had been racing along the roof, had reached the stairs to the level below.

'Well, that was entertaining.' The Emperor's amused voice was so close to Brann's left that it was easy to forget that there was a line of spearmen between them. 'A merchant whose financial success raises him to a form of nobility is usually more of an onlooker in my court than an integral part of such excitement, and his children will be delighted with their inheritance, I am sure. And I suppose it is nice for you to have a thrilling distraction to take your mind off your execution.'

'It is more than a distraction,' Brann blurted. 'Whatever happens to me, at least I know that my friend will live and our ship will carry news of this atrocity to our people.'

'Oh dear boy, your naive optimism is endearing. Under other circumstances, I might have been minded to let you live merely to watch how long you could maintain it in the face of reality.' The Emperor sounded as if he would have ruffled Brann's hair. He sighed deeply. 'These are not, however, other circumstances. And my men will capture those two before long.'

Brann was defiant. With his fate decided, he found he had strength to snarl at an Emperor. He stood. 'Those two have a head start on your men.'

He received a shrug in reply. 'Fine. Say they evade all and somehow escape to the city. Say they reach the ship before the units I have already marching on the docks. Say they somehow gather the crew, still before the soldiers arrive. They will not clear the harbour, and will be forced to settle in the city. What matter to me another few foreigners added to those from throughout the world who have made a home in the districts of this city of a thousand thousand souls? Another few dozen who want me dead? Most here are content to live their lives, and the malcontents either are lost in the crowd or rooted out by my good servant Taraloku-Bana and his excellent people.'

Unconcerned about the drop, the Emperor peered over the edge. 'That unfortunate man has scattered his blood over quite an area. If you are bored on the way down, you could always see if you could manage to land in it.' He nodded, and the spears moved forward to force him and Grakk over the edge. Brann found himself considering the irony of the prospect. While never having any fear of heights, he had always suffered from a morbid terror of the feeling of dropping, of the helplessness of the fall. When his friends had spent summer afternoons jumping from a rocky ledge above the river that ran through their valley, he had splashed in the water below encouraging them. Now he was being forced from the top of a building higher than he could have imagined was possible to build.

He eyed the spear points. Throwing himself forward at the right moment would be a quicker death and wouldn't involve the drop. Bracing his legs to lunge, he found an overpowering self-preservation freezing his muscles. Whatever the logic of his head, his instinct was to fight to survive at all costs, and he cast about instead for an opening, a chance to pass the metal points and inflict any damage he could before they put an end to it. But the spears came on. His mind whirled and his body took over, his legs tensing for movement born of panic.

An order barked out and the soldiers stopped. Brann froze, then glanced across. The Emperor was standing with his arm aloft.

The Scribe was standing behind him, as was Loku, though a respectful distance further back than the slave. The Emperor seemed delighted. 'My Source of Information has just offered a suggestion through my Chief Scribe, my Recorder of Information. It seems an excellent idea to me, a fact that has a bearing somewhat on the likelihood of it coming to fruition. You see, we have a fine tradition of gladiatorial contests here in Sagia, occasions that provide much-loved entertainment for the citizens of this city. There is one such occasion tomorrow, and I would be most grateful if you two would be a part of it. My friend Taraloku-Bana feels that it would be most entertaining to see the bald native fight, and even more entertaining to see you, the talkative one, die. You will both, of course, still die, but,' he smiled warmly, 'you have another whole day of life ahead of you. Is that not a wonderful gift?'

'Why do you want so much for us to be dead?' Brann's voice was almost a hoarse whisper. 'You didn't care when my friend escaped. You don't care if the crew are captured or not. Why are you so set on seeing us die?'

The Emperor's smile remained, but his brow creased in puzzlement. 'Oh, you don't actually understand, do you? I have no interest at all in whether you live or die. Your existence is a thousand levels lower than mine.' He smiled. 'You see, you were only going over the edge as a matter of convenience. You were unnecessary, and someone would have tidied you away at the bottom. But now it is time for you to leave in a different manner, and we are promised some entertainment. This day has proved far more pleasant than I had anticipated.'

Without another word, he walked away, conferring briefly with his Scribe and pointing at the soldier whose spear had been knocked aside by Hakon. A squad surrounded Brann and Grakk, escorting them away without fuss, walking behind the crowds. Before the Emperor had retaken his seat, the soldier had been flung from the roof.

Chapter 2

The two slaves gestured from their hearts to him before leaving him at his door. He wondered if they really did extend their hearts to him; whether they cared at all for him beyond the orders they were given. He wondered if those orders were to provide the escort to his chambers that his status demanded, or to ensure he didn't wander the passages aimlessly on a path formed by mindless old age.

She waited by his chair, water ready for his return.

'You saw him?' Her voice whispered across the room.

His feet scuffed the dust into a dance as he shuffled to his chair. 'I saw him.'

'As did I. Will you visit him? Or have him brought here?'

'Are you mad, woman?' He was torn between incredulity and anger at such stupidity. 'When did I last travel into the city?'

For the first time since she had entered his life, there was uncertainty in her voice. 'It is not the lordling? The one held in this building? But you said you had seen the one we await.'

'I did. And I will see him tomorrow. At the Arena.'

'So you will travel to the city after all?' Her feeble attempt at scoring a point betrayed her disconcertion.

'You know as well as I that it is hardly a trip to the Pleasure Quarter or the market. Being borne across the Bridge of the Sky into the Emperor's section in the Arena will not even see me leave the Royal precincts.'

She poured water for him, the time she took appearing less due to care and more to the need to gather her thoughts. 'You seem sure about this, but I cannot see the one we await being a native of the Tribe of the Desert. It has nothing of the right feel.'

'Your feeling is correct. It is not of the tribesman that I speak.'

'The boy? Are you succumbing to your years after all?'

His voice was calm. He was enjoying this. 'My sword arm may be weak, but my mind is still sharper than those who think they are rulers and, it seems, than yours. You see the whole tapestry, crone, but you do not focus on the individual stitches that form the images. I saw, today. I noticed. He is the one.'

The ewer shattered on the stone floor. 'A wind stirs the mist of my vision,' she gasped. 'I see the face. You are right.'

He smiled.

****

The walk through the streets was longer than their travel to the citadel had been, and was considerably less salubrious.

The soldiers encased them in a shell of armour and sharp edges, with no option but to tramp along between them on a journey where time was stretched by never knowing when the end would be reached but always knowing that misery waited at that destination.

He was a slave again. He waited for despair that never came. He steeled himself to suppress an anger, futile anger, anger that never rose. He prepared to resist a wave of injustice that never washed over him. He wondered at their absence, but all he felt was relief.

He was still alive.

Right now, at this moment, he walked in captivity, but he walked feeling the ground beneath his feet and the sun on his head. He lifted his face to feel the heat, to catch the slightest breeze on his skin, to see the endless blue of the sky. Movement caught his eye and he saw Grakk looking at him in question.

'Better a slave who breathes than a corpse who is free,' Brann said.

'Some would differ.'

Brann shrugged. 'There is no freedom in death, only a certainty of no more life. Death steals the chance of change. To choose to die nobly rather than live to seize an opportunity to make things better, well...' He shrugged. 'I can only think that those who make such a choice would think otherwise should they consider it longer than the impetuous moment. I fear stepping from a great height in despair and finding halfway down that I wished I could fly.'

Grakk grunted. 'You are quite the philosopher today. That is good, I was preparing my words to drag you back from despair and let you use all available time to prepare for tomorrow, but you have spared me that.'

51

The thought of tomorrow settled both into silence. Brann turned his face to the sky again. *While I live, I will fight to live. What other way is there?*

He was unable to see much of the city past the bulk of their escort, but it was clear that the more they travelled, the more the affluence melted away. The areas they began to pass through became dustier, the white of the walls was more cracked, the footing was increasingly uneven. They passed through a great old gate in the city wall, one not frequented by merchants and in fact, if the current level of activity was typical, not frequented by many people at all other than a couple of bored guards who pretended not to be close to dozing when they noticed the approach of the soldiers. They descended a wide ramp, its surface weathered and flaking in places, carved into the face of the bluff that Sagia sat upon and, a short distance after they had left the city proper, the houses started again, some with a small untended garden area, some crammed against each other, and all little more than shacks. A length of empty land had wild shrubbery, gnarled, twisted and fighting the dry ground, growing alongside the road where it was fed by the occasional use of the gutter, before they passed in front of a long wall, around the height of a man and a half as much again, its top a series of curving dips that was itself topped with railings cut to set the spiked tips at a uniform level. While dry grasses and wild plants gathered at its foot, matching the determined but sparse plant life of the scrubland that stretched into the distance opposite, the metal of the railings was well tended and the wall looked solid.

They stopped at an arched gateway midway along the wall's length, and one of the soldiers banged on a door cut into the wood of the gate. A symbol was burnt into the smaller door, two short horizontal lines crossing close to the end of one longer vertical one, forming the simplistic shape of a sword with a flat pommel, with that symbol beside an inverted version of itself. Above it a grill was filled with the glower of a guard's face as he checked the source of the knocking. With an unimpressed grunt, he opened the door and was passed a note. Spear points were levelled and Brann and Grakk were prompted through the doorway, where three more guards waited, all in identical red tunics with the same symbol on the front and back as was on the gate. Shields, both round and squared, lay carelessly to the side but swords of simple quality were strapped to their hips. Without a word or a glance, the soldiers marched back the way they had come, their feet beating an even beat on the hard track.

The guard, as tall as Hakon but even broader of shoulder and chest, looked them up and down. 'Not the most impressive arrivals we've ever had, I must admit. Still, you're here, so I'd as well introduce you to the boss.' He glanced at the note in his hand, and grinned cheerfully. 'I see you are fighting death bouts tomorrow, so you could probably get away with not bothering to have to try to remember everybody's names until after that, if you see what I mean.' He slapped Brann on the back. 'Every cloud, and all that, eh? But if you can remember one name, you might as well make it Cassian's. He's the boss. Hence the name of this place: the School of Cassian. Makes sense, eh? Why not? If you can remember another name, I'm Salus. Salus the Silent, on account that I'm not. I like to remind the world that I'm alive. Especially myself.'

He steered them up a wide straight pathway of white loose stones that crunched with every step. It ran a short way to a wide, two-storey building, as white-walled and red-roofed as every other structure in the city. The path widened at the building and, to one side, a cart of provisions was being unloaded. Brann looked appreciatively at the two horses in the traces, their heads bowed into buckets of water and the tail of one lifting to drop shit on the carefully maintained path.

After coming so close to death, giddiness was coursing through him and he laughed as he nudged Grakk and nodded at the scene. 'So much for order everywhere and everything being controlled!'

Grakk looked at him through narrowed eyes. 'You forget you will most probably die tomorrow?'

Brann shrugged. 'I just can't forget that I should be dead just now. But I'm not.'

Grakk was unconvinced.

Salus, however, was more appreciative. 'That's the spirit, lad. Take each moment as it comes, and don't plan too far ahead. Cassian likes a happy place, that he does. Uncle Cass, we often call him, as he's like the favourite uncle you hear about other people having and wish you had yourself. Well, you do now. For a day at least. Come and let's find him.'

They entered the cool of the building and were directed by a servant along a side corridor. 'Down here we go,' Salus informed them. 'I forgot the time of day. The boss is bathing.'

'He's what?' Brann thought the word sounded a bit rude.

Amusement had started to break through the melancholy in Grakk's eyes. 'It is similar to washing.'

'Well why didn't he say that?'

Grakk did actually smile this time. 'You will see.'

A guard stood before a heavy door. Salus nodded to him and entered, motioning for Brann and Grakk to wait where they were as a cloud of steam drifted past. Moments later, he reappeared, affable as ever. Wary as he was after the encounter with the Emperor of words delivered with a smile, still Brann couldn't help but warm to the man. He frowned slightly at that before his thoughts were interrupted by their subject. 'You can come now,' Salus said, beckoning.

The steam swirled as they entered but was filtering quickly out through vents in the ceiling, allowing Brann to see a tiled antechamber, the walls on either side stepped back in two stages to allow wooden benches to run the length of the room and then, higher, a shelf that bore a pile of towels at one end. A pile of clothing lay strewn on one bench.

Salus strode across slatted wooden flooring that kept their feet raised above the treacherous-looking slippery tiles of the floor beneath. An opening at the far end saw them descend two steps into a much bigger room, the source of the steam with three large water-filled tanks producing more swirling clouds that rose to similar vents in this ceiling, every inch of the space around them covered in more of the wooden flooring. High-set windows, long and narrow, let further steam out and dazzling beams of sunlight in, sparkling the water in the tanks that were square, set in line and each around the size of the Captain's cabin back on the *Blue Dragon*. Brann resolved to find a new unit of measurement – the thought of the excited anticipation of the voyage to this city had stabbed a pain in the heart of his chest. He clenched his fists to steady his thoughts.

The centre tank held a man. Sitting on what must have been a ledge and arms spread to either side as they rested on the edge of the pool, his face split into a huge toothy grin as he saw them enter. 'Welcome to my school, however long or, I suppose, short your stay may be. Your presence here may be enforced, but is no less appreciated for it.' He looked through narrowed eyes. 'You know, do you not, that the Empire intends you to die tomorrow.' The matter-of fact delivery from a stranger cut to where Grakk's words had not and Brann's spirit was sucked from him in the instant. His knees buckled and only the reactions of Grakk and Salus allowed them to grab his arms in time to keep him upright. The older man smiled gently. 'It therefore, of course, becomes our greatest desire to see the Empire disappointed. Many of our guests here arrived as a result of the will of the Empire, but you two are the first to face a death match.' His smile faded slightly. 'In your case, we are not allowed over-much time to assist you with this, but should you return tomorrow, you will be afforded our full hospitality.' He smiled broadly again, and Brann began to wonder if he and Salus were related or even if everyone in this compound had been partaking of the sort of fungi that grew in certain areas of the woods near his village. 'I trust Salus the Silent has taken good care of you?'

They nodded, and he beamed in return. 'Good, good.' He slapped the water in delight and stood, climbing from the pool as he spoke. Brann heard the noise but was oblivious to the words. Completely naked and puce from the heat of the water, Cassian eased himself out of the tank and trotted over to the third pool, launching himself without pause or shred of elegance into it with a resounding crash of splashing water. He emerged like a sea monster of legend, drops flying in all directions, whipping water from his face with both hands and gasping for breath. Brann watched the man, mouth agape and eyes wide. Grakk watched Brann, mirth creasing his face. 'Oh, that's good!' the man exulted. 'There's absolutely nothing like a cold plunge to get the blood flowing.'

He walked up steps at the far end of the pool and came towards them. The boy's despairing panic from just moments before was overwhelmed by a very different horror. Brann eased back against the wall to give him as much space to pass as possible, a move that almost caused Grakk to double up with suppressed laughter.

The elderly man beckoned with a finger as he headed towards the door to the antechamber. They followed, Brann fixing his eyes on the pelt of curled grey hair covering a latticework of old scar lines on his broad shoulders and trying desperately to avoid letting his gaze drop to the sagging and jiggling parts lower down. Cassian took a towel from the shelf and started vigorously drying himself, causing far more jiggling than Brann was prepared to endure. He stared determinedly at the man's face as he spoke, hoping it would appear courteous rather than an attempt to avoid noticing anything he would really rather not see.

'Now, you have this fight tomorrow, each of you, don't you?' He sounded as if he was discussing a polite gathering of old friends in a tavern, and Brann's spinning brain was so overwhelmed by the sight, and the potential but so far avoided sight, before him that he was able to listen to the words this time without terror paralysing his mind. 'It is not much time, not much time at all. So we must prepare you as we can, and hope to see you again afterwards, should Barollon will it.' He noticed Brann's puzzled look. 'You are from the Islands in the Cold Sea, yes?' The description was apt enough for Brann to assume he was talking about his homeland, and nodding seemed the easiest response. 'Yes, of course you are. Your god of war Arlod, is our god Barollon, though we see him chiefly as the god of good fortune, for in the chaos of every battle, that is the biggest factor in whether or not a man will be there to face the next day. But without good preparation, you won't be around to benefit from any good fortune that comes your way, so we will prepare as we can, won't we?'

Brann at last found his voice. 'You mean you are going to teach me to fight?'

Cassian had pulled a tunic – identical to those of the other men he had seen here, but white where theirs were red and with the symbol in red where theirs were white – over his head and was securing a broad belt around it that bore a scabbarded short broadsword, similar to the weapons carried by the soldiers they had seen at the citadel. He laughed. 'No, no, no, my boy, in the time we have, we could teach you nothing to the standard needed for it to be of use in the situation you face. You would forget all of it as soon as the first blade swings and any that you did somehow remember would not be natural. No, we must try to remove the unfamiliar. Then the rest is up to you, the gods, and your fate. But mainly you.' He smiled happily yet again. 'The good news is that in this sort of fight, you will be free to choose your own weapons.'

He walked over to Grakk, studying the tattoos. 'You are of the Tribe of the Desert?' Grakk nodded. 'Scholar?' Another nod. He took Grakk's hands in his, turning them palm up, looking them over and rubbing the area between thumb and forefinger on each hand with his own thumb. 'And your preference is to fight with dual swords?' Another nod. 'Though you are trained in many weapons.' Before Grakk could answer, he clapped him cheerily on the arm. 'You need not answer that one. You are a Scholar of the Tribe of the Desert. I expect I will see you here for dinner tomorrow. I have no worries about you. Should you need a practice partner, let my friend Salus know.' Grakk nodded his thanks.

He turned to Brann and examined his hands. 'You are not trained in arms.'

'I am a miller's son. I did not choose this.'

'Oh, dear boy, few in this city chose the life they live. It was an observation, not a criticism. You are what you are. I am merely trying to determine what it is that you are.' His fingers traced the thick line of hardened scar tissue under the boy's hair. 'And what you are is someone who has survived some sort of action, I see.' He pulled the neckline of Brann's tunic to one side to peer down inside at his upper arm. He whistled softly as he saw a portion of the tattoo. 'Oh my.' He looked at Grakk. 'Survived with some distinction, I see.'

The tribesman's voice was even. 'He has his moments.'

'Let us hope he has one tomorrow.' He turned back to the boy. 'You have a weapon of choice?'

Brann shrugged. 'A sword, I suppose. I don't know anything else. To be honest, I don't really know how to use a sword either.'

'Hit with the sharp edge, stick with the pointy bit, that's a sword for you. You should indeed choose sword and shield then, they are simple solid basics. Good.' He looked at Salus. 'Would you mind, good Salus? Make the unfamiliar familiar?'

'Of course, boss. Now?'

'The sooner we start, the better. Then we must attend to their jewellery, or the authorities will be most displeased with us. Thank you all.'

And with that, he wandered out of the room.

Brann looked at the other two. 'What in the darkest depth of hell was that?'

Salus was beaming as always. 'That was your welcome.'

Brann shook his head. 'Is my land the only place that exists where people *don't* wander around bollock naked without a care in the world?'

Grakk wiped a tear from the corner of one eye. 'No, young sheltered one, customs and sensibilities vary around the known world more than you can imagine, and I expect they vary even more in the unknown world. In this city, it was the fashion not long ago for the well-to-do ladies to wear robes that left their right breasts exposed, in other countries within the Empire men and women cannot show their faces in public once wed, in yet others a woman will take many husbands, and in another men and women are clothed from the waist down only.'

Brann's jaw dropped as images took hold. Salus also had a faraway look in his eyes. 'Ah, yes, Posamia. I dream of retiring there.' He shook his head, as if flinging away images. 'Anyway, things must be attended to. Come with me and we shall attend to them.'

Brann frowned. 'It seems that much of the public nudity involves women. Are there not places where men show off their... bits... as well?'

Grakk shrugged. 'Some, but very few.' He looked pointedly at Brann, stopping his next question. 'You have just witnessed the sight you did, and yet you are about to ask why so few? And you refer to it as showing off? You do realise, do you not, that there is an extent where the ridiculous and the ungraceful aspects outweigh all others?' Brann shuddered. 'Precisely, young Brann.'

Salus coughed, though it was hard to tell if it was to attract attention or cover a laugh. 'Anyway, if you wouldn't mind coming this way? I think we have exhausted the necessity for this conversation.'

He led them out of the back of the building into an open-ended courtyard formed by two long wings that extended back from either end of the main building. Boulders and rocks, paths and small bridges, streams and ponds, bushes and trees whose branches dipped down to the ground under their own weight combined to create an area of such unexpected beauty and tranquillity that Brann stopped dead in wonder, the second unexpected vision of the past half hour driving all other thoughts from his mind as much as the previous one had done.

'Does Cassian have a wife, then? Is this her doing?'

'He does,' Salus admitted, 'but this is his doing. It is his passion, a world he has created from his own head. Lady Tyrala has other talents. Important and useful, but not this.'

A winding path took them through to the far end, where they emerged through a green arch of leafy vines to see a collection of low buildings and, beyond, hillocks and walls that prevented a view of the full area. Low hills on the horizon were far on the other side of the surrounding arid scrubland that lay beyond the unseen far wall of the compound, though it was clear Cassian's school extended over an impressive area. To the right, the buildings on the outskirts of the city showed where civilisation began its mass existence.

Brann became aware of sounds as his mind adjusted to the overwhelming sights that had swamped him. The clash and bang as metal met metal or wood beyond the buildings – and presumably, from Salus's lack of concern, from practice rather than assault; the shouts of people going about their daily routine; the clang of the smith at work; the high-pitched noise of the insects that were unseen but omnipresent and seemed creatures of the oppressive heat. Other than the insects, it was the sound of village life. Brann felt a pang for home but the memory seemed now so much like that of a different life, almost as if he had dreamt it, that the pain failed to stab through him as it had before. There was a sadness to that realisation, but also a hardness in his mind's response to the sadness: deal with now, or the past will weaken your ability to do so. Especially when the only now that was left to him would probably be measured in hours.

A stout building with a stouter door and thick iron grilles over its small windows sat beside the smith's workshop. Salus waved, cheerily of course, at the squat man in the leather apron who hammered relentlessly at the anvil and unlocked the iron-studded door with a key on a large jangling ring that he unhooked from his belt. They entered a cool, dim, treasure trove of weaponry. Every variation or combination of edge, point or club that could be invented to do harm to man, and still more that Brann could never have imagined, lay on or stood in racks in orderly rows of metal and wood. Salus told Grakk to select whatever he wanted to practise with and the tribesman immediately selected a pair of long, slim, gently curved swords.

Brann headed for a rack of broadswords, oiled and gleaming from obvious care. Salus's large hand landed on his shoulder and steered him to a separate area. He eyed the boy's height and felt his shoulders, arms and chest with an expert touch. Brann felt like a horse at market.

Lined in front of them was a row of practice swords fashioned from dark wood. Salus tried a few for weight before selecting one. He walked over to a selection of round wooden shields and plucked one as he passed with less consideration, then took the boy to the other side of the room to pull a heavy, padded, sleeveless tunic from a shelf. Metal clips were set into the front and back and, after pulling it over Brann's head, Salus used the clips to fasten lead weights onto it at several points.

Brann looked at him incredulously. 'Have you felt the heat out there? Are you trying to kill me today instead of tomorrow?'

Salus smiled, quietly for once, and drew a couple of leather thongs from another shelf. He held up the shield to allow Brann to slip his hands through the straps and handed him the sword.

The weapon dipped and almost hit the floor before Brann caught its movement. 'This isn't the right weight,' he pointed out. 'I'll never be able to practise properly with this.' He tried swinging it from side to side, his movements slow and awkward. 'I can't even control it properly.'

With a few deft movements, Salus used the strips of leather to bind Brann's hands to the sword and shield.

Brann stared at him. 'What are you doing? How is that...?' Salus placed a large finger on the boy's lips.

'This. This. And this.' He touched the sword, shield and tunic in turn. 'These are your best friends right now if you want to have any chance of living through tomorrow. These, and water. Plenty of water.'

Brann just looked at him. The big man continued as he led Brann back to Grakk, took Grakk's selected swords from him and then led the pair out the door, locking it behind him. 'Make the unfamiliar familiar, remember? You will wear less in the Arena, even if armoured, so if you can become used to the heat and weight of that tunic, you will benefit. Likewise the sword and shield you have now are heavier than you will be armed with tomorrow, so you will carry these, whatever you are doing, between now and then. You will feel their weight, you will feel the way they try to drag you, and you will start to adjust to control them.'

Brann held up his hands and the weight trying to drag them down left him doubting he would become used to the feeling in a month, never mind less than a day. His stomach lurched at the thought.

Salus turned and whistled sharply through his teeth. A skinny boy detached himself from a group of three youths who were sweeping the area between the buildings and ran over, all tanned skin, white teeth and enthusiasm. 'Yes boss?' He swept his hair away from his eyes.

'Young, er...' He looked at Brann. 'I didn't ask your name, did I?'

'Brann.'

'Yes, young Brann here requires an assistant. You know what to do.' The boy nodded and fell in behind Brann. Salus spoke again to Brann. 'Marlo here will be your hands. When you need to eat, he will feed you. When you are thirsty, and it will be often, he will lift the drink to your lips. When you approach a door, he will open it. When you need to piss...'

'I'll manage that one,' Brann growled. 'However I have to, I'll manage.'

'Very well,' Salus beamed. 'That's that sorted, then. Your arms will learn to feel the weapons. Your legs will learn to bear your clothing. Your head will learn to forget the heat. Now for your jewellery.'

They were standing in front of the forge and the heat within stunned Brann beyond even what the sun had already managed. How the smith could breathe, let alone work metal, Brann couldn't fathom. Even just from standing, sweat was already running down every surface on his body. His eyes started to sting and he twisted one way then the other to wipe the shoulders of his tunic against them, almost battering Marlo's face with the wooden sword in the process.

'Sorry,' he blurted. He had only just met the boy and he was nearly braining him already.

The boy's teeth flashed. 'Good training for me.'

Brann wondered if everyone at this compound was relentlessly cheerful. It didn't take long to find an answer.

The smith looked up from pounding a battered sword-blade flat. 'What?' More a grunt of irritation than a question.

'Garlan, my friend,' said Salus. 'I have two new arrivals here, who require new neck decoration.'

The smith spat into the hot coals beside him without the ring of his hammer losing a beat. 'Friend. I am your friend when you need something. As you are mine, except that I never need anything from you. Except peace, so if you want to be my friend, bugger off. I'm busy.'

'It is urgent, I am afraid, good Garlan. These two will fight in death matches tomorrow.'

The smith stopped hammering and looked the pair up and down. 'Hardly worth my while, then, by the looks of it.' He spat again. 'Since I'll be getting the iron back tomorrow night as it won't stay on a neck with no head, I suppose I may as well oblige you. Consider it a loan.' He pointed his hammer at Brann. 'You.' The hammer moved to indicate further inside the forge where a heavy block sat on the floor, a rounded section cut from its top surface. 'There.'

Brann walked nervously across as the smith fetched a length of heavy chain. 'Kneel.' The chain was looped round his neck. 'Head on the block.' He leant forward, placing his face against the smooth surface. 'Oh by the gods, are you trying to suffocate yourself, fool? Head to one side.' He did so, and felt the chain drawn tight until it sat snugly. Rough jerks were followed by a snipping sound and the unneeded length fell to the ground. The chain pulled against his throat as it was manipulated before heat seared the back of his neck. He gasped and the metal hissed as cold water was thrown over it. The smith used his metal pincers to drag the chain, and Brann, to his feet. 'Next,' he grunted.

Brann moved to one side, his right hand automatically starting to reach for the chain. The swinging sword brought a glare from the smith and prudence suggested that he use his shield arm. His fingers found the chain and explored for a moment, though there was little to discover. The links were thick, it was heavy and he could fit only one finger between the metal and his neck.

Within moments, Grakk had been similarly fitted and they had obeyed Garlan's second instruction to bugger off.

'A skilled man,' Grakk observed.

'More even,' Salus said, 'than you saw there. Much more. You should see his silver-work, and his swords would sell for a fortune on the free market. But Salus saved his life many years ago, and he feels he cannot leave him until he has repaid the debt. A noble sentiment in his heart that his head appears to dispute on a daily basis. Still, he is here and our metal is the better for it.'

Brann fingered his chain again. This time his shield arm was the one to move first, and his fingers found the metal with ease. 'So I am to die a slave after all,' he grumbled.

'Maybe, but maybe not, young pessimist,' Salus pointed out. 'Do you know how many killing blows cleave their way into a neck? Even a chance shallow slice there is likely to be your end. More than a few slaves have been glad they were not free men when they fought.'

Grakk nodded. 'It does you no harm, son of the miller. Better a living slave than a dead free man. It is possible for a slave to wake as a free man someday, something a dead man cannot achieve.'

'Better wrap me in chains, then,' Brann muttered.

'Funny you should say that,' Salus beamed. He looked up at the sun. 'Near enough mid-day. You should eat. You will need the strength of food.'

Marlo ran to one of the nearby buildings to fetch slices of cold meat that had a sharp tang to them and fresh fruit that Brann had never seen before but that had a juiciness and flavour that made it difficult to stop eating them and easy to forget the awkwardness of being fed by another. He grunted around a mouthful and nodded to Marlo that he was ready for another bite.

'Enough,' Salus steadied him. 'It is pleasant to see a healthy appetite, but you will be sick before long if you continue. This is to give you strength, not slow you down. And so we now have work. Come.'

At his request, Grakk was given his swords and directed to a quiet spot where he could initially work by himself. Salus told Marlo to fill a waterskin and catch up with them, and took Brann beyond the buildings where the view opened up to reveal around a score of men and half that number of women working in groups or pairs with a range of weapons on a flat area that extended to the undulating ground, broken by walls and obstacles that he could barely make out and affording only the occasional glimpse of the far boundary of the compound. There was much shouting, some laughter and universal dedication.

Salus called over five of them and, at his instruction, they gathered lumps of the hardened earth and ranged themselves in front of Brann. Salus stepped away from him and, at his instruction, a clod whistled through the air and shattered unerringly against his forehead. He scarcely had time to yelp in surprise and pain before more followed.

'You have a shield, you know,' Salus offered helpfully, just as Brann began himself to try to fling the shield to meet the missiles hurtling at him. Soon he was managing to deflect as many as made it past the shield as he tried to jerk the unwieldy wood in a dozen directions in the space of a few breaths.

'Well done,' enthused Salus when the hail had finished. 'You managed to be hit by only half of them.'

'Fantastic,' glowered Brann, feeling as if his head, arms and legs had been beaten with staves and wondering if his left arm would ever lift a cup again, far less the shield. He rested his encumbered hands on his knees, fighting for breath and watching the sweat that dropped from his head dry quickly where it spotted the ground.

'Don't worry, I'm sure you'll do better next time.'

'Next time?'

'You think tomorrow will be easy? We will do this several times. You must be as ready as you can.'

'They are going to throw lumps of earth at me in the Arena?'

Salus looked long at him, as if dealing with a small child. 'Whatever comes at you, you must be able to move your shield to meet it. Preferably without bothering your brain, though that may not be the hardest part for you.'

He thanked the throwers, who declared themselves enthusiastically available for the repeat sessions.

'Now the sword. But first you drink.' Water had never tasted so good.

They walked to a wooden post half again as tall as Brann and wrapped in thick rope.

'The rope?' Brann wondered. The lack of breath, the heat and the heavy tunic had combined to let him decide that the effort of speaking was worth keeping to a minimum.

'Wood against wood tends to damage at least one of the woods. Rope absorbs the blow on both woods and is easier to replace if it wears. Now strike, left and right.'

When Brann felt like he could lift the sword no more, he made to stop.

'Yes, you may stop with the post. But now you swing at nothing.'

'At nothing? Why would I want to practise missing?'

'Because you need to practise coping with missing. That is when you are at your most vulnerable. Off balance and out of shape. And it happens most when you are tired and least able to deal with it. Like you are now, and will be more before we finish. So swing right hard, stop it as quickly as you can, and swing back as soon as you can. Then right again.'

It wasn't long before his arm started to seize up and forced a halt.

'Not bad for a start.' Salus lifted the water to Brann's lips and he sucked it in greedily, feeling as if he could drink for ever. 'Steady now.' Disappointment surged as it was pulled away, scattering drops down his front. 'Enough to keep you going, but too much and it'll be coming back up before you know it. Now back to the shield work.'

A hard lump of earth exploded against the back of his head, his shocked flinch bending him over. 'Splendid! Our helpers have saved us the trouble of walking back over there.'

And so it continued, relentlessly. And worse each time. More clods flew, and in faster succession. He was urged to hit the post increasingly, not harder and quicker but longer and more. When he was striking at nothing, Salus would pick up a thick rod and poke him in the chest between swings, hard enough to cause pain even through the thick padding of the tunic. He started trying to bring up his shield following each missed swing, but only succeeded in hitting himself on the forehead. And the rod still poked him. Still, it seemed a decent move to attempt, and the rod would come at him whether he tried it or not, so he felt it was worth persevering with it.

And then back to the shield work. And again. And again.

While stopping for water, Brann stopped in mid-swallow. 'I had forgotten about the heat.' He was astonished at the realisation.

Salus clapped him on the back. 'You see. Your first achievement! Now the post. Left then right then left.'

There was movement behind him. He whirled, crouching behind his shield.

'Very good,' said Cassian. He stepped forward and, with a finger, lifted the tip of the wooden sword so that it was held in readiness beside the protection of the shield. 'Like a snake, ready to strike.' He noticed Brann's puzzled look. 'Like an arrow drawn and ready to fly. No use fending off a blow if you are not able to exploit any opportunity, should it present itself.'

His eyes squinted slightly and he cocked his head. Twisting the strap on Brann's right wrist, he turned the hilt a fraction in the boy's grip. 'This way, yes? Now you will swing more easily. Now, drop your sword then turn to face Salus.'

Brann whirled, and stood poised, shield and sword ready. Cassian adjusted his elbow and stepped back. 'Good feet, good balance. Deliberate but almost right. And lead with your eyes. Dizziness is not a benefit when someone seeks to kill you. And you will see more, sooner. Now to me.'

He faced the old soldier again, who moved to correct his sword arm, then stopped with a shake of his head. 'No, it's fine. Now thirty more times doing it right. If you get it wrong, you start again.'

Brann got it right. By ten, the position didn't feel so awkward. By thirty, his arms were following the pattern themselves.

'Good boy.' Cassian looked delighted.

Brann looked at him. 'When do I start practising with an opponent?'

The man leant on a plain staff, for all the world like the shaft of a spear without the head. 'Did you not listen earlier? You cannot learn to fight in one day. Your brain would not accept it. We must train your muscles. You are not used to the movement of a shield or sword, but your muscles learn and remember on their own. They do not need the brain to work out what is best and waste time telling them. If they do it often enough, they do it themselves. So we are teaching your arms to remember. If you come back tomorrow, we can start to teach your head.' His hand patted Brann's head then, almost absently, ruffled his hair. 'Listen to Salus. He is a good man, and has won many fights, inside and out of the Arena. You will most probably die tomorrow, but his words will reduce that possibility a little each time you hear them. Now, the post. Left then right then left. And always with the shield ready to protect.'

He nodded at Salus and ambled away, smiling benignly at the gladiators he passed. No matter their activity, they stopped as he passed and greeted him with their right hands on their chests.

Salus's face dropped into a glare of an intensity that tightened Brann's chest. 'You see the respect and the affection that man brings from those gladiators? That comes from his achievements and his knowledge, yes. But it also comes from his simple acceptance of everyone who comes here to live, and his passion to protect them by improving them as fighters in every way he can. Already he does that for you, so if you want any chance at all to live tomorrow, you will listen and remember every word he says, and waste no time questioning him.'

Brann nodded through his embarrassment.

Salus's smile returned like the sun emerging from a cloud. 'Good. Now, face that post and show me you heard the man.'

By the time Brann turned from the post to take the next clod on his shield, the old man was gone. But the fatigue had eased just enough to see him through to dusk.

Before he allowed him to eat, Salus took him into the main house, leading him through to the room with the pools where he had met Cassian. Brann wondered if the master of the school ever met anyone in his house with clothes on, but found the room empty, little light entering by the windows but lamplight glowing on the still surface of the water.

He turned to Salus. 'Where is he?'

The big shoulders shrugged. 'No idea. Now let Marlo take off your clothes.'

'What?'

But before he could object, the padded tunic was unlaced

72

at the shoulders and fell to his ankles under its considerable weight. Brann felt as it he was rising off the ground.

'Oh, that feels so good.' A flash of a blade saw Marlo expertly slice his clothes until they, too, lay on the floor. Brann dropped his shield to cover himself. 'Oh, that's just great. Now what will I wear tomorrow?'

Salus looked puzzled. 'You think we have no clothing to give you? What you had was nice for visiting the Emperor, but not so suitable for the Arena. And if you are to live or die as a man of Cassian, you must be seen as one.' He patted the symbol on his own tunic. 'Now, into the first bath.'

'The what?'

'Bath. The pool of water nearest you.'

Brann tilted the sword and shield pointedly. 'With these?'

'Why not? They are wood. They will not rust.'

The water was warm and, he had to admit, extremely pleasant. He started to relax, the wooden weapons lying on the surface until, to his shock, Marlo stripped as well and slipped in. He recoiled in horror, but the boy just grinned.

'Don't flatter yourself, Northerner. You have two things missing from your chest and something extra between your legs. Not my type. My duties only extend so far.'

He rubbed a block of soap on Brann and eased the lather through his hair, then scrubbed at him with a hard-bristled brush.

'Good,' Salus nodded in approval when he was clean. 'Now for your muscles. Into the second bath.'

He gasped with the heat of the water as he sank into the middle pool. Sitting neck-deep, he felt his arms and legs grow weak and his head light.

Salus stood over him. 'Thirty breaths in this bath, then thirty in the next. Six times in each.'

Brann rose and emerged from the water, deep pink on all but his head. He stepped into the third pool but snatched his foot back with a yelp. 'You are not serious! That's like ice!'

Salus shoved him between the shoulders and he was launched headlong into the water, the sudden cold constricting his chest and tensing every part of his body. As he surfaced, spluttering, the man said amiably, 'Better to endure shock for one second than to drag it over many. Thirty breaths, then back in the hot.'

'I'll have to start breathing again before I can count them,' Brann gasped.

Marlo patted him dry with a thick towel at the end.

'If that was meant to make me feel better, it was a waste of time,' Brann grumbled. 'I feel as weak as ever.'

'You are tired because you have worked; water cannot fix that. It is unfortunate, and you would have benefited from a rest day today, but you will be better tomorrow tired with muscles that know how to move than fresh and flailing.'

'So how does this help then?'

'This, curious one, is to let you move tomorrow. Were you merely to sleep now, you would wake with limbs stiffened to immobility. The hot lets your blood flow, the cold tightens your muscles in. One then the other flushes the blood through the muscles, like bellows sucking in air then shooting it out, taking with it all that should not be there. Your muscles will be clean and ready for tomorrow.'

'If you say so.'

'I do. Now, clothing, food and sleep.'

As soon as he woke, he could feel the wisdom in Salus's words. He started a stretch, and was immediately reminded of the heavy wood attached to his wrists.

He had slept soundly. Even the prospect of what lay ahead when he woke and the awkwardness of having a wooden sword and shield strapped to him hadn't managed to stop him from sinking into deep slumber as soon as he had laid back. That was the benefit of exhausting himself. He had no exhaustion now to overwhelm his thoughts. His breathing quickened and his stomach clenched. Today was when it happened. Today, he could push away the prospect into the future no longer.

He had been wakened by the sound of the men in the cots around him waking and rising, and he grew jealous of the ordinariness of their actions. He ached with a yearning for mundane daily life and felt tears of despair fill his eyes. He sat up, swinging his legs to the floor, and blinked in time to see two familiar figures approaching, wiping the back of his right forearm across his eyes before anyone could notice the moisture, and cursing silently the stupid blunt weapons he was forced to grip.

'Excellent, you are eager for the day,' Salus boomed. Brann didn't feel it was worth disagreeing with the assessment, though it could not have been further from the truth. His guts were trying to force themselves up through his throat and he lurched slightly.

If Salus noticed, he chose not to acknowledge it. 'Marlo, if you could be so good as to help our young friend dress?'

An under-tunic, open almost from armpit to waist, allowed him to dress without removing the shield, and the weight-laden padded tunic was laced onto him once more. Numbly, he followed Salus to the rope-wound post, stopping only to eat briefly the same food as had been his lunch the previous day, turning away from those around him to mask the sight of Marlo feeding him like a baby.

The movements against the post were fluid, much to his surprise and Salus's delight. When he swung at fresh air, it seemed easier to drag the sword back than it had been just the evening before. Right, then left, than right again. As he started to bring the heavy wood back again, Salus flashed the rod forward. He flicked up the shield, knocking the rod skywards, then crashed the sword into it on the swing that followed. He wasn't sure who of the pair of them was more astonished.

Salus waved away the clod-throwers who were about to start launching their missiles. 'Thank you, but if he can do that with his shield, not necessary.' He turned to Brann. 'What made you think of that?'

Brann managed a small smile. 'I thought of it yesterday, but my arm wouldn't do it. To be honest, I had forgotten it again until my arms did it.'

'Today is a good day to start doing it.' Cassian's voice behind him made him jump. There was a woman with him this time, tall and willowy, dark of skin and eyes and with hair that was a mass of thick tendrils, halfway between black and white. 'Thank you, good Salus. Your work has been well done. The results have exceeded expectations.'

Salus nodded his head. 'You are kind, boss, but the boy did it. I hope there is a chance I will see him again today.'

Brann felt his eyes filling up again. He suddenly felt very young. Too young to be facing this. But Salus could not have done more to help him. He turned to the large man. 'I, er, I...'

Salus grinned. 'I know. You love me, of course you do. Now come back and make me my dinner tonight.' Before Brann could answer, he was walking away.

The woman cut in, turning the boy by the shoulders and

looking him over. 'Strong for his size. You have rowed?' Her voice was cool and measured. Brann nodded. 'That helps. Let us visit the pig.'

Brann wondered who warranted this name, but was almost disappointed to find it a literal description. He was taken to a side room in the building where he had eaten and found the carcass of a pig hanging from the ceiling.

Cassian nodded to Marlo. 'Relieve our young friend of his practice weapons.'

Considering the ease with which the boy's knife sliced through the leather straps, the knots having been tightened beyond unpicking by the bathwater the night before and the movement before and after, Brann was relieved that his speed of use was matched by a surety of movement. The wooden weapons fell to the ground and Brann looked at his hands in surprise as they rose towards the ceiling of their own accord, as if he were a puppet operated by an invisible giant.

Marlo laughed. 'Fear not, they will settle in a moment. But wait till you feel this real sword.'

A broadsword of simple but functional quality was tucked under his arm, and he offered it to Brann.

'Take it, and strike the pig,' Cassian prompted.

He grasped the hilt and swung. His eyes widened as the blade, feeling as light as a switch and just as manoeuvrable, slammed into the side of the carcass, biting deep into the flesh.

'Now you see the value of the heavy wood, but also the problem,' the old soldier said.

'The problem? What problem could there be in swinging a sword like that?'

'Pull it out.'

77

Brann dragged it back the way it had swung, but it stuck hard and tried to pull the full weight of the pig with it. He wrenched it straight towards him and, eventually, as he grunted in triumph, it squelched free.

'Now stab it.'

He thrust, the blade sinking deep. Again, when he tried to pull it free, the flesh sucked it close. He rolled his hand right and left as he hauled it and the pink meat reluctantly released its grip on the blade.

'You see?' Cassian's look was earnest. 'This is most important. Were this a man, not a pig, while you were fighting the grip of the body, all of your right side would be inviting him to hit you as many times as he liked. I have seen men killed after striking a killing blow. Not every fatal strike kills instantly, and a dying man will fixate on taking you with him as his last furious act.' He took the sword. 'Strike shallow and fast, like this.' His blades flashed in and out, stabbing twice on the front of the pig. 'And this.' Surprisingly quick on his feet, he moved in and swung fast at the side of the carcass. The blade bit, he twisted his wrist and withdrew, and he was back at Brann's side in an instant. 'As you started to do, twisting releases it quicker. And causes more damage, which is helpful. Remember that blood vessels, ligaments, sinews and muscles are often near the surface, so damage is caused as soon as you strike. There is seldom a need to go deep.'

He picked up the practice shield. 'Don't forget, either, that you have two weapons. This has a face that can smash,' he slammed it straight into the pig, 'like so. With the shoulder and the hips. Drive from your legs.' He angled it and swung it sideways into the solid meat. 'And an edge that can bite. This is a fight where he will die or you will; there is no other outcome. You must fight any way that presents itself.'

He handed over the weapons. 'Now you try, over and over.'

Cassian stopped him, however, as soon as he was satisfied the technique was right. 'Good. Now we are done. Let us eat. Lightly, in your case.'

They stepped from the doorway, the light bright. 'Cassian, sir,' Brann said. The broad frame turned. 'How did you learn...?'

A roar burst from Brann's right. Steel flashed on high.

He pivoted, dropped into a crouch and brought up his shield, blocking a blow that jarred his arm to the shoulder. In the same movement, his sword thrust forward. The wooden practice sword swung down and Cassian knocked Brann's blade aside before it reached his attacker. He looked up to see Salus's grinning face.

'Not bad, though your opponent will not hold back as Salus did.'

Brann flexed his shoulder. 'He held back?'

Cassian ignored the comment, and patted him on the back encouragingly. 'You will not die overly easily. Now, you were asking?'

'Oh, yes.' Brann cast around for other attacks as he spoke. 'How did you learn all that? The things you showed me in there. Was it in the army?'

'I learnt to swing a sword in the army. I learnt to fight on the battlefield. I learnt to survive from opponents and comrades who didn't.'

'And the stuff about sinews and tendons and blood... things?'

'From my wife.'

Deep in the corridors of the Arena, the noise from the crowd above was muted but was all the more terrifying for it.

When it loitered on the edge of your hearing, it caught your attention all the stronger. And reminded you what was coming.

Brann had spent the journey to the massive stone-built amphitheatre in a daze, carried with three other fighters in a small covered wagon pulled by a single horse. Grakk was presumably in another, similar one. His throat wouldn't let his voice emerge, but one of the men had noticed him looking at the canvas cover.

'It's for the way back. We might not present such a savoury sight on that journey.'

The way back. That seemed like a fantasy. He felt like he was going to his execution. He felt that he *was* going to his execution. Back at the compound, he had been occupied by work and distracted by novelty. The Arena had seemed a world away. Now it was close; now there was no way back. His head closed in, as if a vice for his brain. His guts were like a snake wriggling in his belly. His eyes stared blankly. Why was this happening? After everything, why? He hadn't asked for any of this. He was only a boy, learning a miller's trade. And, somehow, it was going to end like this. In a land where everything was strange and unreal, not least that he would die at the hands of a man he had never met. For sport.

Now, shuffling through the corridors, the cool felt dank and foreboding rather than a welcome respite from the searing sun. He was numb, but not from the temperature. His mind tried to stretch every second, as if he could prolong the time before he must face his fate; his opponent; his death.

They walked alone, just him and the guard. He and Grakk were fighting in the only two death matches that day. They were rare, and conversations overheard from the other side of the wagon's canvas had attested to the excitement brewing amongst those whose blood would not be risked but whose hearts beat faster at the prospect. Those fighting in a death match did not await their moment with the mainstream fighters. They were treated as different. They were different.

He was shown into a room with a domed ceiling of bricks, dark-flamed torches sputtering for air and casting light and shadows equally.

'We meet again, young Brann.'

Grakk sat cross-legged against one wall, a simple breast-plate lying beside him and the two swords he had chosen the day before lying across his lap.

Brann said nothing. His mind was blank. He looked around the empty room and found his voice. 'Where are the others?'

'Our opponents? We will meet them on the sand of the Arena. Until then, it is just you and I. You are feeling fit?'

'What does it matter how I feel now? In a short time I won't feel anything.'

Grakk unfolded himself and stood in one fluid movement. He stood in front of the boy and looked into his eyes. 'You will die today, undoubtedly.' He tapped one finger against Brann's forehead. 'If you think in this manner. Should you enter the Arena already defeated, you will exit it dragged by the feet, trailing your blood behind you. But you are a silly boy, for I feel you will win. Unless your thoughts defeat you.'

'You think I will win? Are you mad?'

Grakk shrugged. 'Some say so. But in this I have reason. I have seen you fight. You are perfect for this. You do not know your opponent. You cannot plan for his style, his methods. But you do not plan anyway – you react, you

81

adapt. There is an instinct in you, a voice that speaks to your hands before your head has heard. But not just this. Your eyes also notice things, chances, opportunities that others do not see. This is a good combination.'

'But if he is better than me? I am on the far side of the world, dragged halfway as a slave and the other half as a silly naïve boy thinking he was on an adventure. Only to die in some stupid entertainment.'

Grakk gripped his head and stared into his eyes. For the first time since they had met, Brann heard an intensity in his voice. 'Listen to me, young Brann, and listen well. There are no rules, no restrictions, no limitations. You will face a criminal, whether it be a former soldier who will show no mercy or a gutter rat who lives by fighting dirty. Whatever or whoever he may be, he will do whatever he can. You must do the same. You must face him with a craving for life, a desperation to keep a heart beating in your body. You must do anything, use anything, to stay alive. The man in front of you will be wanting to kill you. To kill *you*. Feel rage at that, turn it on him. Don't believe you will die, but don't think about winning. Don't think at all. Live in the moment. Live each action and reaction as it happens, then live the next. Live. Always fight to live. Always fight.'

Brann nodded.

'Good. Now you get dressed.'

'Dressed?'

'Dressed.' Grakk turned him around, and he saw the sword he had used against the pig's carcass, a shield – similar to the one he had practised with but studded with iron and emblazoned with the symbol of Cassian's school – and a shirt of chain mail.

Grakk saw him looking at it. 'It is a…'

'A hauberk.' Brann looked at him. 'We don't fight naked where I come from, you know. Just because we choose not to fight every day, it doesn't mean we are centuries behind the rest of the world.' He remembered a conversation with Einarr on the trip to the city, when the wind had filled the sail, the oars were rested and life seemed good. 'Our smiths are renowned, you know.'

Grakk was pleased. 'That is more the spirit you need. And your smiths are indeed regarded with admiration. This mail is a good choice. Light enough to afford mobility and, while it will not stop a weapon used full-strength, it is strong enough to deflect a glancing blow. For it is the small wounds that are often the lethal ones.'

'I know, I know. Tendons and blood vessels and things like that.'

'Good boy! You see, your prospects are more than you thought.'

As they had been speaking, Grakk had lifted the mail over Brann's head. It reached to his mid-thigh and was short-sleeved. Grakk was right, he could move freely. He could feel the weight of it bearing down on his legs, and Grakk smiled. 'Now you see the reasoning behind the tunic with weights.' He fastened a belt around Brann's waist. 'This will keep it from shifting at an awkward moment.'

Brann tried moving in it. It felt awkward, but reassuring. He looked around. 'No helmet?'

Grakk shook his head. 'The good people of this city like to see the faces of those who may die. They like to see the faces as they die. Any sort of light armour is permitted, but only light. In heavy armour the combatants may die of exhaustion before a single drop of blood is spilt. That would not do at all.'

'I feel ridiculous. Like a child at play.'

Grakk grunted. 'Well I suggest you play at being a winner.'

Satisfied with Brann's preparations, he moved across to the breastplate and slipped it on. Brann moved to help him fasten it. 'It is fine. Pick up your sword and shield. Become accustomed to the movement in your new attire. Do not put them down from now until the fight is over. They are a part of you for this time, and they must feel as such. And remember this. Lengthy fights, ebbing and flowing and replete with excitement, they are for the sagas. In life, it is the most exhausting time you will ever live, even were you not encumbered by mail and baking in the heat. It will last minutes, but it will feel like hours. Take your chance whenever it presents itself. Kill if you can; if you cannot, weaken; if you cannot, worry. Learn quickly of his style. Trust your instinct, and act.'

Brann looked at the lean tribesman, a man he had grown close enough to call friend over the course of months and through more than a few deadly situations, and realised that he barely knew anything of Grakk from before the moment they met. And now he may know nothing more. He pushed down the surge of emotion and replaced it with simple curiosity. 'Have you fought in a death match before?'

Grakk stared calmly into his eyes. 'Not precisely as this. But, yes, I have fought to the death in circumstances of many varieties, and I have watched men fight also. One thing I have noticed often: it does not always finish the way onlookers would expect at the start. Do not panic at the sight of a man in front of you with sharpened steel, for once it starts, your mind will empty of all apart from the danger you face. Move, anywhere and in any way, and you will not freeze. Your desire to live will do the rest.'

Brann nodded, at a loss to imagine any way that he would not freeze, but grateful for the words. If nothing else, they had filled the time. He tried a few experimental swings and thrusts, and, to his surprise, the mail afforded him more freedom of movement than the padded tunic had the day before. Grakk merely flexed his shoulders and resumed his cross-legged position.

A guard appeared in the doorway. 'You two. With me.' Brann jumped, feeling foolish at being seen practising his sword strokes. The guard ignored him and turned on his heel.

'Advisable to follow him if we don't want to get lost, young warrior,' Grakk suggested from beside him. They did so.

The noise of the crowd, borne on the constant draft blowing down the bare passage, was different. A chanting that, though the words were indistinct, lent a primeval atmosphere to their journey. Brann felt his legs dragging and his knees buckled slightly. He felt Grakk's hand in the small of his back, a steadying presence.

'Hold your head high, and your pride will follow. If your father, and his father, and his father, and his father were in the crowd, here to see you, how would you conduct yourself? Well, those who have passed to the next life, they are watching you today. Show them what you can do. Show this crowd, who are here to see you die, that you will not bow to their will. And show Loku, for there is no doubt he will wish to see his designs for you succeed, that he cannot beat you.'

Brann felt an anger begin to grow in his chest. His eyes felt an intensity he had not experienced before. But still his stomach heaved, his hands shook and his legs were weak.

They stopped before heavy double doors. The chanting was like a drum beat. Six beats in two threes. Over and over. And over. And over. Growing, swelling, pounding the stone structure till it shook in time.

Grakk turned to him. 'All is order in this land. In a death match, for every killing, there is a life. For every life, there is a death. In a death match there are no rules, you do what you do to make the life yours, and the death his. There are no rules, but there are two laws: it finishes only when your opponent dies at your hand; and for every one that falls, another must stand. If two fight, one only must die. If a hundred fight, fifty only must die. So if four fight, two only must die. We both win, we both live. So think on this: I will finish my man as expeditiously as can be achieved, then I will join you. No rules, remember? I will help weaken him, but the killing blow must be yours. Stay alive and it will be so.

'You will live, young Brann. You will live.'

Horns sounded, and the chanting burst louder still in response. The guard nodded to two men at the doors, and they were swung outwards, flooding them with light and noise. Grakk stepped forward and, with a shove from the guard, Brann stumbled after him.

The chant was a hammer blow harder even than the wall of heat. But now the words were clear.

'... walk out. Four walk in, two walk out. Four walk in, two walk out...'

Huge drums, spaced evenly around the circular stadium, thundered out a steady beat but were almost drowned out by the voices they sought to lead. Brann realised his feet were keeping time, as were those of the squad of eight soldiers marching in line immediately to their right.

86

The floor of the combat area was wide and hard with packed sand, and Brann felt the vast bareness opening away from him. Never had he felt so exposed, so visible. The spectators crammed the benches, a mass of teeming humanity so vast that he was unable to register individuals. The sight and the sound combined to make them a single entity, all seeming to watch him, all seeming to hate him, all gleeful for his death.

From directly opposite, their opponents had entered. Both looked like common criminals, but of the most ferocious and murderous sort. The type of men who killed for a purse rather than stealing it by guile, who fought others for their spoils and who survived amongst others of their ilk by being nastier and more brutal than those they fought. Brann was sure they were not a random choice. Both were lean and strong, one with a moustache that reached the bottom of his chin and a scar that ran vertically from the corner of his mouth to bisect an eyebrow and finish at his hairline, carrying a sword and shield similar to those Brann bore, and the other larger and more powerful, turning as he walked to wave a longsword and an axe high to the crowd. As the groups closed, both men leered at Brann and Grakk with obvious pleasure.

The two pairs, with their escorts, met in the centre and turned to walk together towards one side, where Brann noticed a more sparsely populated area. Rather than the bench seating elsewhere, this section was furnished with individual chairs of a size and ornateness that grew further, the closer placed they were to the centre. Perfectly in the centre was a plain stone throne. Lounging in it was the Emperor, smiling as benignly as if Brann were being presented as a desirable suitor for his daughter, waving his hand absently along with the chants. Behind him stood his impassive Scribe, to either side sat the four who had sat with him the previous day, to the side of them sat the frail old man Brann had seen near Loku at the Throne Room and behind them sat Loku himself, his smile triumphant and his eyes bright with anticipation. The chanting had reached a crescendo.

A horn cut through the roar, silencing the throng in the beat of a heart. The silence was just as overbearing as the noise had been.

A herald, fat, shiny with sweat and lurid in a shirt, pantaloons and imperial tabard of colours that clashed so violently they jarred the eyes, stepped forward onto a platform at the front of the Emperor's section. His voice, though, was as true to the ear as his clothes were offensive to sight.

Almost singing, such was his lilting tone, his words rang to every nook of the Arena. 'What is your purpose today before His Magnificence, Emperor of the all the Civilised World?'

The other three started to respond, and with a jolt Brann recalled the words taught to him by Salus shortly before they had left the compound.

'Lord of Lords, our lives are yours. We fight, win, die for your glory. Death is our master, Death is your servant. Our blood is your power.'

The Emperor smiled down at them, genially.

The herald continued. 'Today we witness a death match. Four walk in, two walk out.'

The crown thundered in response. 'Four walk in, two walk out.'

Silence lay heavy as the herald paused to build the tension. He looked at the four fighters standing motionless. 'Today you walk the red path. But who shall you fight? Now we shall discover.' Both arms aloft, he held on high four balls. 'At this hour of death, we see the four colours of life: the amber of the sun, the green of the leaf, the blue of sea and sky, the claret of our blood.'

A soldier walked over with four strips of cloth, dyed to match the balls, tying one to each of their right biceps. Brann received the claret, Grakk the amber, the moustached man the blue and the large man the green.

The herald dropped the four balls into a bag. 'Our Emperor, the heart and soul of ul-Taratac, shall divine the selection.' The Emperor's Scribe descended to fetch it, but instead spoke briefly to the herald. 'In his beneficence, and in recognition of recent service of great value, our Lord of Lords has invited his loyal and trusted advisor, Taraloku-Bana, to make the selection.'

Loku stood and walked down to the herald's platform, his face solemn. He bowed to the Emperor, receiving a warm nod in reply, and turned to face the fighters. The herald held out the bag and lifted out a ball. The fat man's voice rang out once more. 'Claret will fight...' Brann's stomach lurched. The hand dipped again. 'Green.'

The larger man. Brann was sure the selection was no coincidence. Loku smirked.

The herald continued. 'And so Claret will fight Green, and Blue will fight Amber. Today we witness death matches, not one, but two. No rules, no limitations, just one truth: four walk in, two walk out.' The crowd roared the response. 'This contest will be fought as two matches, separate as the sun and moon. Two men, and two men only, fighting alone, twice over. Pure and simple as death itself.'

A fist of panic squeezed Brann's heart and he looked at

Grakk in alarm. The tattooed tribesman leant in close. 'It is what it is. We cannot change it, so waste no time wishing it different. Deal with the fate you face. You have survived much. You can do so again. What is it you say? Just do what seems right.'

The large man, grinning, exchanged his axe for the shield of his companion. The smaller man started to object but was silenced by a growl. He took the axe, swung it experimentally, and shrugged, apparently satisfied.

Brann's eyes narrowed. The man was adopting the same weapons as he had – he was making them as similar as possible so that the only difference left would be his size and, presumably, experience. The fact that he was alive attested to the fact that it had been successful experience.

The spears of the soldiers separated them into the pairs who would fight, and directed them to the centre of the Arena. Strangely, a hush had descended over the crowd, and they could hear their own footsteps and the clink of metal.

An unexpected calm had settled over Brann also, as a blanket over a fire. His stomach still churned but, with no option left to him and his immediate future certain, a coolness enveloped him. His senses were heightened, but also focused. He lost awareness of the crowd, of their very existence. He examined the man, slightly ahead and eager to start. He was tall and broad shouldered, tending to a bulk that spoke of power rather than speed. Similar to Grakk, he wore a breastplate but he had added matching protection on his forearms and shins. He was never still, banging his sword on his shield or raising both on high and roaring to the crowd. Not that it mattered, but Brann couldn't help but notice that whoever had shaved his head had done a patchy job.

They approached the centre and the man wheeled and hissed at him. 'My name is Balak-dur. Remember that when you die. Do not be ashamed, for it is an honour to die at the hand of The Reaper, the victor of forty-nine duels. A fortune awaits me, and your death will buy it, little man, so feel your worth. My fortune has been promised, and I will have it.'

'Promised by whom?' If he could place even a seed of doubt, it may distract the man.

'Promised by whom?' His high-pitched repetition was mocking. 'By none other than the Emperor's own Master of Information, so there is certainty in the promise. Remember the name of Balak-dur, and take it to the next world.'

A rage began to build within him, but it was a cold fury, washing against his fear. The soldiers stopped, two lines back to back and with spears levelled, separating the fights. The fighters faced each other at a distance of around five spear-lengths. The silence deepened. The Emperor rose from his throne of stone and raised one hand. He held it there for a long moment. The air felt thick, almost humming with the anticipation of thousands.

The hand dropped. The crowd erupted. Shield up and sword poised, Brann moved into readiness. His opponent, though, turned his back and faced the watching masses. As when he had walked, he held his weapons to the sky, roaring over and over. *He wants me to attack,* Brann realised, *and I will run into a full swing of that big sword.* Fighting the nerves, trying to draw on the anger, he waited, dropping both arms to his sides. Why waste energy holding them up?

He glanced across at Grakk, his fight in clear view between the widely spaced soldiers. They were already engaged and the tribesman's swords danced before him, weaving a net of bright metal as they parried and struck at a speed hard to follow. In seconds, the axe had fallen from nerveless fingers. Grakk swayed back just enough to see a wild swipe send the sword slicing the air in front of him, then leapt forward, arms crossed over each other and extending the twin blades forwards like a heron spearing a fish. The arms flung wide and Grakk sprang back, swords up and ready to defend. There was no need. The neck had been sliced from each side, opened from the front halfway to the back. Blood sprayed and squirted high, bright against sky and sand. The head flopped back, and the body hit the ground. The crowd bayed with lust. Grakk faced Brann, looking for all the world like a dog straining on an invisible leash.

Brann's opponent turned towards him. 'See that?' he screamed. 'That's you bleeding your life out into the dirt.' He pointed his sword at the masses watching. 'Except I'll take your head clean off and give it to them.'

He charged.

He came at Brann at a loping run, measured paces that built momentum but kept balance, his weight thudding into the hard ground with every pace. Power, not speed. But changing direction might be a problem. Especially if Brann sidestepped at the right moment. It wasn't much of a plan, but it was a plan. His nerves filled every fibre of his being. He had to get it right.

The plan evaporated. Just short of him, the man leapt skywards, dropping in front of Brann, his impetus down instead of forwards, his sword smashing down with all his weight behind it. Brann dropped to one knee, his shield raised on instinct. Muscles built in months fighting the sea with an oar resisted the blow, but the sword still crashed into his shield so hard that the wood slammed against his head. His own sword was moving, cutting right to left at the large leg in front of him. Just before it struck, the man, still catching his balance from the jump, twisted and Brann's blade caught the edge of the metal greave and sliced across the flesh of the calf rather than biting into tendon and bone.

His nerves evaporated. The cold calm that had crept up on him before now flowed over him. He knew nothing but the man in front of him. His movements. His noise.

The man screamed in fury. 'You little bastard. I'll cut you bad for that. I'll cut you bad before I kill you.'

He came at him in a flurry of hammering blows. The first, backhanded, hit Brann's shield so hard it nearly knocked him off his feet and he staggered back, barely keeping his balance. The next came hard on the first, swinging down from his left. His shield came up to meet it. As it struck, he turned his shoulders to the right, angling the shield the same way. The blade deflected away to his right, the unexpected direction unbalancing the man and giving Brann a fraction of a second. Again he dropped to a knee, but this time hammered the rim of his shield down on top of the man's foot, smashing into the fragile bones. The man screamed. Brann drove up with his legs, his sword vertical. He thrust. The blade speared into the man's throat and ripped up and through to emerge from the back of his head. The man arched back and collapsed into the dirt.

The crowd were suddenly silent, shocked as much by the brevity of the contest as by its outcome. Then shouts turned to roars, and roars turned to the chant, this time louder than ever before. 'Four walk in, two walk out.'

Brann stepped up to the man. Mindful of Cassian's warning about the danger of dying men, he stood on the wrist that still gripped the large sword. He leant over and stared into the contorted face, dark blood flowing from mouth, nose and wounds and expanding the pool already on the ground. Brann's teeth were clamped tight, but the words came out nonetheless.

'I have forgotten your name already. But know this: my name is Brann. Remember that as you die. Be ashamed, for you die at the hand of a boy who today fought his first duel. Remember the name of Brann, and take it to the next world.' He spat red blood onto the baked earth.

He had no idea whether the man was still alive or already dead. He didn't care.

A soldier leant past him, placed a foot against the man's chin and drew Brann's sword from his head with a sucking squelch. He wiped it on the corpse's tunic where it emerged below his unscratched breastplate, and handed it to the boy. 'You might want to keep this, lad. You use it well.'

He took it absently, unable to move his foot from the wrist, unable to move his eyes from the face, the fury lifting from him and, in its place, a horror at the reality of gruesome brutality fixing his gaze on the corpse with a force he could not break. Grakk appeared at his elbow. 'When I said to finish it when you had the chance, you certainly took the instruction to heart. You surprised us all. And, I must say, pleasantly.' He eased him away and the soldiers turned them to face the royal section. The crowd still chanted in acclaim. The Emperor stood, smiling and – as Brann and Grakk bowed on one knee as Salus had instructed when he had taught them the words of the greeting – applauding. Brann's eyes sought, found, Loku. His face was contorted in fury. Brann smiled.

Then the shaking started.

Chapter 3

'You still think me mad and old?'

He had begun to sense her presence when she approached, before even he heard her. He didn't turn as she filled a glass goblet and sipped at the cool water. The Arena lay empty and silent, soft wind and hard shadows reaching across it. Still he sat, eyes fixed on the smudge in the centre, the stain of blood a guide to his thoughts.

'Of course. Are you not?'

He grunted.

Her hoarse whisper was like a voice in his head. 'You do little to dispel that notion. Anyone seeing you sitting here alone, staring into nothing, would be certain your wits had preceded your body to the grave.'

'Those of us with wits call it thinking. It's what people who don't make assumptions do.'

She moved alongside him and followed his gaze. 'And what do you think?'

'I think you will have seen that I was right about the boy.'

'*You think he is capable.*'

'*Not yet. There is much he must learn. That which is within him must be set free.*'

'*Can it?*'

'*There are ways.*'

'*How can the ways come to pass?*'

'*That is what occupies my thoughts.*'

'*Will they come to pass?*'

'*They will.*'

She put a hand on his shoulder. He ignored it, but did not remove it.

A softness crept into her rasp. '*They must.*'

****

When Brann woke, his head was in pain more than his body. Moving his eyelids was too much effort. Groaning was beyond him. The last words he remembered saying were, 'Wine? What is wine?'

Now he knew. It was what demons created for times when ale wouldn't cause enough pain the next morning.

He was too hot, so he pushed the blanket to his waist. He needed the feel of something against him, so he pulled the blanket back over him. He curled on his side, but his limbs were restless. He squeezed his eyes shut against the pounding in his skull.

He sat up with a shouted gasp as icy water crashed over him.

'Good, you're up,' Salus said, as jovial as the water was cold. 'You can carry your bed out to the sun. It needs to dry off.'

He wiped water and fringe from his eyes and waited a

moment before lifting his head. Marlo held a dripping bucket, and wore a sheepish grin that Brann wanted to smash from his face. Except that he wanted even more to never again move a muscle. He made to roll back onto his mattress, but Salus stretched out a big arm.

'No, you don't. Cassian's orders. You do your recovery today, then start training tomorrow.'

Brann managed a groan and slowly stood up. His head felt like it had been filled with lead that was expanding with a relentless thumping pulse.

'Boss wants to see you first of all. Probably wants to see if you survived the second attempt on your life.'

Brann looked up sharply and immediately regretted the sudden movement. 'Second?'

Salus nodded solemnly. 'Your own attempt, using excessive amounts of alcohol. It was a most valiant attempt, I must say.'

'Was I in a bad state?'

Marlo laughed. 'Entertaining mostly. Then bad.'

'How bad?'

'Couldn't even bite your finger. That's when we took you to bed. Well, when I say *took*, I mean *carried*.'

Brann grunted and shuffled towards the door. Salus coughed pointedly. 'Your bed.'

Brann turned and lifted the end of the wooden cot, dragging it behind him, screeching against the tiled floor. Marlo stepped beside him and helped to pull it.

Brann looked at him. 'Would you not be better taking the other end?'

'I would if you looked capable of steering on your own.'

'Why are you here anyway? You were only helping me because my hands were full.'

97

Marlo grinned. 'I won the chance to handle the bucket.'

Brann's reply was snatched away by the stabbing pain of the sunlight as he stepped from the doorway. He dropped his side of the bed and clutched his hands to his eyes, yelling in misery. Marlo dragged the bed to one side and left it to dry in the heat. By the time Brann had eased his eyes open to slits, the boy had gone.

'If you're ready?' Salus was waiting.

'Never felt less like it, but don't feel like it's changing any time soon so I may as well,' Brann grumbled.

Cassian was watching his fighters spar when they found him. Brann was still trying not to vomit from the smell of the food cooking in the kitchens that they had passed on the way, but still managed to curse inwardly that the Master of the School could not have been occupied in the cool shade of his residence.

'Ah, my young warrior!' The old soldier beamed. 'I'm so glad to see you again. I did tell you this last night, but you didn't seem to be taking much in at that stage. Did you enjoy your introduction to wine?'

Brann rubbed the heels of his hands against his temples. 'Even my hair hurts. Why could you not have had a normal drink, like ale?'

'If we had expected you to return, we would have ordered some in.'

'Oh, very funny.'

Cassian frowned. 'It was not a joke.' He beamed and clapped Brann on the shoulder. 'It was a surprise, but be assured, it was a surprise of the most pleasant sort. And you certainly seemed to like the wine when you were drinking it.'

'Well I don't now.'

'Your dancing on the table was most amusing, though

not as amusing as your spectacular fall from it. And it did serve to cure your shaking last night. Although I see it is now causing the shaking this morning.' He handed Brann his waterskin, old leather that still had a feel of high quality. 'My victory present to you. Drink and refill it regularly.'

Aware that his mouth was tongue-sticking dry, Brann drank greedily. Cassian tipped the waterskin back down. 'Easy, easy. Build up slowly or it will hit your stomach and bounce back with all it finds there.'

Salus grinned. 'That might actually not be the worst thing that could happen.'

'Perhaps.' Cassian clapped Brann on the back. He was sure it caused his head to burst. 'What will be, will be. In the meantime, our friend Salus will introduce you to my good lady wife. She will take care of you today. We will start improving you tomorrow.'

Brann swayed slightly, waiting for his vision to stop dancing. It didn't, so he accepted that he would just have to follow both of the two Saluses that were walking back towards the main house.

After a while, Cassian's final words sank in. 'Improve me?'

'You can always improve.'

'But I thought what I did yesterday worked.'

'It worked against him.'

'Yes, so I was thinking I would just be...'

'You will not fight him again.'

'Oh. That's true.'

They were about to enter the house, but Salus wheeled to face him. He placed his hands on Brann's shoulders and bent to look into his eyes. For once, he looked stern. 'The day you stop learning, is the day you die. Dying stops you

99

learning; stopping learning makes you die. Some you will be taught, some you will notice yourself. But you must always look to improve.'

Brann nodded solemnly. 'I do tend to notice things.'

'Well keep doing it. And do it more. Now come, and let us have no more of this seriousness.'

He led Brann down into the centre of the house and turned down the same corridor that had taken them to the bathing pools. Before they reached the pools, however, Salus knocked on another door. A slave, clad in a simple white tunic and with a silver chain of slender links around his neck, opened the door, his head shaven and his arms and legs as smooth as his scalp. The sailors on the voyage to Sagia had filled the nights with tales, and some had spoken of such men who had, as boys, been robbed of their manhood for any number of reasons –through religion, for practicality, as punishment or to break their spirit – and in many cases all body hair followed of its own accord. Whatever the reason for the cutting, Brann thought it abhorrent and he found himself stopping and gripping the man's arm in sympathy as he passed. The slave looked at him quizzically.

'Don't have any designs on my staff.' The tall, striking woman Brann had seen with Cassian just the day before stood to one side and looked up from a potion she was pouring into a cup. Her voice was low, soothing, measured. 'I know of at least one culture that believes sex to be the cure for a hangover, but I find this to be more effective.'

He took the cup from her. 'Staff? Designs?' He frowned, trying to move his brain at normal speed. 'Cure?' His eyes widened. '*Sex?*' Realisation flooded his face with colour. 'Oh, no. I was just so sorry for him.'

'You think he suffers working with me?'

He was stammering now. 'No. I mean... no, no. I just think it's awful, what has been done to him.'

'You think I mistreat him?'

He was starting to wish he had entered the room head down and silent. 'I mean what happened to him as a boy.' He glanced at the man, who seemed unperturbed and was arranging pots and vials on a shelf above a cabinet.

She leant on a padded table, facing him. 'I have known him since he was a boy.'

'Then you know what they did to him.'

'Did what to him?'

He walked closer and lowered his voice. 'You know... when they, er... when he had his...' Of all the experiences he had been through since arriving in this land, this was becoming the most excruciating. He decided he just had to go for it. 'When they cut off his balls,' he blurted.

The slave dropped a pot. Salus spluttered. The woman looked at him. 'Nobody has cut off his balls.'

Brann looked at the man. He still had his back to the room but his hands were braced on the top of the cabinet and his shoulders were convulsing. Convulsing, Brann realised, with mirth.

'But his lack of hair. I thought...'

'We all know what you thought. Hair loss is not always a symptom of castration. You should know that Mylas chooses to shave all his hair. All who work specifically with me must adhere to the highest standards of cleanliness, and some of the men find that removing their hair helps them to facilitate this. In my case,' she shook her long tendrils of hair, 'I wash myself, but beyond that I choose to bind up my hair and cover it, while all Mylas has to do is wipe his head. I do shave my chest and back, though.'

Brann's eyes widened. 'You shave your...? You...?' His brain caught up. 'That last bit wasn't serious.'

She nodded at his hands. 'Drink your drink.'

He took a sip. And spat it back into the cup. 'By the gods, that's foul!'

'It will work.'

'It would need to work very quickly because it will be coming straight back up.'

'It will not. Drain the cup. That way you will not experience the taste for so long.'

He stared at the cup, the pale-orange liquid sitting there and doing its best to look like poison. He looked at the eyes boring into him. He had no option. Taking a deep breath, he downed the drink.

Surprisingly, when it hit his stomach a soothing warmth rose through him rather than the contents of his guts. He felt better. Still not great, but better. 'Is that an old soldier's recipe?'

'It is my recipe. Are you calling me an old soldier?'

'No!' Oh gods, not this again. 'But haven't you been a warrior at some point? Women don't go to war among my people, but I have heard that in several countries they do.'

It was difficult to tell if she was more bemused or amused. 'Quite the opposite, young man.'

'But you taught Cassian how to fight.'

She laughed then. 'I have taught my husband many things, but it is good to hear he has admitted it for once, even if it was to a boy widely expected to take that knowledge to his grave the same day. I cannot lay claim to teaching him to fight – he became accomplished at that all by himself.'

He shook his head in confusion. 'He told me, when he

said about tendons and muscles and shallow wounds. He said he learnt that from you.'

'My expertise does lie in that area, but in putting them back together, not in taking them apart. However, when you know how to fix something, you also know how to break it. And talking of fixing things, let us fix you.'

He had forgotten about his self-inflicted malaise. Forgetting was a good sign in itself, but now that he thought about it, he realised he could move his head without wincing and could even contemplate breakfast.

'Actually, I feel much better, thank you. That disgusting drink has really worked. I'm not perfect, but I could actually do with some food. Thank you very much.'

He spun on his heel to head for the door. Salus put a hand on his chest. 'Are you serious?'

Brann turned back slowly, trying to think what he may have missed. 'My apologies. Should I have bowed, or something?' He bent awkwardly at the waist.

Her elbows were on the table. Her head was in her hands. 'By your gods and mine, I am close to doing what that oaf failed to achieve with you in the Arena.'

Salus's hand closed on the neck of his tunic and propelled him from the room. 'It may be best if we start again.'

He closed the door then immediately knocked on it. Without waiting for a reply, he walked in, dragging the stumbling Brann with him. Mylas was walking across in front of them, carrying a tray of shining instruments. Salus guided the boy around the slave. 'Not a word to him,' he growled.

He jerked Brann to a halt in front of the table, where she still stood, leaning again with both hands on the surface, her head bowed.

Salus's voice was quiet. 'Lady Tyrala, may I present Brann the miller's son, recently emerged from the Arena.' He slapped the back of his head. Brann winced. The potion had not yet fully cured him. 'Though the gods only know how he found the wit to achieve that.'

She looked up. 'On the table.'

Without a word, he lifted himself onto it.

'For your information, Brann Millerson, my function here extends slightly beyond helping the excess-induced sore heads of idiots; that was a bonus for you. I choose to spend more of my time helping keep the bodies of our residents here in a condition where they work.'

'I... er... I'm sorry, I...' He was stammering again.

She ignored him. 'The day of a contest we look to any wounds. To everyone's surprise, you escaped without a scratch or anything more than a slight bump on your head that you managed to inflict with your own shield, far less the fatal result that, incidentally, was universally expected.'

'It's nice that everyone has felt the need to remind me I was expected to die.'

'Try not to talk for a while. It would probably be to the advantage of us all. Thankfully your friend this morning was perfectly co-operative. Had he been like you we could have been here all week. If there are no serious wounds requiring attention, what we do today, the day after a contest, is to ease the bodies back to a state suitable for a return to training. Now, lift your left arm out to the side.' As Salus took his leave, her fingers started to probe Brann's shoulder. 'You took a bit of a battering on your shield, so this is a good place to start.'

And so began a session that seemed to make her use of the word 'ease' highly inappropriate to Brann. Relentless stretching, twisting, pulling, kneading, pressing and, worst of all, gouging with her surprisingly powerful thumbs seemed to owe more to the principles of torture than recovery. When Marlo appeared at the door more than an hour later, he felt as if he would be barely able to walk.

'Good.' Tyrala turned to a basin to wash oil from her hands. 'Now you bathe as yesterday. Return here this afternoon.'

'Return?' He couldn't have sounded more horrified if she had told him he was due back in the Arena.

'You haven't grasped yet that this is to help you.'

'I wish it felt like it.'

'Trust me.'

'Do I have a choice?' She turned and glared. He jumped from the table. 'Didn't think so.'

She let the door close, but not before he thought he might have glimpsed a smile ghosting onto her lips.

The hot and cold pools restored enough movement to allow him to walk with Marlo towards the courtyard where they had first met. The garden seemed even more beautiful today. Perhaps it was because he hadn't expected to have the opportunity to be here. To be anywhere.

He looked at the young boy, ambling amiably beside him. Although they were much the same age, the events of the past year felt like they had moved him beyond the stage his companion was at. He envied him his youth. 'Why are you here, anyway?'

'Youngest of three brothers and father could only afford to support two.' Marlo shrugged. 'It seemed as good a move as any, to enrol here. It is not the worst life. While Cassian does not run one of the big schools, and while he does have a certain reputation, I had heard good things about him.'

It was not what Brann had meant by his question, but he could come back to that. His curiosity was roused. He stopped and sat on a small bench, enjoying the feel of the warm stone beneath and a slight breeze on his face. 'Do you mind?'

The boy grinned. 'It is your rest day.'

Brann felt himself smile back. The sun, searing when they had first started to sail into these climes and blistering when he had come ashore and away from the sea winds, was becoming more familiar. Eyes shut, he let the warmth soak into his muscles. 'Reputation? What did you mean?'

Marlo sat beside him. 'What is the word? Eccentric? Many call him mad, but when you are around him enough, you can see past that. He is a bit odd in many ways, but that is his way. He was in the army, earned great renown, then was captured during a campaign across the sea. They said he was dead. His body had even been paraded by his captors at the time. It was more than a year later that they came across him at the gates of a town, escaped, broken, hanging over the back of a mule.'

'What did they do to him?'

'Who knows? Who wants to know? He certainly didn't. His mind shut off from his body. He sat in inns, squares, brothels, parks, but he never drank, never whored, never spoke. He collected his army pension, he paid for food, and he sat and stared. No one robbed him, not even the scum – he was Cassian, after all. But also no one spoke to him – he was Cassian the Mad, Crazy Cassian, the Insane General. The smell didn't help, or the look in his eyes. Or so they say.'

'But he seems content, maybe not bouncing with life, but at least chirpy. What happened?'

'Tyrala happened. She had met him in the army, when she was working with the other physicians during one campaign and he had wounds needing tending. Whatever their relationship then, whatever the effect he had on her or the regard she held him in, it was enough to prompt her to leave her home and travel most of the length of the Empire to find him in the depths of this city. She had been conscripted to serve her time with the army, but she volunteered to serve her time with him.'

'What did she do?'

'Brought him here. It was a small abandoned farmhouse with failed crops on the infertile wild land beyond the city, but it was all they needed. She needed time alone with him, and he needed her. Whatever it did, it brought him back. Maybe he's a bit bonkers now instead of the inspiring general they say he was before, but we kind of like the bonkers. And he still knows his fighting. He decided to give back what he knew, to help those who he could. So he took in fighters unwanted by the other schools, slaves down on their luck, all sorts, just as long as they wanted to work, and improve. Always to improve. And because they improved, they started winning. And that brought the means to build this place. The Big House, the quarters we need, the training areas. His school. People respected his results, but the big schools resented his presence. The Big Seven are generations old; he was a newcomer. The smaller schools are just meant to scrabble for the scraps. His fighters don't win as much as theirs, but they win, and they hate that. It upsets the order, and you know how we like order here. Cassian doesn't care. He just wants to give people a chance. People like me. That was what I liked; that was why I came. Even at that age, I knew he was a good man.'

'What age were you?'

'Six.'

'Six?' He was incredulous. 'I know your family were poor, but you were sold into slavery at six?'

Marlo laughed. 'You really do know nothing of where you are, don't you?' He pulled his tunic collar to one side. 'No chain. I am no slave.'

'But are all fighters not slaves?'

'I am not a fighter, not yet. Next year I start training. At least two years later, if Cassian feels I am ready, I will start in the smaller contests, the ones where the merchant caravans camp or in the poorer districts. I hope to work my way to the Arena one day.' He nudged Brann playfully. 'Not all of us start our career there. But then, not all of us catch the eye of the Emperor on our first day in the city.'

Brann was confused. 'That's all very well, but as I said, is it not only slaves who fight in these contests?'

'Of course not! Anyone can fight, though you must belong to a school. That was why you and your friend were placed here. You needed to represent a school. But usually people join a school for one of three reasons: they are bought from the slave markets, they are criminals sentenced to slavery as a fighter or they enrol as a free man or woman.'

'Why would anyone want this?'

The boy looked at him, no lightness in his eyes this time. 'Sometimes it is all you have got. Sometimes it is better than you have got. And fighters who are citizens keep half their prize money, whereas all of the winnings of slaves go to the schools, so it is a living. And there are worse livings, believe me.'

Brann shrugged. He had seen the truth in that, and imagined there was far worse than he had seen. 'Do you ever think of leaving though? I mean, now that you are older, going out and finding a craft?'

The boy frowned. 'And this is not a craft? Cassian's school gives me almost all the memories I have in my life. I am happy here. And soon I will start learning my craft in earnest. Why leave now?' His eyes narrowed, but a smile creased their corners. 'What put that thought in your head? Are you thinking of taking your leave?'

Brann's laugh was hollow. 'I don't have much choice at the moment, do I? But if things change, or if they don't and an opportunity presents itself...' He picked absently at a leaf. 'I have friends somewhere in the city and two more held in the palace. The others may be planning something to help the two hostages, or they may not have the chance at this time, but either way I cannot stand the thought of doing nothing. It is just not me.'

Marlo caught at his arm and spoke quietly. 'Be careful. Cassian is a benevolent man, whether from his experiences or just because he cares for people. But there are laws that maintain this city, and above that there do seem to be, from what little I have picked up, powerful people who have your worst interests at heart. Do not give them the chance to act severely, and severely they will act against a runaway slave. You would be an example to others and would not be given the luxury of a death match, believe me.' He turned Brann to look directly at him. 'Just, please, promise me that you will not do anything without telling me. I know this city and I still know people in it who are not fond of the authorities. If you are going to do something stupid, let me help you be less likely to be publicly butchered.'

Brann looked at him. He knew he could trust no one, but he also knew that he was in a city of strangers and alien customs. Trust or not trust, either path carried grave risks. He would decide when the moment came. If the moment came. Right now, he just raised his eyebrows. 'You would do that for me? Knowing the consequences if it went wrong?'

Marlo shrugged. 'I know everyone here. But I only have one friend.'

Brann's breath caught in surprise, the answer touching at his fragile control over the sadness that sat within him, pushed deep and out of sight. Then Marlo brightened, his grin lightening the mood. 'You must be hungry.' Brann realised he was.

They followed the smell of lunch even above the perfume of the garden and, when they emerged with hands full of steaming bowls to sit on a bench, their backs against the building wall, Brann felt almost content.

'No training today,' Marlo grinned, stirring the meat of his stew with a hunk of freshly baked bread, 'so this lunch-time you can stuff yourself.' Brann already was.

They ate in silence, if silence meant no words. Such was Brann's hunger that he ate with a desperation that produced a noise similar to the feeding pigs in the pen where old farmer Donnuld had kept them just south of his village. Even the thought of his village was unable to curtail his anger, however.

'Oh, how good it is to see a young boy eat with such healthy gusto!' Salus stood over him, beaming as ever. 'You are feeling better, then?' Brann nodded without missing a bite. 'The lady of the house sort you out?' He nodded again. 'Your young companion given you the guided tour?' He frowned in confusion. Marlo's foot kicked his ankle. He nodded vigorously. 'Good, good. I'd better get in there while you two have still left some food for the rest of us.'

Brann studiously mopped up the last of his gravy with

the last of his bread until the big man had disappeared inside. 'Guided tour?'

'I was supposed to do that before you ate, but you wanted to spend too much time gossiping and sitting amongst flowers.' He sat his empty bowl down, stretched and burped. 'Anyway, this,' he slapped the wall of the building they were resting against, 'where they store the food, prepare it and serve it, is the Food House. Down across the end, where you woke up this morning, is the Sleeping House, and separate from the rest, of course, is the Shit House.' He waved a hand straight in front of them. 'Over there, where you got your weapons, is the Weapons House and beside the end of it, where our cheerful smith works away happily, is...'

'Is the Smith House,' Brann cut in. 'I think I get it.'

Marlo looked at him. '... is the Forge. Who would call it a Smith House?' He shook his head. 'Down behind the Sleeping House is the Practice House, where the fighters can train if the weather drives us all inside, and beyond that are the Training Fields where you, well, train. Oh, and up at the top, where you were this morning, that's the Big House. There you go. Guided tour done. How hard was that? Let's get some cake.'

Food and a doze in the sun took them to the time to return to Tyrala. As they walked through the garden, Brann was reminded of the question he had unsuccessfully tried on their journey down, and reworded it.

'Why are you with me? Were you not just supposed to be there when I couldn't use my hands? And anyway, if I am a slave and you are free, why are *you* told to help *me*? Should it not be the reverse?'

'Not in here. Slave and free are alike in here. All are men

and women, all are members of Cassian's School, no matter how we arrived here. You are further ahead than me, and so I help you. All apprentices are assigned to a fighter, to shadow them so we know what is expected when we start training. Normally we also clean any weapons you use but in your case, Cassian has decided that you should do that as weapons seem to be woefully unfamiliar to you and he thinks it will help you to get to know them.'

'You have got off lightly, then.'

'Not really. I also have to help you with the things you don't know. Given your lack of knowledge so far, cleaning a few weapons seems trivial.'

Brann couldn't deny it.

The afternoon session with Tyrala, he was delighted to discover, was more to ease his muscles rather than batter them back into shape. Still, he surprised himself at how early he felt ready for bed.

It was barely beyond dawn and scarcely with any warning when he found himself shouted awake. The routine for all fighters was the same, falling out of bed and following Salus on a run six times around a well-worn track immediately inside the perimeter of the compound, then wash shoulder to shoulder at a stone trough that ran the length of the outside of the Sleeping Building. Brann counted around two score fighters, a dozen of them women. They did everything as a group: sleep, wash, run, eat. Or, at least, they tried to. Brann had found himself detached behind the group by the time they completed two laps.

A leather-clad woman, almost as tall as Salus and broader, glanced sideways at him as she splashed water from the trough onto her face and rubbed it under her armpits with vigour. 'Pity you're not as good at running as dancing. Or maybe you need some wine to help you along? Even my arse was in your vision, when I should have been looking at your scrawny effort.'

His chest still heaving, he mumbled, 'I'm just not a natural runner. I can walk up hills all day, but I'm not built for running.'

She snorted. 'Not many hills in the contest circles. And your legs'll need to go faster than a walk.'

A voice spoke up on his other side. 'Leave him be, Breta. We were all new here once.' It was another woman, but one who couldn't be more different in size and shape from the first, her slender body that of a young boy and hair cropped to match. She grinned at him. 'Mongoose.'

'What?'

'Mongoose. That's what they call me. You know a mongoose?' He shook his head blankly. 'They bring them here for the shows, all the way from the lands over where the sun rises. Small, furry, cute things. But put them in front of snakes and they're different. You know, the snakes that do this,' she lifted her hand and formed her fingers into a wedge that darted to jab Brann on the cheek, 'before you even see it coming? Well, the mongoose is quicker.'

'What's your real name?'

She returned to the trough. 'Don't know. Don't care. I like Mongoose. It fits.'

Salus clipped the back of his head. 'If you've finished trying to charm the local talent, new boy, I'd get to the food before it is gone.'

On the training field, Salus took them through a series of exercises that stretched every part of their body. They were a mixed lot, Brann saw. Men and women alike looked drawn from the length of the Empire as well as many of the free countries in the direction of his homeland. Shapes and sizes differed as much as colours of hair and skin, bit all moved through the exercises with a grace that spoke of familiarity. He, by contrast, constantly felt on the verge of toppling. They were watched all the while by Cassian and Tyrala, sitting in the shade of a canopy atop a small man-made ridge that afforded them a view of every person. Brann felt that neither pair of eyes missed a thing, and his balance grew even worse with the thought.

A shout from Salus split them into four groups. 'Light sparring,' he shouted, throwing a selection of wooden swords and shields beside each group. 'Winner stays on.' Four circles were marked out by ropes and the groups gathered at each one.

The first two bouts in Brann's group were won by a short, stocky man with a curiously effective style. He had selected two swords and held both vertically in front of him. From the first instant he would march forward relentlessly, always presenting his front that snapped out thrusts and, with a flick of his powerful wrists, parried any attack.

Salus's rod tapped Brann from behind. 'You next.'

He picked up a sword and shield. After all, they had served him well in the Arena, and he had worked out his opponent's weakness. The man was effective in a straight line only. All he had to do was attack from the side and it would be over.

The man's advance was faster than it had looked when Brann was spectating. He caught the first two blows on his shield and scampered back to compose himself. As the man advanced after him, he was ready. He would feint an attack from his right and slip left, leaving it simple to cut back handed at the man's unprotected left side.

He lifted his sword to his right and swooped left. From the first moment, it felt awkward. The man's right sword knocked his weapon downwards, useless, and his other smacked Brann on the back of the head. It could only have been more humiliating had he slapped him on the rump.

'Too quick,' Salus snapped. 'Go again.'

Brann was annoyed at his clumsy execution of his plan, but was still convinced of its worth. He would learn from his mistake. Quicker, and more clever. He would distract the man better before he made his move. His opponent was already advancing and he raised his shield into the first thrust and hacked three times quickly at the man's left sword. He spun to his right, all the way round to take himself to left of where he was and emerging with a swing of his sword at the man's right side. The right sword flicked his harmlessly into the air and, as his face completed the turn, it met the flat of the left sword.

Expressionlessly, the man returned to his starting position as Brann wiped his hand across his face to clear the blood emerging from his nose. Salus handed him a rag and turned to the trainer assigned to their group, a slender giant whose skin was the colour of his hair and as white as that of a two-day-dead body and whose pink eyes blinked as much as those of a dead man. 'He will learn nothing from such short bouts, will he, Corpse. Give him one bout out to regain his few senses and put him back in.' He wandered off to the next group.

Mongoose took his place and showed him what he was trying to do. She bore a light sword and a curious shield, as round as his had been but smaller and held by a hand alone rather than a forearm. She used her light weapons to her advantage, though, darting and swaying back and forth with a speed and agility that drew out the swords of the burly man in vain attempts to catch her as she moved. She waited for her moment, then dipped and slid, appearing at the man's side and flicking the point of her sword to touch his ribs. The man lifted both hands in submission and wordlessly walked out of the circle.

Brann walked back in, more confident this time. He wasn't as predictable as the burly man, and he was sure he had the advantage in strength. If he rushed her he could overpower her.

It was over quicker than the first two. As Mongoose darted forward, he slammed his heavy shield into her attack. She bounced back and, as he raised his sword to shoulder height and thrust forward hard, all his bruised pride powering the blow that would knock aside her small shield and finish the fight, she twisted and brought her sword up to meet his. With a flick of her wrist at the moment of impact, his sword flew from his hand. Before it had stopped spiralling high in the air, her sword was at his throat.

'Next,' the impossibly deep voice of Corpse intoned.

Miserable, he trudged from the circle. He couldn't resist looking up at Cassian and Tyrala. As expected, both were looking at him as they conferred. Cassian beckoned Salus to them, and the three of them spoke briefly before Tyrala pointed at Brann then waved at another group. She handed Salus a strip of fabric and, whatever instruction accompanied it, it was enough to cause surprise in Salus that was quickly replaced by a respectful nod.

He loped down the steep incline and brought a fighter from another group to Brann's. Taking the boy by the arm, he led him to replace the man at the other circle. The next

116

combatant there was not yet chosen and, before he was, Brann was blindfolded. Feeling as vulnerable as if he had been disarmed and bound, he listened to the clashing, thumping and grunting of the next bout, trying to learn from the noises but finding it impossible. The sounds stopped and a hand between his shoulder-blades propelled him forwards. Vulnerability turned to panic and he brought up his shield and swung wildly with his sword. Laughter rippled round the circle as strong hands from behind steadied his arms and Salus's voice steadied his nerves. Slightly. 'We would not be so cruel as to make you fight without eyes, young warrior. Especially given your lack of success with the use of them this morning.'

Panic turned to embarrassment and the tension dropped from his muscles. In the instant that he relaxed, Salus whipped the fabric from his eyes and stepped away just in time for him to see a lean fighter, not tall but taller than him, heading straight for him, a blunted wooden spear whirling high and low two-handed as he came. He barely had time to raise his shield to meet a swing of the haft at his ribs, and swiped desperately with his sword. It bought him the moment he needed to back off slightly but the deflection off his shield had taken the spear high and the shield wide. Deftly, the man shifted his hands and the spear point streaked towards Brann's open chest. Brann dragged his front leg back and to the side, turning him just in time to let the spear pass. Overbalanced by the lack of resistance to his weapon, the man was unable to stop it hammering into the ground. In the instant that its point bit, Brann's foot smashed down on the shaft, snapping it in two. The man was defenceless and, eyes wide, Brann swung the rounded edge of his sword at his opponent's torso. His wrist jarred as the half-spear knocked the weapon flying and, before he could react, the jagged end was at his throat. The man leant in, teeth bared, to hiss in his face. Tossing the shard of the spear aside, he swaggered away to collect another weapon for the next bout.

Brann's head sank along with his heart. He trudged to the side of the circle and stood, despondent, close to despair. After the Arena, after battling Loku in Halveka and Boar on the ship, after everything he had been through, he had thought maybe he had something. Maybe he could be a warrior, maybe there was some sort of a talent he could be proud of. That could help him find a way home. Three experienced fighters had shown him the truth. His arms sagged by his side, weapons still clutched but forgotten.

He jumped as Salus clapped a heavy hand on his shoulder. 'Well done, young lad.' Brann looked up and was astounded to see a grin.

'Well done? I would be dead if that were a real fight.'

'Silly boy. Death bouts are rare. Fighters are far too expensive to throw away to their death. Most fights are contests of ability, where skill or strength prevail. Or both. We do not need a killing blow to see the victor, only the demonstration of one. But,' he said cheerfully, 'you are right, were you facing an opponent with no restraint, you would be dead.'

'So I am useless. Three times over.'

'So you look to improve. Many times over. That is why we have the practice circles.'

'But even so, you say well done.'

'Of course. I will say it again if you like.'

'But I lost.'

'Ah, you did.' He clapped him again on what was threatening to become a bruised shoulder. 'But this time you took longer to lose.' He pointed to the pair sitting above them. 'That was what they wanted to see.' Cassian raised a finger to Salus. 'And now they wish to talk. Come.'

Brann had been born in a valley and became used to climbing hills almost as soon as he could walk. Even so, he found his legs shaking on the steep, but short, incline. He suspected it was not from the effort. He stopped in front of them. A slight wave of Cassian's hand allowed Salus to return to overseeing the training.

Two pairs of eyes stared at him for long moments. Drained of all emotion other than disappointment, and all energy other than the ability to stand – and even so, barely – he found he didn't care about the examination. It brushed past his attention like a breeze past a rock.

'So,' Cassian said, unexpectedly brightly given the silent stare that had preceded it. 'You present us with a problem.'

'I know.' Brann stared at the ground. 'You have a fighter who keeps losing.'

'We have a fighter who loses but should win.'

'I was well beaten.'

Tyrala leant forward. 'You were beaten in the first because you could not transfer plans into natural movement. You were beaten in the second because poor technique negated strength. In the third, you should have won but failed to anticipate the desperate move and strength of a beaten man. You have natural movement, you have natural agility, you have natural strength and, most of all, you have natural reactions. But when you disconnect your conscious brain, you win. That was what this,' she held up the fabric Salus had used as a blindfold, 'taught us. You had no idea of the type of fighter or the weapon he carried, so all you could

119

do was react, and you were successful almost to the point of victory.'

Cassian beamed. 'My wife has a perceptive eye for strengths and weaknesses, and not just those of the body. She sees what I am blind to.'

The slender woman angled back in her chair, sinuous as a cat and with as much expression revealed. 'You notice, you think and you plan – it is what you do, you cannot help yourself. But you are also an instinctive fighter, you win when you react.'

Brann shrugged. 'I just do what seems right.'

This time she did smile. 'Exactly. What seems obvious to you in the moment would not be apparent to most were we to stop time for them. That is also what you do, and you cannot help yourself either. But nor can you make yourself do it. You are two people in one: the thinker before the conflict and the intuitive fighter during it. We must find a way to marry the two, for at the moment they battle each other and leave you useless when they do.' She looked at Cassian. 'My husband has a knack for working with the strengths and weaknesses. He improves where I can only see.'

Brann wasn't convinced. 'But natural this and natural that counts for nothing if I cannot keep a sword in my hand.'

Cassian waved a hand dismissively. 'That is nothing. Poor technique is easily fixed. Good technique is the basis of everything we teach our fighters. It is pounded into you until you cannot move your weapon, hold your weapon, move your body, hold your body, any other way. For most, that is almost all they have with a vital touch of natural skill or speed or strength, or some of each, and for them, for the level they reach, it is all they need. You, as my lady has seen, are all instinct and not technique.'

She cut in. 'Which is where the problem lies.'

His smile was broad. 'Indeed. We pound the technique and we kill the instinct. But we leave the technique and the instinct is vulnerable. A conundrum indeed. I shall think on it today, and we will start with you tomorrow. But you are very lucky.'

'I am?'

'Absolutely! You are fortunate indeed they did not send you to the army. There, you would have been ruined. A thousand men drilled to move the same way, react the same way, think the same way is good for the battlefield but bad for you. We will find a way, my wife and I. We shall marry the two Branns. They shall feed each other with strength, not leach it. You have any questions?'

Brann looked down at the fighters, who were now in small groups of two, three and four. His eyes scanned them, and he nodded. 'Where is Grakk?'

Cassian's surprise filled his face. 'You listen to all of this, and all you wonder is where your friend is?'

The boy shrugged. 'You sound like you know a lot about this, and I have proved I know little, so I'm best doing what I'm told, I can see that. But I cannot see my friend.'

'Listen, boy, and listen well: do what you are told but never only do it. Always think as well. Take advice, but understand it. Question it within yourself, and if you agree it will serve you even better; if you disagree, you may find you are wrong, but if you are right then others may learn from you. We all learn to improve, and almost as destructive to that aim as being deaf to advice is to follow it thoughtlessly.' He sighed. 'As to your friend, he is no longer with us.'

The horror that struck Brann must have been evident. Tyrala leant forward. 'Panic not, young warrior. My husband does not mean to say that this man has left behind his life. What he is clumsily trying to tell you is that the tribesman has moved to another fighting school, a more prestigious one than ours. We received a request from the palace for an exchange to take place.'

'He has...? An exchange...?' Brann's senses were thrown and he found his thoughts whirling to the detriment of his mouth. 'Why?

The lady's eyes were fathomless. 'We did not query it. Some requests are not requests.'

Cassian nodded. 'It makes sense in a way. The man's abilities were far beyond anything we could teach him. He is better there, where he will be a showpiece, a treat for the climax to a show. They like their spectacle.'

Brann felt numb. Every time he felt he couldn't be more alone, fate proved him wrong. He nodded down at the activity below. 'Shall I rejoin them, then?'

Cassian's eyebrows shot towards his stubbled grey hair. 'Do you not listen, foolish boy? You shall work in your own way, as I devise. Lunch will be soon. Eat, drink, wash, then you can run around the track another six times. Rest, then six more.

'This is important. Of all you did today, you were most rubbish at that.'

He trailed even further behind Breta on the next morning's run. The previous day he had started with a day of recuperation behind him. Today he had not replenished the energy drained from him by the bouts and twelve circuits of the compound.

Mongoose winked at him as he tried to avoid Breta on his way from the trough to the Food House. 'Perseverance.'

He blinked at her. 'What?'

She grinned. 'It will seem like it gets worse and worse. Then, one day, you will realise it has just been better than it was before. Then Breta can get her wish and stare at your arse. But only if you persevere.'

Marlo was waiting at the building, chomping happily through an apple. 'The boss is waiting for you in the garden. You should eat as we walk.'

Brann did so, cramming down a pastry and a handful of his latest discovery: grapes. They found Cassian pruning some bushes, the wide brim of his hat flopping to drop his face into shadow. His expression lit up at their approach.

'Boys, boys! So good to see you.' He straightened, pressing his hands into the small of his back with a slight groan. He looked at Brann. 'Yes, today you start the training that helps *you*, not the training that helps others who are not you.'

Brann nodded.

'So, you will go with your young friend here and select two practice swords, one heavier than the other. Marlo will take the heavy one.' He picked up a clipped twig and held it at various angles as he spoke, some high, some low, twisting into assorted shapes. 'You will do this. And this. And this. And this. With one hand, yes? And each time Marlo will take his sword in two hands and hit yours with all his might. Good, good. See you at lunchtime. Enjoy yourselves.'

He turned back to his bushes. Brann stared at Marlo, who looked much as he felt. 'Is that all? What else should I do?

The elderly man was quizzical. 'You want to stop that exercise early?' Brann shook his head. 'Well, silly boy, how could you have time to do anything else?' He raised a finger. 'Ah wait, you are right, there was another thing. My good lady was worried about your skin. Not the bruises caused by bad fighting. You children of the North grow a different hide, and it does not like the sun god so much. It seems my lady likes her meals well cooked, but not her young charges.' Bending to a canvas bag, he pulled out two small pots and offered them one at a time to Brann. 'This has rice bran, and you apply where the sunlight can reach. This has jasmine, and you apply after your evening wash where you turn red. Rice bran and jasmine, you know these, yes?'

'Rice bran and jasmine? Are they animals?'

He leant in close to the boy and whispered like a conspirator. 'They are not animals, no, but other than that I know no more than you. But my wife has the knowledge and she hails from the land of the Delta River, where pale skin is prized and the well-to-do chase that beauty for themselves. She knows. What you must do yourself, you learn. What others can do for you, let them learn. Use your time how best you can.' Smiling broadly, he patted Brann's upper arm, where scarlet had already started to spread, and ignored the boy's wince. 'All you need to know is that it works. Their vanity is your salvation, young Mr Snow. Embrace it.'

Brann was surprised. 'You know snow?' It seemed so incongruous in a land of constant baking heat.

A calloused finger tapped at Brann's forehead. 'An army does not campaign within the shadow of its own city, does it?' He lifted over a small stool and settled down in front of the bush, blade in hand. 'Now go, before the sun climbs to lunchtime.'

A glance at the sky showed there was no lack of time before then, but the boys took their leave, Brann starting to spread the lotion on his arms as they walked. 'I wish I had this on the ship,' he said wistfully. 'The sun was only really strong for the last two weeks before we got here, but for that time all we did was cover up and bake ourselves.'

Marlo dipped a finger into the vial and spread the smooth lotion on Brann's forehead, forcing him to stop. 'Well, you have it now,' he pointed out. Brann couldn't argue.

They fetched the wooden swords and set to work. Marlo showed no hint of mercy and hacked like a woodsman felling a tree, sending Brann's sword flying at the first attempt, and the next dozen. Circling his wrist to try to ease it, he moved the sword to his left hand and nodded to his companion to continue.

'Right hand not strong enough to carry on?' the boy grinned.

'No, I just want to learn with both hands. What happens if my right arm gets wounded? At least this way I wouldn't have to resort to letting someone batter my shield until they exhaust themselves or die of boredom.' In reality, it was both his and Marlo's reasons.

By midday, both hands were numbed. Even on the odd occasion when he had managed to keep hold of the sword hilt, his arm had been jarred to the shoulder. Washing was hard enough but eating was a particularly slow and awkward affair, and more than once Marlo had to return to his previous job and be Brann's hands for him. He managed to use the waterskin that Cassian had left with him.

Cassian was waiting in the garden, this time sitting in the shade and picking from a bowl of assorted fruit, only some of which Brann recognised. He looked at Marlo. 'He did well?'

'He dropped it a lot.' The boy's teeth flashed in enthusiasm. 'But he tried really hard not to.'

125

'Excellent, excellent. Delighted to hear it.' He turned to Brann, gesturing for his waterskin and taking a long swig. He wiped his mouth with his sleeve. 'Well done. That really is excellent.' He returned to his food, sorting through the fruit until he found what the boy had learnt was called an orange. Brann's mouth watered. He had not only discovered the name of the fruit, but also its taste. And that it was very much to his taste. And that they were in short supply this week.

The boys waited patiently. Cassian dug a thumbnail into the thick skin of the fruit and began to peel it. Pausing, he looked up. 'Yes? Was there something else?'

Brann cleared his throat. 'The training? What shall I do this afternoon?'

Cassian's face brightened. 'Ah the training, yes. Marlo, be so good as to take your friend to the Field of Rocks, would you?'

'And will I come to see you when I have finished?'

'Of course. In the evening, five days from now.'

'Five days?'

'You can count to five can't you? We always have the occasional one who struggles with that. Is that a problem?' He spat a grape seed into the flower bed.

'No, no, it's fine. But what training shall I do tomorrow?'

Cassian looked as if it were the most absurd of questions. 'Why, the same as today, of course. And so on, until six days have been achieved. Then you have earned your rest day, and you will be given your instructions for the next six. Why would it be otherwise?'

Brann shrugged. 'Why indeed? But will you not need to see me?'

Cassian wiped his hands on his tunic and beckoned Brann closer. He drew a knife with a cross-hilt from his belt and pressed it into the boy's hand. Brann's fingers closed around it automatically, and the man altered the angle slightly. 'This is how you held a sword this morning.' He twisted it slightly. 'You see? Like so? Like I showed you on your first day. If you remember this time, you are more likely to hold onto your sword.' His large hand closed around Brann's, locking it tight. 'Close your eyes. Feel it there. Think only of the shape in your hand.' They stayed like that for several long moments. 'Lock that feeling in your head. Practise holding anything, any time, to capture your hand in that shape.' He tapped the back of Brann's hand. 'Now, if I may have my knife back? It was a present from my wife, and she would be most displeased if I gave it away, especially as you already have a present this week.' He handed him the waterskin. 'I hope you weren't going to forget this.'

Brann smiled wanly. 'I have a feeling I am going to need it.'

Cassian just held his knife in his hand, keeping his eyes fixed on the boy. With a slight move of his fingers, he rolled the blade very slightly to a new angle. 'Hmm?' He frowned. It rolled to a new angle. 'Hmm.' He smiled. A slight roll and a frown. 'Hmm?' A roll back and a smile. 'Hmm.' He patted Brann on the shoulder. 'You do not need to visit for me to see.' Picking up his fruit basket, he walked into the house.

Brann was right about needing the waterskin. The Field of Rocks was as aptly named as everywhere else seemed to be. Lying beyond the practice area where Brann had been so soundly beaten, a memory that prompted a shudder as they walked past, it was an area of uneven and rutted ground strewn with what appeared to be a random selection of rocks, from stones the size of a head to others that were nearly boulders.

Marlo walked to a medium-sized one and squatted, wrapping his arms under it. 'Always with the straight back, always with the legs,' he grunted, lifting the rock as he stood.

Brann nodded appreciatively and moved to a rock half as big again. His knees bent and, almost in the same movement, he rose with it clutched to his chest. The ground shook as he tossed it a good couple of yards from him and a bird taking flight in alarm caused Marlo to jump.

Brann grinned. 'Maybe you joined a fighting school when you were six, but I started working with my father when I was five. There are plenty of sacks of all sizes in a mill, all filled with something or other and all needing to be lifted. If there's one thing I'm well used to, its that.'

'Good,' Marlo said brightly. 'Lifting and holding need not be explained, then. We are not practising to carry flour to a cart, however. We are not practising to lift at all. We are lifting to practise. We build the strength to move the way we would in a fight. Like this.' He held two smaller rocks in front of him at shoulder height and swung his right arm to the right then back to the front, then mirrored it with his left, over and again, sometimes with the rocks facing up, sometimes down, sometimes centre. 'And if we work a front muscle,' he took a bigger rock and, elbow at his side, lifted it to his shoulder and back down, 'we work a back muscle.' He held the rock straight up then dropped his hand behind his head and back up.

'Then we also get the big ones, like you were throwing about before, except we walk across the field with them.'

Brann smiled and lifted the same big rock, starting to stroll away. 'Now this is like taking grain to the cart.' He took two steps, caught his toe on a rut and sprawled headlong, the rock bouncing away from him.

128

'You probably had a flatter floor in the mill,' Marlo pointed out helpfully. 'This exercise also builds balance and, er, awareness.' Noticing Brann's expression, he quickly grabbed two rocks and tucked them under the other boy's arms. 'Now squat. Head up all the time, look ahead, back straight. Right down, and up, and again and again many times. Curiously, although you feel your legs in this one, it really works you here.' He slapped his hands all around the bottom half of Brann's torso. 'Lady Tyrala says this is the most important. She calls this the Core of our Whole. She says all real strength comes from there.' He was as solemn as Brann had ever seen him. 'And if the Lady Tyrala says it, it must be true.' Brann didn't doubt it.

He showed him a dozen other ways of using the rocks, and they worked through all of them, then started again, and repeated until the sun started its drop towards dinnertime. As Marlo headed for the trough to join the other fighters at their final wash of the day, Brann excused himself.

On a balcony at the Big House, Cassian stood watching the small figure dragging his legs at a laboured jog around the perimeter track. Every step was clearly a torture, but every step spoke of grim determination. He only slowed to a walk after staggering to the completion of the sixth circuit.

'Good boy.' The old soldier sipped his wine, savouring the taste for a long moment before swallowing. 'Good boy.'

The weeks merged without a sensation of time. There was no goal other than the incessant quest of improving, of being better than the day before, of teaching his body to move before his mind had time to wonder. Once mastered, one exercise would be changed for another, all aiming to develop a skill from new sensation to automatic movement.

Initially basic technique dominated, working single moves over and over with one weapon after another. Occasionally, there would be a double move, where the initial thrust or swing would expose him to attack and he needed to become automatic in shifting into a defensive position in an instant, smoothing the two movements seamlessly into one. Using swords defensively, using shields as weapons; stabbing and parrying with spears and throwing, throwing, throwing them until something that had all his life been an inability to the extent of embarrassment became a strength. All the time, he was guided by the relentless drone of Corpse, his meticulous eye missing nothing and his capacity for repetition never dwindling. He did seem amused – or so Marlo told him, though he couldn't see it himself – at Brann's insistence that whatever he did once with his right hand, he would do twice with his left. Brann didn't care whether he was amused or not; it was his one stipulation that he did so and Corpse never objected as long as his technique became perfect, whichever hand he used.

Once the movement had become as unthinking as breathing, the boys moved to drills aimed at bringing together the learnt movement and unthought reactions. The painstaking presence of Corpse was no longer necessary: the boys were given an exercise for the morning. Six variations, one for each day, a different day each week. Movement of body had become automatic, but the mind had to adjust to the unpredictable circumstances. Over and over, and over.

In one drill, Marlo would have two sticks with cushioned pads on the end with which he would try to whack Brann on random parts of his body. The catch was that Brann was to close his eyes and only open them in the instant that his companion told him the blow was coming. Sometimes he had a sword, or shield, or spear, or knife, or axe, or mace to ward off the blow, sometimes just his hands and arms. For another, Marlo was given a ball the size of a fist that was made, he said, from the mixing of the sap of two trees that grew in a country across the sea. When Brann wondered where, Marlo shrugged and said that the Empire was a very large place. Whatever its origin, the result was an object that, when Marlo threw it with gusto, would ricochet around a small bare room like an enraged wasp. Brann's job was to strike it with a weapon before it stopped bouncing.

Sometimes he would see Cassian watching, other times not.

And every morning he would run with the other fighters, every afternoon he would visit the Field of Rocks with Marlo. And every evening he would run again, a solitary figure in the haze of the dusk.

And he missed Grakk. The eloquent tribesman of the savage appearance had been his last link to his life of recent times, and his absence brought home to Brann how much he had come to rely on his calming advice and reassuring presence. He filled the gap with work, forcing himself almost to exhaustion. After all, what else did he have? He fell into a routine of exertion, embraced it, letting it define his days and fill his mind.

Until a simple question was unexpected enough to jolt his mind from its habitual daily path.

'Can I try?'

Brann leant against the wall of the small room at the end of the Practice House, sweat running into his eyes and the bouncing ball drumming to a halt close to the far wall. It was a particularly hot day, even by the local standards, and he wiped the sting of the sweat from his eyes as he reached blindly for the waterskin.

'Thought you'd never ask,' he grinned, handing Marlo the wooden sword. 'My breath went somewhere and I could do with a chance to find it.'

Marlo scoffed with a fake laugh. 'Your breath is right there with you. I've watched you. It's not just Breta who can now see your arse on the runs.'

'I'm still not a natural runner.'

'So what? No one is a natural at everything. It's your attitude to what doesn't come so easily that makes a difference.'

'Did you come up with that?'

'I overheard the Lady Tyrala. Except she put it better. Still true though.'

'It is, so take it to heart for yourself.'

Marlo shook his head. 'You're wasting your time.'

'I thought we talked about that attitude.'

With a trudge of resignation, the boy retrieved the ball, tossed it to Brann and made himself ready. Brann hurled the ball at the floor so that it flew up against the side wall and across the room. Marlo managed to swing desperately four times as it pinged about the space, and managed to miss four times. Brann threw it five times in all, with much encouragement from him, much enthusiasm from Marlo and much failure from the efforts.

The boy sat down hard, slumped against the wall. Brann leant against the wall and slid his back down it till he was beside him. 'How will I ever be allowed to train? I cannot even hit a ball. It can't even hold a sword to hit me back. I cannot be a fighter. I just don't have it in me, like it is in you.' Marlo's head dropped and he let out a long slow breath through pursed lips. 'For ten years, almost all of the life I can remember, I have watched the fighters during the day and at night I have lain awake and dreamt of the day I would be one of them. But dreams are dreams and life is life.' The wooden weapon dropped out of his fingers. The noise of it hitting the floor was loud in the small room.

Brann reached forward and lifted the sword, the hilt falling into his grip exactly the way that Cassian had shown him what seemed like a life ago. Left hand slipping under the blade, he opened the fingers on his right and let the hilt roll back and forth in his palm as he stared at it. He spoke slowly, forming each word as he thought it. 'Do you remember the first day I came into this room, when I chased the ball the whole morning, and the delight when I actually managed to clip it, and even then by accident with a badly controlled follow-though?' A smile flickered through Marlo's melancholy. 'And on the Field of Rocks, when I thought I was so strong but really didn't have a clue? And all those times you adjusted my sword until I could actually get it right myself? And when I was so bad with the spear that I tripped over it, and you had to show me how to switch hands without nearly braining myself? And with the mace, when I nearly...'

Marlo laughed and held up a hand. 'Don't remind me. I would have lost the chance for there to be little Marlos gracing this world if I hadn't jumped so quickly in panic.' He sighed. 'But I get it, I was patient with you. But if you are telling me you are willing to be patient with me, I can save you wasting your time.'

Brann nudged him. 'Don't flatter yourself, I wasn't intending to spend that much time on you.' He fell serious again, eyes fixed on the rolling sword, the mesmerising twirling back and forth of the edges of the blade. 'What I meant was, you had

133

faith in me. You believed that I would get there. And then you were patient until I did. But sometimes it is easier to believe in someone else rather than in yourself.'

'Sometimes you don't because you know yourself. Or you've come to know yourself.'

'Don't talk like an idiot. Shut up and let me think.'

'It's you doing all the talking!' But he fell quiet.

Brann stared intently at the sword, picturing Marlo chasing the ball and trying to compare with his recent successes. He was unable to envision himself. When he did it, he was lost in the moment. He didn't know what exactly he did, he just did it. He found it hard even to remember the moments of striking the ball once they were done.

So he had to get into the moment with Marlo.

'Take the sword.' He pressed it into the boy's grasp. 'Up you get.'

'Have I not tortured you enough with my ineptitude?'

'No.'

He got up.

Brann picked up the ball but, as he threw it, he thought himself into Marlo's place, trying to see what he would see. The ball pinged across and Marlo lunged at it, behind its passage. He whirled, flailing at it as it bounced back and then, in desperation, reached for...

No! Brann's instinct shouted. It felt so wrong. So awkward to think of doing it like that. *No, like this!* 'Yes!' his voice shouted.

'I think,' Marlo panted, 'no is the word you are looking for.'

'It was, but now it's not.' Brann grinned. 'You're coming at it from the wrong end.'

Marlo was confused. 'Of the room?

'Of your body. Of your intentions.' He took the sword. 'Look.' He reached forward, extending his arm, and waved the sword to the side. 'You are starting with the sword.'

'But that is what I want to hit it with.'

'But it is you who is doing the hitting, the sword is just the part of you that makes contact. You make it happen. But you are leaning beyond your feet, one part of you is fighting to keep you from falling so not all of you is trying for the ball. And you can do less, react less, control less when you reach and stretch like that.'

'Right. So it is like I said. I am hopeless.'

'There is hope. One of us here believes in you.'

'Aye, believes in an unbalanced over-stretching failure.'

Brann shrugged. 'Then we fix it. As I said, you are starting with the wrong end. See, not like this.' He reached forward again and flapped the sword. 'Like this.' He stepped into the swing. 'Start with your feet, and the rest of you has no choice but to follow. Step into the strike, and it will hit harder, and faster and, most of all, it will feel right.' He shrugged. 'If it feels right, it probably is.' He handed over the sword and nodded. 'It's at least worth a try.'

Marlo shrugged. 'I suppose.'

Brann paused before throwing the ball. 'The first couple of times, don't try to hit it. Just move to where you think you would.'

But when the ball flew across and Marlo's feet turned and slipped to meet its path, the sword came up and clipped it, shooting it off the ceiling. The boy whooped with joy.

Brann smiled. 'Again.'

The next time he missed it, and the next three. But each time only by the width of an eyelash. The next time he struck it, solidly.

135

Marlo's eyes widened. 'I did it! *You* did it.'

Brann took the sword. 'You did it. It wasn't me moving the sword. Now let's get it back to the Weapons House.' He barged him playfully. 'Success on the sixth, eh?'

The beaming boy nodded. 'I think we have earned our lunch today, both of us.'

As they stepped from the building into the sunlight, though, a voice stopped them. 'So who is it who is training who? Please remind me?'

Cassian was resting a shoulder against the wall beside the doorway. His broad-brimmed hat hid his face as he looked down at the rake he was toying with.

Brann felt himself colouring faster than the exertion in the heat had managed. He had let down the one man who had helped him more than any to remain alive. 'I, I didn't, I was just...'

Marlo cut in. 'It is my fault, sir. It was I who asked...'

The hat lifted with the head to reveal a smile. 'Panic not, little ones. It is a good thing, a good thing indeed.'

Both boys chorused, 'It is?'

'If I say so, do you not believe me?'

Both boys nodded. Then shook their heads. Then stopped, oblivious to what the correct answer might be.

'Listen to an old man, boys. You,' he straightened from the wall and stood in front of Marlo in one fluid movement, 'improved yourself today and, more importantly, showed the desire to do so. Your official training and next week both will start together. And as for you,' he turned to Brann. 'Some can do it but not explain it. And some can explain it but not do it. They seem opposites, but really they are the same: in each case, that person has reached the limit of their own abilities. But if a person can do both, then that person can always take on more learning. They can still improve. Which in your case,' a finger jabbed Brann's chest, 'may keep you breathing. You, too, can move onto your next stage next week.' He smiled beatifically. 'It's all right. I do not need your thanks. Do not express them.'

Both boys were stunned enough to comply but, as Cassian walked away, Marlo found his voice. 'Sir, what did you mean about *official* training? It is my only training.'

Cassian turned, puzzlement layering his face. 'You did not know you were learning every morning and every afternoon you spent with your young friend here?' He smiled and patted the boy's cheek affectionately. 'Of course you didn't. That was the point. That was why you did learn.'

Marlo thought on it for a moment. 'But if I am to train, who will work with Brann?'

'Your concern for your friend is touching, but now I need someone who can test him rather than help him work. He has a fight to train for.'

Brann's eyes widened. He realised he had become so immersed in learning that the purpose had slipped away from his thoughts. 'A fight? Back at the Arena?'

Cassian and Marlo looked at each other in amusement. The old man smiled. 'The Arena is only for the cream of competition. There are contests on a regular basis across the Empire, and across the city. The standard varies from one fighting pit to another, depending on the sum paid by the pit owners to bring the fighters. All new fighters build experience from the lower levels and rise according to their merit. You are a new fighter. Your fleeting appearance at the Arena was as a novelty attraction.' His smile grew broader. 'Though the surprise turned upon those who organised your appearance there, did it not?'

Brann's mood sobered at the memory. 'When will it be, this lowly fight?'

Cassian shrugged. 'I don't know yet. When you entered this building, you didn't have one. Now I have decided you do. How fast do you think I can arrange these things?' His eyes narrowed. 'And do not belittle this *lowly* fight. The gladiators in such contests as these are mostly of hardened experience, many having spent years in the millens and more in the pits. They know as much as it is possible to learn, but just lack the speed they once had or the little extra talent they were not born with. There are no easy opponents for you.'

The boys looked at each other, thoughts whirling in their heads. 'Now I can't believe you two would rather talk here with an old man when lunch awaits. I know I am starving.' Before he walked off this time, the burly old grey-head reached forward with both hands and ruffled the hair of the pair.

Brann was still stunned. But not so much that he hadn't noticed the smooth movement of the old feet and the fleeting moment it took for the rake to be tucked against the old side to let Cassian's arms reach out to them, and then returned to his grip, within his control all the while.

It was with considerably less confidence than on the last occasion that he approached the sparring circles. Then, he was fresh from a win in the Arena. Now the memories fresh in his mind were of an ignominious triple defeat.

A shadow fell in front of him. A large shadow. He stopped and Breta's breath was hot on the side of his face. 'So Cassian's little pet is returning for another lesson in the circles? That is good. Pets need to be chastened to remind them of their place. Breta hopes you face her. Blunt weapons

138

can still break bodies, and the novelty of little pets grows less as they are out of sight mending their bones. Soon you will be one of us, and a little pet no more. You are nothing special now, and you will be nothing special then.'

Brann didn't know what to say. He was sure she was right.

Salus approached and she growled in Brann's ear and moved away. The tall man gave her retreating form a look. 'You certainly have to fight off the women, don't you?' Brann almost laughed at the irony. He nodded towards the Big House. 'Boss wants to see you in the garden. I think you know your way there on your own by now.'

Brann found Cassian with small shears in his hand and a pile of long branches beside him. Tyrala sat in the shade close by, sipping water that looked as cool as her perpetual demeanour.

'You return to the sparring circles today,' Cassian said without preamble. A nod was the only response Brann could find. 'How do you feel?'

'Fitter. Stronger. Quicker. More knowledgeable. And terrified.'

'Terrified, you say? And why would that be?'

'They have such confidence. They know their abilities and are so sure of themselves. The only thing I am sure of is that the last time I was there, I was rubbish.'

'You were. Worse than rubbish, in fact. But...' Cassian paused, looking as if he were trying to find the phrase to fit his thoughts. He shook his head instead and picked up four straight stiff sticks and expertly trimmed away the leaves, cutting them to the same length. He handed two to Brann and, tossing aside the shears, held the others like a pair of swords.

'Now, you have learnt your moves, yes?' Brann nodded.

'Good, good. Now, as it is your first time with a combination of this sort, I shall furnish you in advance with the moves I will make. Defend against a thrust with the right, the left coming overhand at your head, the right cutting forehand at your left side. Then you counter at once with a backhand with your right, a thrust from wide left with your left as you turn, and a thrust, straight, with your right. Six moves, three from me, three from you. Picture them happen. Got them?'

Brann closed his eyes briefly, then nodded.

'Good. But never close your eyes when the man in front of you has a weapon. I will not let you off the next time.'

Brann nodded again. With his eyes open.

Cassian smiled like a grandfather about to hand over a present, then swept into action. Brann clumsily fended off the first two blows but received a stinging welt on his ribs from the third. He dropped his hands in despondency.

'And never drop your guard until you know it is over. I will not let you off next time with that either.'

'But it is over. That was a finishing blow.'

'This is not a fight, it is a lesson. And you were given three moves of your own.'

Determination to redeem himself brought the moves to the front of Brann's thoughts. Cassian blocked when he swung with his right and, before his left could thrust, a stick shot through and poked him on the chest. Brann shook his head, at a loss what to think.

'Again, we go. Come, come, get ready.' The old soldier was in a stance, waiting.

'Same moves till I get it right?'

'Of course not. This is not training, it is a lesson.'

'But I...'

Cassian came at him, in a flurry of blows almost too quick to follow. Brann stepped back in surprise, fending them off. In seconds it was over. One of Cassian's sticks lay at Tyrala's feet, the other was a broken stub in his hand. Brann had one stick at the man's throat and the other laid across his chest.

Brann jumped back, dropping the sticks. 'I'm so sorry!'

Cassian and Tyrala both laughed. 'Sorry?' the lady smiled. 'You have made my husband proud. You know what he has shown you?'

Brann shook his head. 'I just kept his swords... I mean *sticks*... away. When there was an opening, I just took it.'

Cassian beamed. 'See! You do understand.'

'Actually, I don't. I'm sorry.'

Tyrala picked up the stick at her feet. 'The fighters down there, their confidence is built through *knowledge* of their ability, but yours must be based on *trust* in yourself. They have been taught according to their abilities and strengths and know how to deal with certain stations and moves, but your mind works in a different way. My husband just showed you that you cannot fight their way any more than they can fight yours. You must submit to trusting yourself. This is more frightening and more vulnerable, but also more deadly.'

'And in any case,' Cassian said cheerfully, clapping him on the back, 'it is all you have. Now take it down there.'

Brann felt no more confident awaiting his turn in among the fighters around the sparring circle, but at least he felt no less. He supposed that was better than he had expected. His first opponent from the last time, the man with the two swords held upright, was again in his group and was grinding down a wiry man, all sinew and darting speed, who fought with a sword and a long knife. This man had a plan that

Brann approved of, and thought might just be successful: drawing out the stocky fighter's right sword. Brann guessed he would eventually try to slip to the left under it and come into the then-open side with his knife. It was similar to the move Brann had thought to try, except that with the knife it would be a quicker strike than the back-handed swing with a sword that Brann had thought to attempt. It might well be quick enough.

It wasn't. The flat of the sword clapped the wiry man on the back of his head and left him dazed and defeated. As he stumbled ruefully from the ring, Corpse intoned, 'Breta.'

The large woman picked a wooden axe and a large round shield from the pile of weapons. The axe spun in her hands as if it were a child's toy and, with a smile of relish, she swung her arms to ease her shoulders.

A voice cut across them. It was Salus. 'No. You go next, Breta. Brann, you're in.'

'Oh, by the gods,' he muttered. It was either suffer the humiliation of a fourth loss in succession (five if you counted both losses to this very opponent that had been counted as only one bout) or by some miracle win and be rewarded with a fight against the monster who had already made her intentions clear. And who knew that this first opponent didn't share her view of him, too? *One thing at a time,* he said, as much trying to clear his mind of Breta as to concentrate on the man before him.

There was a gasp at his stupidity when he picked from the pile the very same weapons as the man who had just been defeated. But he had a plan. It wasn't much of a plan, in that the man would expect him to be thinking he could try to repeat the tactics, but that he would be a foolish boy whose youthful arrogance had led him to believe that he could be quicker and succeed where the other had failed. He also had one move in his head, but that was it. After that, he had to rely on Cassian's lesson. And as it meant that he hadn't a clue what would come next, it wasn't overly reassuring at the moment.

Still, he had the arrogance of youth to portray first of all, so he attempted to saunter with a smile to the ring. Seeming to be carved from a tree, the man's face didn't even flicker.

Brann took up a confident stance, knife in his left hand forward, and sword poised. The man advanced with short steps as he always did, his strength fixing into the ground with each pace. Brann stepped to meet him and swung back-handed with the sword at the man's right sword. Short powerful muscles in the man's arm bunched as he met Brann's sword head on. Brann had intended to fake the block, as if he had jarred his arm, but the ruse wasn't necessary. His arm went numb for a moment, and he threw himself back as the hilt fell from fingers that jumped in response. The sword dropped as he did and, letting go of the knife, he grabbed the larger weapon with his left hand as he rolled and rose.

Dropping the pretend arrogance was easy as he let his right arm hang by his side, flexing his fingers as if trying to deal with the jarring. He tried to make the sword seem as awkward in his left hand as his confidence felt in the hands of the unknown. His one move was made. He hoped Cassian was right. He was certainly right about one thing: it was about all he had.

The man closed in to finish it. Brann circled to his right, trying to keep his feebly waving one sword between him and the two swords of his opponent. The man attacked, swinging back-handed with his right, aiming to knock

Brann's weapon wide or even out of his hand completely and open up his side to the other sword. It was the logical thing to do. The obvious thing to do.

Brann's hand shifted slightly, dropping the hilt into what was now a familiar grip. His feet shifted and his knees drove his wooden blade into his opponent's, knocking it high. The other sword was already coming at his chest and he swung his sword down and away from him as he twisted his right shoulder forward, letting the sword pass him much the same way as the spear had in his last bout. He had even more time on this occasion though, as the solid man, unaccustomed to being unbalanced, stumbled forward slightly. He didn't take the time. Even as he had the thought, the edge of Brann's blade was laid across the back of the man's neck.

Impassive, the man looked at him, nodded once, and walked from the circle.

There was silence. Then one fighter started clapping his right hand against his chest, slapping it over his heart. Others followed until the fighters watching around the other two circles turned to find the reason for the applause.

Brann stood, chest heaving, and felt a smile start to find its way towards his lips.

Corpse's drone boomed across the noise. 'Breta.'

Brann's heart sank. That was the problem with taking things one at a time. You could forget what was coming next.

He left the knife lying and hurriedly grabbed the first decently sized shield from the pile, a round one similar to Breta's but thankfully not as huge.

She marched into the circle, banging her axe against her shield. If it was meant to intimidate him, it was working. He had no plan. He revised that. He had one plan: avoid that big bloody axe.

The axe swung at him. Breta didn't believe in preamble. He jumped to one side and had to step back sharply to avoid a remarkably quick backswing.

She grinned. 'You can't jump out of the way forever, little gnat. It will only take one strike to swat you.' He knew she was right.

She stepped forward again, the axe slicing the air from high to her right. He flung up his shield but, instead of blocking it head on, he threw his left shoulder round, striking the axe at an angle to knock it off its trajectory while continuing its passage. With luck, the lack of expected contact would unbalance her and leave him an opening.

He should have known better than to hope for luck. Her movement was effortless as she stopped the weapon's swing and brought herself around to face him once more.

'You can't do that for long, little gnat. You have to get lucky every time.' She had a knack for the simple truth. He had to try something.

He dropped his shield slightly. She was unable to resist the temptation. The heavy weapon swiped at alarming speed towards his unprotected shoulder. But at the instant the swing had started, he had dropped a knee. He dived forward and left and, as she stepped into her blow, he shoved his sword blade between her legs to trip her. He rose and wheeled, desperate not to miss the chance to deliver the finishing blow as she fell.

But she did not fall. With fearsome determination in every thunderous plant of a foot, she grunted her way upright. 'You.' One step. 'Little.' Another. 'Bastard.' She was up and turning. 'But not good enough. That was your one chance, gnat. Now it's gone.'

She flexed her shoulders. And, abruptly, came forward at

a rush. The shield was up like a battering ram. The axe was held high and already swinging. Her right toe caught in a divot. She hurtled headlong, legs trailing, eyes wide and mouth wider in a wordless bellow and arms flung of their own accord wider still. Brann had once seen a child frozen in shock, unable to move his legs in the face of a bolting horse and snatched to safety at the last gasp by a desperate father. Now he knew that child's paralysis. But he had no saviour to pull him clear.

Desperation pulled his shield and sword across his front an instant before she hit. He was lifted clear off his feet and the two flew as one to land in a cloud of dust. The breath burst from Brann as if pushed from bellows. Silence fell across the watchers. One ran for a healer, and Tyrala started down the hill. Corpse loomed over the pair, and carefully examined the layers, lying perfectly in vertical order: ground, boy, shield, sword, throat.

'Sword to throat. The boy wins.' He turned and walked back to the edge.

Breta rolled off him, allowing Brann to drag in an almighty breath. She grinned at him. 'Well I'll be buggered.' One huge hand grabbed his arm and dragged him to his feet with her. 'The gnat has bite.' She slapped him on the back and almost knocked him to the ground again. Chuckling, she walked to the side of the circle.

He wasn't sure exactly what had just happened. But at lease *little gnat* was better than *little pet*.

'Next,' Corpse's voice intoned.

Brann hardly saw his opponent before the flat of a wooden blade tapped the side of his head. His vision starred and unfocused, he wobbled to the side to be welcomed by grins and slaps of praise. The way parted, though, when Tyrala

146

approached. Firm fingers felt their way around his ribs and examined his scalp for bumps. With a grunt of approval, she led him away from the bustle and sat him down. Crouching, she handed him a waterskin.

'Just winded. Rest, deep slow breaths and many sips of water.' She stood. 'Lucky boy. The shield saved you from being crushed.'

'Luck is nonsense.' Cassian was standing over him. 'He saved himself. Instinct pulled that shield across.'

Brann didn't have the breath to correct 'instinct' to 'terror'. So he smiled instead.

Marlo walked him back to the Food House after the sparring had ended. They walked in silence until Brann stopped him, a thought that had nagged him for a while slipping into his head.

'Why six?'

Marlo looked at him, head askance. 'Because that is the age I was when my life took this turn.'

'No, I'm not talking about you coming here. I mean everything here.' Brann waved his arm around. 'We train for six days at a time. We do things six times over when we train. There are six buildings around the courtyard. There are six trainers for the fighters. Six times in the hot and cold baths for recovery. Whenever this school competes, we have sent six fighters to the contest. There are even six bloody benches in Cassian's garden!'

'You're obsessed,' Marlo laughed. 'But you are right. And there are more examples if you can see them.' His finger jabbed Brann's chest and he looked at the school's symbol on his tunic. 'Six lines form the two swords.'

'Oh, by the gods,' Brann groaned. 'This is driving me mad. Why six?'

Marlo's eyebrows flicked up and down mischievously. Six times. Grinning, he beckoned Brann off the path and crouched on some looser ground. 'Look,' he said, and Brann knelt beside him.

Marlo poked one finger in the dust to make an impression, then two beneath it and three beneath them again. 'See, six dots in precise balance. Walk round it – whichever way you face it, the sides are the same, the points are the same. Three equal sides plus three points at the same angle: six again. Perfect balance. It is the symbol of the lady Tyrala. It was her belief, the Balance of Six, that brought Cassian back from the world his misery had taken him to. This,' he laid his hand on the double-sword emblem on his tunic, 'is the outward sign of this school but this,' he thumped a fist into the centre of the six dots. 'This is at the heart of everything we do here. This is how we live.'

Chest heaving, Brann knelt, his sword lying against the chest of the barrel-chested man on the cracked and rutted ground before him.

The crowd was loud with the sounds at the end of a fight: the delight of wagers won and the disgust of those lost. Loud enough to almost drown his opponent's words, ranged as they were around the lip of the wood-lined circular pit that was large enough to hold twenty men in line, arms outstretched and fingertips touching, but at this time home to only two. One kneeling, one on his back looking up.

'Gods, but you were quick. I never saw that coming.'

'I had to be. I would have run out of energy long before that.' Brann grasped his wrist to pull him to his feet. 'I have to say, you seem remarkably cheerful. I don't want to poke the wound, but you did just lose.'

148

The man shrugged. 'I fought my hardest, and them up there could see that, whether they moan or cheer. I thought I had you a couple of times, but I have fought on this circuit for long enough to know when I just come up against a better man, simple as that.'

Brann blew out a breath, shaking slightly from the rush of the fight. 'I thought you had me more than a couple of times.'

'Never in doubt, if truth be told, though I always hoped for a slip that might let me in. Just one thing, youngster. You have a tendency to dip your shield slightly before you strike. An inferior fighter will use his experience to read these signs and close the gap between your talent and his.'

The boy smiled. 'Thank you.'

'It is no disadvantage to me to tell you. I doubt we will meet again in the circle. I found my level long ago, but you are destined for higher venues than this. May fortune be at your back and not in your face.'

'You too.'

The man grinned and slapped him on the back, oblivious to the rivulets of blood trailing from the line across his chest and the nicks on both arms, his left thigh and right ear. He ambled towards a ladder that had been lowered into the pit. Brann smiled and headed to a similar ladder at the opposite side, reflecting that there are just some people you come across who cheer you up just by being in their company. Another of those waited at the lip of the pit.

'Your sixth victory from six since Cassian entered you in these contests in the city pits,' Salus beamed, helping him up. 'You know the boss'll be happy at that.'

Brann glanced over at Cassian, who was in conversation with a Scribe, and a high-ranking one from the look of him.

And the old soldier looked far from happy. 'Really? Doesn't look like it.'

'Oh, that'll be the scribbler's words doing that. The Boss will have been pleased with your performance. Not much wrong with it.'

'Apparently I give away when I'm going to attack by dipping my shield.'

Salus shrugged. 'That's easy to work on, but hard to spot. Good of Altan to mention it. He's been a good honest pro for a number of years, now. His words are worth a listen.'

'That's something I never imagined.' The next fight was starting and Brann moved a few paces back from the crowd and took the chance to sit for a while.

Salus settled beside him. 'What? That Altan would give good advice? He's a good lad.'

Brann laughed. 'No, no. Believe me, there have been many who have been less than pleasant when beaten by a newcomer, or when watching their colleagues be beaten, either in these pit contests or even in practice at our own school. But I have come across one or two decent ones like him.' He stared at the cloudless blue of a sky that seemed to stretch forever and thought how different it was from home. 'When we heard the stories growing up of the gladiators, as the storytellers called them, it was enormous titanic contests that always ended in one man lying slaughtered.'

'Too expensive. Stories are stories and this is real life. If fighters are bought in, they are not cheap. And once they are in a school, they work a lot, so they eat a lot. Weapons cost to maintain. There are all sorts of things I don't even know about need to be paid for just to keep a school going. It takes a while to train a new fighter to the standard and style of your school, so it takes time for him or her to earn.

The contests pay the schools to bring contestants, and we can hire out fighters as bodyguards on short contracts, but the income just gets a school by. We can't afford to keep replacing fighters who go off and get killed. When you think that this circle, in this gathering point for caravans, is replicated in other caravan points, market quarters, docks, living areas, anywhere that people gather all over the city, that's a lot of fighters who would be cast aside on a regular basis. That's why the death fights create such interest. Such entertainment is kept for certain occasions, or for the depravity of the... well, whatever. They don't happen much. The entertainment is in the contest, the skill or strength that wins them. The main risk in most contests lies in the winning or losing of the wagers laid by those watching.'

Brann saw in his face that there was no point in asking. He grunted. 'And I can see why the enormous titanic fights are an exaggeration. I'm knackered after just a few minutes. And that's after training hard enough to get ahead of Breta in the runs.'

The man's head nodded in an amused snort. 'You should maybe think of raising your standards a touch.'

'You will have to raise your standards very much.' Cassian stood over them, his tone unusually grave.

Brann scrambled to his feet. 'I know I dip my shield. I'm sorry, I'll work on it.'

Cassian's eyebrows raised, but he didn't pursue the detail. 'You'll work on a great deal more than that. And quickly.' Apprehension started to churn Brann's stomach. 'They want to move you to the Arena. I tried to tell him that any fighter would need a year at this level before we could even judge if they were ready, not the half of it that you have had. You could be badly injured, not through the fault of an opponent, but from your lack of experience. But he was just a Scribe, he only carried the message.' The man put a hand on Brann's shoulder. 'My poor boy, first they put you in a death fight with no preparation, and now this. I don't know who, or why, but someone influential is hunting you. And we have no choice but to send you out to run before the hounds of their plans.'

Brann knew who. And why. But he merely shrugged and looked at the cart that would take them back to the compound. 'Better get started then.'

Chapter 4

'He fights well, this boy of yours.'

She had taken to drawing a chair beside his as he lost himself in the view from his window and the thoughts in his head. Even his wife had never dared as much. But she was not his wife.

He had long since stopped wondering who she was, or had been. Or why she was there. Or what her reasons might be. There was an acceptance of her presence. It had grown, but he could not tell himself when it had started. That was the thing about acceptance: you did not tend to question it.

But that voice, that dry whispering voice. It seized his attention with an irresistible power and ease like nothing else he had encountered in his years. And he had encountered a great deal in a great deal of years.

'He does.' It could not be denied. Seven victories in as many months since graduating from the peripheral pits to the Arena was a feat that would make an experienced fighter proud, never mind that they had been against fighters of seven different sizes and styles. Whoever they put before him, he *had found a way to beat them. He took no acclaim; where others postured and played to the crowd, he would walk out with a brief wave of respectful acknowledgement and, at the conclusion of each fight, would face four ways in turn and place his hand on the symbol on his chest, homage to the school that trained him to claim these victories.*

And the masses had warmed to him. They loved him. They flocked to his fights like no other, the pale young boy from the North with the unpredictable style that entertained beyond empty showmanship.

'But he needs more.'

'Have you seen him?' The astonished uncertainty in her voice was a rare pleasure.

'He is only half of what he must be.'

'How much more need he be? How much more can he be? What more must he gain, must he prove? When you expect too much, failure is the only outcome.'

'Fate expects,' he snapped. 'Situations demand. If he cannot bear the load, he is not the one we seek and we must cast our net again.'

'He must be the one.' She stood and paced closer to the window, her eyes distant. 'I feel it too strongly for it to be otherwise. But can what is needed be brought from him? Can it be done?'

'It can.'

'He will need to grow, to learn, to change.'

'I will ensure it.'

She shuddered, as if a chill had lanced through the heat. 'I fear for him.'

'You should.'

****

Brann was emerging from his cold plunge in a cascade of dripping water and a gasp that rang against the walls as Marlo stuck his head around the corner.

'By the balls of the gods,' he spluttered. 'Well the male ones. Gods, I mean. Male gods, not male balls. Although they are male as well, I suppose.' He heaved himself quickly from the pool. 'Anyway, it doesn't get any easier in that pool. There's something just not right about doing that.'

Marlo laughed and threw him a towel. 'I thought you Northerners were used to the cold. Is it not always that way there?'

Brann's laugh was abrupt. 'Sometimes it seems like that. Sometimes it heats up, to as much as just "chilly". Occasionally, we get a few days of sunshine, and then we make all the usual jokes about that being our summer. But mostly we get rain. Sometimes as snow, but mostly rain. A lot of rain.'

'Snow?'

Brann smiled at him. It was always a slight comfort when, in a land where he found so many things to be strange and unknown, there were still some crumbs of knowledge he had that would hold mysteries for others. 'It's like rain, but colder. And whiter.'

Marlo pondered it. 'I would like to see this snow.'

Brann grunted. 'Catch it while you're young, then. It's fun for children and an irritation for adults. And it's cold, much colder than you ever know here.'

'And yet you find the plunge bath unbearable?' Marlo's curiosity wouldn't let this go. 'When you were born into this cold wet land?'

'Believe me, when you are born into it you don't seek it out. We spent our lives trying to avoid it, under several layers of clothing or near a fire.' He wrapped the towel around him. 'Anyway, what are you here for?'

Marlo fetched his tunic. 'I have a surprise for you.'

'That's hardly what you want to be saying to a semi-naked man.'

'Enough. I've just had my lunch. Put your clothes on.'

Brann grinned and adjusted his belt. 'So?'

Marlo turned and walked towards the door. 'We have an adventure to go on.'

Brann was used to the other boy's infectious tendency towards exaggerated enthusiasm, so he followed without great expectations of the surprise involving anything remotely exciting. But, still, he followed with a smile. He found it impossible not to do so with Marlo.

When they left through the front of the house rather than the rear, however, he was thrown. 'Where are we going? You do remember, don't you, that I was fighting yesterday? I have an afternoon session with Tyrala and her manipulation torture.'

'You don't,' Marlo said over his shoulder. 'It was the lady's suggestion that you take some time away from everything. It is just as important to let the head recover as the body, she said. Come on, keep up.'

Brann trotted alongside him. 'So where are we going?'

'You'll see,' was all Marlo would divulge, and proceeded to chat cheerily the entire way into the heart of the city about anything but the destination. Brann did notice, however, that the areas they were passing through were becoming less and less salubrious. A few curious glances were thrown his way as they walked, as if he seemed familiar but, out of the context of the Arena, up-close and devoid of sweat, blood and grime, they just couldn't think where

156

they knew his face. He was only vaguely aware of it, though, his own attention drawn away from them by the bustle of the city. His eyes darted constantly, drawn by a whirl of shifting movement, colour and sound. Buildings seemed so close, people so numerous. They turned a corner to a narrow street, wide enough to allow a cart in only one direction should one choose to enter it. Not that any cart driver would attempt it, jammed as it was with stalls along one side, sellers stationary behind them and, in front of them, those buying or perusing or haggling or chatting or passing through or waving or arguing or, presumably, thieving swirled amongst each other like grains of sand caught in eddies of wind. He stopped, the scene as much a barrier as a stone wall.

It took Marlo a moment to realise Brann was no longer beside him. He wheeled round with a look of alarm that faded to a smile. 'It's funny, isn't it?'

Brann frowned, staring at the crowded street. 'Really? Why?'

'No, not the street. And not funny that way.' The boy moved closer to Brann to let a baker carry past a tray that trailed the most appetising of smells in its wake. 'I mean the feeling you get after living in the compound for a while. How everything outside it seems so strange when you come back to it. I grew up in this city and it only takes me a month in the school before I feel weird when I come out of it. You've had a lot longer than that. Don't worry, it'll pass before long.'

It was true. Brann hadn't realised how much the boundaries of the compound had become the boundaries of his world. Even when he had travelled to the Arena, he had done so in a covered wagon, hidden like a prized asset.

Now the humdrum routine of the city seemed alien to him. That it was so visibly normal to all around him left him feeling apart from them, distant, detached, as if watching them in a dream, moving among them unseen and unnoticed by all around, just like he had felt in the aftermath of...

... his brother's death.

The image of Callan flooded Brann's vision: jolting with the impact of the crossbow bolt, the claret stream of the life draining from him and the way his arms, his legs, his head all hung as he carried him. Shivering became shuddering, and his right hand grasped at air repeatedly. He reached his left hand for the wall of the building, fell against it and sank to the ground, the rough surface drawing scrapes of blood from the top of his arm.

Marlo stared helplessly at the boy, stunned into indecision by the sudden nature of his transformation. A deep voice spoke casually at his side. 'Gladiator?'

Marlo saw a face beaten by the elements into creased leather. Stubble that looked as rough as the wall Brann had scoured himself against was equal on the lower half of his face and on his scalp. Marlo found himself stammering. 'No. I, I'm just a trainee. But he is.'

'I was talking about him.'

'Yes, he fights in the Arena. Have you seen him there? Or maybe before, in the local pits?'

The man grunted. 'I have not seen him in any of those places. The theatre of steel lacks allure when you have lived its reality. Some memories are best not stirred.'

'Then how did you know? About him? That he was a gladiator?'

'The hand.' The man nodded at Brann's fingers, opening

158

and closing in relentless hope of success. 'Those who have known the sword reach for it without thought in times of unease. Those accustomed to wearing a weapon grasp at their hip, whether they carry the blade or not. But a gladiator never wears a weapon, never sees a sheath or a scabbard. The only weapon a gladiator knows is the one he carries, the one he holds.' A broken wooden rod, still bearing scraps of the cloth that once had been rolled around it, lay in the dust beside them. The man crouched before Brann and put the rod in his hand. The fingers seized it, knuckles white, but the hand became still. The man smiled. 'You see? Now his hand is content.'

Marlo bent over them. 'It is more than just his hand that needs tended. I have never seen this before.'

The man stared, almost gently at Brann. 'I have. Many times. In the aftermath of battle. Or sometimes before it, sometimes during it. Or sometimes even months in its wake. Any time, really. New recruits or old survivors, the basest slogger or the grandest general, there is no telling who it will strike. Memories? It seems that, for this young man, some memories have indeed been stirred. And sometimes when the memories are too much, the person in the head shuts down for a short while, lest they be destroyed, leaving the body to fend for itself.'

'Can he be helped?' Marlo looked up, his tone pleading. 'Can you help him?'

Brann became aware of a grip, firm but gentle, taking hold of his head, both sides held by calloused hands as the thumbs stroked his forehead from centre out in a soothingly repetitive movement. A voice was low and calm, the words indistinct but the tone soothing. Gradually, Brann's body stilled and, in the same moment of uncertain haziness as between asleep and awake, his cloudy gaze lifted. He blinked several times before clarity returned and found kind eyes looking at him from amid a jumble of creases so numerous that it was hard to tell which were wrinkles of age and which scars of violence. The eyes were familiar; very familiar. He blinked in an attempt to regain focus. 'Cassian?'

A broad smile multiplied the creases. 'No, Ossavian. But I do have a young brother named Cassian. And you,' he peered at Brann then looked up at Marlo, 'are a Northerner slave boy with a troubled past, who is in the company of a trainee fighter, who knows someone called Cassian who in turn looks at least vaguely like me. I am thinking you would be Brann of the North Isles, the darling of the Arena, the one I have been hearing about.'

The boy shrugged. 'I'm Brann.'

Marlo beamed. 'He is that Brann. I call him the Brannihilator.'

Brann looked at him. 'No you don't.'

'I will now that I've thought about it.'

'No. You won't.'

'If you two have quite finished?' Ossavian pulled Brann to his feet with surprising ease. He looked the boy up and down. 'I thought you'd be bigger.'

Marlo nodded. 'His opponents thought that, too. That was their first mistake.'

The big man laughed a slow laugh, his shoulders rising and falling as he did. 'I'm sure it was.'

With one hand against the wall and the other arm supported by the man with a grip that suggested strength held in store, Brann eased himself to his feet. 'What just happened?'

Concern still filled Marlo's eyes. 'You left us for a short while.'

'You left yourself for a short while.' Ossavian's voice was matter-of-fact. 'But you are fine now. You have been through more, I suspect, than even your young friend here knows, and sometimes that catches up on the best of us.'

Marlo started to speak but was halted as the dawning of realisation widened his eyes. '*Cassian's brother*. Oh, gods, how could I have forgotten?' He dropped to one knee, head bowed. 'Your Radiance, forgive me.'

'The only things that will need to be forgiven will be you continuing to grovel down there and if you ever again address me as a high priestess,' the man grunted, nudging Marlo with his foot. 'Get up before I knock you all the way down.'

The boy jumped to his feet, his eyes shining as he turned to Brann. 'This is General Ossavian. One of the only two brothers ever to have commanded the Imperial Host between them. While Cassian, you know, our Cassian, led the Army of the South on its campaigns, this man commanded the Army of the North, defending our borders and the city itself.'

'Yes,' Ossavian said drily, 'my thanks for reminding me that my younger brother got the better job.'

Marlo's cheeks flushed. 'And you would have been given that post in time as well, had those who claim to rule made even just one appointment based on merit, as was done in Cassian's time and before, and not based on who fawns best over them or has been spat from the womb of whoever had filled their bed from one moment to the other.'

'Calm down, youngster, calm down. It's far too hot to get yourself even more heated.' He drew Marlo in towards the wall and continued in a lower tone. 'It is a fine thing to know your own mind, but little use if the head your mind inhabits finds itself separated from your shoulders. Think what you will, but have a care what you say, and where. Those of whom you speak have many ears and few scruples in dealing with those who have opinions that differ from their own.' He faced Brann. 'And while I'm in the mood for advice, you should remember that this is a big city around you, and you have, you hope, a long life ahead of you. Whether a city street or the path through the years, think not of the entirety of the journey nor the thousands who will surround you upon it, but only as far as you can see at the time. Deal with what is there in clear sight – it will usually provide enough to occupy you. The rest is conjecture and chance, and there are no two better devourers of good time and thought. Worry about what you have not or wish was otherwise, and you waste the opportunity to attend to improving your situation.' He gripped Brann's shoulders. 'Plot only the course you can see, and you will suffer less of,' the big hands shook the boy rapidly, 'this.'

'But what about...?' Marlo's curiosity was halted by a calloused finger on his lips.

'There are always exceptions. Exceptions are your executioner or your tutor. Try to be the pupil, not the corpse.' He turned Brann to face the street that had daunted him. 'One step at a time.' A gentle shove encouraged his feet. 'Starting now.'

Brann turned to thank him, but the broad back was already ambling in the opposite direction.

Marlo grinned. 'You heard the man. Keep it going.'

He steered Brann into the throng and they weaved through the bodies, the way more open than it had looked from the corner. Before long they were several streets away and Marlo handed him a fresh apple, taking a bite from one of his own.

Brann looked at it. 'But we didn't stop at a stall? You didn't...'

'Some old habits never leave you.' His cheer was so infectious that Brann couldn't help but laugh with him. But still, alongside it lingered unease. Whatever that episode had been, would it strike again? He thought back to Ossavian's words. There seemed sense in them. In any case, they were the only advice he had on this.

The white of the buildings around them had become more faded and patchy and the footing more uneven. The smell of the sea now mingling with that of the human refuse flowing down a channel in the centre of the street led him to think they were closing in on the docks, but the trading area he had been carried through on the way up from the ship had enjoyed a look more in keeping with the affluence of the business conducted there. Here every second frontage seemed that of a bar or a whorehouse, or sold some sort of stew served from a vat and seeming to be locally popular, though from taste or price it was hard to tell.

It was curious the way that attitudes had changed as they had moved through residential areas of decreasing prosperity. Where it had been well-to-do, they had passed almost unnoticed, as if their existence was beneath the interest of those who belonged there. As they moved further in, and the mass of the city wrapped itself around them, they were viewed with suspicion as strangers, watchful eyes following them until they had moved far enough from property or possessions to pose no further threat. Here, however, the people around them showed as much interest as the wealthy had done, but from the opposite end of the spectrum. The residents were wrapped in their poverty as much as the rich had been wrapped in their opulent comfort, but the weariness in their faces and their tread spoke of an existence that considered only the day before them and left little room for anything other than what directly affected their own lives. Some had retreated into silence, some shouted their boisterousness to the world, and most were at stages between, but all were worn by life. *It must take a special kind of strength to live like this,* Brann realised.

Marlo's grin flashed at him as he led him into an alley. 'I know what you're thinking. How could I ever think to leave the delights of a place like this to scratch my way through life at a hellhole like Cassian's school?'

Brann's eyes widened. 'You lived here?'

'Well, not strictly here. My home was in the poor bit.'

'In the *what*?'

'Oh, you dream of moving to here in Dockside when you grow up in The Pastures.'

Brann spluttered. '*The Pastures?*'

'Your sense of humour relies a lot on irony when it is all you have to keep your strength to live another day.'

Brann looked at him appraisingly. There was much in his friend that was hidden by his cheerful demeanour.

Marlo led him down alleys that led off alleys that led off alleys until not only was he certain he could never find his way back alone, but he wasn't even sure which way he was facing. They were in a narrow street lined by buildings of three stacked storeys, the glare of the sun barely reaching the ground where a stream of liquid that he didn't dare inspect in any greater detail than the smell that cloyed his

164

nose ran past their footsteps, when Marlo abruptly stopped beside a door much like all the others. Frowning, he looked up and down the street.

'Yes, I'm sure it's this one.'

'This was your home?'

He rapped a specific and careful knock before he pushed the door open and stepped through, beckoning his companion after him. 'Not mine.'

Brann followed, his eyes adjusting to the deeper gloom enough to let him see the back of a large man at a plain table, spooning stew from a large serving bowl into a smaller eating one.

'Well bugger the gods, look who's come to visit,' a voice shouted from the side.

Brann almost staggered in surprise. That voice. It could only be: 'Hakon!'

He had only managed to half turn towards the boy before he was enveloped in a suffocating bear hug. He found just enough breath to gasp, 'I see you haven't lost any of your strength, then.'

The hulking boy grinned and released him enough to give him a gentle slap on the back that sent him lurching forward several paces. 'I see you haven't gained any height, little mouse.' He fingered the heavy chain around Brann's neck. 'Though you have gained some new jewellery.'

Brann shrugged. 'It is what it is. I don't intend to stay in this city forever. Whenever I get away, I will have to stay alive till then. And it could be worse.'

The man at the table had risen and came to grip him by the arms, looking him up and down in an unconsciously similar way to another old warrior with cropped grey hair not too long before. 'At least they seem to be feeding you fine,' Cannick said. 'Good to see you, boy. And good to see you're alive, despite their best efforts.'

Hakon drew up a chair and dropped onto it, threatening its condition. 'Not just alive, but a legend of the Arena. You have tales to tell, young farm boy.'

'Mill boy,' Brann corrected him before he saw Hakon's grin. 'Anyway, there's not much to tell. Someone tries to beat me, I try to beat them and, so far, I've come out luckier.'

'No such thing as luck,' Cannick growled, sitting back at his stew, 'just what happens and what doesn't, and what you do and what you don't. I managed to get in for your last fight but one. Not much wrong with what you did there.'

Brann smiled, pulling up a chair for himself. 'Aye, that was quite a good one, I suppose. He was tricky.'

Cannick levelled his gaze at him. 'He was more than tricky. It's just a pity Einarr wasn't able to see how his page has improved.' He grinned. 'Well, improved a bit.'

Brann's face fell at the sound of the Captain's name. 'Have you heard how he is? And Konall?'

Cannick shrugged and spat on the floor, scrubbing the damp spot on the dusty boards with the sole of one boot. 'Not a peep, but you wouldn't expect to hear anything. They'll be kept in comfort, probably extravagance, but with a locked door on their room and an escort when they leave it. Imprisoned in luxury, that's the lot of a hostage.'

'And the others? The crew? Grakk?'

Cannick spat again, this time staring at his rubbing boot as he spoke in a low tone. 'The bald one is also faring well in the Arena, though I don't think your contests have been on the same days yet.' Brann shook his head in confirmation, relieved but not surprised at Grakk's fortune. 'The rest? Mixed. Scattered. Living how they can. Those who got away were lost, just more faces in the masses of the city. You and Grakk were the Emperor's example, Einarr and Konall are his assets, and the rest of us seem irrelevant. According to a palace servant Hakon met in a tavern shortly after,' the big boy grinned at the memory, 'the word is that they see only those of you who travelled to the palace as part of a conspiracy. Apparently simple seamen are, well, too simple to be mixed up in any politics. In a city of a million souls, the grumbles and gripes of the common man are as numerous and of as much consequence to the lords and ladies as the drone of the flies.' He waved a hand in a wide sweep. 'About half a dozen of us stay here and labour at the docks where we can find work. Others found other roofs to put over their heads. Some come and go – we've got plenty of space here. About half the crew have a new life here in the Heart of the Empire, thanks to the Emperor's welcome. Remember our soothsayer from the ship? Our Lady is upstairs; we keep her as well as we can. She asks for little, as is her wont, but deserves more than we can give. And Einarr would kill us himself if we let anything happen to her.'

'And the other half of the crew?'

'The ones who didn't escape the ship in time? Thanks to the Emperor's welcome, they found death in the Heart of the Empire. That was the Emperor's other example.'

'Half the crew? Slaughtered? As an example?'

Cannick nodded gravely. 'A powerful example, you must admit. They like their little reminders. A bit of random death here and there by the authorities is less work than keeping tabs on everyone.' He sighed. 'A lot of good men are gone. Galen? Remember him?' Brann did. Of course he did, and his breath caught in his throat at the thought, followed closely by tears catching in his eyes. 'Took six of the bastards with him, and only had a long knife on him when they came. Died a hero, so he did, but hero or not he's still dead. Still, that would have been all of us but for the warning we got. Maybe half of us died, but half of us lived.'

Brann wiped the back of a hand across his eyes and smiled at Hakon. 'You managed to reach them, then? When you escaped the citadel?'

The large boy looked hurt. 'Of course I did. You doubt my skill and prowess?'

A cool voice slipped from above. 'Such skill and prowess would not have got him beyond the first courtyard of the palace.' Brann looked up to see a slim figure on a high windowsill, sitting side-on with knees drawn up with a casual relaxation that was almost feline. Dark eyes regarded him. 'A touch of help did aid him along the way.' A bright blade cut a slice from an apple. 'Every step along the way, if truth be told.'

'Well, yes,' Hakon admitted. 'She did help a bit. I allowed her to, so she would feel of some value.' He yelped as an apple core smacked his head square on the crown. 'Oh, that's Sophaya, by the way.'

Brann smiled. 'My pleasure to meet you. I'm...'

'If I didn't know who you are,' she said, her tone as languid as her posture, 'I would have to be deaf to that one beside you with apple in his hair, prattling on about your exploits in the Arena. I would have grown to hate you without having to go to the trouble of meeting you, had I not been in the stadium crowd to see it was actually based on truth, even if his fawning prattle was hugely over the top.' She produced another apple and sliced herself a piece with an adroit twist of a wrist. Hakon moved to the other side of the table, where he could see the flight of any missile from her perch. 'So your slate with me is clear. For now.'

Brann looked at Cannick. 'What about Einarr and Konall? You have a plan?'

The grey head shook. 'We are too few. We are gathering our strength, but we are new to a foreign city, and while I said they aren't actively looking for us, if you bring yourselves to their attention then they do take notice. Even if it is just a petty official, too stupid to look for an opportunity but too greedy for the opinion of his superior to risk one when it is presented, it is still a noose that he dangles for you and a carrion cage that awaits you afterwards.' He grunted. 'Anyway, you were always the one for a plan, and we don't have you yet.' He saw Brann's look. 'This is a fleeting visit, and you are lucky to have that. You will not be here often enough to be a part of anything and your life is too removed from ours to make this more permanent. Don't worry, if an opportunity presents itself in the meantime to help you or the two up in the big stone house on the hill, we'll take it.'

Brann looked into his eyes. 'Einarr is the priority. If you get the chance, you take him and forget about me.'

Cannick reached across and gripped his arm. 'Rest assured, if there is any way to get Einarr and his young cousin out of here, he'll be on his way back North before you know it. But we won't forget about you. There will always be some of us in this city as long as you are.'

Brann nodded, but then his eyes hardened. 'And Loku? We forget him?'

'Never. But this is his ground. He is too strong here. The

priority is to get Einarr home. Every battle has its day to be lost, and its day to be won. We have to choose the day with sense.'

Brann nodded. It was true. But Loku refused to leave his head. His eyes bored into the table-top with a fury that shook his body. Cannick's grip tightened on his arm, pulling at his attention, and he looked up. The man nodded. 'Don't worry. I know what you feel. We all do.'

A knock on the door, the same as Marlo had made, sounded and Gerens slipped in, all gangly limbs that should have moved awkwardly but, through corded muscle and sinew, afforded him a smoothness of movement that spoke of menacing control. The dark eyes, burning with cold fire as ever beneath wild hair that would always remain untamed, settled on Brann immediately.

'Good to see you, Chief,' he said, as if he had last spoken to Brann earlier that day, and walked to the table to help himself to a bowl of stew.

Brann smiled. He felt almost complete now. 'It is good to see you, too, Gerens. Very good, actually. But you do not seem surprised at seeing me.'

Gerens didn't look up from his bowl. 'Why would I? I followed you from the edge of the city.'

'You were following me?'

He tore a hunk of bread to dip into his stew. 'Of course. How could I ensure you were safe if you were not in my sight? I was glad that the old man was able to stop you shaking though, else I would have had to reveal myself.'

'Thank you, Gerens, but you don't have to keep me safe. It wasn't as if we were back in the bandit camp in the mountains; I was only walking through the city in broad daylight.'

'Even were you to be walking among the Sisters of Peace

170

in their Garden of Tranquillity, still I would feel better to see with my own eyes that you were safe. It irks me that I cannot look into that training school of yours, but Cannick said it would risk too much.'

Brann's smile was fond. 'Why, though, Gerens?'

The boy shrugged with inconsequence. 'I don't know. I just feel that I have to do it. Thinking about it won't change it, so why bother?'

Cannick grunted. 'More to the point, where were you after you had seen the boy safely here?'

'I paid a visit to he who would be our landlord, to persuade him to change his opinion on whether he does, after all, own this building that has been unattended in all the time we have been here.'

'And did you?'

Gerens shook his head, the hair that exploded like black fire waving in time to the movement. 'He wasn't in his chambers. Then the guards came and one of them died a bit noisily, so I had to leave.'

Sophaya's cool voice floated down. 'He wouldn't have been there because he would have been looking for this.' A streak of gold flashed across the room to be snatched from the air by Gerens's hand. 'I imagine his search would have been fairly frantic.'

She slipped from the high sill in one movement and landed noiselessly on the wooden floor, the fingers of one hand brushing the dust from the rough planks as she steadied her landing. Cannick took the object from Gerens, a broad and ornate golden bangle that hinged open and had a tiny keyhole and a small but sturdy lock where it would join shut.

'A marriage cuff,' he mused. 'You took this from his house?'

'In a general sense.' Cannick raised his eyebrows. She shrugged. 'He was in his house when I took it from his wrist.' She raised her arms in exasperation. 'Well, how else could I get it? The whole point of these things is that they aren't taken off. He wasn't going to leave it lying around, was he?'

'So he now thinks it has fallen off,' Hakon said. 'So how will that help anything?'

Cannick began to smile. 'It won't. But it could.' He looked at the girl. 'So where is it going to be found?'

She cut a sliver from her apple and studied it. 'He has a lover. She has a divan. It may have dropped there. Married men do endearingly tend to remove reminders of their married state when with their unmarried lovers. It would be most unfortunate were it to be found by someone other than the married man or his lover.'

Cannick's smile was broader. 'And who might find it there?'

'His darling wife has a powerful father. And the father has a powerful temper.' She sauntered around the table to run her fingers gently through Gerens's unruly locks. 'And the temper may be roused by a rumour that might be circulating the tavern he frequents of a certain woman of low repute who had caught the eye and opened the breeches of his darling daughter's husband. A rumour that would not, of course, have been planted by a handsome man with hair more wild than the sea.'

Cannick caught Brann's eye. 'This is the level of our battles at the moment. We look to grow, but the pace of growth is governed by what is possible, not just what we wish for.'

Gerens looked at the girl, his voice as matter-of-fact as

ever. 'You are magnificent.' He looked at Brann. 'She is, you know. Magnificent.'

'And your perception,' she kissed the top of his head, 'is your most endearing quality.'

Cannick barked a laugh and slapped Brann on the back. 'That look on your face is worth every bit of the effort in getting you here.'

'So how did you come to know my friends?' Brann looked back over his shoulder as they strolled back through the city. He knew Gerens was there, somewhere, but the boy was as visible as he had been on the way down. He smiled at the thought of the time he had spent with people he had thought he would never see again. Hardening his heart to loss and focusing on the present had not become anywhere close to easy, but it had become more familiar, to the extent that rediscovering that which he had thought was lost had become an unexpected pleasure. A delight that he could now look forward to whenever his duties allowed.

'They found me. I was on an errand for Cassian, and they had been watching the compound, waiting for someone they felt safe asking about you.' Marlo smiled. 'I guess I'm not one of the scary-looking ones.'

'And you just told these strangers all about me?'

Marlo frowned. 'You think I am simple? They were sleeping rough, under crates at the docks, unable to find work because they looked the way they lived, and unable to pay for lodgings because they found no work. It is funny how you are drawn back to the area you are born to, and in recent years I had become aware of an abandoned building. It suited them and, in dealing with them, I learned they were men to be trusted. That is the first judgement a child learns in an area like The Pastures.'

'What of those who don't learn it?'

'The ones who learn it, live. Therefore all the children you see running around have learnt it. Anyway, it was only when I knew this about these men that I told them everything about you. Including how you dance on tables when you are drunk. And how you fart in your sleep.'

'I don't!'

'I know you don't. But it made them laugh. And they have travelled with you on a boat so they know it isn't true.' He looked sideways. 'Is it?'

Brann punched his arm, drawing the attention of more than a few passers-by. Grinning, Marlo slapped him hard on the back of the head. 'Just for the sake of appearances,' he pointed out. 'A slave striking a free man doesn't go down well, you know.'

Brann snorted. 'Free *boy*, more like.'

'And that,' Marlo smacked his head again, 'is for your cheek, slave.'

At the look in his victim's eye, he spun on his heel and made good his escape up the street, his laughter preventing any words. Brann laughed and took off after him, almost catching him twice before they approached the compound. The road across the school's front became a racetrack as each boy tried to reach the gate first, Brann's determination running Marlo's naturally fleet feet close, but not close enough to triumph. The pair collapsed breathless but snorting with laughter against the wood of the gate, alerting the guard on the far side.

As soon as they stepped through the door, the guard stopped them, an unusual stern look to him. Not one of disapproval of their boisterous arrival, not admonishment. There was concern, but more: almost sorrow.

When all he said was, 'You are to see Cassian immediately on your arrival. So now,' they waited not at all to reply but raced to the house, no laughter pulling them this time but the more powerful force of fear and worry. What could have befallen their beloved mentor?

When they burst into the house, however, Cassian was descending the stairs in as rude health as ever – but unlike every other time, there was no smile on his eyes.

'Oh, my poor boy,' he said softly, coming to put his hands on Brann's shoulders. 'Why can they never leave you be? The hunter in the high place has returned to have his beaters steer you towards death once more. What enemy have you made to be so relentless that when you survive one trap, they must set another?' He smoothed the hair away from Brann's forehead as if to see his face more clearly, a tender gesture that left his hand cupping the side of the boy's head. He sighed, as if he had no more excuse to delay what he wished he didn't have to say. 'They want to see you fight for the ultimate stakes once more. There is to be another death match.'

Brann stiffened. He was silent for a long moment, the words growing to fill his thoughts. When his words came, the tone was flat. 'When will it be?'

'In one full turn of the moon.'

His shrug was one of resignation in the face of fate. 'At least this time they have given me more than a single day to prepare. I suppose I will have to get to work, then. I wonder what monstrous criminal they will present me with this time.'

Cassian's breath caught in his throat. 'The monstrosity is

not in the opponent himself, but in the choice of who it will be.' He stared at the ceiling, as if silently imploring the gods. 'It has been decreed...' His voice was a whisper, almost too faint to hear. 'It has been decreed that you will fight the Tribesman of the Desert. You will fight your friend Grakk.'

His arms folded around Brann as the boy's knees buckled, holding him tight to his broad chest. From the side, a moan of despair escaped from Marlo.

'What will I do, Cassian?'

'You will do what you must.'

'But I cannot kill him.'

'We will train you to give you every chance.'

Brann pushed himself back enough to look into the old man's face. 'I don't mean I have not the skill, although that will undoubtedly be the truth. I mean I cannot bring myself to do it.'

The man's eyes were moist, but a hardness crept into them. 'You will do what you must. As will he. Should you both not do so, to the utmost of your ability, you will both be killed. Such is the tragedy of this story. One will die and the other will most likely be broken.'

Brann drew a long slow breath. 'Whatever transpires, then one thing is certain.' He looked at the old man and the young boy. 'I have a lot of work to do.'

The days that followed merged into a timeless blur. He woke, ran, trained, ran and slept, interspersing it only with eating and washing. The effort served to fill his consciousness, allowing him to block thoughts of what lay at the end. When he sparred, it was always against fighters bearing two swords, and never against a single opponent. Sometimes he faced two, sometimes three; always Cassian sought to

176

heighten his reactions, his awareness, his speed, his stamina. When he died, he would die well and not easily.

His mind was still numb on the ride to the Arena, and in the walk through the oppressive passages to the room where he would await his call. What had become familiar and routine about the place was now surreal and strange. He responded vaguely to those he encountered, their presence immaterial to his awareness.

It was when he donned his mail, though, that the thought of Grakk became irresistible. The image of the little tribesman caringly helping him into the mail on his first visit to the very same room swept over him and the emotion started to rise. Panicking, he grabbed a wooden sword and thrashed at a wooden practice post set in one corner of the room, battering the feelings back down with every stroke. He couldn't afford any weakness. Not a trickle, never mind the deluge that had threatened to engulf him.

Even the stone-shaking chant of 'Two walk in, one walks out' drifted at the edge of his reality as he walked with his escort to the gateway to the Arena floor. He walked into the blazing sunshine with detached curiosity wrapping him like a cloak on a winter's day. The roar was thunderous. Never in all of his visits, even the first, had the Arena been more full; tokens for this day had passed hands for many times the value of their original sale, and more blood had been spilt over many of them than would be soaking into the sand at the end of this fight. Not a seat lay spare, and many were supporting more than they had been designed to hold. The atmosphere thickened the air, and Brann noticed all with a dispassionate interest.

But when he saw Grakk walking towards him, all of that changed.

Like a veil being lifted from him, the noise, the sights, the feel of everything around him hit him with a clarity that knocked his stride. Everything was accentuated: the faces of the crowd were as defined as the crunch and slightest give of the grit beneath his soles; the heat through his soles from the sand was as forcible as the shine from the blade gripped tight in his hand; and the edge of the blade was as keen as the fear pulsing through every part his body.

Not fear of dying. Not fear of his opponent's skill. Not fear of the Emperor, or the crowd, or Loku. Not fear of pain, or of failure.

Fear of looking into Grakk's eyes, and knowing his friend was looking back.

He stopped. That friend was standing before him. He had been lost in the moment so much that he hadn't realised how far he had walked.

He looked into his friend's eyes, and Grakk looked back.

'I can't kill you,' Brann whispered.

Grakk barely blinked. 'Nor I, you.'

'So what do we do? If I refuse to fight, I condemn us both.'

Grakk smiled slightly. 'So we fight.'

'But they want a death.'

'So we fight. And we see where that takes us.'

Brann felt as if he were in a recurring dream as they walked towards the Emperor's section. The same party surrounded the Emperor as on his first visit. The same horn blasted the chanting crowd into expectant silence. The same fat herald stepped forward, inviting the same response of the death-match combatants.

'Lord of Lords, our lives are yours. We fight, win, die

for your glory. Death is our master, Death is your servant. Our blood is your power.'

The Emperor was, as always, every bit the genial uncle dispensing treats to his nephews, and the formalities were quicker on this occasion, with no selection of opponents needing to be drawn. Sooner than he realised, before he was prepared, Brann found himself back in the centre, again facing Grakk. No soldiers accompanied them this time – there was no other fight to separate them from – but the chant of the crowd booming around from every side was familiar.

'Two walk in, one walks out...'

He swung his sword and shield in now-familiar patterns to ease his muscles and settle his mind. His muscles eased. His mind did not settle. He blew out a long, slow, deliberate breath. His mind did not settle. He banged his sword against his shield. His mind did not settle.

Grakk lunged. Brann's mind settled.

His shield deflected the strike and his sword the next from the other sword and he danced back out of range for the shortest of instants before darting back in to probe with an attack of his own. As he had become accustomed to happening, his whole being fell into the fight, but this time with an intensity he had never before known. His whole universe became his movements and Grakk's, steel and bodies twisting and sliding and weaving and angling in a whirling dance of death and the will to survive.

He had planned to thrust and cut close to Grakk but, if the opportunity arose to kill, he would turn the blow the merest extent to inflict instead a shallow wound. There was no need. The pair were so evenly matched in every respect that neither could create such a opening. It wasn't for the want of effort, attack and defence merging into one and flowing into the next as the battle raged around the Arena.

There was no memory attached to the fight. Everything was in the instant. As soon as that instant passed, so too did awareness of what had transpired, supplanted by the new instant. And so it went on. Brann was unaware of anything other than three blades, one shield and two bodies. Unaware of time. Unaware of the rips in the mail on his right shoulder and left hip, and the red drips from each. Unaware of the half dozen slashes on Grakk's bare torso and legs. Unaware of the stunned silence that had engulfed the crowd.

Unaware, almost until it was too late, of Grakk's intentional dropping of his guard to let Brann's sword streak towards his heart. Almost. He threw himself at an angle, as if he had caught his toe, and his blade went with him, cutting a red line across Grakk's ribs and creating a line of trickling crimson streams, but missing the fatal blow.

As he hit the ground, he rolled, one of Grakk's swords spearing into the earth where his neck had been. As Grakk's head bent over him with the movement of the blow, he hissed, 'Foolish boy.'

Brann grinned. 'Told you I couldn't kill you. You can't even make me.'

'One of us must die. I have already seen much in my life. So now should you.'

Brann was still smiling. But it wasn't Grakk's words or his own that were the cause. In the moment of Grakk's attempted sacrifice, Brann's concentration had been broken by the surprise – and he had noticed something. Two things, to be precise. A groan from the crowd at the sight of the killing blow. And a sigh as it missing its mark. A groan of disappointment, and a sigh of relief.

180

Brann had continued his roll and transformed it into a crouch, then straightened. The other consequence of the break in concentration had been realisation of the tiredness in his muscles, the slight slowing of Grakk's movement and the sheen of sweat coating the pair of them. And of the heat.

He exaggerated a stagger as he backed off, and held up a hand as if to pause his opponent. He threw down his shield, drawing gasps from all quarters of the Arena and, reversing his sword, sliced the straps of his hauberk and pulled it over his head, his tunic following it into a heap on the ground. Retrieving his shield, the pair faced each other once more, one in only a pair of breeches and the other even less clad, in just a loincloth. It was combat on its most basic scale.

He stared at Grakk. 'They wanted a fight and a death.'

'I tried to give them one.'

'*Wanted*. Now they want the fight more than the death. They don't want it to end.'

Grakk groaned, but with a smile. 'A pox on them, I'm exhausted. Just kill me.'

Brann almost laughed. 'I told you, I can't. So you'd better bloody find some energy from somewhere, old man.'

He circled his head to flex his neck and, with a movement of his shield, beckoned his opponent onto him again. The crowd roared. Their weapons clashed.

Grakk had told him before his first fight that lengthy fights were for the sagas, not real life, and his experience since then had proved the truth in those words. But this fight was one for the sagas. They fell to it anew, as intensely as before, and the mob shouted and gasped and cheered with every blow. Over and over, move after move, fast and intricate, strong and fearsome, the contest raged on.

But the blows became slower, the movement more deliberate, until the moment when the two of them threw themselves at each other and spun in opposite directions with the impact, stumbling and falling hard onto their backs on the hard-packed and burning sand in almost choreographed unison. Brann stared at the deep endless blue of the sky, chest heaving and sweat stinging his eyes and his wounds. It was then that he heard the chant begin.

'Two walk in, two walk out... Two walk in, two walk out... Two walk in, two walk out...'

Fatigue flooded through him. Sudden immobility had brought a dead weight to his limbs. He rolled to his side and forced himself into a half-sitting posture, then got his feet under him. He heaved with his legs, managing to push himself upright. Grakk, he saw, had done the same, and was standing in a similar pose, exhaustion written clear in the hang of his head, his shoulders and his weapons. The chant of the crowd engulfed them, booming back and forth from every quarter of the Arena, shaking the very air around them. The pair slowly spun in shuffling steps, absorbing the scene in weary wonder.

'Two walk in, two walk out.' The chant continued, over and over.

The horn cut through it, and the Emperor stood. In seconds, the noise had petered to a silence as heavy as the clamour had been. A twitch of a regal hand brought his Scribe to his side, and the tall slave in turn moved to the fat herald. A grunt from Grakk seemed all the sound he could muster, but it successfully caught Brann's attention. The tattooed head nodded in the direction of a soldier who had advanced towards them and was waving them to approach the royal section.

They stopped where they had earlier recited their homage,

and dropped to one knee, waiting, as did the masses, for the herald's words. The sing-song voice rang out.

'His Magnificence, Emperor of the all the Civilised World, has spoken. Never before has he seen such a contest. Never did he expect such a spectacle. Two warriors, of styles differing but ability perfectly matched. We have witnessed a duel the likes of which will spawn ballads and fuel the tales of legend.

'But the gods have spoken. These two cannot be separated, and His Magnificence will not gainsay the gods. If their will is that these men shall both live, these men shall both live.' The roar of the crowd was instant and tumultuous. The herald raised a hand and the horn demanded silence once more. 'The gods have spoken, and so has His Magnificence. Such a match is seldom, if ever, witnessed, and as such cannot be matched. These two men shall fight no more, but shall walk from here free men, living in your memories through the sight you have seen today.'

If Brann had believed the previous noise was as loud as it got, he was proved immediately wrong. Any disappointment at the thought that they would not see either of these men fight again was overwhelmed by the privilege of being present at an occasion that grandchildren would recount to their grandchildren. The cheers washed over them in waves, and the Emperor stood, waving genially as if he himself had fought out on the sand. Loku, his face flitting between shock and fury, had pushed past an elderly man with a long beard and was remonstrating with the Emperor's Scribe who, implacably, waved him back to his seat, clearly reminding him of life-saving etiquette. Brann half-rose, wondering if it was permitted to do so, but the hand of a soldier on his shoulder ushered him back down.

'My apologies, sir,' he blurted.

'No need for that, lad,' the man, a wiry grey-head with all the marks of a veteran, said cheerfully. 'A free man has no need of that sort of speech. I just need you down there because it's easier for both of us. But if you want to stand, I'm certainly not going to argue with you or your friend there on any matter, rest assured of that.'

Brann saw a pair of long-handled cutters in the man's hand, and nodded, remaining on his knee. In seconds, the chains had been cut from his neck and Grakk's, and the pair stood staring at each other. Brann grinned as he realised they were identically massaging the absence on their necks of the accustomed weight of the chain.

The Emperor gestured towards them, prompting a concerted cheer from the crowd, and the two bloodied fighters bowed to all sides of the Arena, starting and finishing with the royal section. The Emperor sat down and started chatting to the man seated at his left.

The soldier who had cut off their chains ambled up beside them. 'I guess that's your cue to take your leave, lads.'

A chant started in one area of the throng and was quickly picked up by all. 'Two walk out, two walk out, two walk out, two walk out...' Brann found it hard not to let his feet start marching in time to the words. The shouts demanded a response and the pair waved and smiled their way across the Arena.

'Did that just happen?' Brann said to his companion as the events started to sink in.

Grakk smiled. 'Your assessment of the mass feeling was correct, it seems.'

Brann wiped sweat from his brow with a forearm, leaving a smear of blood across his face. 'I thought I wasn't going to get up at the end. I was glad when you decided to fall over as well.'

'There was no decision involved. I have not experienced so exhausting a physical encounter since my final fight in training as a youth.'

'You fought someone to that standard as part of training?'

'Three someones. And it took a fraction of the time for me to be able to triumph. On that day, the challenge was in the number. Today it was in the quality. You have improved somewhat since our last meeting, young fellow.'

'I had a clever teacher.' Brann's smile held a tinge of sadness. He would have to leave Cassian's school now that he was no longer a competition fighter. At least he could live with his friends in The Pastures. Or maybe Cassian would let him help train the fighters. Or perhaps he could do both.

'And that was a clever man up there.' Grakk nodded at the royal section and saw Brann's eyebrows rise in question. 'He not only listened to the crowd, but he was aware of the danger of allowing us to fight on in future. Rulers do not sit easy when citizens, or even slaves, become too popular.'

'His Source of Information did not seem to agree.'

'His Source of Information was blinded to logic by his hatred.'

Brann smiled. 'That may prove a useful weakness to be aware of.'

Grakk smiled in reply. 'You think well, young Brann.'

They had reached the gateway and with one last wave for the crowd, they gratefully accepted the cool of the torchlit passages. As the heavy door swung shut, Brann enveloped Grakk in a hug with the power that could only come from the heart.

'I can't believe we are seeing this, this reality. I can't believe we are both here, standing, breathing. Alive!'

Grakk pushed him back. 'I won't be for long unless you let me breathe.' But there was a smile in his eyes.

A guard met them and led them to the familiar Room of Baths, where the blood, sweat and grime of countless fighters had been washed clean. Grakk, as in everything, was quick and efficient in washing. Brann preferred to soak and savour the experience.

'You want to linger here? You will no longer belong here when you leave,' Grakk pointed out.

Brann smiled. 'That is exactly why I want to linger here. I will miss this place.'

Grakk frowned. 'I will not. And you should not. There is more to life than this, young Brann.'

'Not in my life. First and last visits apart, this has actually been a place of happiness – and even those two visits ended well, even if they were awful for the first part. I have never felt as valued as I have here; I have never felt as natural as I do when I fight.'

Grakk regarded him through narrowed eyes. 'Have a care, young man of the North. Do not grow to love the violence, lest it usurp you as the master of your life.'

'But, Grakk, do you not feel it? The thrill of doing something you are so skilled at, and people loving you for it.'

'The love of many for the figure is worth far less than the love of the few for the person.' The bald head shook slowly. 'And do not think that because I can fight with skill, I therefore enjoy it. I can do more than that, and my enjoyment lies in other areas. I only fight when I must, and if I never have to do so again, I will be a happier man for it. But we are all different, and we are what we are. So long

186

as you do what you do for the right reasons, and with a good heart, that is what matters. There will be times in this world when you have to do a bad thing for a good reason, or because the choice is taken from your hands – it is then that you will need to draw on the memories of the good things you have done to remain the person you are, else you will be lost and only know that fact when you are unable to find your way back.'

Brann looked at him. 'Well, that's a cheerful thought for a day that was taking a turn for the better.'

Grakk laughed and ruffled the boy's wet hair. 'You are right. That is talk for another day. I merely care for your wellbeing, boy, and would see you happy. There is a big life ahead of you, and you will find contentment in many ways. Do not close yourself off to them.' He pulled on a clean tunic and spoke quietly. 'I will take residence with your friends from the Northmen's ship and we will wait, ready to provide any assistance the hostage lord may require. Should you wish to find us, I believe your friend with the wild hair and the wilder eyes will find you. I hope to see you soon.'

And with that, he left.

Brann soaked for a while, thinking on his experiences in that building and on the sand in its centre. It was hard to make the move to step out of the pool, because he knew it was the first step towards a leaving that would be a wrench. But there came a time when the water started to lose its allure, and he stood at the side, waiting for the drips to stop. He padded into the next room to fetch a towel.

'I thought you would never emerge.' He jerked in surprise. The Emperor's Scribe stood impassively in the corner.

Grabbing a towel, Brann covered himself. 'Oh, your modesty is touching. But then, you are full of surprises.'

Brann grunted. 'As are you. I nearly had to clean myself again. What do you want?'

'Modest and blunt. Well, I have waited long enough to speak with you.'

'You waited all that time when you could have stepped through the doorway and told me whatever you want to tell me without delay?'

The face was impassive. 'That room is for fighters alone. Rules are there to be obeyed, or order is lost.'

'And order is everything?'

'Correct.'

'Talking of order, or rather orders: yours are?'

'My orders are to deliver the following message.' Implacably, the Scribe drew a sheet of paper from his satchel. Peering down his nose at it, he intoned, 'Brann, of the Northern Isles, as a free man you are invited to take up the position of personal guard to the Lady Myrana of the Royal Court of ul-Taratac. Your acceptance is requested by sundown tomorrow.'

Brann stared at him. 'My acceptance is requested? I'm afraid I have other plans.'

The Scribe's expression never flickered. 'You need not be afraid. You no longer have other plans.'

'Come on, Narut. You live by order and precision. Free man? Invited? Those words have a definite meaning. It is my choice. This is not for me.'

'The words hold one meaning, but reality holds another. Order governs all life, not least the standing of one man to another. You should know that the Lady Myrana is niece to the Emperor of the Civilised World, and as such any appointment to her personal staff must be sanctioned by the ruler himself. Emperor Kalos has decreed that you may become personal guard to his niece. To be specific, he thought it an excellent idea.

'Therefore, as I said, you no longer have other plans.'

'Why in the names of all of your gods and mine would he trust me with his niece? The last time he spoke directly to me he wanted to push me off a rooftop.'

'That was not personal. It was expedient. At that point, you were an untidiness that required disposal until his Master of Information found a better use for you. Now your situation has changed unexpectedly. As a free man of some renown, there would be avenues open to you to become an irritant to the order of the city, especially when you have friends still guesting at the palace. But as one in the employ of his niece, you will be surrounded by eyes and steel at every turn. You will be in his control, which is one of the places where he likes to have potential irritants. The other place is in the next world, but the public reaction to your death in the near future is the unknown outcome that has, I would say, saved your life.'

Brann's heart sank and, with it, his resistance. He slumped to a bench, his towel across his lap and his forearms on his knees. 'I really have no choice, do I?'

'You do not. Other than the choice between the Lady Myrana and the executioner. Your taste in beauty may be your own, but it is likely that you will find the executioner less pretty.'

The comment was undoubtedly devoid of humour, but it still drew a weak smile from Brann. 'This just sums up my life.'

The Scribe cocked his head, looking more bird than man

as he considered the comment. 'Not fully. You have spent much of your time as a slave. Now you are a free man.'

Brann snorted. 'In name alone. A free man has choice.'

'You can choose to live or die.'

'That is the choice of a slave.'

The Scribe picked up a soft cloth and dipped it in a stone basin set into the wall, soaking it in cold water then carefully squeezing away the excess. 'Not always. Whenever you have the choice to live, it is a valuable decision to be able to make.'

'Fine.' There was a resigned finality in the word. 'I will spend a final night in Cassian's School and, in the morning, will gather what belongings I have and present myself at the palace.'

'You need not trouble yourself. Your belongings have been transported there for you.'

Brann looked at him through narrowed eyes. 'The *sundown tomorrow* bit. That was words versus reality again?'

'Your own transport awaits you.' He gave the cloth a final squeeze and walked across to examine the nicks, scrapes and cuts Grakk had inflicted. He began to wipe them with a surprising gentleness. 'But it is transport furnished by the palace, and it would be unseemly to bleed on the cushions.'

Deft and careful as his movements were, they brought a thousand stings to every part of Brann's body. It was a pain that was now familiar, and the boy sat in silence. A murmur of disapproval signalled the Scribe's unhappiness.

'What?'

'Three of them require further attention.' He placed a finger in turn on his calf, ribs and bicep beside three of the gashes, deeper than the rest.

Brann started to rise. 'I'll see the physician, then. Where will I find you afterwards?'

'You will go nowhere near those butchers.' Brann's eyebrows rose, bringing a wince as he aggravated a bruise on his forehead. The Arena physicians were highly regarded among their caste and valued by all who had fought there. 'Sit still.'

He produced from his satchel a small flat pouch. Unwrapped, it revealed a small medical kit, from which he selected a needle and a length of cotton thread. The needle he thrust into a brazier at the far side of the room, ignoring the searing heat of the glowing coals, and moments later he had it threaded without a fuss.

His stitching was quick and neat. It was another sensation that Brann was well accustomed to and he watched in interest, forced to admit that the Scribe's skill did indeed outdo that of even the esteemed healers of the Arena.

'I am impressed, Narut. Your work is excellent.'

With pursed lips, he surveyed his work. 'Not excellent, as I'm sure my boyhood tutors would attest, but it shall suffice under the circumstances.' He noticed Brann's look. 'I did not grow up a Scribe. And you are lucky that this one,' he tapped the cut on Brann's bicep, 'is on the arm that does not bear your artistic but primitive adornment. No amount of skill could have kept that unblemished.'

Brann ran his finger over the tattoo of the dragon. The girl who had designed it and the boy who had earned it seemed part of another life, strangers both. His touch dropped to the runes, reminding him of their message. *Dare to dream. Trust your heart. Let your soul fly.* The first two were still possible, but his soul was more caged now by another than it had ever been. He sighed, drawing

191

his attention back to the room and the man before him.

'Still,' Brann looked over the areas of treatment, 'it is work that I am more than happy with. Thank you.'

The Scribe looked surprised. 'Your spirits seem to have risen.'

He shrugged. 'A man told me that there are no better devourers of good time and thought than conjecture and chance, and that worrying about what I have not or wish was otherwise will waste the opportunity to attend to improving things. He said I should plot only the course I see before me.'

'A wise man.'

Brann smiled. 'He was. And I'm sure he still is.' He looked at the man before him, his height accentuated by his overly slim and angular frame. 'So what is my course from this room?'

'Prior to leaving your berth, and here I must leave behind the ship analogy, you may be best donning a tunic.'

Once Brann was dressed, the Scribe led him through the passages and up what seemed like endless flights of stairs until he realised he was in an area behind the royal section of seating, but facing out over the city. Where the sun was dipping towards the horizon there was a copper glow to the sky that bathed the white buildings stretching before him in a soft glow. Brann stood, transfixed for a long moment. 'It is beautiful.'

'There are many beauties here, particularly where prosperous people reside, but they cannot rival those that are free to all and created by the hand of nature.'

Brann grinned. 'Oh Narut, you are quite the philosopher now.'

'As I said, I was not always a Scribe. I had many tutors,

all of whom bestowed the knowledge that has allowed me to rise in my field. One important fact amidst that knowledge being the need for punctuality. Come.'

He turned on his heel and walked towards an archway. Brann caught his breath as he followed him through it. Before him lay an impossibly tall bridge leading from their level, around two-thirds of the way up the giant Arena, to a corresponding archway set into the outer wall of the citadel. The width of two carts set side-by-side and supported by what seemed impossibly tall and slender arched columns, the bridge had a fragile grace despite being constructed of massive blocks of stone, carved to offer an almost perfectly smooth surface to the eye.

'The Bridge of the Sky,' the Scribe intoned expressionlessly. 'Our passage to the palace and travelled only by the rulers of this city. As you will serve one of those rulers and may have to accompany her on this route at some point, it would be helpful for you to be familiar with it in advance.'

'Helpful for the future, maybe, but easier for us right now,' Brann suggested.

'Perhaps.'

Brann paused. 'Wait. I thought you said that my transport awaited me. Where is the transport?'

'It stretches down from your torso to the ground.'

'My legs?'

'They transport you, do they not? I was making a point at the time. The definition of the word was wide enough for my purpose.' He pointed at the length of bridge stretching before them. 'Do you have a problem with heights?'

Brann grinned. 'Just as well I don't. Just jumping off them, so as long as that isn't involved, we're fine.'

He could have sworn he heard the Scribe mutter that it

was best not to tempt him as he turned and started onto the bridge. As Brann trotted to catch up with him, a thought entered his head.

'Isn't this a defensive weakness?'

'We are not a stupid people. The columns were constructed in a way that allows for them to be collapsed fairly easily by our military engineers.'

Silence fell over them for the rest of the journey. The bridge led through the outer wall of the citadel and to a series of smaller versions from wall to wall until they had entered the royal levels of the keep. The Scribe took him on a similar path to the one on which he had led Einarr's party at the start of their visit to the city. The familiarity was disorientating and Brann could not prevent his eyes from expecting to see the others if he only turned his head to look behind. Before long, though, they had reached the hallway where ten stern soldiers stared at them in front of the massive golden doors. Only their eyes moved, however, as the Scribe passed between them and through the doorway. Feeling vulnerable with no weaponry about his person amidst so much naked steel, Brann followed him quickly.

He entered an oasis of opulence. The sight that greeted him rendered the luxury of the areas he had already witnessed as plain as a military barracks. Shining white stone formed the walls of a corridor that was as wide as most rooms, reflecting light from ornate lanterns that stood on tall slender stems or hung in clusters from the ceiling. The ubiquitous statues lined the walls or formed features in the centre of the passage, but were of such quality that it seemed that only the addition of colour to their whiteness would be necessary for them to come to life. Some were even carved into the very stone of the walls. Water trickled into basins cut into the walls, over stone leaves or from ewers held by petrified maidens from mythical tales, as much a source of refreshment as it was a visual attraction and restful to the ears. Colour was splashed around the feet of many of the statues in the form of fresh-smelling petals. And the murals: intricate and filling every space on the walls, they were picked out in precious metals and formed of pigments so varied, rich and, in some cases, unusual that they alone must have been worth more than an emperor's ransom.

Brann stood, overwhelmed. As soon as his eye settled in one place, it was drawn to another. His head whirled until the Scribe's fingers clicked in front of his face.

'I would advise accustoming yourself to this quickly. If you think this unusual, their chambers will stun you further. And as a guard, your duties will not include being distracted at every turn.'

Silently, Brann nodded, and followed the tall shape of the man who seemed to glide along the shining floor. Servants, most of them slaves, passed them by, slipping in and out of doorways to either side, in silence and without a sideways glance. He became uncomfortably aware of the quiet, the only sound that of trickling water, and conscious of every noise he made.

The Scribe stopped before a slave girl who had approached from the opposite direction. After a few words, he turned to Brann. 'This one will take you to your employer.' Before the boy could reply, he was already several paces back the way they had come.

Her eyes lowered to the floor, the girl turned silently and led him further down the hall before branching into a short passage to the right. A door lay on either side, and she rapped softly on the one to the right. It was opened by a tall slave, elegantly dressed in a light material that brushed her feet and floated in the slightest of breezes that whispered through the doorway. She dismissed Brann's guide with a look and swept her eyes over the boy.

'He's here,' she called diffidently over her shoulder. 'He's not as big as he should be.'

'I'll be the judge of how well my money is spent,' came a voice from within.

The slave's head tilted to one side and she raised her eyebrows. 'You'd better come in, then.' Brann had fought in two death matches, had razor-edged weapons slicing towards every part of his body and had men and women of all shapes and sizes snarling in his face with intent to maim, but he had never felt as intimidated as he did at that moment.

He nodded and squeezed through the narrowest of gaps that she angled slightly to allow him, and stepped into the room, wondering at the terror that might be instilled by the mistress if the servant was so fearsome.

He could not have been more wrong. A girl looking just slightly older than he reclined in a high-backed chair, one leg draped over the side and her opposite arm hanging almost to the floor, dangling a half-drunk goblet of wine.

'Oh my.' A lock of hair had fallen across one eye but the other was wide enough open to reveal that it was a perfect match of brown to the hair that obscured its partner. The almond shape of her eye and the angular cast of her cheekbone gave her a feline look, and one that her languid pose did nothing to dispel. It spoke of danger; a cat sizing up its prey. Sitting up, she brushed a hand across her face to allow full vision. 'He looks just right to me.'

The tall slave stalked around him. 'Any merchant's guard

is twice the size.' Brann could not have felt more like a lot at a livestock auction. And one destined for the dinner table, not a field.

'Merchants are rich, Persione.' She stood and sipped delicately from her goblet. 'Their guards are meant to be big, to dissuade trouble from starting. The dissuasion on my part is the level of retribution that would come the way of anyone who was discovered even thinking about bringing harm to me, so if someone is determined and mad enough to get close with violence in mind, I need someone who can actually fight.' She trailed a finger down his chest. 'And we all know that this one can fight, can you not, Brann of the Northern Isles?'

All he could think was that her eyes were the largest and deepest he had ever seen. Dumbly, he nodded.

'Oh look,' Persione said in mock wonder. 'His face is changing colour, just like the Hider Lizard. It would only really be any use, though, if we had walls that were a deep shade of red.'

He blushed even harder.

She smiled. 'You will have had a long day, and I have no intention of being placed in danger tonight, so Persione will show you to your chambers. I shall be taking a walk in the gardens in the morning, two hours after sunrise. If you are outside my door for that time, that will suffice.' She touched a fingertip to his forehead as one side of her mouth twitched into a half smile. 'Sleep well, Champion of the Arena.' Brann was certain he would not.

The slave girl walked to the door. 'Come.'

In the hallway, she turned to the doorway opposite the one they had exited. 'There,' she pointed.

Brann found his voice. 'There?'

'Oh, it speaks. Well done.' She was already heading back into the princess's chamber. 'What if there is an incident during the night? You wouldn't be much of a guard if you stayed at the other side of the building, would you?'

It was a simple room, but the fact that he had it to himself instantly rendered it several levels better than the quarters he had slept in for the past year. Or at sea for that matter. He pulled off his sandals, tossed his tunic on top of the pile of his belongings that he noticed had been placed in one corner, and fell onto the bed.

He was wrong about his prospects of sleep, but he wasn't awake long enough to realise it. Though he did dream of huge brown eyes.

Habit pulled Brann out of bed at sunrise, and he managed to surprise himself by finding his way down through the keep to the ground level. He worked his way through the gates to the outer wall where he found what he was looking for, and what he thought he had remembered from his first visit here: a path that ran along the inside of the wall's base.

As the track ran, so too did he. Pushing himself harder than he would have done at Cassian's compound to compensate for the lack of competition around him to drive him on, he pounded along the length of the wall and back to where he started. Six times he did it, thinking all the while of the group of fighters who would normally have been surrounding him as he did so, and feeling alone.

A guard directed him to the marshalling yard where he found a practice sword and a wooden post to batter it against, and enquiries with a total of four other passing servants enabled him to discover the bath house and his route back to his room.

When Persione opened the door to her mistress's chambers, Brann was waiting outside, wearing one of a selection of identical tunics, cream-coloured and emblazoned in dark brown with the hawk sigil of Myrana's family, that he had found hanging in his room.

Her disappointment that he was there on time was obvious. 'In,' she said, looking down the length of her nose at him.

The princess was brushing her hair, and glanced at Brann in the mirror. 'You worked hard this morning.'

'You could see me run?' He was even more surprised that she would have bothered to. 'Er, My Lady,' he added belatedly.

'Don't be silly. I can't see through the curtain walls of a mighty citadel. But I did see the state of you when you walked back up to here.'

'I may just be unfit. My Lady.'

'No one is unfit if they can fight as long as you did yesterday.'

He said nothing. It was a fair point.

Persione took the brush and tended to her mistress's hair with long smooth strokes that spoke of a familiar action. 'As long as he hasn't tired himself out to the extent that he cannot protect you, My Lady.'

Fatigue and unfamiliarity had dulled Brann's brain the night before, but irritation retrieved some of his spirit this morning. 'I'll do my best not to keel over, My Lady's slave.'

He had heard once a fireside tale of a fearsome witch who could set fire to men from the inside out just by meeting their gaze. The look Persione gave him at that moment made him wonder if she was related.

Myrana gave no hint that she had noticed the exchange,

but she stood and walked over to Brann. 'I'm sure you won't, my guardian. But you will need to do more than just stay upright. If you need to defend me, you will find it easier with steel, I would think.' She picked up a length of pale-blue fabric that matched the darker blue of her robe, and Persione wound it around her head to contain her hair and form both headgear and veil with such easy skill that Brann was caught in fascination. 'We shall stop at the armoury on our way.'

The armoury was both a delight and a relief to Brann, being an area of familiarity to him. With the Emperor's niece making the request, nothing was too much trouble for the quartermaster who quickly presented a selection of swords to Brann's specification. He tried each in turn: all were finely crafted but the weight and balance of each varied just enough to let him find one that felt right in his grip. He added a long knife to his right hip and a shorter one strapped to the inside of each forearm. He always felt better with something extra in reserve. Cassian's brother had been right, though: it did feel strange to a gladiator to carry weapons on his belt.

He followed a few paces behind Myrana and Persione as they strolled from the citadel to a nearby market, chatting more in the fashion of sisters than mistress and slave. Wary of every shadow, seeing danger in every movement, his eyes darted constantly until he realised that he was going to exhaust himself before they even reached the next street. Instead, he tried more to take an interest in the surroundings and be open to anything that seemed unusual. The trouble was, when in a country so far removed from the world of your upbringing and where the exotic lay at every turn, the unusual was the norm. He was surprised at first that not one person recognised him as the hero of the Arena until realisation dawned. He had been a distant figure in the middle of the gladiatorial sand, and anyone who had been in the crowd probably would not have had any idea of his appearance up close. And context seemed to be a powerful disguise.

They drifted into a market that was in itself an education to Brann. Birds of sizes and colours beyond his imagination eyed him from cages and added their sounds, raucous or sweet, to the bustle of the market. Some even spoke like men, causing him to almost draw his sword in alarm the first time he heard it. And the smells: the heady aroma of spices at one stall mingled with the enticement of cooking meat drifting over from another, while the effect of a baker's oven being opened as they passed was enough to make Brann drool. The noble girl had been struck by the smell, too, and paused by the stall. A short conversation with Persione and the production of a purse from within the slave girl's robes resulted in a handful of fresh pastries being handed over. At a word from Myrana, one was tossed to Brann and he nodded his thanks, noting at the same time where Persione stowed the money pouch. If he had seen it, light-fingered passers-by would have seen it also, and he moved in close behind the pair as they passed deeper into the throng of market-goers, toying with his left wrist as he did so as if fiddling with his cuff; at the same time, it happened to keep his fingers close to the most easily drawn knife in a crowded situation. Such was his concentration that they were well through the area before he realised that he had not been affected by the situation as he had been when out with Marlo. He remembered Ossavian's advice about thinking only about the distance he could see at any time. In a pressing throng like this, that was what he had been forced to do and once again the truth in the old soldier's words had been demonstrated. He forced his attention back onto the pair in front of him, who had now reached a small stall, tucked behind the main area to the extent that it would go unnoticed if it hadn't been sought specifically. Fabrics were piled in rolls of colour, from bold richness to subtle pastels, and all with a look of quality to them. The merchant nodded and smiled at the girls with more than just friendly encouragement to trade, suggesting that they were familiar customers.

Myrana trailed her hand through the cloth and asked the merchant to pull to the top three of the rolls from deeper in the piles to allow her a closer look. She felt the material between her fingers. 'They are all lovely. So lovely I can't decide.' She turned to Brann. 'Which colour is the prettiest, fighter from the North?'

Pretty colours were not Brann's strong point. 'Why not get all three? You are a...' He realised proclaiming her high rank would negate the effect of the veil disguise and would not help in his role of keeping her safe. 'A lady of means. You could add all three to your wardrobe.'

'Oh, I do like your style, my guardian. I fear, though, that you are missing the point of this expedition. If I buy without choice and just because I can, I have nothing to be excited about.' She swept her hand across the three rolls. 'So, which one?'

He realised his lack of knowledge would not be an acceptable excuse, and stared at the fabrics. With a mental shrug, he said, 'The pale red and the green are very nice, but the soft brown will go with your eyes perfectly.'

There was a snort of derision from Persione, but those

202

eyes flashed in amusement. 'I really do like your style.' She turned back to the merchant. 'The brown it is.'

Persione was clearly a veteran of such situations and, without fuss or delay, determined the length of fabric to be cut, arranged delivery and paid the man. The pair walked again, in deep and animated conversation, until the slave girl pointed down a street away from the market. Two more turns and the area was becoming distinctly quieter and less salubrious. An unease began to creep over Brann, a feeling that grew considerably as the girls stepped into a alleyway, still chatting cheerily.

He stared at crates discarded against shabby walls tall enough to block the sun, deep doorways and open steps leading into shadows on their way to basements. His right hand edged along his belt to sit close to his sword hilt. 'My Lady...' he began.

A man stepped from a doorway in front of them, and another emerged from behind a large crate to lean nonchalantly against the wood. Both looked as if a bath was a more rare experience than a brawl. 'Well, good day to you, ladies.' Persione gave a short scream before covering her mouth with both hands. Myrana just stared at him. A short club swung absently in his hand and the second man carried a sword that, though pitted with rust, looked perfectly capable of causing injury. Brann grabbed at his own sword but a brawny hand moved from behind him and seized the hilt, drawing the weapon for him. A fourth man did the same on his right with the long knife on that hip.

'That will prevent your young warrior from doing anything silly. Not that, you would think, he could actually do anything more silly than allowing you to take a turn like this. Bad for you, but good for us, I would say.'

Myrana drew herself up straight. 'We have coin. Take it and leave us alone.'

'Oh, I will take it, lady. But as for leave you alone? You and your tall friend have far more to offer than just payment for your passage.' He nodded towards the doorway his companion had stepped from. 'Take them.'

Brann's hands slid quietly together, palm to palm, and continued the movement to reach the hilts of the knives strapped under his sleeves. His arms drew apart and brought with them the blades and in the same movement he spun to his left in a crouch, almost kneeling in his attempt to go as low as he could manage. He had no idea what weapons the men behind him had brought with them, so he determined to target first the one he knew had his sword. The crouch proved valuable as something, possibly his own weapon, flashed above him, causing a cry of surprise from the other man and the sound of scuffling alarm as, presumably, he jumped back out of the way of the swinging weapon. Brann sliced his first knife across the shins that appeared in front of him and the second followed an instant later to deliver a jab into the side of the left thigh. The scream was gratifying.

The wounded legs had flipped back on impulse and the writhing body fell to the ground hard, Brann's sword falling with a clang. He rolled away from it though, because the movement took him away from the unseen danger of the second man. Coming to his feet, he saw the man, surprise on his face and a blade more suited to a butcher's place of work in his hand. Brann's sword lay between them and, without hesitation, the boy dived for it, reactions honed in the Arena and on the practice field driving his body. Letting go the knife from his right hand, he came up with the sword.

The man had been frozen in indecision. He was more decisive now. He dropped Brann's long knife and fled.

The remaining two were coming at him. The one with the sword was rangier, more muscled and, it would seem, the more dangerous. There was a crafty look, though, about the other, the leader, despite him being armed only with the club. Brann decided quickly that he was the one to watch. As he had heard many times on the rowing benches in the tales of dockside adventures, more people in street brawls had their heads caved in from behind than died of sword wounds.

He backed off slightly, as much to buy a few seconds as to move towards the spot where he had seen his long knife fall. He felt it by his foot and shoved the shorter blade back in its sheath on his forearm, crouching to feel for his knife while keeping his eyes fixed on the pair approaching. They spread slightly as they came, obviously no strangers to this situation. But neither was Brann: more than a few times he had faced multiple opponents in training as Cassian had looked to improve his awareness, reactions and stamina, and on those occasions he had faced experienced and skilled fighters. However, it was sometimes easier to fight those who fought properly; the unpredictability of the inexperienced can work in their favour, something he knew well from using it to his own advantage against veterans of the fighting circles. The man with the slashed legs lay curled and moaning to the left, clutching his wounds. Brann edged away from him. A wounded man could still lash out.

The two other men closed. The swordsman snarled from behind a grime-smeared beard. 'You won't catch us by surprise, you little bastard.'

Brann just waited, watching. Then, just before they

attacked, he did. He sprang at the swordsman, forcing him back with a rapid flurry of blows. Almost immediately, though, he dropped to his left knee, turning that way and rising to the side of the man who had swung his club from behind, as Brann had guessed he would. His knife cut across the man's wrist, sending the club spinning through the air, and he swung back to the swordsman, leaping forward to thrust his sword-tip into the man's right shoulder, drawing a grunt of pain. The rusty sword fell from spasming fingers and the man spun and ran. Brann had already wheeled back to the leader, who had produced a completely inadequately sized knife from within his unkempt clothing, and his sword thrust towards the man's throat. He caught the movement, the blood-smeared point coming to rest just under his chin. He looked past the face, frozen in helplessness, and saw Myrana, eyes bright with excitement and widening in anticipation.

'What are you waiting for?' Her voice was thick with glee. 'Finish him. And the other.'

Brann's eyes flicked back to the man in front of him. He met his gaze, and nodded at the knife in his hand. 'Put it away. Unless your arm is twice as long as mine, it won't be much use to you.'

Slowly, the man did.

Brann lowered his sword. 'Now piss off. And take your friend with you before he dies of self-pity.'

The man backed off, wariness in every move. He hauled the wounded man to his feet and half-supported, half-dragged him away.

Fury infused Myrana's face and voice alike. 'You let them go? Four men attack the Emperor's niece and you let every one of them *go*? That is as much treason as the attack itself.'

206

Brann retrieved the dagger he had dropped when he had grabbed his sword and found a rag behind one of the crates to wipe each of his blades. 'I don't recall any of them actually attacking the Emperor's niece, My Lady.' His tone was tight with suppressed anger. 'As I remember it, they focused their efforts on me.'

'But they attacked you. Why did you not kill them? Why?' She was close to screaming. Behind her, Persione stood silent and staring, her face having drained white in contrast to that of her mistress.

He stared into the eyes, so attractive previously but now slitted in rage. The violence had, however, presented perspective enough to dispel the awe he had felt in her presence.

'I do not, My Lady, kill for your entertainment.'

'You killed in the Arena, and before.'

'In all my fights in the Arena and elsewhere, I killed only once, and then because it was the only way to stay alive. And before, for the same reason. On this occasion, you and your... companion came to this area looking for just this sort of encounter. Men do not deserve to die to assuage your boredom.'

'You *dare* to speak to me like this? *You dare?* I will have your head.'

He shrugged. 'If this,' he swept an arm around to indicate the alley, 'is an example of your bloodlust, I would not be surprised if you would. But you will have to tell your headsman to move fast to perform his duties before I take my leave from your service. Those men will be long gone now and my priority is to see you safely back to your quarters. I will do so and then gather my possessions and leave. I clearly do not meet the requirements you have in mind for a personal guard.'

'The headsman is as quick as I want him to be,' she snarled. 'Come, Persione.' She whirled away and stalked up the street. On the direct walk back to the citadel, he was as watchful as ever. But a weight had also lifted from his shoulders at the thought of leaving to meet up with his friends. Myrana's uncle had said to him that once miscreants disappeared into the mass of the city, he lost interest in them. He fully intended to take advantage of that attitude.

He had almost finished the short task of gathering his belongings into a bundle when he heard the perfunctory rap on his door.

Persione stood there, having recovered the haughty demeanour that had deserted her in the aftermath of the fight. 'She wants a word before you leave.'

'Why not?' He watched her back as she walked past Myrana's door and continued out of sight, leaving him to knock on the door alone. On the command from within, he entered to find her on a small couch, her legs tucked up beside her, a goblet of rich red wine in hand and garbed in a robe made from the very material they had bought that day.

She noticed the direction of his gaze. 'Our seamstresses can be extremely quick when they work for the Emperor's niece.' She smiled softly. 'You were right about the colour. Let me thank you with some of this delightful wine from one of our more distant provinces.' She indicated a small table at the other end of the couch, holding a second goblet and a clear decanter of the ruby liquid.

'I'm not thirsty.'

'Wine is not drunk to quench thirst, but to bring a warmth from within.'

'This is hardly the country where you would seek to add heat.'

'It is not that sort of heat. But,' she shrugged, 'it is your choice. If you wouldn't mind, though...' She held out her empty goblet. 'Persione has duties elsewhere.'

He was not her servant. He was not even her guard any longer, as far as he was concerned. But the sooner this was over, the sooner he would be on his way, and replenishing her wine would take less time than arguing about whether or not he should comply. He took the goblet, unable to prevent himself admiring the quality of the heavy glass.

When he handed it back to her, the princess's hands closed over his. He couldn't withdraw his fingers without jerking the drink, so he waited and met her eyes.

Her voice was quiet. 'The offer of the wine was not, in truth, to thank you for choosing a colour of cloth. It was a selfish attempt to make it slightly easier for me to start an apology.' She slipped her hands up to take the goblet from his grasp. 'Please, indulge me. I will not keep you long thereafter, I assure you.'

He stared at her for a long moment. Why not? If he indulged her, he could leave her service without rancour on her part, and his disappearance into the anonymity of the city would be much the easier. He filled a goblet of his own. She swung her legs down and he sat beside her, stiff and awkward in every movement.

He took a drink to ease his discomfiture and immediately knew the truth of her words. A warmth spread from his belly and another sip quickly followed.

'Apologies do not come easily to me.' Her eyes stared at her finger, drawing circles on the fabric between then. 'My upbringing teaches that admitting wrong is revealing weakness that can be exploited. But today,' she paused, biting her lip. 'Today I was too wrong to avoid saying what must be said.'

She stood and paced a short distance. He took another drink as he watched her stand with her back to him, her eyes staring into her own goblet as if the surface of the liquid held an image of the subject of her words. 'I know not why I did what I did. But I did it, and that cannot be undone. What cannot also be undone is the position I placed you in.'

She walked to the table and lifted the decanter. 'Allow me.' It was only when she started to pour that he realised his goblet had been empty. He thanked her. She was being kind, after all, and the wine did have a very nice taste. He took another sip. She sat beside him, curling her legs up beside her again, but this time on the other side so she was leaning close. He assumed it was because she wanted to be heard and thought it polite not to interrupt what she was going to say, so he took another drink instead.

Her head was tilted down in embarrassment but the big eyes looked up into his. He could see them over the rim of his goblet, and there was a pleasantness to looking into them, so he happily stared. 'What was I saying?'

'The position,' he offered helpfully. 'The one you put me in.'

She smiled, a sad smile that made him feel sad, too. 'Of course. It was a terrible position. I asked you to do something terrible, and worse...' A tear welled up in one eye. 'What was worse was that you could have been hurt yourself.' The tear escaped her eye and started to trickle down her cheek. Her voice was a whisper thick with emotion. 'You do not deserve that.'

He felt her sorrow. He wanted more than anything to soothe it. A finger stretched out to halt the tear, then moved slowly up her soft cheek to gently wipe the trail of its passage. 'You shouldn't be sad,' he reassured her earnestly. 'You didn't realise, that was all.'

Moving to a cabinet beside the bed, she pressed on in a voice hoarse with remorse. 'But I should have realised. What if you had been badly hurt?' She placed her drink on top of the cabinet and opened it to lift out a fresh decanter. 'What if you had been...?' Her eyes filled with tears.

It was more than Brann could bear. Swigging down the rest of his goblet so as not to spill any as he moved, he strode quickly to her. One foot stubbed his toes on the short leg at the end of the couch as he passed, but the pain went unnoticed. His goblet was left on the cabinet as he moved close, using both thumbs to wipe the tears as he tenderly cupped her face in his hands.

'But I wasn't hurt, and neither were you, which is the main thing. Please don't cry. I hate to see you cry.'

She looked into his eyes. 'You are such a kind man.' Her voice was as soft as her skin. Her face lifted, and her lips brushed his. He pressed back slightly, and when she didn't pull away, he pressed more. Her hand slid behind his head and the kiss became deep.

She pulled away slightly, just enough to speak. 'Does this mean you'll stay with me?' He could feel the breath of her words on his skin.

'Yes. Yes, of course.'

She smiled and stepped back, taking his hand. She stepped back again, towards the bed.

'Then stay with me.'

He woke in the early hours before dawn.

Only a single lantern still burnt on the far side of the chamber, filling the room with shadows and the gentlest glow of light. The second decanter lay empty, and Myrana lay peaceful on top of one of his outstretched arms.

He watched her breathing until sleep claimed him once more.

Chapter 5

'You asked for me, my lord?'

'You know I did, else you would not be here.'

'My apologies, my lord.' The lamp threw her shadow against the wall from where she stood respectfully behind him, allowing him to see her head drop in embarrassment. A voice within him said, 'Don't fret, child, all you need do is speak with plain and simple truths.'

But instead: 'Two things I ask: your obedience and your wits. One alone is no use to me; if you cannot supply both, another will serve better.'

'I will serve, my lord. It is my honour.'

'Your honour be damned. Obedience and wit.' But it had pleased him to hear it.

'Obedience and wit, my lord. You have them.'

'Should I not have to remind you again, you may serve. So, now, serve.'

'He was leaving, but now he stays, my lord.'

'While you serve me, you stand before me.' He waved a hand. 'Come, I would see your eyes as you speak.'

The tall girl stepped forward, awkward in his sight. That pleased him. Comfort bred complacency. Complacency bred sloppiness. Sloppiness devoured details. And details were the building blocks of plots.

'You honour me, my lord.'

'Is your honour not damned enough already? I wish...'

'You wish to see my words. To see what they mean to me.' Her eyes widened in horror at the impulsive interruption. 'My lord, I...'

'And so the wit appears. Not ahead of time. So he stays?'

'He stays close.'

'How close?'

'Skin close.' There was something in her tone. She was trying to hide it, but it was not born of happiness.

'You disapprove.'

'She deserves better.'

'She deserves you?'

She coloured. 'My lord, I...'

He waved a hand dismissively. 'It is of no consequence. Right now, it is they who interest me. How long?'

'Three weeks.'

'How often?'

'Every night.'

He nodded. So not just skin close. Oh, to have the energy of the young once more. He almost smiled. 'This is acceptable.'

She could not have looked more shocked. 'Acceptable, my lord? But she... With a...'

'Do you wish to serve me?'

'Of course, my lord.'

'Then set aside your sensibilities. Absorb, analyse, assess, remember, use. Aught else is a misuse of information and time.'

Her face hardened. 'Yes, my lord.'

This one may learn after all. It was more than a genera-tion since he had trained a new one. He had forgotten the enjoyment.

'It is acceptable because...'

'...Because it may be of use, my lord.'

'Correct. And he can use a weapon outwith the bed? In real life, not the sterile Arena?'

'He can, my lord. But...'

'But?'

'She toyed with him. He is not a killer, my lord. Though he knows his own mind.'

'The second is a boon. The first a weakness.'

'And so, my lord? Will he not serve your purpose?'

'He may yet. But he will need to learn.'

'How do you change a soul, my lord?'

'You cannot. You break it, and it grows anew.' He closed his eyes. 'Girl.'

'My lord?'

'You have served. Now I must think. I will call when I need you again. And girl?'

'My lord?'

'Obedience and wit.'

'Yes, my lord.'

The door clicked softly behind her.

His brow furrowed. 'He must learn.'

****

Sunlight flooded the room in soft peace and Brann watched through the open window as a bird wheeled lazily against the early morning sky.

He had risen, run, washed and returned, and still she slept. She looked so tranquil and content that he hadn't been able to resist slipping back into the bed. Soon he would fall into her daily routine, accompanying her as she performed her state duties, entertaining and enchanting the womenfolk of the high-ranking visitors, an activity that was as important to a congenial approach to the discussions of the men as the words of the Emperor or his brothers themselves; and attending her in whatever leisurely pursuits took her fancy, from riding, with or without a hawk, to strolling the streets or merely sipping wine and watching the world from the shade of her roof terrace. He saw little of the Emperor or any other member of the royal family, a fact that he was perfectly happy with. And while Persione was clearly not by any means perfectly happy, still she seemed to have thawed somewhat. She was attentive to the princess almost to the point of obsession, but then it was her role to be around her unless dismissed. Brann mused that the public side of his life was good. And then there was the time they had alone, which was better.

He raised himself on one elbow to see her better. The strand of soft hair that had fallen across her face. The gentle rise and fall of her ribs. The slightest fluttering of her eyelids. The...

The crash as the door was smashed open.

Before Myrana was even able to scream, Brann was already on his feet, sword in hand. His eyes scanned the intruders as six heavily armoured men rushed in, rapidly forming a wall with rectangular shields. Movement behind signalled brief activity before the shield wall knelt to reveal the four archers with bows drawn and wickedly pointed arrowheads aimed in their direction.

'Behind me, Princess,' Brann shouted, moving to position himself between her and the danger. He stared at the soldiers. To rush them directly would see him pierced by four arrows before he could complete a pace; to dive to one side to try to avoid the shafts would expose Myrana to their deadly hail. He was trapped. As his eyes fell upon the Hawk symbol on the chests of the archers, Loku walked in behind them.

'Get away from him, Princess,' the man shouted. She scampered across the bed, dragging on a gown before she left the cover of the bedclothes. He looked at Brann. 'You knew we could not shoot if the Emperor's niece was anywhere near you.' His voice was contemptuous. 'You are pathetic.'

'I was protecting her,' Brann snarled.

'With what?' Loku's tone turned mocking as he looked up and down the boy's nakedness. 'It's a pity for you that you only have one impressive weapon on you.' Several of the men sniggered.

Brann's rage was rising. 'Come out from behind your coward's barrier and we'll see how many weapons I need.'

'Oh, my concern is for the Lady Myrana, not a petty duel.' He looked over at the girl. 'I only wish I had arrived in time to prevent the attack on your virtue, My Lady.'

'Attack?' Brann was aghast. 'I would never hurt her!'

The man roared. 'You dare imply that a member of the royal family would willingly surrender her body to a base-born common guard?' His voice turned to a hiss. 'To do so would bring public humiliation on the Emperor himself. Her standing would be destroyed. At best she would be cast out from the family, at worst, public confidence in the ruling family would be rocked. Should a member of that family be capable of such stupidity, what other misjudgements might the family be capable of? No, the only explanation is for the princess to have suffered a violation of her honour of the worst sort.' He walked around the far end of the soldiers to approach the princess. 'It could only be that he attacked you.' His eyes stared into hers. 'Is that not so, My Lady?'

She looked at Brann, her eyes wide and starting to fill. Her head moved as if to shake, and he readied himself to defend her, no matter what followed her denial. He automatically started scanning the space he had around him, the positions of the soldiers relative to each other, the eyes that would betray even the slightest nerves, the work of the past year capturing the situation in one sweeping glance. He looked back at her.

It was then that he saw it. The tightening around her eyes; the hardening within them. The clench of her jaw. The slightest straightening of her back, settling of her shoulders, raising of her chin.

'Yes,' she said.

Loku's voice rasped, though he didn't even turn to look. 'Seize him.'

The soldiers braced themselves and began to edge warily forward, his reputation competing with the fact that he was naked and held only a sword.

But there was no need for their caution. His blade had dropped to his side and hung listlessly. He stared without comprehension. She had drained the fight from him with a single word.

His arms were grabbed and held fast by two men on each side, but he offered no resistance. He watched numbly as Loku stepped closer to Myrana, studying her. 'Of course, yes,' he said, his tone matter-of-fact and analytical. 'The

218

evidence is compelling, is it not? Take, for instance the gown.' His knife cut a small nick in the neckline before he used both hands to rip the expensive material to the hem. He threw her onto her back on the bed, her nudity casually open to see for anyone who cared to look. 'Take the bruising of the violation.' The hilt of his knife thumped into the inside of her thighs, raising angry marks that promised imminent darkening. He hauled her back to her feet, the marks of his rough grip left on her upper arm. 'Take the result of her initial resistance.' The back of his hand struck her face hard enough to send her spinning and flying back onto the bed. She picked herself up, her cheek and eye already starting to swell and a trickle of blood drew a line from her burst lip and down her chin.

Her expression had not flickered throughout.

Loku examined his handiwork. 'The evidence, as I said, is compelling.' His tone was satisfied. 'Anyone could easily determine what has transpired here.'

Drawing the torn gown around her, Myrana picked up Brann's tunic. She turned it inside out to hide the family crest and tossed it to a soldier. 'Clothe him. His nakedness is an affront to me.' It was pulled over his head then one arm at a time was pulled through. She waited until he was fully restrained before she came to stand before him. 'Tell who you will, what you will. There are lunatics and taletellers beyond number out there who have fanciful stories aplenty of scandal at the palace. What matter one more? What matter when the truth has already been proclaimed and,' she touched her fingertips to her swollen cheekbone, 'displayed.'

He stared at her, shock still pounding inside his skull. 'Why?' he whispered.

That drew a puzzled look. 'Why, you ask? Why?' She

laughed harshly. 'A princess in the palace or a former princess in the city? And you ask why?' She snorted. 'What else would you expect?'

'Nothing.' It was a hoarse whisper. 'When would I ever expect any more from this life?'

She turned and walked to her wine decanter on the other side of the room. 'I have no time for his self-pity. You may take him.'

One of the men who had held a shield bore a sergeant's insignia on his tunic. He looked at Loku. 'To the dungeons, Lord?'

The head shook. 'He must disappear from the palace. There must be no reminder to the princess of this horrific incident.'

'Where shall we leave the body? In the wasteland for the animals? Or floating in the docks?'

Loku spoke too immediately for it to be anything but a premeditated decision. It was as if he had waited too long for this moment and could wait no longer. 'Death is too quick and forgiving for this dog. He should be left to rue his actions every minute of every day he has left.' He smiled, cold but triumphant. 'Sell him to the first pitmaster you can find. No name, no explanation.'

'Very good, Lord.' The sergeant nodded and one man on either side started to drag Brann from the room.

'Wait.' Loku's voice stopped them at the door. 'Do not sell him. He is worthless. Give him to a pitmaster. Now go, the sight of him is sickening me.'

He flung a last glance at Myrana. Her eyes blinked. Did he imagine the fleeting burst of anguish in her look? The coldness had settled over her by the time he looked again. He would never know.

Reason began to return to Brann as he was bounced against the doorway on the way out. How had Loku known? Who had told him? As he was being led down the corridor movement at the edge of his vision caught his attention. Persione watched his passage from the shadows. And those questions were answered.

Brann huddled in the cell carved from rock, thick bars separating his space from the corridor. The cells were all on one side of the passage, affording from each a view only of the bare rock wall opposite, glistening in the torchlight as it wept subterranean moisture.

His wrists and ankles had been shackled in heavy manacles before he had left the royal quarters and been led shuffling deep below the keep, past the dungeons with their screams and shouting and silent stares and along a passage lit only by the torches borne by those who dragged him.

The only words spoken to him had been in that passage. 'He is a clever man, that lord,' the sergeant had said. Brann barely looked at him but the man took the slight head movement as an indication that he was interested in the reason for his opinion of the lord's intelligence. 'The giving, not selling. Should the pitmaster have exchanged coin for you, he would have wanted to keep you well enough to earn back at least his investment. Now you are nothing to him. If you die of disease or in your first seconds in the pit, what matter? He has lost nothing. Should you prove yourself in the pit, you may have a chance of him caring about the remainder of your life – although life can be short down here.'

Brann did look at him this time. 'You saw what happened up there. How can you live with that knowledge?'

The man looked at him. 'Waken up to the real world,

boy. I can live. Your hope died the moment the lord knew he had his chance. I take his truth forward, and my life is still my life.'

Much like Myrana. He just stared again at the ground and his shuffling feet.

His shackles remained as they emerged into the city by way of a door into a storm drain, and a grating unlocked by the sergeant at its exit cut into a small bluff just inside the city wall, a couple of hundred paces outside the citadel. The city was at the start of its waking and soldiers with a prisoner attracted little interest from citizens still to fully shake off the sleep of the night before. Brann lost count of the number of alleys and backstreets they passed through until they arrived at a derelict building, its door half hanging off its hinges. In a back room, a large opening in the floor revealed a broad stairway that switched back on itself over and over until he had lost all concept of the depth they had descended.

Lanterns numerous enough to rival the star-filled sky revealed a new society in the tunnels and caverns beneath the city, one that was moving towards sleep as the world above wakened. Stalls that had sold meat and wine had covers drawn over their fronts as the merchants packed away their wares and the few people they passed headed in subdued silence in the opposite direction to them. The man he had been handed over to was clothed in a ridiculous exaggeration of opulence, his gaunt bald head protruding from voluminous robes of green and yellow as his small eyes regarded his new possession. He looked for all the world like a giant upright tortoise and it would have been hilarious had Brann been in the mood for laughter. Instead he regarded him dispassionately, a sour resentment the closest he felt to any emotion. As the man moved, he sparkled in the flickering torchlight and Brann noticed that gold and gems, real or imitation it was impossible to tell, adorned him in every way possible – dangling from, piercing or entangled in almost every part of him.

The man had shrugged and indicated to a companion, equally bald but twice as large in every dimension and only a fraction as extravagantly presented. The soldiers had turned quietly back upon their path as the bald pair set off down a passage leading to a heavy studded door, the larger one dragging Brann with them. The door had opened on their approach to allow them entry to a private area of several passages, one of which led to his current location.

The big man, his job done once Brann had been deposited in the empty cell and had his manacles removed by reaching his limbs through the locked bars, had left. The colourful man remained, staring without sound or expression at the boy. Brann stared at the floor. When he eventually raised his eyes, the man had left. Brann had never caught his new owner's name. He found he didn't care.

He was just starting to doze when he heard the voice. 'Boy. Boy?' It sounded close enough to be coming from the cell beside him. A whining oily voice that slithered round the rocky wall between them. 'Hey, boy. You hear me?'

Why not answer? What other pressing matters were calling on him? 'What?'

'Welcome to the eighth hell.' A cackle of a laugh.

Brann grunted, remembering the tales of the men on the ship. 'Some believe in just one hell. Some in none. Some in two or four or whatever. No one believes in more than seven hells.'

The cackle again. 'You've just found what doesn't exist, then. Welcome to the secret hell.'

223

'If you are trying to scare me, I'm not in the mood.'

'Oh, poor boy. If you ever can find your way to my little home here, I'll comfort you. I'll comfort you so nice.'

Brann ignored him. The silence was broken only by the sound of dripping water.

Then: 'Boy? Know you where you are, boy? Know you your purpose?'

He may as well find out. 'Not a clue.'

'You are in the Rat Runs.'

'The what?'

'The Rat Runs. The city under the city. Some choose to live here, some have no choice. And some visit, attracted by the pleasures on offer.'

'The pleasures?'

'There are no laws here. No power other than what one man carves from others with his strength or his wits. What a man wants, he will find here. What a woman seeks, she will find here. If they have a trade. Coin, services, secrets, possessions, people. If two have what each other wants, they have a trade. But the biggest pleasure is us. The pit wretches.'

'Us? The what? What do we do?'

There was a scrabbling, and a rattling as the man grabbed at his bars. His breathing sounded so close he could only be at the closest point to the wall between them; so close that Brann involuntarily shrank back. 'You jest, no? No? Really? You know nothing of the Pits?' The cackle scratched at Brann's ears again. 'The city is the shining heart of the Empire, but the Pits are the diseased beating heart of the city. They all come to see them, to see us. The poor come with what they can save to feed on the thrill; the rich come more easily, but with the same desires.'

Despite himself, Brann was curious. He felt a sick foreboding, but his interest was sparked. 'So what happens in the Pits?'

'You have seen the fighting circles above? You have heard of the Arena?'

'I know something of them.'

A snort of derision. His tone hardened. 'Pale imitations.'

Brann shrugged to himself. If that was all it was, at least it was familiar activity.

A deeper voice, a rough voice, rasped from further away. 'Savyar, you degenerate, leave the boy alone.'

'Oh, you care for the young one yourself, do you?' The voice slithered like a snake of sound once more. 'Starting to find a taste for the softness, are you?'

'I don't give a whore's arse for the boy. I want to sleep. If I hear one more word I swear I'll find a way into your cell myself.'

'You flatterer. Well, if you do your hair nice, I may welcome you.'

The voice became impossibly deeper and the bars shook in fury. 'I'm warning you...'

If Savyar had a further smart answer, he had reached the point where he considered it better kept to himself.

Brann was wakened by the harsh clang of the door in the cell bars being flung open.

The large bald man stood outside while two unkempt men with the brawny build of grapplers gripped his arms and cut his tunic from him. A loincloth that wound around his waist and under his crotch was dragged on and he was hauled into the passage.

Savyar's voice slipped from his cell. 'So someone else desires you, not just I.'

The harder Brann tried not to look on the way past, the more it was inevitable. A pinched face and feverish eyes looked back. And a moist smile that spoke of a disquieting hunger.

He was led through passages within the private complex to reach another door that opened directly onto a cavernous hall teeming with life. Concentric circles cut from the rock rose to the ceiling and supported row upon row of people, crammed into every space and filling the hall with noise as much as with their bodies. The smell of so many people in a confined, hot place mingled with that of hot food as vendors wriggled their way through the crowds. The atmosphere had at the same time a palpable feel of excitement and a primal hunger that he couldn't quite place.

He was dragged towards the centre of the area, where the flamboyant bald man waited at the side of a pit carved into a rough circle. He held his hands high at the sight of Brann and slowly spun in a circle. The crowd fell quiet. His voice rang out. 'The final entertainment of the night is upon us. I, Carcydon, Pitmaster of the City beneath the City, bring you new flesh. Will he fail quickly, or will he surprise us and last long enough to delay our journeys home by a few extra breaths? Or will he astound us and triumph? We can only know if he has one to oppose. We will only know if a Pitmaster is present and willing to offer flesh of his own. Is there such within this chamber?'

A voice roared out from the other side of the pit. 'You know there is, you hairless bastard!' The man who stepped forward was huge and, by contrast, had a mass of hair on head and body that was covered only by a simple tunic. One hand gripped a chain that ended at the neck of a capering wild-eyed man, similar in general appearance to

Grakk but as far as could be from the demeanour of Brann's friend. 'You know well I love a chance to humiliate your worthless self.'

Carcydon ignored the insults, but merely turned to the crowd. 'We have a match. Only the placing of your wagers delays the start of the entertainment.'

A flurry of activity broke out as bets were placed either with neighbours on the terraces or with men who moved among the crowd, accepting them on behalf of some agency. In a remarkably short time, the business had been concluded.

The two Pitmasters faced each other across the pit. From beside Carcydon, Brann saw the wild man straining at his chain like a dog eager to run. A hooded figure, robed all in black, stepped to the lip of the pit midway between the waiting combatants and, to the roar of the crowd, tossed two long knives high into the air to land randomly on the sand floor below.

'Your turn, boy,' said Carcydon, and pushed him from the edge.

The large man on the other side let go of the chain and his man leapt with flailing arms and legs and bounded for a knife. Brann leapt for the other and both rose at the same time. Brann readied himself as the other cavorted manically, now on all fours, now upright, the chain flailing from his neck like a misplaced tail. Entertainment meant nothing to him. He must make this quick, if he could. He slid his left foot forward and held up his left hand ready to ward off an attack. His right held the knife back, poised to strike.

The man launched himself at Brann, his blade flashing one way then back the other in an instant. Brann swayed out of reach. Cassian's words were ingrained in his mind, the repetition of his training rendering conscious thought unnecessary. Watch the eyes and the arm. The weapon will move too fast for sight. The eyes and the arm betray the weapon's path.

When the man thrust at him he stepped to the left of the attack. The point of his own knife jabbed into the back of the wrist and the fingers spasmed wide, sending the weapon arcing away. In the same instant Brann's left leg swept hard at the back of both the legs before him and his left forearm smashed into the throat. The man flipped hard onto his back and, as he landed, Brann's knee was on his chest and the edge of his blade drew a thin line on the man's throat as, vanquished and utterly surprised, he coughed in rasps and fought to regain his breath.

Brann stood and walked away, looking for the rope that would be dropped to let him exit. 'I win,' he said flatly, tossing his weapon to one side as he moved back towards the spot where Carcydon waited.

There should have been something in the noise of the crowd that would have alerted him, but everything was so strange to him in this place that nothing seemed unusual enough to catch his attention. It was instead the heavy links of the chain smashing into the side of his head that caught his attention, and dulled his reactions as his vision swam and his skull rang. He forced his legs into a stagger to one side and he hit the wall, grabbing it with two hands as the man sprang to his back. A face appeared over the edge of the pit, fleshy and pampered and contorted with rage. 'Finish him, you fool. If I lose my wager now I'll come in there and kill you myself. *Finish him.*'

Streaks of pain were dragged down his back as fingernails scrabbled at him, trying to gain purchase on sweat-soaked skin. Then he was on him and Brann shouted in agony as teeth sank into the top of his shoulder. Growling and snarling, the man worried at him. He felt for a moment that a mouthful of flesh and muscle was going to be torn from him but the bite released as the man went instead for his neck. In panic he thrust his head down to the side and nose or mouth or both mashed into the hard bone of his head. By chance his defensive movement had caused the grip to loosen slightly and desperation drove him around hard to crash the man on his back sideways into the rock wall.

The impact knocked them both to the ground, but separately, to Brann's relief. Gasping, he dragged warm damp air into his chest. *Get up,* his head told him. *Always get up.* Too late, though, he realised that the other was quicker of thought than he and was scrambling to start towards the nearest knife. Brann grabbed at the end of the chain but it was slippery with blood and he had to keep grasping at it hand over hand. The man was stronger than he looked, though, and all Brann could do was slow his progress. Inexorably the snarling man dragged himself forwards. Brann knew the other was faster. Should he let go and turn it into a race, it would be one he would lose along with his life.

He forced stiff fingers to hook through links in the chain and yanked back, the sudden movement catching the man by surprise and halting his progress for the moment Brann needed to launch himself. This time he was the one on the other's back, knocking the man flat. The chain fell before them and he grasped it, wound it around the man's neck, pulled it. The man resumed his crawl, dragging himself forwards, eyes fixed on the waiting knife.

After a few meagre feet, though, his movements slowed.

His hands stopped grabbing at the sand and instead grabbed at the chain. His movements became more frantic as his eyes bulged and his head darkened to a deep angry red. Brann wriggled and shifted a knee to between the shoulder blades beneath him, bracing himself and, snarling, dragging the chain tighter. The man's back arched and his feet drummed on the ground.

Then he was limp.

Brann stood, chest heaving and legs barely able to support him. His head spun and he was oblivious to all around but for the rope that lowered and the hands that reached to grab his wrists.

When he woke that night, the hard floor of his cell beneath his curled body, he stayed awake. It was not the howls of the crowd that kept his eyes wide, staring into the darkness, nor was it the hiss from the man as his life had slipped out of him. It was the sound of the snarl that had escaped his own gritted teeth as he had dragged the chain tight.

'You did well, lovely boy.'

Three days he had barely slept, and now the voice slithered around into his cell once more.

'I did what I had to do.'

'That may be so, but you did well. Every time you are carried back breathing, you do fine. Every time you walk back here, you do well.'

'They never told me it was a death match.'

The cackle cracked against the rock walls. 'Oh, lovely lovely boy, you do delight me.' A melodramatic sigh. 'This is the Rat Runs. You now belong to the pits. There are no matches or death matches. There is no glorious triumph or valiant defeat. If you see a man in the pit before you, he is

230

either there for the first time or has won every single fight.
And sooner or later, we all lose. The trick is to not be the
one who dies for as long as you can. You choose: live or
die. If your choice is to live, you do anything, *anything* to
make that so.'

Brann shrugged. 'For what, Savyar? To entertain *them*?
Those who would faint if you faced them with a fruit knife?'

The voice went soft for once. 'For you. All you have left
is yourself. Guard it with your life.'

Before his second fight, he sobbed into the stone of his cell
wall, but they took him nonetheless.

The man before him was a common criminal, but not
without some skill, and Brann had to concentrate to
prolong the fight. They both had swords, and the familiarity
of the weapon made it easy to let the man look good, but
still he could not chance a lucky strike slipping past his
guard. If he could make it last long enough, maybe the
crowd would react as they had done when he fought Grakk.
He watched the man closely, and fought with style to win
them over.

The longer the fight lasted, though, the more the crowd
grew restless. And the more they grew restless, the more his
opponent grew restless. The danger he posed increased with
his desperation, as his attacks became more frenzied.

Brann had no option.

He sidestepped one wild attack and slammed the pommel
of his sword onto the man's wrist with a sharp crack, his
opponent's weapon falling from numb fingers. As the man
tried to readjust his balance, it was easy to kick his legs
from under him. Brann dropped to one knee with his right
foot on the man's left wrist, the broken right posing no

further danger, and his reversed grip on his sword let the point rest on the man's heaving chest.

The crowd howled.

If he thought the man had been desperate before, it had been nothing to what filled his eyes now. Except that this time, it was born not of a desire to win but of despair. Of misery. Of terror.

'Please,' he whispered. 'Please don't.'

Brann looked at him. The crowd fell silent. He couldn't. Then he heard the bow strings drawn.

He looked around the lip of the pit. At least a dozen archers stood at all sides, arrows trained not on the man beneath him, but on him. Carcydon stood with one hand raised. He looked at Brann, and a single eyebrow lifted in question.

Brann knew the choice. One dead or both. He placed his left hand on the top of the pommel.

'I'm sorry,' he whispered.

He tried to make it quick.

That night, he again sobbed into the stone of his cell wall.

Several fights later, he began to lose count of their number. And he began to forget how to sob. The world became his cell, the pit and the passages between. He ate, he slept, he entered the pit, he stayed alive.

The fights merged into a haze of actions, a mix of weapons, a crowd of opponents. The metal gauntlets with the wicked spikes. The huge twin men from the East. The even bigger twin women from the South. The axes. The chains. The bare hands. The wild mountain cat, as long as he was tall. The neck he broke, the leg he shattered, the chest he opened.

With every one of them, a little more of his humanity leaked away. But he lived.

Every night, he whispered to himself, 'I live.' Every time he woke and breathed, he whispered, 'Still, I live.'

The voice crept through from the next cell, like tendrils of noxious fumes. 'You are building quite the reputation for yourself, lovely boy.'

It meant nothing. He knew a response was expected, so he grunted.

The voice continued, but the words were irrelevant. They washed over him like fog over rocks. They spoke of another world, but there was no other world. There was only what there was. He stopped listening.

The voice had stopped talking some time back. He heard it no more, other than when the food men came, talking to them.

He ate eagerly. He always did. It was the good part of life. That and the people who cheered when he lived.

A bald man in bright colours stood on the other side of the bars that marked the edge of his home, regarding him. The man spoke the same words several times until some meaning entered them. 'What is your name? Do you know where you are?'

He replied, 'I still live.'

What else was there?

The large man pushed the tray under the bars then backed off in a hurry as the boy moved to pick up his meal.

He wiped the back of his hand across his mouth to smear away the remnants of the blood from the man's throat he had ripped in the pit, and fell to eating. It was good.

Finished, he settled down in his home, waiting for whatever came next.

A different man crouched on the other side of the bars.

A long plain cloak, hood thrown back to reveal a bald head, designs covering the scalp. And eyes that knew things. Such eyes were dangerous.

The remains of the boy's dinner lay beside him. He grabbed the plate, picking intently at the gnawed bones. Maybe the man was just there to look at him; it was not unusual. Maybe if he took long enough over his food, when he looked up the man would have gone. Without rising he shuffled across the few feet of his shallow cell, pressing his cheek against the wall as his fingers worried at the left-overs on the plate. The cool dampness of the rock felt good, felt familiar, felt reassuring.

The man spoke. 'My poor boy, what have you endured?'
The boy looked at him warily. 'I still live.'
'That you do, that you do. Which is the only scrap of a saving grace in this whole repugnant affair.' He produced a pair of slender rods and bent to the lock at the bars. A soft click sounded just like the noise the key made when the others came, so the man must be official. The gate swung wide as the man walked slowly in. Where were the others? Always when the gate opened there were three of them. Recently, five or more.

The boy eyed the man from his crouch as he walked calmly towards him, hands open to show he carried no weapon ready to use. That was no guarantee of a lack of danger, though, and he remained on his guard, a wary tension filling his limbs.

The man squatted before him, then sat cross-legged. His face was sad, and had a look of kindness. But dropping your guard leads to death. *And I still live.*

The man dipped a hand into a bag at this side. The boy tensed, and gripped the metal plate. The edge, if striking in the right place, would serve as an effective weapon. The free hand came up, open and palm-forward, in a placatory gesture and the other hand inched slowly from the bag, bringing with it a round object of bright colour. A word stirred in the boy's head. 'Orange,' he said.

'Orange,' the man confirmed, a slight smile creasing one corner of his mouth. He offered the fruit to the boy, who snatched it eagerly and tore at the skin with his teeth and nails, discarding the peel in the space of a few short breaths. In a similar space of time, the fruit itself was gone, the only remnant being juice running down his chin. He grabbed the neck of his tunic to wipe his face clean.

'Good?' the man asked.

He nodded. 'Good.'

The man smiled. 'More where that came from.' The boy looked up eagerly and reached out a hand. 'Easy, young fellow. That's for later. Just now, we have to go.'

He rose and held out a hand. The boy took it and let himself be pulled up. He had to go, the man had told him to. It was good to obey. If he obeyed, he was given food. If he obeyed, they let him fight and the crowd would cheer. He followed the man out of the cell. The man with the thin face in the next cell roused from his sleep as they passed, blinking at them in confusion.

They started along the passage but, at the sound of voices ahead of them, the man halted and pulled the boy back the way they had come. The man in the cell hissed as they passed.

'The one after his chamber is empty. In there.'

The bald man nodded and grasped the boy's wrist, pulling him on. The boy tried to walk into his own cell but the man dragged him into the next one.

'No.' This was wrong. He tried to pull back, but the man smiled and put a finger to his lips.

'It is a game,' he whispered, pushing the gate shut and pulling him into the shadows.

As the voices drew nearer, however, the man in the other cell started shouting. 'Hey! Here, quick! The boy has escaped! He has gone!'

The boy felt the bald man tense and one hand stole under his cloak. The boy tensed also, but the man patted his shoulder reassuringly and squeezed the two of them tight into the corner.

Footsteps thundered along the passage and stopped in front of his cell.

'It's true, it's empty.'

'How did he get it open?'

'You can't have locked it properly. Carcydon will put you in the pit for that.'

'Not if we catch him first.'

The thin man in the cell cut in. 'He ran there. Down that way.' Three men hurtled past their cell, not one of them looking in. 'Remember me to Carcydon when you find him. Tell him how I helped.'

As soon as they were out of sight, the bald man rose and led the boy out. Pausing in front of the man with the pinched face, he drew out the thin rods he had used on the boy's lock and raised his eyebrows.

The man in the cell shook his head. 'I have nowhere to go. I have... urges that offend. My life expectancy is longer here than up there.' He looked sadly at the boy, and then at the man. 'I loathe you for taking the sweet thing from me before I could have a taste, but I love you for giving back his life.' His eyes turned to the boy and he wiped a hand across his mouth. 'Stay safe, my lovely. Take this gift and treasure it for many years. I will think of you.'

The boy looked at him. 'I still live.'

The man smiled, his lips forming a thin line. 'You do, and may that thought be my gift to you. Now go, before those dolts realise their mistake.'

The bald man nodded. 'Come,' he said to the boy. The boy obeyed.

It was strange moving with just one man rather than five, and this one man moved differently. The five would hold him tight and march him along the passageways. This man moved in a strange way, sliding along walls and peering around corners, waiting and darting, crouching and creeping. But then, in the pit people moved in many different ways. It was just what people did. He followed.

They followed a different path from the one he knew. Occasionally he would be taken to a different pit. This must be one of those times. He could feel the fighting joy start to build in his chest, and his fingers flexed.

But when they approached a wide ramp that rose sharply, he paused.

'Up?' He was not used to up. Or down. It was always flat in his world.

The man nodded. 'Up it must be, young friend.'

He looked around. The area, wide and long, was empty. 'People?'

The man smiled. 'It is daytime. When the City wakes, the City Beneath sleeps. Let us go, my young friend.'

He obeyed. Even up.

But when they reached stairs, he paused. This did not happen. The man ushered him up, though, and he obeyed. At the top, the man pushed open a door.

Daylight stopped him dead. He shrank back, covering his eyes and the man moved quickly, an arm around him, soothing words murmured. He pulled out a cloak and draped it around the boy's shoulders, pulling the deep hood far enough over his head to shield his eyes. Hunched against the brightness, he allowed the arm around his shoulders to lead him out.

They walked and turned and walked and turned. Eventually, they stopped before a door and the man rapped on it in a deliberate rhythm.

They entered and noise erupted. Bodies pressed around him and smiles and laughter swept over him. He lurched backwards, eyes wide, striking a wall and sliding fast along it until he met the corner. He dropped into a crouch, pulling the hood down over his face.

He felt movement in front of him and the hood was gently lifted. He recoiled but saw the bald man, kind eyes and caring touch on his head.

'I still live,' the boy whispered.

'You still live,' the man whispered back.

He didn't want to wake anyone in case they were angry, so he crept along the corridor, the wooden boards threatening to creak with every step. Darkness lay beyond a window, but he knew not when these people slept. In his cell, he slept when he was tired, fought when he was told, ate when food was presented. But he could hear voices downstairs, so he headed the way he had been brought when he had entered this place, when he had been tired. Now he was hungry and the voices would have food. So he followed the voices.

Part of the way along the corridor, a door lay ajar, but only by a crack. Something within called to his senses, an urge that brought him to push open the door and step through into a gently lit room of draped cloth and soft surfaces. A woman older than he thought possible sat propped by cushions in a high-backed chair, her head tilted to one side in slumber. Was she dead? He stepped quietly closer until he was near enough to see her chest rising and falling in tiny, but definite, movements. His brow furrowed. She stirred the feel of a memory, and a feeling of comfort. He reached towards her face, and traced the back of a forefinger lightly down her cheek.

She stirred, her eyes half opening. Staring for a moment, a glimmer of comprehension showed through her drowsiness and she reached up and grasped his hand in strong fingers. A smile ghosted over her lips.

'My boy, you have returned to us.'

He stared at her, trying to make sense of her words.

'How fare you, child? Are you well?'

His eyes had been wandering around the room, but now they returned to her. 'I still live.'

'And it gladdens me that you do, so it does.' Her eyelids grew heavy and her voice fainter. 'It gladdens my soul.'

A hand fell on his shoulder and he spun to his right, coming to a stop in a fighting crouch. He faced an older man, broad of shoulder and face and grey of hair. He did not attack the man, but remained poised, alert to any movement towards him.

The man backed off two paces, arms held up and palms forward. A toothy grin wrinkled his eyes and he moved a single finger to his lips and nodded towards the old lady. The boy watched as slowly, keeping his gaze locked on the boy, he moved beside the lady and rearranged a pillow to better support her head. Then he crept to the door, and the boy followed. Why not? If the woman slept, what was there for him here?

When they were both in the corridor, the man closed the door with care and spoke quietly. 'She is one of a kind as, I suspect, are you. I can see the attraction.' He reached a hand towards the boy's shoulder and he tensed. The man raised his eyebrows and showed his empty hand, then the boy felt it fall on his shoulder. It felt strangely reassuring. Strange because the only hands he was used to feeling on him were dragging him under force from cell to pit and pit to cell, or were trying to kill him; reassuring because... He didn't know why. He just felt it.

He trusted the feeling, and let the man lead him towards the stairs. 'There are others would see you, too. Friends of yours.' Friends? People only either fed you or tried to kill you. 'And they have food.' He relaxed. Then they were not the killing type. 'You have slept right through to the evening meal, so good fare awaits you.'

They descended the stairs, which doubled back on themselves at the halfway point to face him towards the large room below. A long table filled the centre, four people seated on the long benches that ran either side of its length, spooning from bowls something that appetisingly looked and smelt very much like a stew: a huge boy with an honest face; a rangy boy with untamed hair that writhed from his head like tendrils of black flame; a slight girl in an easy pose that spoke of suppleness and balance; and a young boy of more sallow skin than all but the girl, and with a relentless smile.

A large hearth with an inviting fire burning was surrounded by a selection of chairs and stools, no one of them matching another, and on one of them was the bald man who had led him to the daylight.

In scanning the room, the boy's eyes had not only seen the people; they had also noted the poker by the fire, the scabbarded sword by one wall, the butcher's blade that had been used to cut the meat on a bench at the far side, a stool small enough to be wielded, the knives on the belts of the large boy and the one with the wild hair, the spear leaning beside the door, the stacked logs, some of which would fit nicely in a hand, even the discarded metal spoon on the table. Noted them and their positions, and how many paces it would take to reach them.

The man with the hand still on his shoulder continued with him down the stairs and the boy's eyes were drawn back to the faces in the room, all now turned towards him and seeming happy at the sight. It seemed as if he had seen them before. Perhaps they had been in the crowds who had cheered him.

The man led him to the table where a large steaming bowl held what proved to in fact be stew, and one rich with meat. It was ladled into a feeding bowl and the boy's eager hands took it while his wary eyes watched the others. One of them patted a space on the bench beside him, but he shrank away. He ate alone. He was only among other people when he fought.

He took his bowl to the hearth and sat with the bald man, who regarded him solemnly but said not a word, leaving him to eat. He ate.

The older man who had brought him down came also to the hearth but, at an inclination of the bald head with the markings, he nodded and sat with the others at the table.

They chatted cheerily, and their conversation enveloped him. He was not used to much speech, only commands. Over the course of consuming half of his bowl, he began to find an interest in listening to the words. He did not know the people they spoke of nor why certain things would make them laugh from time to time, but there was a comfort to the sound.

'You know them?' The man nodded at the group.

He shook his head.

'You did. They are your friends.'

'I do not know them.'

'Maybe not now. But once you did.'

'When was once?'

The man sighed, a sad sound. 'You were below, in the tunnels, in the caverns. You remember?'

He nodded. 'Home. I fight there. People like me when I fight.'

'There are people like you for much more than that, young fellow.' The man smiled gently. 'It was not always home. You had a lot of life before that. You were only in there for a short part of your life.'

'How long?'

'Close to nine months.' Those words meant nothing to him, and it must have shown. 'A short part of your life, but a long time to be there. You fought more than thirty fights. No one has ever lasted more than three months or ten fights and still lived.'

'I still live.'

'That you do. And now you will live longer, should we be successful. Somewhere in there,' he tapped the boy's forehead. He felt the finger and was surprised that he had not grabbed the wrist before the hand had reached him. It just felt right to allow it. He couldn't remember feeling that way before.

242

'Somewhere in there is the boy we know, the boy who knows us. We will find him again. You will find him again.'

He looked at the man. 'More food?' He held out his bowl.

The man smiled. 'One step at a time, Grakk.' He took the bowl.

The boy's hand on his arm stopped him. 'I am Grakk?'

This brought a smile. 'My apologies for my rudeness. I spoke to myself. I am named Grakk. You are named Brann.'

As the man filled his bowl, he tried the sound of the name. 'Brann.' It fitted well on his tongue. He looked again at the faces around the table. Memories swirled faintly in his head, like shapes in smoke. He strained to see them, but always they were just vague, just shapes, visible enough to know they were there, but just too far into the murk to discern. He shook his head at the frustration.

He took the bowl when the man returned, and finished it quickly. The heaviness in his belly extended to his eyes, and he felt them closing. He looked at the bald man.

'You are a good man.'

The man, Grakk, stared at him and, strangely, one of his eyes started to water. The boy understood that. It sometimes happened to him near a fire.

He looked at the fire, and it looked inviting to his heavy eyes. He curled on the floor before it and the man settled a cloak over him. 'It is winter,' the man said. 'There is a touch of chill at night.'

It felt good. He let his eyes close.

'Brann,' he whispered. 'Brann still lives.'

When his eyes opened, the room was silent. A single candle burnt still on the table, casting a wavering amber glow over the room.

The door was barred by a heavy beam, he saw, and the windows more permanently. Just one other person remained, the large boy. He slept, bent over the table and head resting on forearms, but an axe lay on the surface beside him. Were anyone to try to break through the door, he would be up and armed long before the intruders gained entry.

Brann cast around for the other potential weapons he had seen earlier, or for others that may have appeared since. Only the poker remained, propped beside the hearth. He rose quietly and took the heavy metal rod, automatically swinging it in each hand to test it.

The fire had burnt to its embers, but he left it. The room was mostly wooden and had retained enough heat. It was certainly warmer than his cave home.

He curled again before the hearth: he liked that spot. There was the comfort, and attackers could come at him from only the way he faced. As a bonus, thrown embers could make a useful weapon and, if stirred, they would put the light at his back. It was a good spot.

He sat the poker quietly on the floor, beside his hand. He could have taken the axe, but that belonged to the large boy, and the man with markings instead of hair had said he was his friend. You care for friends. You don't leave friends defenceless. You protect them.

He watched as the others, freshly arisen, arrived in the room, the dawn sun just starting to lighten the high windows. He remembered the sun. It was a good memory, even if it did hurt your eyes.

Back resting against the warm wall beside the fireplace, knees drawn up and shins clasped in both arms, he saw the girl descend first, feet hardly seeming to touch the stairs as she passed. She had barely wakened the boy at the table before the one with the hair of black flames came down, heavier of tread but a different sort of balance: a stronger one. The older man was next, scratching his cropped hair and rubbing his weather-beaten neck.

'Was your sleep a good one, young fellow?'

Brann's head snapped around and the poker was in his hand. The man who had helped him sat in the chair by the fire. How had he reached it unseen? Brann's eyes narrowed as he relaxed. This was a clever man.

'Grakk,' he said.

The man looked pleased. 'Are you hungry?'

He nodded.

Grakk looked across to the far side of the room, where the large boy was preparing food. A stone box had a steaming pot hanging over it that the boy was stirring, breaking off only to add a little water to the pot or open a door on the front of the box to add small pieces of wood to a fire within. The man called across, 'Ensure you have enough of your famous peasemeal for our returned friend.'

The boy flashed a good-natured grin. 'Of course. How could I omit the guest of honour?' He beckoned with his head. 'It is ready, Brann. Come and get a bowl before these other vultures finish it before you can start.'

Hunger roared through his belly and he rose quickly.

The man smiled and gestured at his right hand. 'I think a spoon will be more use than that poker, young Brann.'

He scanned the room. There was no immediate danger, and the hot pot could be grabbed if need be. A knife also lay on the table beside a half-remaining wheel of cheese. He replaced the poker exactly as he had found it and let his feet lead him to the food.

The stone box had an opening in the top that let the heat warm the pot above it, and the steam was still rising, bringing with it the smell of the food. The pungent aroma filled his head and he stopped dead, his eyes widening and his finger pointing.

'Hakon.' It was a statement, a flat fact, but the joy it brought to the large boy's face was instant.

The finger swept round. 'Gerens. Cannick.' It stopped at the girl. 'You, I don't know.' A frown creased his brow, then cleared. 'Sophaya. Marlo is missing.'

Cannick collected two bowls and handed one to Brann. 'Marlo stays here seldom. His home is elsewhere.'

'You are my friends.'

Hakon slapped the surface before him in delight. 'You remember us!'

Brann shook his head.

The big boy was clearly confused. 'But you know our names. How?'

He thought about it, tried to find an answer. 'I just do. They came into my head.'

'Then how do you know we are your friends?'

Brann nodded at Grakk. 'He told me.'

Grakk was walking across to the food. 'Never underestimate, Hakon my young friend, the power smell holds over memory. In this case, your peasemeal unlocked a door. There are many doors our Brann must have opened for him, and some will be unlocked more easily than others.'

Hakon smiled. 'Glad it was useful.' He took Brann's bowl and slapped a brown sludge into it. 'But you should all take advantage of its original use before it gets cold.'

Brann took his bowl to the table. As he lifted a spoonful, though, he paused, looking at the others. 'Milk.'

'Correct,' Gerens said, handing him a ewer and sitting beside him. 'Well done, Chief.'

'My name is Brann. I am not Chief.'

The dark eyes regarded him emotionlessly. 'You are to me.'

He looked around the room. 'I lived here? Before... before *Below*?'

Cannick sat opposite, carving cheese and placing it on a plate beside a torn hunk of bread and a selection of fruit. 'You did not, but that is a story for another day, I think. Suffice to say, lad, it is your home for now.'

'It is a nice home.'

The older man grunted. 'I'm glad you think so, but right now this part of this home stinks of that pease-crap and I must take my leave and my breakfast to a distant room.'

'You do not like it?'

The man headed for the stairs. 'Tell you what, you take my portion.'

'Thank you.' Brann rose, lifting his empty bowl. 'You are a kind man.'

As he finished his second bowl, Hakon chatted amiably, filling him in on the washing arrangements, the layout of the building, the duties and responsibilities of the occupants and the work they did to bring in the coin. 'After you've eaten, I'll show you where we shit and piss, but if you've forgotten how to do those activities, that's one thing I won't be helping you with.'

'You do not have a bucket?' It seemed strange that they should be adequately equipped in every other respect, but not in this.

'We do not have a bucket.'

'A bucket would be helpful. It is convenient.' If they were

helping him, it seemed only fair to try to educate them in return.

Grakk put a hand on his shoulder. 'Thank you, Brann, but we'll maybe just persist with the arrangements we have.'

'In the meantime...' Cannick was descending the stairs. His arm shot out and an object flew towards them.

Brann rolled back off the bench and came up with Gerens's knife in his hand. Sophaya's arm extended and plucked the object from the air. Gerens looked at Brann and then at the empty sheath at his belt. The girl showed Brann a small pouch. 'Among friends, remember?'

Gerens held out a hand, and Brann placed the knife in it. 'Sometimes I do first, then think.'

Hakon laughed. 'You always used to do the opposite. Either way, just try to remember who's on your side and who is not. I have a feeling that this will prove important to our health.'

Sophaya's eyes narrowed. She looked at Cannick. 'Can we trust him?'

The older man shrugged. 'I believe so. And who would he betray us to, anyway?'

'I mean, are we safe from him?'

Hakon leapt to his feet, his voice impassioned. 'Brann would never harm us. Never.'

Gerens looked at her and nodded. 'He is right. I believe it.'

Sophaya grunted, grabbed a bowl and sat. But she sat where she could see him, Brann noted. She was sensible. Never turn your back on someone new.

Cannick cut in. 'What will be more important to your health in the short term is whether we have enough food or not. Our young friend should be reacquainted gently to the world above ground. Take him to the market.' He rhymed off a short list of essentials. 'Young lady, you take charge, as you have the coin as well as the only sense among this group of hare-brained cubs.' Gerens looked pointedly at him. 'Fine, hare-brained cubs and a remorseless achiever.' Gerens looked pointedly at Brann. Cannick sighed. 'Right, a remorseless achiever, a danger-obsessed pit-fighter and a hare-brained cub.' Gerens looked satisfied. 'Regardless, I think that lends even more credence to my choice of the most responsible among you. But,' he tapped the pouch in the girl's hand, 'please do pay for them. We do not need any more enemies, nor to attract attention.'

She smiled sweetly. 'Of course, dear Cannick. Whatever do you take me for?'

He grunted. 'The most natural thief I have ever known, that's what. And I have known a few, believe me.' A look of alarm struck him and his hand shot into the low neck of his tunic to emerge with his own pouch in his hand and a look of relief on his face.

Sophaya's smile never wavered as she turned to walk backwards shortly before the door. Her wrist snapped and a knife embedded itself in the table top. 'Our Brann is not the only one who can relieve someone of the blade from their belt.'

Brann pointed helpfully at the quivering knife. 'It is true. Look.'

Cannick's reply was short, but highly uncomplimentary.

Their walk to the market was a source of wonder to Brann. He swung his arms, unencumbered by a heavy grip on each of them. He stared at the blue of the sky, the faded and cracked white of the building walls. He listened to groups of people talking, rather than chanting, screaming, howling or cheering: just talking. And through the myriad smells, there was one that cut through them all to his core.

'Sea,' he breathed. He smiled in delight. 'The sea!' It was almost a shout. He branched off abruptly in the direction of the smell, but was halted by a huge hand that grasped his tunic between the shoulder blades. He permitted Hakon to hold him. *Friend.*

'Calm yourself, little one,' Hakon said. 'Plenty of time for that. Right now we have a mission of shopping, and Sophaya has been given responsibility and Gerens has been given a task. Neither should be tested on those scores.'

They entered the market, a bustling collection of stalls surrounding an open square where some brightly dressed men and women cavorted acrobatically while more than a few passers-by stopped to laugh and throw coin appreciatively. Sophaya proved to be as adept at gathering the required supplies as she had been at relieving Cannick of his knife, and soon Gerens and Hakon had their arms filled. 'As the new boy, you are excused bearer duties,' she had told Brann. 'This time.'

While the girl paid for their last items, bread shaped into two long batons, and called to Hakon to come to add them to his already considerable bundle, a stall behind the rest caught Brann's eyes. His feet took him to it, followed closely by an attentive Gerens. Rolls of fabric were piled upon each other, more colours than he knew existed, but one caught his eye. His fingers felt at the soft brown fabric, a thought nagging at him just out of reach of his mind's grasp. A tall slender slave girl stopped beside him to peruse the wares.

'You like that colour, do you?' she asked.

He looked at her, then back at the cloth. He frowned. 'You should choose that one.' He touched a deep green.

250

'This would be nice on someone with brown hair. And brown eyes.'

A shout drew his attention to the square. A wiry man was running along one side, a shoulder bag that was more than half filled in one hand. A matronly woman at the far end of the area was shouting something about a thief, but it was the shining blade in his other hand that Brann's eye was fixed upon. That, and the route the man was taking straight towards Sophaya.

Three paces took him onto the stall between him and the square and he ran along it, scattering spices in clouds of colour and scent, until he leapt onto the next. It was one selling roasted meat and, as he passed, he leant down and seized a heavy-bladed knife from a steaming haunch, sending a spray of hot grease into the face of the stunned vendor, provoking a shout of pain and anger. Planting a foot on the end of the stall, he launched himself. The wooden board jerked backwards, tilting a pot and its contents over the unfortunate merchant, whose shouts turned to a pained screech, and Brann flew past the startled Sophaya to land with a roll to rise and take the running man in the chest with his shoulder. The man staggered back and barely managed to hold his balance, doing so only by flailing his arms. Brann ducked under the knife and, in a movement too quick for most to follow, cut his blade across the man's throat, continued his turn, reversing the knife in his grip and using the heel of his other hand to hammer the end of the handle to spear the point up under the ribs and into the heart. He maintained the spin and used the movement to drag the knife clear with both hands. He skipped a couple of paces to clear arm's length from the body as it folded in on itself and fell to the cobbles in a splash of its own blood.

Brann's arms shot aloft, the blood-drenched knife in one hand, and he spun slowly in a circle to take the acclaim.

But no cheers came, nor chants, nor stamped applause. Only silence.

Then came the screams. A woman, heavy with child, lumbered across the space, her wails hysterical and relentless. She cradled the body and looked up at Brann. 'You monster,' she screeched. 'All he wanted was the bag. All he had was the knife to cut the strap. You monster, you monster, you monster...'

As confusion brought Brann's arms back down, Gerens strode from the stalls and, without pause, took one of those arms in a fierce grip and steered him among the stalls and away from the uproar, into an alley. They were immediately joined by the other two and, once out of sight of the square, they broke into a run. At first, Gerens took them away from their path home, then doubled back until they stood panting at their building. Sophaya rapped the rhythmic knock on the door and, without waiting further, Hakon pushed them through and slammed the door shut.

Cannick leapt from his seat at the sight of Brann, his tunic front soaked in blood and streaks of crimson splashed across his face and arms.

Gerens steered Brann towards the table and sat him on the bench. 'He is unhurt.' He took a damp cloth and wiped his face and arms free of the blood. Brann relaxed. This was an activity that was familiar.

Sophaya looked at Cannick. 'Remember the question I asked earlier? I now agree he will not harm us. Others, however, I am not so sure.'

The old warrior moved around the table to examine the boy for himself. Brann felt expert fingers feeling their way around his torso and testing the movement of his arms and head. Cannick looked at Sophaya as he did so. 'This is what comes of your responsibility?'

She shrugged. 'Everything was fine until one fool started running about with a knife.'

'It seems we have been too hasty in reintroducing our friend to the world. We have more of a problem than we thought.'

'Indeed,' said Hakon. 'You know that thing you said about not attracting attention?'

Sophaya looked indignant. 'That's not my fault. I paid for everything.'

'Enough.' Cannick's voice was a growl. 'I spoke of the task of dealing with the problem within our friend.'

Grakk rose calmly from his seat by the hearth. 'More still than that. Some people see our young friend as a source of great fortune. The loss of that source, they will have taken with bad grace. And now they know the area to start seeking that source.'

A cheery rap at the door heralded a dark-haired boy's entry. He burst into the room with enthusiasm. 'How are we all this fine day? We must hasten to the Crooked Corner Market. Apparently there was some excitement there.'

'We know, and we must not,' growled Cannick.

'Oh.' The boy was crestfallen, but then his eyes fell upon Brann. His smile returned redoubled and he strode across to seize him in a hug. 'Brann!'

Brann frowned. His body wanted to break the grip and target the throat, but a name appeared in his head and he felt himself tense as he halted the urge. 'Marlo.' He lifted his arms and mimicked the boy's hold on him. It seemed important to the boy for some reason. 'You are my friend.'

'Of course I am!' Marlo pulled back and Brann let him go, though his blood-wet tunic was less willing to release Marlo's clothing. The boy looked down. 'You have spilt something on yourself.'

Brann looked at him. 'It is blood. There was a man with a knife. I stopped him.'

'That you certainly did, Chief,' Gerens grunted, but Marlo was frowning at Brann. He stared closely at him.

'Brann?'

This was strange. They had already done this bit. But if the boy wanted to try it again... 'Marlo.'

The slender boy looked at Cannick. 'Is he... you know... all right?'

The man blew out a long breath. 'Physically, yes.'

Concern was plain in the boy's face. 'But...' Cannick nodded. 'Can he be helped?'

Cannick sighed. 'We hope so. We must hope so.'

'What can I do?'

Grakk faced the confused boy. 'What you must do, Marlo our friend, is speak to your Cassian. Whoever Brann's unknown friend in high places may be, he or she must now go beyond facilitating his escape from the City Below. He must aid our escape from this City in its entirety.' He looked at Cannick. 'Would you ask some of our erstwhile maritime colleagues if they would live here for a while to watch over the Lady?'

The veteran's grey head nodded. 'When should they move in?' He was already moving towards the door.

Grakk's face was grim. 'Tonight. We must be out of this place before dawn.'

Chapter 6

The girl fidgeted, awkwardly. It looked even more ungainly on the thin frame that accentuated her height.

'I make you nervous, girl?'

'No, my lord.' The piercing eyes swivelled to meet hers. 'I mean, yes, my lord.' The eyebrows arched. 'I mean, you have a fierce demeanour, but on this occasion it is that which I must report that unsettles me.'

'You bring bad news?'

'I bring news. It is not for me to say whether it is bad or good, my lord.'

'Yet still you are troubled.' He stared at her, assessing. 'You are not at ease with what you saw.'

Eyes down, she shook her head.

'Then spit it out, girl, and be done with it.'

She coloured. 'Of course, my lord.' She cleared her throat, as if to clear the way for the words. 'There was an incident at a market. A man was killed. He killed a man.'

'This troubles you? Men have died at his hand already. As have wild beasts, a couple of warrior women from the

255

Southern Deadlands and various combinations of all of these. This is known to many. And neither is it unknown for men to die in altercations in the city. Yet you come to me claiming such news of disturbing sights.'

'The man was a thief, my lord, no more. He was not a threat, nor a danger. But the boy, he is not the boy he was. No man acts like he did.'

'In what way?'

She paused. 'I engaged him. He is distant. With most people, there is the person on the surface and if you reach, you find the person underneath. With him, it is as though the person on the surface is all that exists. He is... not there. The boy I saw before is not within. Everything seems new to him, to the surface boy, but for fragments of memories, fragments he does not comprehend himself. Distant, yes, as though he watches and hears from far away and without understanding.'

'And within? What of that? He is empty? He is a shell beyond this surface simpleton?'

Her eyes lifted, wide at the memory, staring from a face gone pale. 'Oh no, my lord, not empty, far from empty. Beneath the surface sits a monster, waiting, watching, ready.' She drew a long, shuddering breath. 'The thief, he carried a knife for cutting bag straps, purses, hanging meat, nothing more. But the sight of the blade woke the monster, and the monster became the man. He slaughtered the thief without hesitation.' She paused, reassessing. 'No, beyond that, it was as though he was driven to it, was eager for it. He butchered the man faster than you could clap your hands. And then he sought acclaim. Women were screaming and men were retching, but he saw it as a source of approval.'

'The blade brought out the monster?'

She thought on it, then shook her head. 'I think the blade was just a sign of what he sought, like spoor to a hunter. The fight was his quarry. At the sign that blood might be spilt, the monster emerged, thirsty to be the one to spill it.'

'He fought well?'

'He fought a man who had little or no training and only a small knife. But it was not that he disregarded the ease of his opponent. It was more that it was immaterial to him, that he saw only the fight and acted solely to win it.'

He nodded slowly, lost in thought.

'My report is satisfactory, my lord?'

He nodded again, but absently this time. He waved a hand, a gesture vague in its movement but clear in its message.

She left.

Obedience and wit. She showed promise; already she exceeded his expectations. She would prove useful, if nurtured.

'You are popular with the young today.' The hoarse whisper was so close that he would have jumped had he not been expecting it. 'A young boy and then a young girl. People will wonder where you get your energy from.'

'They can wonder all they like. The less they know of the truth, the more it suits me.'

She poured the customary drink from the water jug. 'And the truth is?'

'You know it fine. It is their energy I need, and their eyes and ears. Facts are the bricks of which plans are built. Rumour and conjecture construct only folly and ruin.'

'And the facts?'

He sighed. 'The boy brought news that discovery is likely, and escape necessary. News and a request also: that assistance may be given to make escape possible.'

'*And will it be given?*'

'*It will. It must. Those who seek them are many and have much to lose. But so, too, do we. So the aid will come their way.*'

'*And the boy himself? I heard the slave girl's words. She spoke truly, and with perception. I saw what transpired. It was as she said.*'

'*He is now a killer.*'

'*He is that, and more.*'

'*You achieved your goal.*'

'*I achieved half of my goal: the portion within my influence. The remainder must be completed by others with skills of their own.*'

'*I saw him. You may have overstretched. He may be lost, too far broken.*'

'*That is the risk we take.*'

An edge crept into her tone. '*It is the risk you have taken, old man. You play with the fate of many when you play with the fate of this one. Should you be proven wrong, we may be lost.*'

Rage burst from him. '*You dare to lecture me, crone? You think me unaware of the stakes we face? Great danger requires great boldness, for only great boldness can accept the challenge of great risk, and without meeting risk face-to-face we capitulate to danger. If we do not have him right, we may as well not have him at all, and then we have nothing. Then we have already lost.*'

She smiled. '*Now who said you had energy no longer?*'

'*It is not energy I need. It is the strength to endure what I most detest. What I now have no choice but to face.*'

She put a hand on his shoulder. '*And what is it that you detest so fiercely?*'

258

He sighed. 'Resting my faith in others. And sitting, unable to play a part, while I wait for news of their success or failure.'

'That is life, old man.'

He placed his hand on top of hers. 'That is as may be. But it does not mean I have to like it.'

****

The small party slipped from the doorway as midnight struck. Clad in the white robes of the Servants of the Moon, they followed Marlo's lead through barely enough light to see the narrow streets before them or the uneven surface underfoot.

Hakon was grumbling. 'Only we would try to sneak unseen through the darkness in bright white.'

'Sometimes the best way to be unseen is to be seen,' Grakk murmured.

Hakon stopped, and Brann peered into his hood to determine the problem. Seeing a perplexed look, he offered help. 'Something obvious draws no attention.'

Hakon grunted, unconvinced.

Cannick hissed at them. 'Quiet, you fools. However we are dressed, we can still talk our way to death. Now form up.'

They arranged themselves into the circle adopted by the moon priests and moved steadily through the sleeping city, the echoes of their scuffling steps the only noise around them.

Then the clamour erupted.

A crash several streets to their right heralded an orange glow that grew to lighten the sky in that direction, and shouts were interspersed with screams of alarm.

From another angle, cries sought to urgently organise some sort of activity, and from yet another, the roar of a beast caused further consternation. Windows lit up in random patterns and the streets began to fill, citizens passing them in a rush and heading in various directions.

Marlo grabbed a barefooted boy of apprentice age by the arm. 'What's going on?' He tightened his grip as the lad wriggled in his eagerness to be on his way. A coin calmed his impatience.

'What's not going on?' he said, grinning through his breathlessness. 'A bear has got loose in the Street of a Hundred Anvils. What is a bear even doing near there in the first place? And the Northern boy, you know, the runaway fighting champion, has been spotted in The Pastures – and him with a fat merchant's ransom offered for his capture alive. And would you believe there's talk of a spinster in the Blue River Quarter taking a turn and throwing coins from her window.'

Cannick nodded at the sky. 'And then there's the fire over by.'

'And then there's the fire over by,' the boy agreed. 'Now unless you want to pay me more to stay and chat...'

Cannick nodded to Marlo, and as soon as the boy's arm was released he was haring on his way.

'That's a happy coincidence,' Grakk observed. 'Four incidents that are commanding a considerable amount of attention and creating even more confusion and, by fortunate chance, every one of them leading people away from the path we follow.'

Cannick nodded sagely. 'Very handy.' He looked at Marlo. 'Whoever your master's contact at the palace may be, he has certainly delivered on his promise to assist.'

The boy nodded. 'It does seem a lot that he has achieved

in a short time. I have to admit, I hadn't expected as much myself. Would you like me to continue guiding you now?'

Grakk pulled his hood more deeply over his head. 'Of course. Please do.'

The disturbances allowed them passage to the edge of the city free of incident and, before long, Brann saw the deeper blackness of a towering wall against the dark of the sky. A small gate was set into it and, to the side of the portal, a brazier lit the slumped form of a snoozing guard, a sword on his belt and a billy club lying by his side.

'Another stroke of luck,' Grakk noted. 'Although on this occasion it is merely good fortune, unless our benefactor was remarkably detailed in his planning.'

Marlo smiled, his teeth bright in the darkness. 'He is, but I think you may be right regardless.'

Sophaya slipped up beside them. 'If we are blessed with good fortune, it would be a sin to waste the opportunity.' Brann nodded. This girl did tend to move directly to the most immediate truth.

It wasn't hard to agree, and the small party crept forward, seven pairs of eyes fixed on the sleeping sentry. Their footsteps were quiet, but the door was not so. Sophaya had relieved the guard of a set of keys and the second one she tried fitted the lock, but the creak as she eased it open could have wakened the surrounding neighbourhood had they not already been disturbed by the excitement elsewhere. There was only one person whose sleep they were concerned about, however, and he floundered to his feet with a cry of alarm.

'Silence him,' Cannick hissed.

Gerens seized Brann's arm barely in time as he stepped forward, naked dagger in hand. 'Steady, Chief,' he murmured. 'Remember what we talked about before we left. Take a breath before acting.' As the man stared in drowsy confusion at a monk intent on murder, Hakon knocked him senseless with his own club.

Brann was still not convinced. Taking a breath before acting was the surest way for that breath to be your last. But with the man now unconscious, it no longer mattered.

Silence was now less important than haste, and they ran through a low tunnel to the thick door on the outer side of the sally port. Hakon swiftly unbarred it and Sophaya found the two keys on the guard's ring that fitted the great locks. Within moments, they were outside the city walls.

'It would have been so much easier to leave in daylight, when the great gates lie open to all,' Marlo pointed out.

'It would be so much easier for those who seek young Brann to watch the gates in daylight. We seek to leave this place alive, and without incident.'

Hakon grinned. 'Well, without incident other than a building on fire, a rampaging bear, a mad spinster and a mistaken sighting of this valuable commodity, that is,' he said, ruffling Brann's hair.

Grakk stepped away, staring into the scrublands. The moon was well filled and, away from the shadows of the tall buildings and narrow streets of the poor quarters, there was enough light for their eyes to adjust and let them see a little of the surroundings. 'Those disturbances will not be directly attributable to us, and will therefore not tend to alert Brann's enemies to our path or our intent. However, it will all be for naught should we not put distance between these walls and ourselves before the sun arises.' He turned to Marlo. 'You have been most helpful, young guide. If you would be so good as to complete the final part of your task, it would be most helpful.'

Marlo stepped towards a shallow defile. 'Most certainly, sir. It is not far, in actual fact.'

They scrambled down the short slope and followed the line of the gulley as it carved a crooked path away from the city walls. Brann walked among them, his head constantly twitching in search of danger and his feet spinning him to watch the way they had come. He stopped once to step aside from the party, sniffing the air and cocking his head to listen before satisfaction allowed him to rejoin them. Forced to leave the gulley's scant cover as it bent back, they emerged warily onto the open plain for a short spell, stepping through the brittle brush that littered the area for miles. Hakon snagged his robe on a branch and, in irritation, started to drag the white monk's garb over his head.

Brann darted forward and grabbed the hem, stopping it with the material bunched over the big boy's head. 'No,' he said, and Hakon stood still, realising that it had not caught on a bush. He allowed Brann to pull the robe back down, but looked at the boy, clearly puzzled.

Frowning, Brann looked up at Hakon, then around the immediate surroundings. The others looked on curiously as he took Hakon by the arm, feeling the solid hugeness of it but also the compliance as the boy followed him into a crouch. He pointed at the figures in their white robes against the darkness of the night sky, and then pulled the bigger boy to a slight rise, giving them more of a downward perspective on the rest of the group.

A broad smile spread across Hakon's face in realisation. 'We see each other against the darkness, but anyone on the walls, looking down, is looking at the ground. Ground that is *light*-coloured, like,' he pulled at his robe, 'our ridiculous clothing.'

The pair rejoined the group to find Grakk and Cannick standing before them, looking at them.

'Now that your brain has caught up with why you shouldn't lose your temper at a bush, maybe we can continue,' Cannick growled. He looked at Brann. 'And as for you, maybe the man is not lost as deep within as we thought.'

Grakk looked at him with narrowed eyes. 'Be not so sure. Animals understand the importance of blending. Animals are attuned to survival. The unique qualities of man are frivolities where surviving is the only concern. Is that not correct, young Brann?'

He liked this Grakk man. He understood things. And he moved in a good way, like one who understood the importance of balance and control in a fight. He smiled. 'I still live.'

Cannick snorted. 'Well, man or beast, we all risk being hunted like either if we are seen out here when the sun brings back the light. Let's move.'

Marlo started to move but, as he turned, he plummeted from view with a startled yelp. They rushed to what they found was the lip of a small ravine, where the light of the moon revealed the dusty figure around twenty feet below, rising from where he had rolled and slapping the dirt from his clothes.

'Down here,' he said, inviting them with a wave. 'This is the way.'

Sophaya spat in disdain. 'Are you just making this route up as you go?'

'No, no, it is surely this way,' Marlo assured them as they scrambled down with more control than he had exhibited. 'We follow this to its end, and then that will be our journey's end.'

Without further delay they stumbled and wound their way through the rocks and bushes that were scattered among the shadows at the bottom of the wedge carved from the plain by a long-forgotten stream. Before long, the murmur of voices became heard. Brann froze, his eyes darting in search of a weapon. His eyes, then his hand, found a jagged rock that fitted snugly in his fist. His mind relaxed at the feel of it, but his body remained like a mangonel straining for release.

'Worry not, young warrior,' Cannick grinned. 'That is the noise we seek.'

Grakk turned to Hakon. 'And this is the point where you may divest yourself of your holy raiment, impatient boy.'

The big Northerner looked at him. 'I may what? With my what?'

Gerens stepped up behind him with a curved knife. A swift and deft movement saw Hakon's robe sliced from neck to hem, and with a yank at the arms, Grakk pulled it from him.

Gerens shrugged. 'It seemed quicker than an explanation.'

'And altogether more helpful,' Hakon grinned.

The rest of them removed their disguises more conventionally and bundled them under their arms. Several more turns brought the sounds more clearly to them until they climbed to emerge from the defile to a scene that widened Brann's eyes in surprise. Roaring fires lit up an encampment that was teeming with life at a time when all should be asleep and in a location where he expected only to see moonlit wasteland. Bodies cavorted or slumped, watched or danced, ate and drank. Instruments provided a backdrop to the movement and noise of men and women clearly determined to enjoy the passage of the night in whatever manner brought each one pleasure.

Marlo swept his arm towards the scene. 'Behold your new friends.'

Brann was surprised. 'My friends? Like you? I know all these?'

Cannick laughed. 'No, the boy means these will be our travelling companions. We are your true friends, so don't be wandering off with anyone else.' He looked at Marlo. 'They do seem overly jolly, however.'

'The caravan leaves in the morning. The custom on the final night is to consume whatever cannot be taken. Of course, that then extends to all sorts of pleasures that might not be so easy on the road, and attracts many from the city who would earn coin by providing those pleasures. It all adds up to an eventful night.'

'I can't disagree with that,' the old warrior said.

Grakk moved up beside them. 'The terrain ahead is not the most hospitable. They know this well and are wise to take what pleasure they can before they leave, although the pleasure brought by wine now may not be appreciated in the glare of the sun tomorrow. Those before us may be weighing the current pleasure heavier than the future pain, and as seasoned travellers of this path, this is their choice to make. We, however, would be well advised to avoid inebriation. The road will be soft underfoot, but hard in endurance.'

Hakon eyed the revels appreciatively. 'So, basically, don't get bladdered?'

'Indeed.' Grakk's tone was implacable. 'Bladderation is not an option.'

A guffaw erupted from the large boy and he slapped Grakk's back with enough force to drive him several paces forward. 'You have a wonderful way with words, my friend.'

Brann was curious. The bald one, Grakk, was a fighter; the way he carried himself betrayed it, as did his quickness of hand and alertness of eye. Yet he had been struck, and had not responded to the attack. The Hakon boy may be large – very large – and as strong as any he had seen, but there was a deliberateness to his movement that would make him predictable should any conflict last beyond the initial few thunderous blows. Brann resolved that he had much to learn about these friends.

Marlo led them into the camp, weaving among the tents and through the throng of staggering revellers, hawkers of pleasures carnivorous and carnal and intoxicants consumed and inhaled, and entertainers ranging from the exquisitely skilled to the pathetically inept and desperate. Thieves, too, although they tended to eye their little party and steer clear of them. Whether it was due to their look of grim determination, their range of weapons or their lack of drunkenness was hard to tell. Hakon grinned in joyful appreciation of every woman who passed, whether fully clad or less so, Sophaya automatically and almost absently increased their travelling fund as they walked while Gerens watched over both her and Brann simultaneously. Brann himself, in one memorable moment, was restrained by Cannick with the older man's shortsword almost clear of its scabbard when a fire-juggler was over-clever and sent a ball of flames on a chain swinging too close to the boy's face. 'That is why we don't give you a weapon,' he advised the boy. 'The smart-arse may have deserved to be tripping over his own entrails, but it's not the attention we need at this time.'

They reached an empty tent, large and circular, with a roaring fire in front to ward off the nightly chill and a young Scribe waiting patiently to one side. Marlo conferred briefly with him, nodding several times, before clasping forearms with him and allowing him to be on his way.

'This is indeed our tent. We will find everything we need for the journey inside but for, of course, our mounts. These also have been arranged and gifted, and I have been given instructions on where they can be found. I can show you to them before I take my leave back to Cassian's compound, if you wish.'

Grakk stepped forward. 'We do so wish.' He placed a hand on the boy's shoulder. 'Our gratitude will go with you, not only to your master's contact, our benefactor, but as much to you. You have risked much and helped even more. It will not be forgotten, my young friend.'

Marlo grinned and shrugged. 'I would have been bereft had I not been permitted to help. And he who has aided you asks only one thing in return.' He looked at Brann. 'That you take our broken friend and return him whole once more.'

Brann looked himself over. He could find nothing broken on him. Perhaps they talked of someone else. He wandered towards the tent, led by curiosity.

Grakk smiled. 'It will be our pleasure to pay that price. Now let us two go see our mounts while these others take their rest, and then you can be on your way home.'

Inside the tent, Brann found a treasure trove of supplies. Food and drums of water were piled at one side, and at the other were clothes, weapons and an assortment of the mundane essentials that keep a traveller alive. The only thing that drew his eye, however, was the selection of swords and knives carefully propped among several spears, small round shields and two short bows with full quivers alongside.

Cannick entered as he was trying out two swords for

weight and balance, one in each hand. 'Well, don't you look happy, playing with your toys?' The veteran ambled over to him, seemingly unconscious of the danger of two naked and sharp blades. He held out a hand. 'May I?'

Brann handed him one, as the others ducked under the tent flap. Hakon whistled appreciatively, Gerens's dark eyes scanned the equipment and Sophaya slipped to one side to sit cross-legged on a rug. Brann watched carefully as Cannick examined the sword, sighting down the blade and running his hands over its parts. He felt a trust in this man, but you never take your eyes from anyone carrying a drawn weapon. The hilt of the other sword was still snug in his right hand.

Cannick grunted. 'Basic and simple in design, but good quality. Better than we have managed to gather over our time here. We should exchange ours for these.'

Brann looked for a scabbard for his, but Cannick laid a gentle arm on his. 'Not you, youngster.' Brann felt himself tensing, the point of his sword rising. Cannick smiled a disarming smile. 'Do you trust us, Brann?'

He felt for his feelings. He imagined a fight, a mass brawl. In the picture in his head, he saw these people in this tent protecting him. He nodded.

Cannick gently took the weapon from his hand. It was a bad feeling. For as long as he could remember, he had only ever let go of a weapon when it was embedded in a corpse. He did not like this feeling.

The grey-haired man smiled sadly. 'You don't understand, do you?' He shook his head. 'You are too skilled. But you are going into situations where you will find strange things happening, and your instinct is to fight. Sometimes it is not right to fight. But you are too skilled for us to be sure of helping you to stop before it is too late. Do you see that?'

269

It was true. He was faster than any of these. He had seen enough to know. They could not stop him. But... 'People like me to fight. People cheer me.'

'In the pit, they cheer you. It's a lot less simple outside the pit, young man. You will learn this, but until you do, it is dangerous for us to make you even more dangerous with a few feet of steel.'

The dark-haired boy, Gerens, had moved beside him. He was very quiet on his feet, Brann had noticed. 'In any case, I will ensure you come to no harm, Chief.'

Brann looked into the dark eyes. There was no emotion there, nothing to read. But there was something that spoke to his instinct, he could feel it like a silent voice in his head. 'I believe you.'

'In any case,' Hakon grinned, 'you have a knack of finding a weapon when you need one.' The flat of one hand slapped Brann on the shoulders. The boy stood unmoving and Hakon's eyes widened. 'Gods, but you've got strong.'

Brann looked at him. 'I practised. I fought.' He looked at Cannick. 'In the pit.'

Cannick's face creased into a smile. 'Good boy.'

He felt a yearning. 'I like the pit. I will find one.'

'No!' Gerens and Hakon chorused.

'Wait.' Cannick's voice cut through their protests. 'You others stay here and look through this lot. I'll take him to find the pit here.'

Gerens stepped forward. 'Are you sure?'

Sophaya's voice soothed him. 'Has Cannick ever struck you as a man of rash decisions, my Gerens?'

The boy nodded and the man returned the gesture. 'Trust me, lad.' He looked over at Hakon. 'But you stay here, for you *will* get us into trouble. Not in the pit but in some

270

trollop's arms. Busy yourself here and start with throwing those priests' robes on the fire. We take nothing we do not need and leave nothing that can tell any story.'

Brann allowed the man to steer him from the tent and they worked their way through the encampment, guided by Cannick's occasional questioning of the more conscious of those they passed. Brann felt the man's fingers tighten on his arm as they rounded a tent and a shouting crowd filled the space before them. Torches guttered on tall poles arranged in a wide circle, bathing the area in a wavering glow of shifting shades of orange. Man argued and pointed, and scraps of paper were passed between them, held aloft in triumph or crumpled and tossed aside in anger or despair. This, he had seen before. He had seen it at...

'The pit!' His eyes lit up and he made to rush forward.

Cannick's unyielding grip halted his progress. 'Slowly, carefully, youngster. You must learn to assess a situation before you act.'

This was not right. Watch your surroundings but act on a situation. Otherwise you let your opponent act. But the Grakk man had said this man was his friend, and so he nodded and let himself be led forward more cautiously.

The crowd was not so thick as to impede them, and Cannick threaded a way through to a space at the lip of the pit. Two men with similar swords but differently shaped shields – one a long rectangle and the other round – hacked and stumbled their way around the circle, enthusiasm and effort replacing any hint of skill or thought.

Brann frowned. 'This is not a fight.'

'This is a fight. It passes for a pit contest in these places.'

'I could have them dead in two beats of a heart. Both of them.'

271

'Which is why you do not fight here. Ever.'

'But the people cheer when they die.'

'Not the people here. No one will die.'

'No one? In a fight?'

Cannick pulled him back from the spectators. 'These people want to see a contest, not a kill. Even when you remember fighting, were not your opponents always enough to make you work?'

He felt his mind go distant. He could not remember every fight, but his head quickly filled with a succession of scenes – memories that were jumbled but vivid enough to to let him understand. He nodded. 'Most. Some were easy. But mostly the next one was harder than the one before.'

'Exactly. If a lion fought a dog, who would win?'

'The lion.'

'Sometimes?'

He frowned. 'Every time.' This was silly. A child would know this.

'Were you to go in that pit, you would be the lion. Everyone would know you would win. So no one disagrees. But when it is hard to say who will win, people disagree. And then they argue with coins, and the one who guesses best wins the money, just as the fighter who fights best wins the fight. This happened in the pits where you fought, too, but where the fight is to the death, the fighters become even more desperate and the end is harder to predict.' He shrugged. 'And then there are some who just like the blood.'

He thought about this. Fighting with no skill. Fighting with no death. He stepped back towards the pit and cast a glance at the two men, one on his knee and the other hammering at the upraised shield. He spat in disgust. 'This is not fighting. I do not like this pit. I will find another.'

'There is no other, lad. This is it in this place. And in many others. There are two places where you will find the level of contest you seek. The Arena above ground, where skill is prized, and the pits below, where death is sought. You have triumphed in both, a unique achievement.'

Brann felt a surge of interest. 'Then I will go there.' He started walking.

Cannick fell in beside him. 'Should you go to either place, there are those who would kill you before you had a single contest.'

He shrugged. 'Then I will kill them.'

'You do not know how.'

This man was stupid. 'I know killing.'

Cannick smiled. It looked sad, which was a strange smile. 'You do indeed. But you need to learn how to do it without getting yourself killed by them at the same time. That power is inside you, but it is hidden. You need to learn that even a lion may be beaten by dogs, if there are enough dogs. You need to learn to think.'

'I think when I fight.'

'It's a different sort of thinking. For when you are not fighting.' Brann frowned in confusion. The man's words did not make sense, but Cannick continued. 'Grakk is taking you somewhere to help you learn what you need.'

That, he could understand. 'Then we must go there. We must leave.'

This time the man's smile was a proper smile. He looked happy. 'In the morning, you shall get your wish. Now, we should return to the tent to prepare for that.'

They reached the tent as Grakk was returning with an excited Marlo. Hakon looked up. 'Welcome back! How was the pit?'

Brann thumped onto a thick rug beside Sophaya, who was toying with a small stone, rolling it between each finger in turn at a speed that was hard to follow. 'It was not fighting. It was pathetic.' He pointed at Grakk's head as he ducked into the tent. 'He will take me to learn to think so I can kill people but not die.'

Grakk looked at Cannick. 'A rather simplistic description.'

The veteran's mouth twitched in a half smile. 'You wanted me to try deep philosophy?'

The tribesman nodded in acceptance.

Sophaya flicked the stone at Marlo's head. 'Someone looks surprisingly cheerful considering they have come back here to say farewell to their darling friends.'

The boy's grin grew even broader. 'Did you notice? There is good reason.'

Grakk stepped over to the supplies and started picking through them, selecting some and discarding others. 'He will be accompanying us.'

'What?' Cannick clearly didn't like surprises.

Grakk straightened. 'The young Scribe returned and caught us at the livestock merchant. A messenger had found him as he returned to the palace. The word around the area we have so recently vacated is that a boy of a description matching Marlo, and known by many who have lived there for some years, has been seen in the company of the boy gladiator who is sought. There is now coin offered for news of either boy, and should young Marlo be found, they will have their particular methods of asking questions.'

Several of the swords that were native to this region were of a slim, slightly curved variety and so several of those left for them were of this sort. Grakk sorted through them as he spoke until he found two that satisfied him. While Brann was happy to fight with any weapon that came to hand, he found he had a liking for the straight swords. He supposed he had preferred them in the time before his memories started. The tribesman continued, while pulling on a harness which would allow the blades to sit crossed on his back: 'He has been released from his duties with Cassian and will travel with us for his own safety. Comparative as that safety may be.'

Brann felt pleased. The boy seemed to want to be helpful, and he smiled a lot. He wouldn't like him to be harmed.

Cheerfully, Hakon slapped Marlo on the back, which seemed to be his main form of communication. 'Welcome to our happy band,' he said, steadying the boy's stagger with his other hand. Gerens nodded once in acknowledgement and, grinning, Sophaya unerringly flicked another stone that pinged off Marlo's head.

Marlo beamed. 'This is going to be exciting!'

A grunt came from Cannick. 'Give me boring and uneventful any day. Let's just settle at the moment for all of us getting back unharmed by man or nature.'

'Starting now, select what we need,' Grakk commanded. 'Clothing suitable for the path ahead is over there.' He looked at Sophaya. 'Same for everyone. We will not be dressing in fashion for the court.'

The girl rose in a single smooth movement. 'When have you ever seen me dress anything but functional, dear Grakk?'

'At the court. On our first day, if you remember.'

She smiled sweetly. 'That was with purpose, too, do you not see? Were a leopard able to dress as a gazelle, would it not do so?'

Grakk stared at her. 'Indeed.' Brann noticed that there was amusement in his eyes, though he knew not why, for she had merely stated a fact, and one that made sense. 'In any case, find clothing that fits, then take a spare set. There are packs there, also. Then weapons, a blanket, for the night is colder where we are going than in the city, and anything else you see that you may need, though do not take any more than you do need. Our mounts may be hardy, but they will need energy more than we will, and we should not overburden them. Cannick will assist me with the food provisions and cooking equipment.' The old warrior nodded. 'Of that which you leave here, anything that can identify you goes on the fire outside. The rest can be left here and will be removed on the morrow when our benefactor sends his people to take the tent. Soon we must sleep for what few hours remain of the night, as our start is early.'

As Brann pulled his tunic over his head, his eye caught a design marked on his arm: a strange and fierce beast and writing he was unable to read. When they had washed blood from him after fights, these marks remained, so they must be a part of him. He looked at the shapes adorning the bald man's scalp. They seemed the same sort of thing, just different shapes.

Grakk turned at his approach and looked at the arm Brann proffered. 'You have lines on your skin,' the boy said. 'I have this picture on me – do you know what it is?'

The man nodded. 'You were brave, very brave, and you helped a lot of people. This symbol was an honour from them, a way for them to say thank you.'

Brann considered this. 'I like helping people.' If that was why it was there, he was happy. 'And the writing?'

Hakon stepped beside him. 'They are runes. It is how my people write down their letters. It says, "Dare to dream; trust your heart; let your soul fly."'

Brann's eyes narrowed. That stirred a memory, but only the start of one, like a picture forming in the smoke of the fire that swirls to nothing just as your eyes try to grasp it. A name remained, though. 'Valdis.'

The room fell silent. He looked around the staring faces, and settled on Grakk. He was good with answers. 'Who is Valdis?'

The bald man drew a slow breath. 'She is a friend. She chose those words in the runes for you.'

'Then she must be a good friend. Is she?'

'She...' Grakk looked past him at Hakon.

The large boy smiled gently. 'She is. She most certainly is.' He clapped a hand on Brann's shoulder for a moment, then turned back to his preparations. Satisfied, Brann did likewise.

Without being asked, Marlo assisted Brann with his clothing – loose-fitting trousers and tunic and a light cloak with a broad strip of cloth hanging from one side of the hood, all in dark shades of blue, and a pair of light but sturdy boots – and tossed him a blanket. The boy was indeed most helpful.

'Thank you. You are a good friend.'

The boy's eyes grew moist. It seemed a strange reaction to Brann, especially as there was a quiet smile on his face. 'Friends help friends.' He gripped Brann briefly on the arm, then turned to his own belongings.

Following the lead of the others, Brann stowed his meagre belongings in a pack but kept out the blanket for the short rest ahead of them. Hakon had happily festooned himself with steel: a longsword, a fighting axe and a throwing axe on his belt, a spear and a large round wooden shield beside his blanket, and more knives than could be counted, stowed in more places than could be seen. Brann looked longingly at the swords, and Cannick caught his eye.

He stared solemnly back at the man. 'I know,' he said. 'It is not permitted.'

'Not yet,' Cannick grinned. 'Maybe in a few days if you behave yourself.'

'Behave myself?'

Gerens looked up from where he crouched over his pack. 'Not kill anyone.'

They settled down and Brann let sleep come to him. Taking rest whenever he could, he was used to. In his cell home, there was no sky that darkened and lightened, and you never knew when your effort would be required.

When he woke, it was instant. That was also a beneficial ability in the City Below. The others were being roused, and in moments the tent was bustling with the brief activity it took to ready themselves. Brann looked at them, at their weaponry. Hakon carried more than most men could bear the weight of and Grakk had his crossed blades on his back; Marlo bore a curving blade similar to Grakk's pair, while Cannick and Gerens had on their hips the straight swords that had caught his eye, with the boy also having chosen a small, but heavy-looking club and two knives: one a familiar-looking long dagger and the other a slim blade that, even in its sheath, promised a needle-like point. Sophaya was the only one who had not taken a sword – she had answered Hakon's surprised look by asking why she should want the extra weight of something she had no ability to use – but had managed to equip herself with a selection of knives of a startling variety, including a harness that extended down the front of her torso to hold a rack of throwing blades, their handles facing alternately to suit each hand. She had also picked up one of the local bows, a short one that curved and curved again, as had Marlo, while Hakon had been particularly happy to have discovered a much longer, straighter bow.

Bann had understood the words from the grey-haired Cannick, and he was familiar with the feeling of being without a weapon among armed men, as every man he had encountered from his cell to the pit and back again had carried a blade of some sort whereas he had only been permitted what had been thrown to him in the pit and retrieved at the fight's bloody conclusion. But still, to be part of this group, and yet to see them with weapons to hand while he buckled on an empty belt, left him feeling uneasy. It was not a fear born of vulnerability, for all he could remember was fighting with whatever came to hand; it was more a sense of being different among those who called themselves friend. Perhaps if he behaved. Perhaps, as they had said, if he didn't...

'I will try not to kill anyone.' He was standing before Cannick, looking into the man's honest face.

'I know you will.' The man's voice was solemn, genuine.

'I do not seek to kill. It finishes a fight.'

The man frowned, but strangely he did not seem angry. 'It does indeed, lad, it does indeed. But sometimes it is better not to finish a fight that way. And sometimes it is better not to fight at all.'

'What are these times?'

'That is what you must learn for yourself. Once you knew these things yourself, on occasion better than the rest of us. Which is why we make this journey, to reach someone who Grakk believes may help you remember. And which is why, until you remember, it is best that your access to weapons is not overly easy.'

279

Brann nodded, and turned away, but the old man continued: 'You can, however, keep what is tucked into the back of your breeches.'

His hand went instinctively to the knife hilt. 'How did you know?'

Cannick's eyes smiled. 'I have spent a lifetime staying alive. It helps to be able to notice these things. And it would be overly cruel to deny you absolutely everything, I think.'

Brann nodded again and moved across the tent to take his pack. He liked this man. But he would also have liked a sword.

'We should collect our mounts and be off,' Grakk suggested. He paused, though, as Hakon hoisted a water cask to his shoulder with a grunt and stomped out of the tent. 'Alternatively, I am thinking, why carry our provisions to beasts of burden when the beasts can come to the provisions? Cannick, my friend,' he said. 'Would you mind waiting here to protect our belongings? We shall return before long.'

Hakon set the cask down outside the entrance to the tent with a puff of relief and held aside the flap to let the others emerge. 'I would naturally have been happy to carry that and more,' he said, 'but of course I am even happier to take the advice of such a learned man.' They left Cannick sitting contentedly on the cask, watching the world pass by.

Brann could smell the livestock before he heard it, and heard it before he saw it, but when he did so it was with surprise at the scale of the animal pens. Horses, oxen, goats and fowl were gathered in a huge area that teemed with imminent travellers who collected and bought animals that would carry them or their goods or fill their stomachs. Grakk headed to a fence behind which a collection of fine-looking horses stood, but his companions were surprised when he passed the pen and stopped at the next, the man waiting at its gate greeting the tribesman with the enthusiasm of a merchant who had been well compensated. They were even more surprised at the pen's contents.

Brann stared at the beasts in astonishment. They looked like several animals had been rearranged into one beast, long of leg and neck, narrow of head and with a hump on the back that looked anything but healthy. In the City Below, a man had come to clean their cells every so often who was bent and had a hump to his back, and these beasts seemed to suffer the same affliction. Marlo saw his expression.

'You do not have camels where you come from?'

'I don't know where I come from.'

Hakon was equally astounded by the animals. 'I do know, and we don't.'

Now Marlo was surprised. 'Then how do you cross desert and deadlands?'

Hakon grinned. 'We don't have those either.'

Marlo shrugged. 'Fair enough. Just be content with the generosity of our benefactor in providing such animals. You will discover their worth.'

'Generosity?' Brann was puzzled. 'These beasts are deformed, they are sick. They have a growth on their backs.'

Marlo laughed. 'That hump is the sign of a healthy camel. Some say it stores its water there, some that it has another sustaining purpose, but whatever is true, the fact is that these beasts can manage far longer than you and I without taking food or water, which make them great friends to have in empty lands. That, and their broad feet that walk well when the sand becomes soft.'

Hakon's face brightened. 'We fit similar lattice frames to our shoes for soft snow.'

'Ah, yes, snow.' Marlo's face had also lit up. 'I would most certainly like to see this snow.'

Hakon's eyebrows had risen. 'You know of snow?'

'Indeed.' He flicked a thumb at Brann. 'He told me of it.'

'I did?'

Grakk's voice cut through their conversation as he beckoned them over. 'We are fortunate enough to have been supplied with nine of these beasts, and all are of excellent quality.' The animal handler beamed in pride. 'There will be one for each of us to ride, and two to carry the extra supplies. Our friend here,' at which the handler puffed up even more, clearly delighted at the thought of friendship with such clients, 'has supplied us with suitable tackle for each animal's purpose. Sophaya and Marlo, are you familiar with such beasts?'

Both nodded. 'Young children from the poorer quarters are *invited* to ride in camel races,' Marlo explained. 'They are light and easily enticed with just a few coins.'

'And,' the girl said drily, 'it matters less if they fall off and are trampled.'

'Then we are grateful that neither of you fell off and are here to help us,' Grakk said. 'We shall lead a camel each, that which will be our own mount, and I will also take Cannick's while you two will each also bring one of the pack animals.'

Brann was wary as he took the corded rope of many twined colours that hung from the harness of his beast. The only animals he had come across at close range were those replete with tooth, claw, muscle and savage rage that had been sent to kill him in the pit, and therefore his only interaction with animals had been to put as many inches of steel as he could into them as many times as possible. The camel regarded him balefully with a sidelong look from on high, as if it knew his history. Nevertheless, it followed willingly enough when he tentatively pulled the cord, and he was able to lead it after Grakk and his two beasts.

They stopped at the edge of the livestock holding area, where a long row of stone troughs sat, brimming with water. Grakk indicated them. 'This is the most valuable commodity in the desert, but here it is free, as is tradition, in gratitude towards those who brave the sands and sun. You will notice a post with a rag by each trough: a black cloth indicates water for animals, and white for people. Take your camels and let them drink their fill and, while they do so, fill up your own two waterskins so we might save that which is in our supply of water casks for the path ahead.'

Brann was impressed at how much the animals could take in. It was small wonder that they could last for so long without replenishing it if they could stock up in such quantity.

By the time they were pacing with their ungainly steeds back to Cannick, their way was made easier by many of the tents having already been dismantled.

Hakon called forward, 'Are we not taking our tent also, Grakk?'

Without turning, the tribesman shook his head. 'We travel light. We seek speed, not comfort.'

When they came in sight of Cannick, the veteran soldier stood and whistled in surprise. 'I haven't seen one of these for many a year. Never got to ride one, either, so this'll be a first.'

Grakk handed him the cord of the mount that would be his. 'Then be glad that our benefactor was far-sighted enough to specify that we should have highly trained beasts. They can be wilful in the extreme.'

Cannick looked up at the animal. 'Given its size, I wouldn't bet against the camel.'

A saddle on top of the hump had what looked like a sturdy blanket woven into latticework draped and fastened over it, and had leather sacks sitting behind it, one hanging either side of the animal. Grakk placed his pack in one and a water cask in the other, then hung his two waterskins on hooks at the front of the saddle. The others followed his lead and found that the saddles also bore a selection of sheaths and straps to hold spears, shields, bows and quivers, and they filled these also as suited each accordingly.

Only a short time later, they were ready. Grakk stood in front of his camel and gave a sharp tug on the cord, at which, to the surprise of Brann, Hakon, and presumably Gerens, though his face was as expressionless as ever, the large beast obediently bent its forelegs and knelt before him. The tribesman nimbly swung himself into the saddle and slipped his feet into two stirrups in front of him so that he was sitting as if in a chair. Another tug on the cord prompted the animal to stand once more, Grakk effortlessly maintaining his balance during the lurching movement. He nodded at the others.

Brann could not remember feeling fear in any fight in the pit. Now, however, nerves drew his innards into a knot. He did not like this. As the others attempted to follow Grakk's example, he determined not to be the one to fail. The animals were indeed well trained, as each one responded without hesitation to the varying degrees of clumsiness. Sophaya was the only one to gain the saddle and bring her camel upright with any sort of ease. When Marlo almost fell as he tried to climb into place, she looked at him enquiringly.

He shrugged. 'When I was small enough to ride in races,

I was small enough to be lifted into place. And not everyone has the natural balance of a master thief, you know.'

'Evidently,' she said.

Brann's camel was the last to rise. As it lurched in all directions, a cry of alarm escaped him and he clung to the pommel in panic, convinced he would plummet at any second, a fate he only barely avoided as the beast settled in a calm stance. His fear remained evident even with the animal still and placid, however. Never had he felt so precarious, perched at the highest point of a living beast, and not even feeling securely seated. It seemed a long way to fall and he decided against looking down to confirm the height.

Once the laughter had subsided, Grakk spoke again. 'That is why we mounted here, and not where we might embarrass ourselves in front of our travelling companions. Now, the camels respond to simple instructions. Pull the cord left or right to turn in those directions, pull back to slow down and keep pulling to stop, and strike with both heels to start or increase speed. Like so.' His heels rose and fell and his animal stepped off.

Brann tried the same and found to his relief that his not only responded, but also followed Grakk's mount automatically. He would be able to learn to steer more gradually. The rest followed in single file, Marlo and Sophaya leading a pack animal each by a long cord.

From his lofty perch, Brann could see the encampment dispersing in various directions. It seemed that the people here had many differing roads to travel, and were congregating according to the paths they would take. One of the biggest single columns was the one heading back towards the city, their business concluded.

On the edge of the town of tents, a band of around two

score men and women were putting the finishing touches to their camels' readiness, checking straps were tight and all was packed.

Grakk reined his animal to a halt and the other camels responded obediently to their riders to form a group around him. He indicated the group ahead. 'Our travelling companions.'

Cannick frowned. 'Is that wise?' Grakk looked at him in question. Cannick looked at Brann then back to Grakk. 'The fewer people who know of our journey to find our friend help, the better our chances of staying undetected.'

Grakk smiled. 'Rest easy, friend Cannick. These voyagers of the desert are the means used by merchants either side of the Deadlands to pass goods from one to another. This group have their journey to take, and our path coincides. It has been many years since I last travelled these sands, and their assurance of the path is better than mine. It is also helpful to have as many companions as possible who are experienced in these conditions when all but I have never set foot in them before today.'

Cannick's eyes narrowed as he looked ahead. 'Can we trust strangers?'

'These are not strangers to me. We can.'

Hakon looked dubiously at the endless expanse of sand, hazed in heat, which lay beyond the settlement of tents. 'Are you sure it is our only option to cross this?'

Grakk nodded. 'It is the only hope I know of in aid of recovering our young friend from the prison he has made for himself.'

The big shoulders turned as Hakon looked again at the sand and then swivelled to regard Brann. 'Fine by me then.' He smiled and kicked his mount into motion.

The group ahead were dressed similarly to Brann's party and, as they drew closer, he noticed that, while the men had the length of fabric that extended from their hoods wrapped around their heads to expose only their eyes, the women all had their faces laid bare. It was a strange distinction.

Grakk had looked back to check that all were together as they neared the other group, and noticed Brann's puzzlement. 'It is ever thus with the Deruul. Respect is everything to them. Respect of women even more so. They consider it disrespect for adult men to show their faces to anyone outside their own home while the sun watches them from on high. They must also veil themselves in the presence of any women outwith their immediate family, at any hour and in any place. Other than the bedchamber, that is.'

Hakon had heard the last comment and his attention was ensnared. 'A curious exception to have.'

Grakk smiled. 'Pleasures of the flesh are considered entirely natural. But, again, respect and consideration of honour prevail. A maiden's bedchamber has an external door of its own, because as long as a visitor enters unseen after sunset and leaves unseen before dawn, no eyebrows are raised.'

'What an excellent tradition.' Hakon's approval was predictable but nonetheless exuberant. 'And if they sleep in from their exertions?'

Grakk shrugged. 'The young man must hide in the chamber until the next sundown or leave and risk the traditional punishment of Planting.'

'Planting?'

'Buried upright with only the head left above ground. It is carried out in the last minutes before the sun rises, and the subject is released as soon as darkness falls. What is uncertain is whether death comes from beak, teeth or sun. What is certain is that death comes, unpleasantly.'

'That from oversleeping?'

'That from dishonouring a woman.'

Brann was still confused. 'But why cover men's faces and not those of women?'

Grakk smiled. 'They say that there is too much beauty in the face of a woman, that it would be a crime against nature to hide it.'

They were drawing up to the Deruul party and Brann's eyes looked over the women as they went about their tasks. Skin the colour of dark sand, high cheekbones and bright eyes the shape of the almonds Marlo had shared after the previous evening's meal not only suggested the wisdom in the Deruul philosophy, but also nagged at the corner of his memory. He glanced at Sophaya, but while pretty, her looks were of a different sort. Had he known someone from these people? He looked again and realised that they were moving among them. Hurriedly, he snatched at the cloth hanging from his hood and pulled it across his face.

Grakk's eyes narrowed in amusement, and something else. Approval? 'You need not, for their sake, young Brann, though your sentiment is noble. Their respect extends to the customs of others. They do not expect you to abide by their customs, just to maintain your own as long as your conduct exhibits respect in its own way.'

Brann regarded him. 'My only customs are obedience and survival. Their custom will be my custom.'

Grakk smiled and nodded, his stare returning to the front. His eyes found a man at the centre of the activity and he steered his camel towards him. 'We will join you soon enough in any case. It will serve us well to appear as part of their

288

party when we leave. Prying eyes will find it harder to spy the road we take. And it will be more practical in the less hospitable land we will cross.'

The man Grakk sought was tall and lean, calm and deliberate of movement and with dark eyes that seemed to probe his thoughts when his gaze locked with Brann's. The tattooed tribesman vaulted nimbly from his camel and the pair embraced like old friends. Brann assumed the reason for this was that they were indeed old friends. He quickly pulled back on his cord to halt his camel before it careered into the two men.

After a short conversation, Grakk returned to the party. 'Icham is happy for us to travel in their caravan as arranged. We will take our place slightly behind the first riders, while those following us will lead several camels each, bearing the shipment of spices and dyes that they take to the far side of the Deadlands. Highly trained as these beasts may be, those without a rider take slightly longer to respond to a command, so take care not to impede them with your own riding. The remainder of their party will bring up the rear, watchful of the need to act, as the shipment they are transporting carries considerable value and the Deadlands are unpatrolled by the soldiers of the Empire's millens.'

Brann was the only one who had remained on his camel. He had not been told he could dismount, and wondered at the attitude of the others. Nevertheless, a greater question vexed him.

He pointed at a group heading away. 'The women are leaving?'

Hakon laughed. 'Oh, you are a surprising one. Fancied your chances of entering by a side door, did you?'

Grakk ignored him. 'They do not travel.'

'They are not permitted?'

Grakk patted his knee affectionately. 'On the contrary, dear boy. It is the women who permit the men to travel. The women run their settlement. Their ruling elders are the oldest generation of women in their clan, and they have no gods, only goddesses. They even see the world as female. After all, it provides what life we have. We plant it and reap what it sows, but it grows and creates. Women, to them, are the representation of that. They can be a direct and, at times, ruthless people but the softness they have stems from and is directed towards their women. It is their thinking and it rules their lives, though not all who regard them from outwith agree or understand.'

There was sense to it. 'I understand. I like these people.'

Grakk smiled. 'Then I have a feeling, my young friend, that they will reciprocate.' He turned to their small band as a whole. 'We leave shortly. There is a pit over there if you feel the need to relieve the pressure on your bowels and bladder. It is a long day in the saddle.' He looked up at Brann, seeming to read the boy's uncertainty on how to dismount. 'At a standstill, pull on the cord. He will kneel.'

Brann was ready for the back-and-forth movement this time, and was marginally better balanced. He noted that the Deruul men close by averted their gaze, but not before he saw the amusement in their eyes.

With little fuss, the caravan left not long afterwards. With their veils drawn across their faces, Brann's party were indistinguishable from the rest in appearance, even if some were less natural than others in the saddle. They travelled through the scrubland along a track that ran straight as an arrow-shot towards the horizon, the hooves of the camels scuffing the dust on the baked surface. Before long, the gait of the beast became soporific and, with the heat of the sun, he could feel his eyelids and head begin to droop as one.

'Drink.' He jerked alert at the sound of Cannick's voice alongside him. 'Take some water. I don't feel like picking you up if you drop off and, well, drop off.'

Pulling down his veil, Brann took a long draught from one of his waterskins, feeling the liquid running down inside him.

'Sip it, lad, sip it,' the man cautioned him. 'It will last longer and benefit you more.'

He took another drink, smaller this time, but already felt slightly revived. He looked about him, but there was nothing to see. Beyond the worn track, the bare flat land was spread with the now familiar bushes, stunted, twisted and gnarled, for all the world appearing long dead but relentlessly forcing their way from the iron ground with a desire to survive that he found familiar.

As the sun approached its zenith and the air itself threatened to bake them, the caravan drew up and the Deruul erected simple shades, cloth stretched between slender poles, to provide some scant protection for travellers of two legs and four.

Hakon flung himself to the ground and pushed back his hood, waterskin in hand and a frown on his sweat-soaked face. 'The air is as hot to breathe here as out there. Where is the advantage in this?'

Grakk was sitting cross-legged and as calm and still as ever. 'The advantage is in the protection from the beating of the sun, not escape from the heat. The glare directly on you at this hour would send you to madness.'

'Actually,' Sophaya said brightly, 'this clothing is surprisingly cooling. These dark hues seemed a strange choice at first, but I am not as hot as I would have thought.'

'The Deruul have travelled these lands for generations beyond count,' Grakk said quietly. 'Even they do not know the reason for everything to work, but they know everything that works. They are renowned for dressing in these shades of dark blue, but it is not for reasons of fashion or superstition. Everything in the Deadlands has a purpose, and every purpose is concerned with survival. We may not be aware of why we feel cooler than we think we should, but it matters not why as long as we know it is so.'

'Are you mad?' Hakon was incredulous. 'Cooler? I am baking.'

Sophaya stretched out like a desert cat. '*Baking* is cooler than *baked*. And baked is a bit final. So baking is better.'

The searing force of the sun seemed to Brann anything but reduced when they resumed their journey, but if they said it was, then he had no basis to argue. The long legs of the camels ate up the distance steadily, but still the land about them was unchanged, leaving the impression that they were marching on the spot. The bumps of hills on the horizon remained no more than bumps no matter how many hours they crept towards them. And so it went for the first days. He was unsure how many, three or four; unceasing repetition played with the concept of time, but it was an experience he was at home with. Time stood still in the cells of the underground city just the same. He let his mind settle, and accepted it.

At nights they huddled around a fire fed by cakes of dried camel dung that the Deruul collected as they dropped and baked during the mid-day rest. The open sky let the heat escape like steam from a lifted pot lid, and although the ground retained some warmth, still an ironic chill set in and the fire became a welcome location as they huddled in their blankets.

Gradually, so slowly that the change was a surprise when it was noticed, the terrain changed. The bushes became sparser until they were non-existent, and the ground started to break up until it was more sand than earth. Then it was just sand.

They followed a track still, slightly firmer by comparison to the rest of the terrain, but to all but the Deruul its path was invisible. Their ability to keep to it was unfathomable, but Brann and his group by now had entrusted their survival utterly to these people, and it was accepted without question. Where the path petered out, the camels' broad feet plodded over loose and firmer sand with equal ease before the native intuition picked up the trail once more.

It was on the second day into the flatness of the sand that Brann was jolted by a cry of warning from further back. He followed the rider's pointed finger to a dark smudge on the horizon; a smudge that grew larger even as he watched. He felt his camel twitch nervously as its nostrils tested the air and, at a command from Icham, the column halted and the Deruul dismounted, Brann's party following their lead. He slipped his feet from the stirrups and dropped from the saddle to land in a crouch; he had found this easier than negotiating the lurching kneel of the beast, no matter how earnestly he had tried to adapt. As soon as his feet hit the sand, the animal folded its long legs beneath it to settle on the ground, as had done its companions already.

A slight breeze was more common than not on the sands and he had become accustomed to it making waves of his loose clothing. Now however, it was plucking more insistently at his sleeves and he could feel its strength increase slightly against the exposed area around his eyes. Sand started to sting that area also and he turned away from it as Grakk called their small group together.

'A storm of sand approaches,' he said without preamble. 'Do not panic: it is not uncommon and may not be the last we will encounter. This is routine for the Deruul, so follow their example. Look at them. I advise that you copy them.' The native men had settled down on the leeward side of their camels, curled hard against the beasts. The animals themselves had bent their long necks to shelter their heads in beside their own bodies. 'First, you may have noticed that an extra length extends from your veil after you have covered your face, so use this to wind it around once more to protect your eyes.' They needed no extra bidding and were already fixing the material in place as he continued, noting that the fabric was thin enough to allow hazy vision.

As Brann peered through it, his hand was drawn to the material across his eyes by a memory just too distant to grasp. A name came into his head.

'Konall.'

Hakon's head snapped round. 'What did you say?'

'Konall. It entered my head.'

'You remember him?'

Brann shook his head. 'Only the name. I know not its owner.'

The big boy shrugged. 'Nevertheless, I don't believe it to be a bad sign. Now, if you'll excuse me...' He ran to the cover of his camel.

With the wind picking up considerably and the sand whipping into them, Brann glanced in the direction of the storm. The darkness was in essence a huge wall of swirling sand, higher than the tallest tower of the citadel in the City Above, and it seized his eyes with a dreadful fascination. Never had he seen such power. And it was almost upon them – the speed it possessed was beyond imagination. The sight was intoxicating. Never since he had left the tunnels of the City Below had he felt so alive.

'I still live!' he yelled into its face.

Cannick dragged him down. 'You won't be saying that in a moment if you stay there, you fool.' He pushed him against his camel and scuttled to his own, his words barely audible as the wind tried to flick them away. 'Now stay there.'

The man had commanded, so Brann would obey. He pulled his knees to his chest and snuggled into the camel's warm body, feeling the steady thump of its heart against his back. The beast made a sound that seemed more welcoming than irritated, and at the least it didn't reject him.

Then the storm hit.

It was impossible to say how long it lasted before passing on its way; every minute was an hour, every breath an effort as they felt the weight of the elemental power that enveloped them, every hint of respite followed by an even stronger gust. When light once more reached them and the wind had drifted off, they lay there for a while, absorbing the over-whelming silence that had fallen over them. One by one, they staggered to their feet.

'Now you can say it,' Cannick acceded.

Brann's senses were too stunned to allow him to say anything.

A drift had built up beside the camels and, as the beasts climbed to their feet, a waterfall of sand cascaded from them. Brann stretched as high as he could reach and brushed the excess grains from his mount, drawing a grunt of contentment from the animal.

'I cannot deny I was close to soiling myself,' Hakon admitted cheerfully. 'Never have I seen a storm of its like.'

Grakk was readying his camel. 'That was a minor one. It is not unknown to have to dig a man and his camel from the sand.'

Hakon was impressed. 'And if the would-be diggers are also buried? What then?'

Grakk's voice remained even as he swung into his saddle. 'The desert makes many graves for the living.'

Hakon let the subject lie.

The greatest effect of the storm was to create a sense of gratitude for the tedium of their ride. Brann now found the plodding of the camels welcome, and appreciated the vast silence as he lay under the startlingly bright stars that night in the scant moments before sleep settled over him.

It was two, maybe three, days later when the monotony was broken once more, albeit in a less dramatic manner, though almost as unexpected. A shape in the distance ahead resolved itself into a structure, tall and slender. On closing, Brann recognised a chimney and, a short distance away, a low stone wall in a short straight line, broken almost exactly in its centre by a space for a long-disappeared gate.

The caravan headed directly through the gateway although it could just as easily have passed around the minimal length of the wall, with each Deruul rider, Brann saw, touching his forehead as he passed through. He copied the gesture: whatever it meant, it meant something to them.

They dismounted and started settling for the night, even though several hours remained before sundown. Grakk gestured for them to come to him.

Gerens was last to arrive after tethering his camel with the rest. 'There is a problem? There are several miles more we could cover today.'

'Not today,' Grakk responded. He swept his hand in an arc. 'This is the remains of the only known settlement in the expanse of the badlands. No one knows who built it, who carried the stone so far, or who managed to live here, but Deruul logic maintains that it could only have been a god. Every traveller who reaches this spot, therefore, shows respect by resting the night in this holy place. Not one passes it by.'

The fires were laid in a precise circle around the chimney, each one lit from a small blaze started in the hearth of the chimney itself: all that remained of the ancient dwelling. Eight fires, one for each point of the compass and one between each of those.

If Brann and companions expected the silence of reverence to be held throughout the duration of their stay there, they could not have erred further from the fact. The Deruul sought to fill the desert with sound into the night, sonorous chants swapping with rousing song. Herbs were cast onto the fire that enveloped them in a thick aroma, and their heads began to swirl with thumping song and swimming vision. Shapes shifted in and from the dancing shadows, until it was a fruitless struggle to determine the real from the trickery of the imagination. Brann did not like this. Comfort lay only in knowing what there was around you, what was danger and what was safety. The world around him lied and he moved away from the fire, seeking clarity in the chill of the night air and free of the treacherous fumes.

The broken stone wall appeared in front of him, the glow from the campfires shifting on its inner surface. It reached to his chest and he leant on it briefly, feeling the cooled stone refreshing against his hands. Turning, he slid down until he sat, his back against it, watching the camp and savouring the chill of the air he drew into his chest in long slow breaths. Leaving the scale of his cell and the embracing surroundings of the tunnels and caverns below the city had not been hard, though Grakk had spoken with concern to him on a few occasions about any effects he might feel at the change. Here, even more so, he could have been over-whelmed by the never-ending terrain and the greater vastness of the sky, but he had survived below ground by accepting each second as it transpired and dealing with whatever lay in front of him, and here was no different.

No, in fact, here it was different. Here he felt a freedom coursing through him, as if he was meant to be like this, even though it was all new to him. He was like a bird he had seen at the travellers' encampment, hooded and immo-bile, cruel talons gripping its handler's gauntlet until the hood was removed and the powerful wings took it circling high into the blue of the sky above.

The man Icham was standing at the edge of the light of one fire, his face lit in flickering orange as if it were itself afire, his voice deep, strong and haunting in the desert still-ness as he intoned a powerful melody. Listeners swayed in time and shadows shifted and jumped around him. Even beyond the reach of the fires, shadows cast by the moon seemed to move as well. Brann frowned. Nothing other than the chimney and the wall protruded from the desert floor to cast a shadow, and the dark from the wall extended only a few short feet while that of the chimney extended towards the far side of the camp where the camels were tethered. He shook his head and drew in a great breath of clean air, irritated that the effects of the herb-fuelled smoke still toyed with his eyes.

But the shadows still moved. And one was moving directly towards the Deruul leader, towards his unsuspecting and unprotected back. It was when the glint of the firelight betrayed a naked blade that Brann moved, rolling to gain his feet in a crouch and running, bent low and silent, his hand reaching for the dagger in his belt. He counted seven in all as he closed from behind on the nearest, then saw two further around the circle.

He was too far from the leading figure to reach him before he was able to strike at Icham, but his knife did what it could do, slicing at the back of the knee of the first man he passed, the victim spinning and dropping with a scream. As he had hoped, it turned the figure targeting Icham and alerted the Deruul leader to the presence of danger, even if he and the others would be too intoxicated by the smoke to offer anything more than flimsy resistance. The other dark figures had turned also, but Brann's momentum had taken him to another and, as he left him behind, so the man's life left him in a spray from his gaping throat. Brann ignored all but the man closest to Icham and reached him in less than a dozen strides, ducking under a wild swipe of a curved sword as the man, his eyes not yet adjusted from looking at the light of the fire, swung in desperation at any potential danger. That danger became real as Brann rose inside his swing and stabbed his knife up through his chin and into his head.

The lifeless body relinquished its sword to the grasp of Brann's left hand as it took the knife from his right, and he turned to see two more approaching side by side. They were too close to be an effective team and he sliced right to left with the edge of the blade across the shins of the one on the left so he fell into his companion in a tangle of limbs and screams. Finishing them was simple.

He shifted the sword to his right hand as the other two closed on him with more menacing caution, while the pair from further off had realised that the screams were from their own party rather than their intended victims and were also moving his way. One man advanced on Brann with a curious weapon, a wooden handle attached to a chain from which hung a heavy ball of metal; the other bore a more conventional sword and rectangular shield. He let the man swing the chain and stepped back, thrusting his sword to let the links whirl around it in a tangle until the weapon stuck fast. In that instant he stepped forward and spun to his left, using the momentum of the man's swing to pull him around and stumbling towards his partner, his hand losing its grip on his weapon. With the chain still wrapped around it, Brann stabbed the point of the blade through his neck but, as he pulled the sword free, the body twisted as it fell and the wound clung at the steel, pulling the hilt from his hand. The chain slid off its length, though, and he grabbed at the strange weapon's handle as it bounced at his feet, rolling sideways in a move that, as it had many times before, saved his life as the other man's sword flashed down into the sand. He swung the unwieldy weapon sideways, knocking the shield wide, and continued the swing in a wild and high circle to aim it backhanded at the side of the man's jaw. His opponent ducked, but not enough and the metal ball crushed the side of his head with a sickening crunch that would have brought hesitation to anyone but those who had fought in the depraved madness of the pits of the City Below. Brann dropped the weapon in favour of the more familiar sword.

The remaining two were now coming at a run, trying to get to him before he could ready himself. He could feel his arms slowing slightly and glanced at his travelling companions, but the Deruul and his friends alike were swaying in stupefied astonishment, spectating being their only contribution. Gathering his efforts, he settled the sword in his grip, and the pair came at a rush, seeking to overwhelm him, one with a short stabbing spear and a round metal shield small enough to double as a clubbing weapon, and the other with a sword and a long dagger.

Hesitation was an invitation to death. He batted the spear to the left and spun into the movement, inside the weapon's range and taking the blow of the shield, which was punched at him as he suspected, on his shoulder blade rather than his face where the man had intended. His elbow smashed into the man's face with a feeling of something, nose or teeth he did not know, giving way to it and buying him a moment to reverse the sword and drive it up under his right armpit into the body behind, more in hope of finding a crucial target than any directed skill. A grunt and then a brief gurgling gasp of desperation sounded into his ear and he whirled away to a safe distance but, for the second time in as many minutes, a sword was ripped from his grasp by a corpse. Weaponless, he lurched as the remaining man came at him, blades long and short poised to strike, and leapt aside, flying at one of the glazed-eyed Deruul. The nomad's instinct turned him away from the hurtling boy and they struck back to back, Brann rolling against him to spin to his feet. His hand had reached as he passed, though, and when he stopped it was with the Deruul's sword in his left hand. With one step forward, a thrashing backhand swing smashed past the knife's scant defence and cut almost entirely through the attacker's neck.

Leaving the blade embedded, Brann strode away, plucking the man's own sword from his lifeless fingers. There was one left, the man he had crippled, the first of the nine he had struck.

'Brann!' Cannick's voice cut through the night.

He stopped immediately and looked to the man for further instructions.

'Wait there.' The older man's voice was laboured and he staggered slightly as he walked. Brann looked around. The Deruul were passing a small glass vial between them, each man in turn holding the unstoppered top briefly under his nose. Their eyes would stream and more often than not coughs and sneezes would ensue, but the effect of clearing their herb-befuddled heads was universal. Grakk and Gerens had, like Brann, been discomfited by the smoke but, unlike Brann, had not moved completely from its clutches, but only to its periphery. Still, they had been ensnared by its effects enough to render them useless during the violence, though the reduced effect they had suffered allowed them to regain full capability moments after inhaling from the vial. Icham, too, seemed unaffected, an impressive feat if it were so, as he had been in the heart of the fumes. The three reached Brann at the same time as the still-unsteady Cannick, though, once satisfied that Brann was unhurt, Gerens returned to check on Sophaya.

Icham looked at him, narrowed eyes and slim nose giving him the look of a bird of prey. He spoke in his own tongue but paused almost as soon as he had started. Haltingly, and with concentration on every word, he said, 'Any who witnessed that, they would see there lives a demon within you. But that cannot be so. A fight on holy ground, it wakens the interest of the gods. The gods play a part in that which

302

interests them. You were favoured by the gods in our most holy of places, and you fought like no man we have seen. An angel of death is within you. Our people will hold you in regard. Those who the gods smile upon, we smile upon.'

Brann looked into his eyes. 'I still live.'

The desert traveller nodded. 'As do I. And we both have you to thank for that.' He knelt before the boy. 'I pray one day the gods will grant me the opportunity to repay in kind.'

Brann's voice was even. The matter was not complicated. 'You keep us from danger in the Deadlands. I kept danger from you. I did not want you to die.' He looked across at the remaining foe, writhing and moaning in the light of torches in the hands of a circle of Deruul, impassive and all the more menacing for it. 'Him...'

Cannick's voice was less slurred, though marginally. 'It is good that he lives for now.'

Brann's brows drew together. 'Good?'

The man nodded. 'It will be helpful to hear from him why they attacked, and on whose orders.'

Brann looked at the faces around him, including the still-kneeling Deruul leader. Each nodded. He reached out a hand to raise Icham to his feet. 'We should ask him then.'

The circle of nomads, around half of their group, parted to allow them through to the wounded man. Some reached out to touch Brann as he passed. He had no idea why they did it, but their manner was not in any way threatening towards him and he relaxed.

Still clutching the back of his leg, their captive had struggled into a sitting position. Cannick placed a boot against his chest, pushing him back down.

The broad face that looked back at them was unusual in its normality. The man could quite easily have been a baker or a farmer rather than a killer sent into the desert on a mission of murder. Normality, but for his eyes. A fanaticism glared from them, a belief that was rooted deep within. The eyes alighted on the blood-streaked and gore-spattered Brann and a macabre grin stretched his mouth.

'Your job is not yet finished, boy. Kill me now.' He sounded eager, certainly not fearful.

Brann looked at him. 'We would like to talk with you.'

A snarl now. 'You would like to kill me.'

'I would. But my friends would like to talk to you.'

The man turned his head and spat into the sand. 'They can talk. I will not.'

Brann frowned. 'That would be rude.'

Cannick leant more heavily on the man's chest. 'Well, let's just chat for now on how your leg feels.' He lifted his foot and kicked where Brann's knife had slashed. The man gasped but did not cry out. He started breathing, slow, deep and deliberate, his eyes unfocusing.

'I will not talk to you, now or ever. You may as well let the boy kill me now.'

Cannick ignored his words. 'Your leg, does it hurt?' He pressed his foot against the wound and the man stiffened, but was silent. Cannick leant close. 'If you think that is sore, just wait. There is pain waiting to be visited on every part of you. Save yourself the pain. Speak.'

The man spat in his face. 'Save yourself the time. Kill me.'

Cannick turned his head to wipe his face and Grakk caught his eye, beckoning him with his eyes. The veteran came close and Grakk spoke low, so low that Brann, even alongside, could barely hear his words. Glancing at the pair, he noticed that Gerens had returned, and was standing close behind, his intense gaze taking in the scene.

'I have seen his type before,' said Grakk. 'An obsessive about a cause, he will descend into a trance that will resist pain. This may take a while.'

Cannick grunted. 'So what do we do?'

'Persist.'

'Not the most pleasant of work.' He shrugged. 'Still, if it keeps us alive, needs must.'

The conversation was cut short by Gerens, shouldering his way through the silent Deruul and striding towards the prone man, now lying still and peaceful as he composed himself, muttering an unintelligible phrase repeatedly. Without a pause, the rangy boy pulled out his slender dagger, leant forward and stuck it into the left eye of the man on the ground. A scream ripped from the man, the action so unexpected and extreme that it had ruptured whatever wall he was building in his mind. Gerens left the knife in place for a long moment as the man's shrieks rent the air over and over, holding the hilt still so that the pinned man dare not move his head a fraction, though his back arched and his arms and legs thrashed and dragged at the ground, gouging long ruts in the hard sand. With a sharp twist, Gerens pulled the blade clear, wiped it on the man's tunic, and walked away.

Before he left the circle, he stopped beside Grakk and Cannick, staring ahead. 'He will talk now.'

Without expression, Grakk said, 'I do believe he will.'

Cannick grunted. 'It may take longer for him to stop screaming than it would have to frighten him my way.'

Gerens looked at the older man, his eyes burning as much as ever with cold fire. 'Tell him I'm going for something to eat, then will be back. He has another eye.'

Despite the horror in the screams that threatened to drown

out their words, Cannick almost smiled. 'That might do the trick.'

Gerens shrugged and continued back to the remainder of the party, sitting by the chimney. Cannick gave Grakk a long look. 'It seems we have two of them to worry about.'

The wiry tribesman shook his tattooed head. 'That one is what he is. Born or made regardless, it is his way.'

'You mean he feels nothing? He is incapable?'

Grakk frowned. 'I think not. His feelings for the girl are clear. There was that stray dog he nursed from a broken leg back at the city. And as for him,' he nodded at Brann, 'there is a loyalty there that is singular and deep, though I know not from where it stems.'

Brann looked at them. 'I don't know either.' He wasn't entirely sure what they were talking about, but it might help them to know this fact.

Cannick smiled and patted him on the shoulder. 'I'm sure you don't, lad.'

Brann looked at the captive, both hands clamped where his eye had been and his screaming lessened, though only slightly. 'He will still die? After he talks, he will die? Yes?'

Grakk looked at him curiously. 'Would you like to kill him?'

Brann's shrug spoke of his lack of concern. 'Me, you,' he pointed to a random Deruul across the circle, 'him. Whoever, it matters not.' He shrugged again. 'Dead men do not seek vengeance.'

Grakk nodded. 'In this case, you need have no worries of that.'

Satisfied, Brann left the ring of Deruul. Gerens's mention of food had reminded him that he had walked away from the smoke before he had eaten.

He found Hakon standing slightly back from the circle, his face seeming pale. 'You can eat?' he said. 'After watching that?'

Brann kept walking and the boy's long stride fell in beside him. 'Why not?'

Hakon looked down at him. 'Of course. You saw worse in the pits.'

He looked up at Hakon. 'I did worse.'

The large boy shook his head. 'I grew up among warriors. I rode out first at the age of twelve to hunt raiders. I have seen much myself, have done much. But I haven't even imagined such... such horrors. How can you think to...?' His voice tailed off.

'Thinking is a luxury, a weakness. You do or you don't. You live or you die.'

Hakon was clearly trying hard to make sense of it. 'The Brann I knew did think. The Brann I knew couldn't have stomached that.'

'I do not know the Brann you knew. But a man taught me.'

'Taught you what?'

'He taught me: I still live.'

'Is that not stating the obvious? If you can say it, it must be true.'

He stopped and looked at Hakon. The big boy stopped with him. 'That is the truth in it. While you can say it, you live. No matter what they do, who does it, you must make sure you are still able to say it. So you learn to do what you must to be able to say it. And when you say it, it is true. It is all there is.'

Hakon's voice was a whisper. 'You had nothing else. They took everything else from you.'

He was puzzled. 'If not for that, what else is there?'

Hakon's large hand clapped him on the shoulder and steered him towards the fire and the food. 'If not, then nothing. But if you have that, if you still live, then there is so much more. But that is something for others cleverer than me to teach you.' He grinned. 'I would just teach you the wrong things with the wrong people. Most of them female.' He walked towards the fire. 'To be honest, all of them female.'

Brann frowned at his back. The boy at times made little sense, but there was something that made him good to be with. That must be why he was his friend. That, and the fact that he could hit hard, which was always useful.

When he reached the fireside, Hakon was talking to the quiet boy with the black hair. He seemed to have nothing but questions in him tonight. 'That thing with the captive. What you did does not bother you?'

Gerens looked at him. 'Did it look like it did?'

'But how...? Why can you...?'

'How can I do such a thing? It needed to be done.'

'Maybe. And I could cut a man in two in battle, but I could not do what you did.'

The cold fire in Gerens's eyes seemed to burn with intensity even greater than usual. 'Hakon, you are my friend and you know well how little I like talking of myself. But as we have been through much, I will tell you this. I was young when my father... when I was left to help my mother raise our family. Killing livestock for the table is not a woman's job, it was my job. It is not easy, often they look you in the eye, often they seem to know what is coming. But if you stick a knife in something living often enough, it becomes just sticking a knife in something, nothing more. So you do what needs to be done. As with tonight.'

Hakon wasn't convinced. 'So killing a pig prepares you for sticking a knife in a man's eye?'

Gerens shrugged. 'If it works...'

The big boy shook his head. He looked in Sophaya's direction. 'You are fine with this?'

She shrugged. 'You would not believe what you would have seen had you grown up with me. Where you come from, the bad people you fight are the ones who threaten your town. Where I come from, the bad people you fight live beside you. Maybe I couldn't do it myself, maybe I could, but I have seen worse.'

'Each to their own, I guess.' Hakon looked around them, and his face broke into a smile. 'You are all bonkers. But I am glad you are on my side.'

Marlo laughed, the effect of the fumes not quite away from his head, and Sophaya raised herself on an elbow to look directly at Hakon with an eyebrow arched. 'All of us, dear Hakon?'

The smile spread across the big honest face and into a grin. 'You most of all. On both counts.'

They realised the captive's screams had stopped, and a group of Deruul were carrying a limp form beyond the perimeter wall of what had once been a garden. They left by the gate.

'The gods knew what they were.' The others looked at him and Brann nodded at the group at work. 'The men who came, they did not use the gate. It is a good thing to show respect.'

Grakk and Cannick sat beside them. Gerens looked at them, and Grakk said, 'He talked.'

Cannick stretched. 'In actual fact, we could hardly get a word in after we suggested that Gerens had nearly finished his meal. They had followed us for days, waiting for this place and the night of the smoke, as they had been told to do. By whom, he did not know, but I think we can all guess.'

Marlo frowned. 'Why would Taraloku-Bana want a Deruul leader dead?'

'He didn't. They had another target.' He looked at Brann. 'You do seem to drive a great determination in this man, youngster. But if bandits, or deserters, or whatever they appeared to be, if they attacked a Deruul caravan for their goods and a foreign boy happened to die in the process, who would ask why that boy had been targeted?' He looked at Grakk. 'So what now?'

'Now,' Grakk said, 'those men will disappear. Stripped, they will be a feast for the animals of the desert. What will burn, will burn, and what will not will be taken if it is serviceable, or left in some remote place if it is not. And as for us, we continue on our path.'

Hakon said, 'We continue as normal? Despite this?'

Grakk nodded. 'You would prefer to wait here? Or turn back on our own? Yes, we continue as before, although I agree that we should increase our vigilance. The importance of reaching our destination is as great as ever, if not greater, given the determination of our enemies to rid us of our young charge. And whoever sent these men will wait in vain for news, as our young friend here has ensured that there is no one to bear it. More immediately, I suggest you sleep what sleep you can in the hours of this night that remain, for we leave at dawn. But first...' He nodded at Cannick, who tossed a scabbarded sword and a long knife to Brann.

They felt good in his hands, and he eased the sword clear enough of its scabbard to see that its blade was clean and its edge sharp. But he was confused. 'For me? To keep?'

Cannick nodded with a smile and Grakk said, 'Indeed. You earned it tonight. Not from the way you fought, which is an ability we already knew you had, but by the way you stopped, which we did not know you would do. And it would be ungrateful of us were we to deny you the arms to defend yourself especially as, thanks to you, our young friend, we have the liberty to sleep tonight with breath in our chests.'

Brann slid the sword back into its scabbard and stared at the fire that was starting to burn beyond the boundaries of the ancient settlement in the emptiness of the desert night. His voice was flat, cold. 'They had to die.'

Hakon nodded his shaggy head. 'That is true. They attacked as cowards, against helpless men.' He grinned. 'Or so they thought.'

Cannick grunted. 'A decent strategy against a more numerous foe.'

Brann's gaze turned to him. This man thought with sense. 'That is true. They looked to gain an advantage.'

Hakon's brows raised. 'You agree with their tactics, but still you say they had to die?'

'Of course.' Brann stared again as the Deruul started to return from their work to tidy the mess he had left, silent and impassive as their torches picked out their progress from the darkness.

'They did not enter by the gate. They should have shown respect.'

Chapter 7

He had ordered his chair moved to the balcony. Once the afternoon sun had moved out of sight, the combination of shade and breeze made for a soothing effect. It helped him to think.

The view was spectacular, but he had to remind himself of that. When your eyes had opened to it each morning for the number of years that his had, it was just the view. But here, on the balcony, with only the balustrade between him and the horizon, it was the vastness that drew him. The endless sweep of the sky and the unbroken flatness of the Deadlands, could combine to throw a sense of overwhelming size that let him drift from distractions. Even the scattered peaks that sat where land met sky in a suffusion that hid the point where one became the other were no larger than his thumbnail.

His eyes saw far, but when he closed them he saw farther. His mind envisioned a small party, inching their way across the vastness, closing on the other extreme.

'You think they still press on?'

He was so accustomed to her sharing his thoughts – and appearing unannounced at his side – that he no longer was even mildly startled.

'*I do. Those sent after should have returned. Not even a single one has yet arrived to speak of defeat, let alone all of them crowing in triumph. Even were they all to be dead, had the boy been killed then what was left of his own party would have returned with the next caravan, for their quest would have had no purpose.*'

'*You know for certain the hunters have not returned to he who sent them?*'

'*Of course. It is he who supplies a helpful share of my information, though he knows it not.*'

'*And you know that he who sent those who followed knew where to send them?*'

'*Of course. It was I who alerted him, though he knows it not.*'

She was unhappy. '*You play a dangerous game.*'

'*All my life.*'

'*It is more than your life at stake in this game.*'

He stood and shuffled the few steps to the balustrade, resting his hands on the wide stone sill. '*You think me unaware of that, crone? If he cannot survive the tests, he will not be of use.*'

'*Even a stacked deck can lose if enough hands are dealt. Do not let your stubbornness kill what might be our only chance.*'

His fingers pressed against the stone and his voice was a snarl. '*You dare instruct me, woman?*' *But she was right. He sighed.* '*This hand, as you would say, lies on the table. But I do not intend to deal again until we see the faces of the cards before us.*'

'*You have played this game all your life?*'
'*In the halls of power, is there any other game?*'
'*And you always win?*'
'*I still live, do I not?*'

* * * *

For days without end the camels strode on with a capacity for relentless movement that would have inspired wonder had not the stupor of repetition without any glimmer of interest from elsewhere reduced it to commonplace routine.

Brann found he had grown accustomed to the heat. He did not welcome it but, like the movement of the camel beneath him, it became *just there*, nothing more. He sank into a trance of thoughtlessness, much like a waking sleep, while they travelled but, at the same time, he seemed to sense when they were due to stop at mid-day or in the evening. Routine must do that. In the City Below, he had started feeding a rat that had started sniffing around his cell. It did not take long for the animal to start appearing shortly before the time when his main food of the day was due to be brought to him. Day after day, it would appear with precise punctuality until it snapped its teeth at his hand as he offered it a scrap, and he dashed it against the wall.

Without warning the hills on the horizon started to grow in his vision. He was unaware of when the change had begun, but as he squinted his eyes, he became sure: they were definitely bigger, more defined. As the day wore on, he was able to see more. The terrain rose from the desert gradually to differing heights, but further back the view was speckled with taller, steep peaks. The camels' steps, too, began to reveal a change as the sand had a firmer feel, as if it sat on something more solid. He considered the way his senses had adapted to feel through the tread of the animal beneath him. It was beneficial to know your abilities and capabilities, to have an awareness of yourself. Sometimes it was what kept you alive. Sometimes it already had.

It was another day and half of one more, though, before the ground rose beneath them and took them to the start of what seemed a new world, startling minds that had become accustomed to endless unvarying sand. And it was a change that was as abrupt as it was different. Black rock made jagged by tiny edges and points that seemed more numerous than the grains of sand they had passed across, sloped up before them at a shallow angle until it was the height of the great outer wall of the city they had left. Marlo reined up beside Brann. 'I have heard of this place. The Deadlands are known as such for nothing lives there. These lands before us, though, are a different prospect. Not only does nothing live, but the land itself seeks to kill you. Rocks that cut, blasts of steam that melt the skin, smoke that chokes, all is danger there. There is no benefit to entering the Blacklands, and many reasons not to.'

'But if the Deruul's route takes us through there...?'

Marlo smiled. 'It will not. It is from the stories of the Deruul that we learn of this place. They will not enter it by one pace – I forget their name for it, but they speak of the land itself holding an evil within it.'

Brann looked at the dark terrain with increased interest. At random points along its front, ravines great and small were gouged from the rock, some reaching as deep as the desert floor, as if an axe-wielding god had hacked at it in a haphazard frenzy. One such entrance to its mysterious interior lay before them, its sandy floor running straight and flat for the length of two good bowshots before it angled out of sight.

But they did not take up its invitation to enter. Instead, Grakk was in deep discussion with Icham and a small group of the older Deruul while the rest dismounted, easing stiff limbs and wetting dry mouths. There was much pointing, studying of the sun and drawing with fingers in the sand before the Deruul leader shouted a brief command to his men and Grakk approached his own party.

'We camp here for the night, and leave at dawn,' he said simply.

Sophaya tugged her camel into a crouch to better reach her pack hanging by the saddle. 'So do we near our destination, dear Grakk?'

'The initial part of it.'Hakon frowned. 'The initial part? Surely we either get to our destination or we are not there yet.'

'For some destinations, you must pass a certain point to reach them. On this journey, there is one such point, and we are close to that.'

The big boy nodded, thinking. 'And when we pass this point, we are close to where Brann can be helped?' He received a nod. 'And Brann will be helped there?'

'If he can be helped anywhere, he can be helped there.'

'And we haven't forgotten Einarr and Konall?'

Grakk moved his camel close and clapped Hakon on one broad shoulder. 'You are a good boy. No, we remember them, but we must deal with one obstacle at a time. And we need,' he glanced over at Brann, 'this young mind and his knowledge of the palace and its inhabitants to help our other two friends within.'

He made to move on, but Hakon hadn't finished. 'And

Loku? We have unfinished business with him. More even than we had when we sailed into this shit-hole.' He shot a look at Marlo and Sophaya. 'No offence.'

Marlo grinned and Sophaya shrugged, unconcerned.

Grakk's look darkened. 'I fear our original objective in obtaining the Empire's aid against Loku will not now be possible. However, that does not mean we do not now have new objectives as far as he is concerned.'

Hakon's brows knitted. 'And that means?'

'The threat his actions pose must still be addressed in some fashion. Should we get the chance, we will deal with him.'

Hakon smiled. 'That is all I need to know.'

They fell into the familiar routine of camp, caring for their camels then settling themselves. While they had become accustomed to the searing heat of the desert, and despite the inactivity of sitting on top of a beast of burden all day, still their energy was sapped by the sun and, as on every other night of their journey, they found sleep easily, little time seeming to pass before they were back in the saddle once more as the sky was painted in a stunning array of crimson and pink by the dawn.

They rode with the front of the rocky rise to their left, seeking what Brann could only guess was a certain passage into its depths. The line of the rock cut in and out on itself like a coastline onto a sea of sand, complete with promontories, bays, inlets and even small islands. All morning they continued and, as the sun approached its zenith, they began to exchange glances, the normal time for a halt having passed with their progress unchecked. Grakk now rode alongside Icham, with a wizened Deruul of indeterminate but advanced age on the party leader's other side. The trio rode in silence but their eyes were set, sweeping the rock formations constantly, seeking only they knew what.

In the same moment, all three seemed to find it. Still they said nothing but they straightened in the saddle and the pace of their camels picked up noticeably. The rest of the column kept pace with them, and an air of expectation spread through their number.

They rounded a headland and Brann saw why. Successive riders stopped in wonder at the sight until the entire caravan spread in a single wide line.

The jagged rock sank back on itself at this point, forming what would have been a harbour to rival that of Sagia itself. Where mighty ships would sail on open water between sheltering cliffs, however, here the space was filled with something altogether different – and unexpected.

Buildings. A city. A ruin of a city. A ruin of a once-great city.

As much life filled this place as filled the desert, the great wall that had stretched from one mighty promontory to the other now containing more gaps than barrier. Midway along its length stood the vertical remnants of a massive arched gateway, the missing sections having collapsed under the weight of time to lie in rubble that blocked passage to the height of a ship's mast.

Brann frowned at the comparison in his head. What did he know of ships and harbours? Still this was an astonishing sight, whatever he might or might not recall. While the gateway was blocked by its own ruin, there was in reality no block to entering the city; even the most casual of wanderers could have picked from any one of a score of openings where once had stood the most daunting of walls, some open to the level of the desert where the travellers stood agog, scattered blocks littering the space before them, others with broken stone forming ramps or steps. More pertinent to them at the moment was the admission granted by the gaps to their amazed eyes: glimpses of the remains of what had once been a city to rival Sagia itself in magnificence if not in size. The wall itself and the buildings beyond were formed from blocks more massive than the imagination could picture being moved the length of themselves, far less across a desert. The stone was of a colour similar to that of the sand before it and slightly darker in hue, giving a sharp contrast against the dark rock behind it, and a beauty lay in the simple, clean, unadorned lines of the constructions. As they started to move closer Brann noticed a remarkable smoothness to the facing and, even more astoundingly, an accuracy of cutting that saw the blocks fit so precisely that no mortar could have made them more secure. Where some force unknown had caused the city wall to collapse, it appeared to have had little or no effect on the buildings beyond, their single-storey design and the rising ground they were built upon allowing the city to be seen as it extended back to a cliff of the enclosing black rock. This was a city built once, with no capability for expansion. Once fully populated, the only hope for any other inhabitants of the region would have been to build elsewhere, were that even to prove possible.

It had the organised look, too, of a settlement that had been formed as a single enterprise rather than the sprawl of one that had evolved. While the view afforded to them was only that of an assortment of buildings, Brann had the clear impression that, were he to shred his skin scaling the jagged rock of the bluffs to gain a perspective from above, he would find an order in the layout that spoke of precise planning. That thought appealed to him.

Grakk halted them before the nearest opening that offered flat passage through the wall and wheeled his camel to face the party.

'Behold,' he called. 'Known now as the City of Ghosts, it is rightly called ul-Detina. Fear not the spirits, for the only ghosts in this place are in the imagination of those ignorant of the truth. And the truth is in the memories that have been forgotten by all but a few. There are empty buildings within this place and history within them, but nothing to make you wary other than the instability of the great outer wall.'

He walked his mount to Icham and the pair clasped forearms as a few low words passed between them. This was apparently as close as the Deruul caravan would pass to the ancient city as, without further comment, they turned their camels and plodded towards the next rocky headland with curious glances into the empty city, though not before their leader had nodded deeply at Brann, his eyes locking with those of the boy. People had been kind to him below ground, feeding him, talking to him, tending his wounds, but since he had been led into the sunlight by Grakk, he had found much that was pleasing in all he had met. But for those who had stolen into their camp, of course.

But the Deruul were now on a separate path, and Brann's party turned their backs to them and entered the city.

Stillness overwhelmed them. The sand was now merely a scant covering on thick flagstones fitted as precisely as the blocks of the buildings. Brann had a sense, though he knew not from where, that it had been centuries since anyone had lived in this place, but brushing away the sand would be all it would take to leave it looking as if its construction had been completed the day before.

The cushioned feet of the camels made almost no sound other than the occasional scuff as they paced between the buildings on a narrow road, where windows and doors felt like eyes watching them pass. The silence was such that, when Cannick sneezed from dusty sand kicked up by the beast in front of him, Hakon jerked so much at the sound bouncing against the close walls that he almost fell from his saddle, causing Sophaya to laugh so hard that she also nearly lost her seating, while even Gerens smiled.

Brann's attention was drawn to the side. It seemed that there had been some inhabitation in the more recent past, the remains of a fire sitting in a small alley between what looked to have been two houses. Bones scattered around it suggested a meal, though the light covering of sand spoke of the time since even the local wildlife had picked them clean after the visitors had left.

He pointed. 'We have not been the only guests here.'

Grakk turned slightly in his saddle. 'Indeed, young Brann. As with every ancient and abandoned place, rumours of treasure draw those who cannot resist that prospect, though even a cursory glance will tell you that there is not even a single item of furniture to scavenge. Only stone remains in this place. Stories also persist about a portal to a fabled hidden city, attracting adventurers of all motives, but none have ever discovered the truth of them. You, however, should prepare to be privileged.'

This last drew the attention of all, but Grakk merely faced the front once more and let his camel take him on its plodding way. They entered a wide boulevard, turning left towards the back of the city. The broad street ran directly to the cliff at the rear, its pale straightness distinct against the towering black backdrop and drawing the eye to the distant end where a building, much larger than the rest before it, sat flush against the base of the cliff. It had the air of a temple and, as the camels drew them inexorably closer, that impression grew ever stronger.

The building was as tall as it was broad, with twenty square-cut columns, each the width of two men lying head to toe, rising the height of at least six of the single-storey buildings that formed the rest of the city and supporting a massive stone roof that, incredibly, appeared to be formed of a single slab to make a portico fit for a giant's giant. The building itself was entered by a single great squared doorway that soared almost to the height of the huge pillars before it. They dismounted and followed Grakk to the entrance, the weight of the slab above them so palpable that it was impossible not to hunch their heads into their shoulders as they passed beneath it.

The interior was a wonder still greater. A multitude of small windows were cut into the walls and ceiling to allow just enough light to form a soft glow that suffused the entire area that extended the full width and height of the structure. But it was to the back of it that their eyes were drawn, where a row of pillars, similar in style to those outside, stretched across an opening twice the height of a man and running from close to the left wall to the same difference from the right. Without a word, Grakk strode towards it, and without a word, they followed. What lay beyond, they could not guess, for whatever it was had been hacked out of the very rock of the cliff itself. Was it tunnels? Was it private chambers? Was it vaults where treasure had once been stored?

What lay beyond was so much more. They stepped into a cavern that was like a hall of the gods, twice again the width and depth of what they now realised must have been a hall of welcome, an antechamber to this wonder. The height, though: it was the height that stopped the breath in their chests, that widened their eyes, that made their heads spin so suddenly that, as one, they staggered and clung to their neighbour for support. The cliff face was not quite vertical but sloped back at the slightest of angles, just enough to hide from outside the apertures cut into its face, openings high, high above that took the sunlight and pointed it in shafts so well defined that they seemed they would be solid to the touch, great beams of light that angled to the back of the vast chamber to pick out the reason why this gargantuan hall had been hollowed from the rock.

The beams drew their eyes to figures, eight in number, carved from the blackness of the very rock of the hill they were within. Eight figures, seated on mighty thrones, hands placed on knees, faces impassive to the cares of men, features fine in stone smoothed to a sheen by skills lost in time where all else was coarse and jagged. Eight figures, at one with the cliff face and each, though seated, taller than the great keep in Sagia. Eight gods.

The sheer scale shocked through them, awe draining their strength from them and sending them to their knees, not in reverence but in crushing wonder. Only Grakk still stood, until he sank to kneel on a single leg, head bowed and lifting the four fingers of each hand to meet in the centre of his forehead, a picture of deepest respect.

'The gods of the ancient ones,' he said quietly, his voice nonetheless carrying through the vast chamber, 'their names lost before memories began but their power everlasting.'

Brann stood and moved slowly towards the figures. It was a long walk, but it felt impossible to rush in such a place. He reached a foot, itself the size of a two-storey house. His hand was drawn to it and, once there, was held in fascination by stone more smooth than he could have imagined possible for man to achieve. Without turning, he addressed Grakk. 'This is our destination?' It was a question that contained no specific desire for further travel. Even were they to be trapped in such a city, a man could die with peace in his soul to have witnessed such magnificence.

But Grakk shook his head. 'This is our passage to our destination. There is a place of fables, fables discovered only by a few, but sought relentlessly by those who know. A place reputed to be a cradle of great knowledge, knowledge with more power for good or evil than whole armies. This place contains a portal to that place.'

Marlo had regained his feet and his voice. 'There is a doorway in this hall to a mythical land?'

'A city, not a land. And when I say *this place* I speak of this city. A gateway exists, but not in this hall, though you would not be the first to make that assumption.' He pointed beyond Brann, and they saw the incongruous marks on the rear wall between the figures, where men had failed to make any more than the merest impression on the surface. 'The tools of the world we know make little more than a scratch on this rock, yet still there are those determined that they only have to find the right spot to break through. Their resolve is admirable, but their efforts are doomed to failure.'

'Still,' Cannick said softly, 'it makes you wonder at the ability not only to craft these gods, but to hollow a cavity of this size in the first place. That such people could cease to exist does beg the question as to who could destroy them.'

'That which is more powerful than any creature,' said Grakk, his voice neutral. 'The world that grants us life can also snuff it at a whim. The beings that move on the surface, on two legs or four or many more, by wing or by fin, are mere irritants to the life that grows without restraint, to be used or ignored, inconsequential to the forces within this world. No matter the power we think we have, compared with the relentless force Nature can command at a whim, it is as a grain of sand to a mountain.'

Hakon had gathered his accustomed lack of gravity, though Brann noticed that he avoided looking at the massive figures. 'So the question is, where can we find this gateway?'

Grakk started walking back the way they had come. 'Not in here, though it would have been a sin greater than most were you to pass this temple and not witness what lay within. Come with me.'

Brann nodded to himself at the truth of the words and trusted this man who spoke them more than ever. There was great power to be felt in such a place, and he found it difficult to leave. But leave he must, for the man Grakk had told them to.

The sunlight of late morning struck them and they made to follow Grakk's back to the camels. A shout from Gerens halted them, and they followed his pointing finger. The steps from the portico of the temple entrance afforded a view down the main avenue directly towards the great gate of the city, but it was what could be seen beyond that caught their breath.

Dust was billowing up, but it was too localised to be a sandstorm. Cannick's voice was a growl. 'Riders. And coming at speed.'

'Could it be the Deruul returned?' Marlo's tone held more hope than suggestion.

Grakk shaded his eyes with one hand. 'Too many. And

straight from the desert, not from the direction the caravan took.'

Brann shrugged. 'Too many to fight? We are seven and we can choose where we attack.'

Sophaya was already moving to the nearest building. 'Let us see what a higher point will reveal.' With four bounds, she was on the roof, hands and feet having found purchase where even the eyes of her companions could not.

Grakk pulled something from his pack, a wooden tube that extended as he pulled on it. 'Here.' He tossed it to her and her sure hands grasped it from the air. He mimed holding it lengthways from one eye, and she copied him, recoiling in surprise.

'What is this magic? It makes them close, but they still are distant in reality. Or does it actually bring them near?'

Grakk smiled. 'They are where they are. It is your sight that is brought close to them. Now count them, if you would.'

The girl grinned and raised the tube to her eye once more. Her grin faded. 'Two score at least. Maybe ten more.' She dropped the tube into Grakk's waiting hands and stepped off the roof, landing in a crouch with as little effort as if she had jumped from a table. 'Headed straight for a gap near the centre of the wall and, yes, they are indeed in a hurry.'

Cannick spat into the dust at his feet. 'I think we can assume they are not here for treasure hunting or worship.'

Brann's hand was on his sword. 'About seven for each of us.'

Hakon cheered up at that. 'Actually, when you put it that way...'

Marlo looked shocked, but Cannick ignored them and

326

looked at Grakk. 'I remember you mentioning a gateway from here? It might be useful, as any other way seems to take us directly towards these new guests.'

Brann glanced at Grakk. 'We do not fight?' It was not a question bearing disappointment, for he felt no eagerness at the prospect. Whether the bald man wanted him to fight or walk through this portal, he would do what was asked. It mattered not.

Grakk's smile was soft. 'I hope to avoid the need for combat, young Brann. Not all of us may survive and I would keep our little band alive if I can.'

'So,' promoted Cannick, 'the gateway?'

'It is close.'

Marlo frowned. 'You do not look as happy as that thought should have made you look.'

The tribesman squinted at the sky, the sun almost at its zenith. 'It can only be opened at mid-day.'

Cannick stared at him. 'Tell me this is your attempt at humour.'

Grakk shook his head. 'Come.'

He led his camel across the front of the temple portico, the animal complaining at his brisk pace. A short way down the road that curved left with the face of the cliff, taking the temple out of sight, a long building sat, a wide opening cut at its front where once doors had hung. It also backed onto the cliff, but as Grakk led them inside they saw that in this case the interior ended where the rock face started.

'The priests' mounts were stabled here,' Grakk said simply. 'Camels or horses, we know not, nor does it matter to us now.'

Marlo peered around the interior, a plain simple place, and as bare of contents as every other building they had seen. Light streamed in from high windows and, in accidental mimicry of the temple's great hall, a crack where the front wall met the roof caused the sunlight to send a slender shaft to strike the back wall. 'We leave the camels here while we seek the portal?'

'We take the camels through the portal,' Grakk said, letting his reins drop and fishing in his pack. He pulled forth a crystal the size of his fist and, oblivious to the admiring sounds that came from Sophaya, he moved to the back wall. 'The gateway is here.'

He placed the fingertips of one hand where the beam of light struck the wall. 'The aperture allowing this light entry is no error of construction or defect from time or mishap. The beam of light is wholly deliberate, and at precisely mid-day it will land on an indentation...' he traced his fingers slightly to the side, '... here.' Turning his hand palm-upwards, he slipped his fingers into the slight dent in the rock and slid them up into what must have been an unseen opening.

'So,' Sophaya ventured with a thief's interest, 'there is a latch in the opening that the light would have directed us to?'

Grakk smiled. 'A latch of sorts. And indication of the location of the aperture is only the first purpose of the light. The second, well, it will become apparent should our visitors arrive late enough to allow it.' He looked at the girl. 'From your observation, do we have time for the light to travel to the spot?'

Her face was dark. 'Not a chance. Not if they come straight up the main avenue to the temple, and their approach appears to be fast and direct enough to suggest they will.'

Marlo slapped a wall in anger. 'Then we are doomed. After all this distance, doomed by a matter of moments.'

'Then we must create time,' said Brann. All eyes turned to him. He frowned, for it seemed obvious. Nevertheless, it seemed he must explain. 'We cannot wait and do nothing, as they will then force us to fight them and he,' he pointed at Grakk, 'has forbidden us to fight them.'

'Not exactly Grakk's words, but carry on,' Cannick said.

'If we cannot do nothing, then we must act. And in acting, we must keep them from here for the time required.'

Grakk was curious. 'And you have a suggestion how we should act?'

It seemed a strange question. 'Of course.'

Hakon beamed and slapped him on the back. 'You see, it *is* good to think.'

'Not when you should be acting. Bring a camel into the temple. I believe we should hurry.'

Leaving Marlo to watch the remaining camels, Cannick led one at a run as they retraced their steps to the holy building. A glance as they ascended to the portico revealed the riders almost at the city wall.

'All the way inside,' Brann said. 'To the big chamber. And then scare the animal.' He looked at Hakon. 'Probably you would be best at that.'

The big Northern boy looked at Grakk. 'Do you think he is feeling all right?'

The tribesman looked back calmly. 'Do you have an idea of your own to offer us?'

Hakon shrugged and ran the camel into the temple, followed by the others. Brann lingered briefly, staring with narrowed eyes at the dust cloud that was almost at the city wall, while a selection of strange human and animal noises emanated from within. He hurried inside to find them in the great chamber, the faces of ancient gods looking down

329

on the strange group halfway across the floor. Hakon must have performed his task well, for the camel was agitated, stepping and pulling nervously and with more than one pile of steaming droppings lying close by.

'Now look what's happened,' Hakon complained. 'We have no fortune but bad fortune already, and now you have had me make the camel desecrate this holiest of places, right before the gods themselves.'

Brann was unconcerned. 'If this is all it takes to anger the gods, they would lay waste to the world every minute of every day.'

Cannick punched Hakon on the arm. 'Shut up and listen to the boy. Whatever he is thinking, if we don't do it quickly you'll be able to ask the gods their opinion when you meet them personally.'

Brann was already moving, scooping up piles of dung and running towards the rear of the chamber, dropping it haphazardly as he moved. He returned for another armful and moved quickly to the back wall, peering at the dark surface until he found the marks where past fortune hunters had attacked the surface. He scattered the dung in front of it and ran back to the group.

There was a slight smile on Grakk's face, as if he suspected Brann's thinking. He started jogging back out of the temple as he talked. 'The camel should go back to wait with the others, as should all but you, you and you.' He had pointed at Sophaya and Hakon. 'You have bows, I remember. You should fetch them. And the smiling boy who was left with the camels: he has a bow. Bring him. The others should wait at the portal.' He looked at Gerens. 'You should wait with me.'

The dark eyes settled on his. 'Fine by me, Chief.'

Cannick grinned at Grakk. 'He's still in there, somewhere.'

Brann frowned and looked back into the building. 'Who is there?'

Grakk rested a hand on his shoulder. '*You* are in *you*.'

Brann dismissed the thought. It was not the occasion to wonder on what nonsense they talked. He stood on the steps of the portico, staring down the long avenue. This was what he understood: judging distances to danger, assessing threats and weaknesses and reacting to each, all in the moment. The road before him was long, very long, joining the very front of the city with the back. So long that the intruders, just now entering the opposite end, were still evident only from the dust they kicked up and not as individual figures. It would be many long minutes before they reached the temple; Brann and his friends had to hope they could make the minutes long enough.

He descended the steps as the trio returned and skidded to a halt, bows in hand. He nodded at Sophaya and Gerens. 'You two need to come with me. You two others, I need here. At that corner.' He pointed at the spot where the area widened to lead off into the street that ran past the stables. 'When I say, step out from there and send three, maybe four arrows each at the riders, and then make for the portal.' He looked at Gerens and Sophaya. 'We should move now.'

They moved off at a run, heading several minutes down the street before he pulled them to the side.

Gerens looked hardly out of breath, while the girl was similarly fit to run still. This was good. He needed their energy as much as any skill with weapons they possessed.

The dark-haired boy eased his sword and the larger of his knives in their scabbards. 'We are to delay them however we can? Right, Chief?'

He nodded. 'First, yes. Then you run when I say, and reach the portal. Second, they must follow me. I hope not for a great distance, for their mounts have longer legs than I have.'

'Should we start from above?' Sophaya suggested. 'There may be more surprise from there.'

'We should.' In the space of a few heartbeats, they were crouched atop one of the low buildings, staring down the avenue.

'Horses.' Gerens had his intense gaze fixed on the riders galloping up the avenue. The hooves pounded like never-ending thunder on the hard street, kicking up decades or, perhaps, centuries of sand into a cloud that rose like a brown halo around the whole group. It was clear that surprise was not their tactic.

Sophaya frowned. 'Then they have extensive resources. If they crossed the desert on horseback, they must have had a large amount of supplies to sustain the animals. More likely they came on camels and bought the horses at an oasis, or that they had access to resources owned by whoever sent them. And they knew where to come.'

'He does.' Gerens didn't turn his eyes from the approaching band, but his voice was even. 'Access to wealth, I can only assume, but power is most definitely his.'

Brann looked sharply at him. He would know more of his enemy. 'You know him? Tell me.'

Gerens stood and eased his shoulders. 'That, Chief, is a story for tonight's campfire. This situation approaches fast.' He nodded at the horsemen, only minutes away from their position. 'What would you have us do?'

He was right. And the answer was fairly simple. 'We must cause confusion. If we cause them to pause for thought, we

332

cause them to pause. Time is the treasure we seek now. Every second we seize is precious.'

The boy nodded. 'You have a plan, Chief?'

'The nature of confusion is that we only know its start, not what ensues.' He turned to Sophaya. 'You will start it. Two arrows into the front riders, then move several buildings closer to the portal before they know where they have come from. Two more when they move again, then you move. You must not be seen, or they will know you are only one archer.' Without waiting for a reply he started moving towards the next building, closer to their prey. 'We will hurt them from behind or the side. Boy-with-the-angry-hair, take note, do not engage any more than you have to. You need not kill, only hurt. I have fought many at once before. Should you be drawn too much to one, another will undoubtedly kill you.'

Gerens jumped to the next roof by his side. 'Makes sense, Chief. You can rely on me.'

Brann looked at him. 'I feel I can. When we have hit them twice, use the street behind these houses to get her to the portal as fast as you can. Wait for nothing, for it will gain you or anyone else nothing to tarry once your job is done.' He glanced about as the rumble of the horses' passage surrounded them. 'They are almost upon us. We should act separately. It will cause more confusion.'

Without bothering with a response, Gerens jumped off the back of the building and slipped into it from the rear. Brann ran its length – it was three dwellings in a single structure – and dropped into a narrow alley. It was unlikely that any of the riders would look down every opening as they passed when they were obviously so intent on their destination, but it did no harm to maximise his chances and he flattened against the far wall. The first of the group battered past him and he drew his sword and knife, letting them hang loosely in his grasp.

Almost immediately the screams and shouts rent the air and the rhythmic rumble of the horses' hooves turned to the randomness of milling and turning. Without waiting to look, he sprinted from cover, finding himself slightly behind the back of the group. Angling across them, he ran as fast as his legs would move, slashing his sword across the backs of the nearest horse's hind legs. Through the fog of the dust cloud that caught at his throat and eyes, he glimpsed a rider dragged from his saddle beside the house that Gerens had waited inside before the wheeling horses and shouting men obscured his view. A jumping horse careered around and the rider's eyes widened as he caught sight of the boy in front of him. Brann ducked under the horse's head, slashed its flank to make it rear and, as the rider fought to keep his balance, stabbed his straight sword up under the side of his ribs. The man fell and the horse bolted to the far side of the avenue, and Brann shoved the handle of his knife into his mouth so he could grab the pommel of the saddle and let it lift him away, its bulk hiding him from the riders close enough to see through the dust. As the horse ran, he managed in three attempts to sheath his sword and, at the nearest building, one that looked like it had been some sort of a place of work with an open front, he pulled himself to the saddle and placed one foot on the leather to raise himself up and grab the lip of the flat roof, gaining enough purchase to hold on just as the horse hurtled away. Scrambling onto the rough surface, he grabbed his knife from his mouth and raced along the rooftops, jumping two alleyways by the time the leaders of the riders had restored order and forced their men to forget the attack and remember their goal. He could see the girl two buildings further up on the original side of the broad street, kneeling with one arrow already nocked.

The riders urged their horses forward again, but just as they reached their full speed once more, two more arrows thudded into them, one taking the lead rider in the chest and the other transfixing the neck of a horse, causing it to rear screaming and crash into the animal to its right, knocking that man from his mount as well. Again the group halted in whirling confusion as the riders sought to identify the source of the danger. This was good. Were they soldiers, their training would have kept them on their course as their orders had decreed. Ill-discipline was encouraging in what it said of the quality of the foe they faced. Still, the horsemen's numbers would prove decisive should it come to a straight fight.

As the horses' stamping hooves raised the dust whirling around them once more, Brann saw the wild-haired boy dart from an alleyway and slash one rider across the back, stab a horse in the throat and leave his knife in the side of another rider before flitting back through a doorway. He glanced further up to see the girl Sophaya slipping off the back of a roof and his eyes swept over the scene below, assessing it as the cries of alarm from men and beasts were split by the screams of those Gerens had attacked. Their attention drawn to those screams on the other side of the avenue, Brann moved. Knife in hand, he leapt, wrenching a man from his mount and leaving him dying on the ground. His knife was left in the man's neck as his fingers slipped from the blood-drenched hilt, and he wiped his hand on his own clothes and reached for his sword as he turned in a crouch. A rider bore down on him, thrusting at him with a short spear. There was no time to draw his weapon. Spinning away from the flashing point, he grabbed the shaft and continued his movement to haul the weapon forwards. Caught by surprise, the man toppled from his saddle with a grunt of rage and landed at his feet. The spear impaled his chest.

The dust was thickening now, and Brann hurled the spear at a dark shape and heard a satisfying scream. Almost immediately he was knocked into the dirt. A horse had careered into his shoulder and the rider now realised that the blood-spattered figure before him was not one of his companions. He shouted, whether in triumph or anger it was impossible to discern, and turned his horse to bring his sword arm to bear. The curved blade sliced down and Brann dived under it, finding himself falling beneath the horse's belly and rolling frantically to avoid the murderous hooves. The move did, however, bring him up on the opposite side from the weapon and surprise the rider. Brann grabbed the small round shield strapped to the man's left arm and, as he turned in the saddle to find his prey, yanked him headlong from his mount. The man was heavy and he felt the effort lance pain through his left shoulder, but the weight meant the man hit the ground hard, the sword spinning away into the dust cloud.

The momentum carried Brann down on top of his foe, both unable to draw any weapons as arms entangled and writhed for an advantage. He felt the spit from the man's grunts of exertion against his face, and his nostrils filled with the stink of a hard ride across the desert. Hatred burned from eyes scant inches from his own, and the struggle turned to a brutal, base fight for survival: one that Brann sank into with familiar ease, feeling he was back in the cherished surroundings of the pit. One way or another, it would not last long. No two men existed who could sustain such effort. Thick fingers clawed inside his mouth and dragged his cheek wide, and he bit hard, drawing a shout and trapping the fingers. The other hand closed on his throat and a rush of triumph surged through him at the mistake. Any attack in this struggle must have immediate effect. His thumb sought and found an eye and gouged it. This time there was a full scream and his mouth released the fingers as the man arched back, both hands snapping to the pain. Brann's right hand scrabbled at the man's belt, finding a knife hilt. He stabbed the blade three times, fast: thigh, waist and upwards into the side of the neck as the man flailed at each previous strike and left himself open to the next. It was over.

He hauled himself to his feet, chest heaving, having to force himself upright. A horse stood nearby in incongruous stillness, from which of his victims he did not know, did not care. Shouts from the front of the group were starting to restore some order and the dust was beginning to settle. It was time to go.

He grabbed the saddle and pulled himself up. His head could not recall ever riding a horse but he must have done so in the time before his months of memories, as his hands and heels remembered for him, kicking the animal into obedient action. It leapt forward and he swept through the group, bursting from the front of them like a rock from a sling. It took moments for the riders to realise he was an enemy, giving him a bowshot of a start. His action achieved what the leaders' shouts had not, focusing the band's attention back on their charge through the city.

The chase was on, and he was leading them towards his own companions, but the speed was no greater than they

337

had been moving at before and their destination was no different. They had, however, been delayed and Brann meant to delay them more.

Bending low, the horse's hot sweat against his cheek every time its jerking head brought its neck close, he urged it on, seeing the corner approach where the big boy and the smiling one would wait. He dared not risk a glance behind for fear it may lose precious yards, but he needed no look to know they would follow with as much effort as he led.

He was upon the corner, and as he passed he screamed above the tattoo of the pounding hooves, 'Arrows! Now!'

He directed the horse up the steps of the temple and stopped under the cover of the portico, turning now to look. The archers had served their purpose and, for a third time, confusion reigned as the larger volley suggested the horsemen had ridden into an ambush. Already, though, the effect had been gained, and a cloud of sand had been stirred into the air even quicker and thicker than before. Now was his moment and he sprinted, aching legs pounding as he followed the disappearing backs of his two comrades as they, too, swiftly made for the stables. Fortune was on his side, and the horse declined to follow him, standing with head bowed and chest heaving, more in exhaustion, he guessed, than any other reason. He grunted to himself in appreciation of his luck. The horse would give the impression he had entered the temple on foot, but only if he could make it out of sight down the side street before a single rider emerged from the maelstrom of dust when realisation dawned that no more arrows rained upon them.

Legs pounding, arms driving, sword slapping his leg, he fixed his eyes on the building corner that offered sanctuary, expecting with every pace to hear a cry of discovery. Running did not feel natural. There wasn't much cause for it underground and he guessed that before that time he had got by on determination rather than grace of movement. More than determination drove him now, though: desperation powered his legs and he closed on safety.

He was no more than ten yards away from the corner when he saw a rider emerge, his horse dancing sideways skittishly, still infected with the hysteria of the crowd. All the man had to do was look to his left and their eyes would meet, but his attention was caught by the waiting horse and he turned to shout over his right shoulder in excitement, forcing his own beast towards the temple at a run. More followed as Brann flattened himself against the wall, head back and sucking at the hot air for breath.

'I still live,' he whispered.

He remembered that he was expected elsewhere. The lane angled away from the temple, taking him quickly out of sight, and he ran with eyes scanning for a route back to the right, towards the temple. Within a dozen steps, a narrow street opened and he thanked the ancient city designers for their practical approach. The lane ran straight and he sprinted with renewed strength, bursting from its end a short distance from the front of the stables. Gerens was waiting in the doorway and he ran to grab Brann and hustle him inside.

They crowded him, slapping his back and shaking him in delight. Sophaya planted a kiss on his cheek and Hakon ruffled his hair, while Cannick stood watching, a broad grin splitting his face. Brann tolerated them but frowned. These were strange people.

'We are not safe yet,' he pointed out.

'The boy is right.' Grakk was the only one who had not

joined the celebrations, and he stood by the wall, the large crystal in hand, where the beam of light had crept across to almost fill the indentation he had found earlier.

He placed the crystal against the rock, turning it until it abruptly slid to fit precisely into the niche. So snugly did it fit that he was able to take his hand away and leave it unblocked from the light by fingers.

The light almost covered it, but nothing happened. Grakk stood impassively, staring at it as Hakon came to stand at his shoulder. 'Should we be doing something to help this portal open?'

'All we should do is wait.' The tribesman's voice was calm, but the tension of his companions was plain.

Cannick tried to be encouraging. 'And hope that camel shit does its trick and leads those bastards to the marks in the temple wall and lets them think we are already away. With some fortune they will spend time trying to work out how to open the gateway they think we went through before they start looking in other buildings.'

Gerens drew his sword and strode to look from the doorway. 'Then we should make ready to fight in case they don't.'

'It would be more helpful to ready the camels.' There was an excitement in Grakk's tone that none had heard before, and it stopped their conversation dead. Gerens sheathed his sword and all eyes turned to the crystal.

The light crept to cover the crystal and a flash of brightness drew gasps as it glowed with a brilliance that was startling. It seemed to fill the aperture and curiosity drew Brann closer, crouching to look up at it. Where Grakk had previously inserted his fingers, the crystal seemed to angle the light, the cut of it focusing the beam and turning it vertically. Just at the edge of his hearing, he thought he heard a faint click and he squinted his eyes, but was unable to see through the crystal other than to tell that it lit some sort of shaft about the width of his closed hand.

'Above, maybe twice the height of this building, there is another stone like this, but set within the rock,' Grakk said quietly. 'It turns the beam of light again to follow the channel straight into the cliff. No one knows how they cut such channels and inserted the crystal at all, let alone so precisely, nor is there any record of the means by which the light achieves what it does.'

'And just what does it achieve?' Marlo was anxious, and with good reason. Shouts could be heard back at the temple. Whatever the intruders believed had happened, it seemed unlikely they would leave without searching the surrounding area.

Grakk smiled, and walked ten strides along the wall. 'This.' He placed one hand against the rock face and pressed gently. With barely a sound, a section of the cliff opened in on itself, revealing a tunnel large enough to take a well-laden cart and lit softly by what they could only imagine were further channels cut subtly into the cliff.

They needed no further invitation. Grakk retrieved his crystal and the camels were led into the passage with alacrity. Once all had passed, Brann cast about the stables for any sign of their presence, and his eye fell on the part of the wall that Grakk had pressed. Six dimples in the stone formed a triangle – the same triangle that Marlo had drawn in the dirt at Cassian's school.

'The Balance of Six.'

Grakk smiled. 'Those who taught it to those who enlightened Cassian did not invent it. He benefited from an older wisdom. Much older.'

Cannick appeared beside them. 'Young Marlo did well by us, keeping the animals calm until he had to go shoot arrows for you. Then he soothed them on his return. He has a way with beasts, that one.' He grinned at Brann. 'Maybe that's why he likes you.' He glanced around. 'No dung here to lead them. Come on, lad, let's go.'

He took Brann by the arm and they stepped into the tunnel. He watched with interest as Grakk swung the massive rock doorway, the slab as thick as a man's outstretched arms and half as much again, as easily as if it were made from paper.

'What sorcery is this?' Hakon breathed.

'No sorcery,' Grakk smiled. 'Engineering beyond compare, my boy. The product of clever minds and precise construction.' The door whispered shut and settled into place with a soft click, the fit as seamless as the set of the stonework throughout the marvellous city. 'And so we are gone. I suspect, young Brann, with this portal, your subterfuge and the violence, we may well have contributed greatly to the myths of this being a haunted city.'

Brann stood near to the closed door, but such was its thickness that no sound could penetrate it. He would never know if the men who had chased them had ever entered the stables or not. He turned and walked away. It mattered not.

They followed the tunnel in silence but for the occasional snort of a camel. The animals' feet padded on the smooth rock with virtually no noise, and likewise those of the humans, who wore the boots of the desert travellers: hardened leather soles and uppers of a soft fabric that let through what air there was and wrapped around their feet, bound with straps for security, and slouched about their ankles.

The unusually cool temperature and gentle light joined with the silence to bring a surreal atmosphere, as if no other world existed. The quiet, in particular, Brann found comfortable. What was there to say? What was done was gone; what would be was unknown; all they could do was be ready.

The apertures admitting the light became close, directly piercing the ceiling of the tunnel a man's height again above them. They must have cleared the cliffs and either the tunnel had risen imperceptibly or the ground level had dropped. The thickness of the rock above increased again, suddenly this time, so it seemed that the surface was what varied. Still, though, step after step, the rock was as dark as ever and the tunnel ran as straight as a spear, with no branches, no junctions, no deviation. One destination alone seemed to have been in mind for the builders.

Hakon broke the silence. The nature of the builders appeared to be concerning him also.

'Dwarves.' Several quizzical glances turned his way. 'This was undoubtedly dwarven-built. It is clear.'

Cannick laughed. 'Next you'll be deciding this was a lair for dragons.'

Hakon shrugged. 'Why not?' He looked at the others defiantly. 'What? The stories have to come from somewhere, don't they?'

'Most likely from the mead you Northerners drink, eh?'

Hakon stared ahead, a glower settling over his broad face, and they walked in silence.

'I still think it was dwarves,' he rumbled. A loose piece of rock lay on the floor and he kicked it against a wall. 'And a dragon.'

The roof opened to the sky and the tunnel became a

man-made crevice, boring straight through the relentless black jagged landscape. The endless blue depth of the heavens, so familiar for so long, seemed a novelty and the heat struck them as if the air had become thick as soup. It was only a short stretch, though; before long the ground level rose again like a god's sculpture of a swelling wave and their passage bored relentlessly once more into the rock.

When the roof disappeared again, the sides dropped until they were only knee-height above the passage floor. They effectively walked along a road in a plain of spiked rock scattered, to their surprise, with flowering shrubs and trees. What held their attention, however, was directly ahead where the road arrowed at a conical mountain that rose, like a crowd of others in every direction, from a landscape that seemed itself alive, great plumes of breath bursting from the ground in myriad spots.

They stopped, unnerved at the sight. The effect of such alien terrain was overwhelming and Brann felt disorientated enough to steady himself against his camel's neck.

Grakk smiled.

'Our destination.'

The road stretched what looked a mile to the foot of the mountain, and they climbed upon their camels to finish the journey, pulling their hoods up as shade from the sun.

Marlo looked across. 'Why did we not ride them in the tunnel? It was high enough.'

Cannick frowned. 'I don't know.'

Hakon looked equally mystified. 'It just didn't feel right.'

'Yes.' Cannick mused on it. 'It didn't feel right.'

'People,' Grakk said, 'stick to the familiar, the normal. Have you ever ridden underground? Or only with space around you?'

344

Brann shrugged. 'I once rode a wolf underground. But only to cut its throat without it biting me.' He looked at them. 'It was in the pit,' he offered helpfully.

'I'd never have guessed,' Sophaya said drily.

'The camels,' Grakk said, 'are used to the expanse of the desert. They are uncomfortable underground and in these enclosed passages and only their training maintains their co-operation as it is. If we lead them, their attention is on us. Were we to be on their backs, there is less reassurance for them and more chance of injury to us should they succumb to panic.'

In that case, it was good that Grakk had enlightened her. Brann settled into his saddle, satisfied, feeling that he was at last fitting in with the strange conversations these people enjoyed.

He turned his attention to the road ahead, the mountain rising higher and drawing closer with each languid stride of the camels. The road ran straight towards its base, and Brann looked in vain for a pathway that would take them up its side. Perhaps they were yet too distant for it to be visible. After all, a path formed of the very black rock it was cut from would not stand out particularly clearly.

On their approach, however, his puzzlement grew. There was no path. The sides of the mountain rose in towering, dizzying, belittling majesty of vastness, unaltered by the hand of man. The road ran its final stretch, the length of two mighty bowshots, across a wide bridge as the ground dropped into a deep chasm, a bridge crafted as strongly as all else they had seen this side of the desert, and held by cleverly angled supports. *Cleverly angled* because their design enabled them to be slender in construction. Slender enough, he mused, to be easily shattered by defenders.

The road ended in a wide circular area, as if for carts to turn or travellers to stop for an ascent, but there was clearly no path: to the naked eye, it was nothing more than a terminus at the base of a mountain, and an inhospitable mountain at that. His thoughts drifted back to the other extreme of this pathway, and the way by which they had passed onto it. There would be balance were a doorway of rock at one end to be mirrored by one at the other. He peered at the bald man, Grakk, looking for him to fetch another crystal from his pack.

No such key was necessary. As they reached the end of the path, a section of the rock face swung inwards as silently and smoothly as they had witnessed back in the stables. The hand that had moved it and, indeed, the person attached to that hand was not revealed to them. Still, entry was preferable to scaling a peak whose surface looked as if it would tear the skin from them before they had climbed the height of themselves, so he gladly rode in among his companions. A tunnel stretched before them. Was the city on the far side of this mountain?

This time they were already upon their mounts when in the tunnel, and this time they remained upon them. The tunnel was identical to the one they had travelled already except that, after a while, there must have been too much rock between them and the sunlight even for builders of such inconceivable abilities, and torches burnt to light the way. There was another difference: a slope. They climbed as they rode, the camels pacing with steady quiet.

Movement caught Brann's eye, and he stared at Grakk. In the pits, he had become accustomed to noticing voices of the body, involuntary and often unconscious movements that betrayed a thought or an attitude. More than a few times it had saved his life, or at least enabled him to serve up death sooner than he might otherwise have done. The tribesman hid it well, but he was agitated. Whether it was positive or negative was impossible to tell, but there was definitely a tension about him. There was another feeling, too. He could not say how he knew, but know he did that they were being watched, over every inch of their progress.

The passage lasted a fraction of the distance of the last tunnel, its end heralded by natural light that grew quickly in brightness as they rode closer. Surely they had not passed through an entire mountain in that space of time? Perhaps they had angled unnoticed and cut across a side of it. But without doubt they had climbed, and the terrain around the mountain had not looked to be of varying level. Certainly not to this extent. Something strange was afoot here.

The truth was revealed as they emerged from the tunnel, the great door here lying wide in a lack of concern. And the truth stunned each of them with as much unexpected wonder as they had experienced at the feet of the great stone gods.

They were at the side of a great circular area, a valley encased in steep walls of stone, the very heart of the mountain open as though a god had sliced off the top and scooped out the insides. The floor was carpeted in life, not only trees and shrubbery, but crops of uncountable variety and livestock quietly grazing. Streams and pools caught the sun in myriad sparkles. The doorway where they stood in mute astonishment opened onto a broad platform cut from the mountain, around a quarter of the way up from the valley floor. Brann moved to the foremost edge, drawn to absorb as much of the scene as his eyes could find. After a journey of sand and rock where not a seed grew, this was a vision that would match the description of heaven in any religion.

His hungry gaze swept to the valley sides, the walls of the hitherto ubiquitous dark rock. But not all was black here. Brilliant in their contrast, buildings of pale stone had been built into the sides that started with a gentle slope but quickly angled to a much steeper incline: a city of soft curves and simple beauty that climbed towards the summit, black roads hewn from nature winding their way between stacked dwellings like ribbons draped about boxes of secret treasures. It was a place of tranquillity, of infusing peace, of content-ment. For the first time that he could remember, he felt relaxed, free from danger, in no need to seek a threat. A calm flowed through him. How could anyone ever want to leave this place?

He looked at Grakk. 'How could you leave this place?'

The man said nothing, but his eyebrows rose.

Brann pointed out over the valley wherever he saw move-ment. 'There. There. There. Everywhere.' His finger stabbed at people, some closer than others, but all, young or old, men or women, dressed simply. And all of shaven head. And all of those close enough to reveal it had pates swathed in tattoos of intricate designs. 'Your people.' He stared at the man. 'Why would you wish to leave this place?'

Grakk's expression was unwavering. 'Perhaps I did not wish it.'

'They do not know?' Every member of the group started at the voice – soft, deep and seeming to come from the mountain itself. 'You have not told them?'

A man, taller than Grakk, more portly and a score or more years further advanced in age, stepped from the rock. Two dozen more appeared around them, unarmoured but each bearing a pair of curved swords in the same manner

348

as favoured by Grakk. The bare steel caught the light as the weapons were held casually, but Brann's assessing gaze knew from the first instant that it was an ease born of innate confidence, a surety that only comes from intense training and revealing testing. Grakk's fingers stilled the boy's hand before his sword had cleared more than an inch from its scabbard, and he nodded upwards at a ring of archers, arrows nocked to short powerful bows, and every one with a clear shot at the group. Brann slid the sword back home. He had known of them already; it was his own movement he had been unaware of.

Grakk knelt, head bowed, and the others awkwardly followed suit. If he who had led them to this wondrous place deemed that action suitable, then it was suitable.

'I have not, Father.' Hakon caught Brann's eye with a grin at the discomfort in the tone of their normally imperturbable companion. 'Beyond the walls of my home, my past is my own.' He rose and the others did so with him, but his head remained bowed.

The older man's voice was still soft. 'Within this place, however, your past belongs to all of us. You did not return when you could have, Guarak-ul-Karluan. Your time has passed.'

Grakk's hand rubbed his neck where a slave's collar would sit. 'I was otherwise engaged. Our choices are not always our own to make.'

'In truth, they are seldom so. Yet now you do indeed return,' he looked around the group, 'and you bring outsiders with you.'

Grakk glanced at Brann. 'I only guided our path. We all brought one.'

The man stepped forward and his gaze fixed on Brann.

'I am pleased to meet with you, for my son deems you worthy of being brought where none is brought. I am Karluan-ul-Turat.'

'I am Brann.'

'Tell me of yourself.'

It was a strange question. What was there to tell? He shrugged. 'I still live.'

'That is indeed true, but not a surprise to learn, as my eyes had managed to determine this fact some time ago. What is interesting, however, is that you felt it worthy of mention.'

His hand rested on Brann's head with gentle strength and the boy felt the thumb brush back his fringe. The eyes looked directly into his for a long moment, and the man turned to Grakk. 'Feral. I am assuming not so by nature.'

His son shook his head. 'Far from it.'

'And that is the reason for your visit?'

Grakk nodded.

'To bring him to the Friend of the Soul?'

Another nod.

The man looked long at Brann. There was nothing to say, so he looked back and waited. The man turned back to Grakk. 'Are you certain? Pain lies down that road. It may be kinder to leave things as they are. Pain such as this can be the death of the sufferer.'

Grakk raised his head and looked his father in the eye. 'Were I not certain, I would never have dragged these people on a journey such as this, nor would I have revealed secrets such as these.'

'And are such secrets safe?'

Grakk looked around his little party, but his words were for his father. 'These are good people, with good hearts.

Once they witness the truth of this place, they will guard that truth with their lives. I am certain of this.'

'And is it worth it? The journey for all, the pain for the boy, the responsibility for your companions, the risk to our home and all it contains? All worth attempting to find a cure for one?'

Brann did wonder at this himself. The man's words did make sense. He had thought all that they did was to flee the city from those who chased them.

Grakk started to speak but was interrupted by Cannick clearing his throat. 'If you don't mind me saying, sir,' he inclined his head in respect but kept talking at the same time, 'much could rest on this. One who can see such things has foretold that much of great import may be finely balanced in the scales of the gods, and the soul that may be saved is the weight that could tilt the balance away from that which many fear.'

Grakk looked sharply at the veteran warrior, who shrugged in return. 'You were not the only one Our Lady asked to speak to before we left.'

Grakk blinked. 'I suppose she asked you to keep him safe as well?'

Cannick grinned, almost sheepishly. 'Not only he. Also the one who had the knowledge to bring us to where we had to go.'

'And yet, ironically, it was the one we were to protect who protected us.' Grakk smiled. 'How fitting. And reassuring.'

Hakon pushed Marlo out of the way to step forward. 'Just as important to me is that I liked him the way he was. It is not right, what was done to him. And not fair.' Grakk's father turned his gaze upon Hakon, and the big boy faltered. 'Well, that's what I think anyway. I miss him.'

351

The girl nodded and the cheerful boy said, 'I only knew him a short while, but I liked what I knew.'

The boy with the dark stare spoke in a low voice. 'The hurt should be undone.'

Brann's brows knitted. None of this made sense. He liked these people, but he hated when they spoke in riddles. Life had been much simpler when all he had to do was eat, sleep and fight.

'Admirable,' Karluan-ul-Turat said, his voice as soft as ever. 'But there are many who are missed, and many more who suffer under misfortune and injustice, yet we cannot risk what is held dear here for the sake of each of them. For the sake of all of them, however, we find the risk acceptable, and what I heard from your older friend here leads me to believe that the fate of countless such people may be influenced one way or another.' He faced Brann. 'And what say you?'

He looked at the man. 'I know only the life underground with others, and the journey here with them. The life above ground and all that fills it is familiar, so it seems not strange to me, but when I think of it, the only people and places I know are those I have come across since this man Grakk led me out of the darkness.'

'That is interesting, but it is not of what we speak. It is not what I asked.'

Brann stared into his eyes. 'I am saying that I don't know of what they speak, so I cannot help you as they have done. But,' he looked at the group, 'they say they are my friends and if they feel as they do about this person they knew, I too want him to be helped.'

The man smiled. 'Then that settles the matter.' He looked at Grakk. 'You shall have your wish.' He turned to the group. 'Now, as you are here we cannot turn you away: we can only either welcome you or kill you to preserve our secret.' Brann felt Grakk's hand stay his wrist again, and let his hand relax away from his sword. 'Fortunately, we have enough of a meal prepared to adequately feed you, so welcome it is.' He turned to walk down a path and beckoned over his shoulder. 'Come. Please come.'

They fell in behind him, and Brann found his head turned by the scene to marvel further as they walked. The path was a ramp that took them down to the valley floor and they walked between rows of vines where men and women alike clipped fruit and smiled at them as they passed.

Brann looked behind and saw that the armed men had melted away as silently as they had appeared. He moved alongside Grakk. 'They do not fear us? We walk among them with sword and axe and bow, they know us not, and yet they trust that we will not visit harm upon them.'

Grakk smiled. 'They know that, should those who govern this place not trust us, then we would not have set more than a pace within it and still be alive. As they trust those who trust us, then they also trust us.'

'And your father is the leader of these people?'

'No, young Brann, a council of respected elders governs this place, and while my father sits on that council, yet he is not even one of those considered senior. However, given the family connection, he requested that it be he who welcomed us.'

Brann nodded. He could understand that. If only all conversations were like this.

They were led to a simple hall just a hundred paces up the side of the slope where a trestle bowed under the weight of the food that awaited them. They fell upon it with the vigour of those who had existed on only the food they could carry for too long, and were soon abed in the rooms above, fatigue they had denied to themselves for long weeks now impossible to ignore.

Brann lifted the padded mattress from his bed and carried it outside building where he could lie and stare at the stars as he had every night that they had travelled. He liked the stars. Although he could never remember a life where he had seen them before the City Below, still from the first time he had seen them after emerging he knew them with a familiarity he could not understand. Just like he knew a horse, though nobody rode underground, and was not astounded by the sight of the sun, and walked streets and passed buildings without wondering what they were. He knew, though he knew not how. It was just the people he had to learn about with each one he met.

He thought about the people he called his friends, who called him friend. The tattooed tribesman who had led them to his home, the old warrior who spoke with straightforward sense, the protective boy with the anger in his eyes, the big boy who found life so simple, the girl with confidence in every movement and the boy with the smile that came as often as he blinked.

He liked them.

And he liked the stars. Whatever happened, good or bad, they were always there. The same stars he had seen in the desert night, he now looked upon in this place of peace, of safety, of calm, and of much more that had been alluded to at times by Grakk and now his father.

Now, if he could just find a fighting pit, it would be perfect.

The screaming had lasted for days until his throat could make no more sound.

Even then, his back had arched and his jaw had felt displaced as his body had refused to admit the futility of trying to make the noise. He had not screamed continuously, nor even the majority of the time, interspersed as it was with weeping dredged from the depths of his being and cold blank staring, lost in his own private hell. But, screaming or not, the days had merged into a daze of horror, a horror that was all the more ravaging because it came from within.

Very little of it, he could remember. His mind had lurched from one instant to the next. What fogged consciousness he had been granted was able to deal only with the torment it faced in the moment. He recalled the scent of a vapour, heady fumes that seemed to fill every part of his body, though he knew not the source of the incense; he recalled the sound of the screaming that sometimes seemed his own, sometimes seemed from afar, though he knew not what ripped it from him; he recalled the hands that had held him and the mitts that had been fastened onto him after he had tried to claw his own eyes, eyes that had been guilty of bringing horrors into his mind, though he knew not the men behind the holding; and most of all, he recalled a face and a voice, a stranger who was familiar, who was soothing as he brought pain, though he knew not the name of the man. He felt the pain in every part of his body and mind, though he knew not the reason for the torture.

He lay in the breaths between sleep and awake, gradually aware of voices around him. Voices he did not know. Unaccustomed softness beneath him. Unusual coolness around him.

Unfamiliar peace within.

He tried to open his eyes, but the effort was still too great. He listened to the voices, a pair of them, one deep and soft, the other older and more grating than the rocks of the land.

'I can do no more.'

'He is lost?'

'Not necessarily.'

'How can he return? They ripped out the man and left a beast in his place.'

'They did neither.'

'How so?'

'There is the beast in all of us. It emerges when it must, the ease and frequency of doing so governed only by the nature of the individual. It emerges to guard what we hold dear: our loved ones, our beliefs, our own survival. Else a baker could not defend his home, a gentle mother her child, yet both can fight with a ferocity they could never otherwise imagine. In this one, whatever he faced required the beast so constantly, so powerfully that the beast assumed the mantle of the body, and the man was buried so deep that even his memories were buried with him. All that the beast knows is that it must fulfil its purpose, and no limits of society or personal restraints will hinder its actions. He became the beast to survive, but such was the work of the beast to keep him alive, and such was the life he endured, that his awareness began in that world and that existence was all he knew. So man did not leave and beast did not invade him; both were always there and both will ever be.'

'He will return?'

'He did return. That was the beginning and the cause of the anguish, of the pain you witnessed.'

'He will be as he was before, though?'

'That we must wait to discover. Never quite the same.'

'The best we can hope?'

'At best? He now has both sets of memories, and the man will have found acceptance of the memories of the beast. Whether it is peaceful acceptance remains to be seen.'

'Acceptance? So the man before will be the man who speaks to us now?'

'We can hope. If he is strong. But there may be situations that will awake the other.'

'In what fashion? He will lose himself once more?'

'That cannot be said until the moment arrives.'

A third voice. 'The pain you put him through. Was it necessary?' He knew this voice.

'It was not I who brought the pain. The pain was the man returning to awareness and discovering the memories of his life as the beast.'

'Such pain can kill.' The voice was concerned. 'And leave damage in those who survive.' And ever more familiar.

'It can. Which is why the herbs use sleep to limit the exposure. Think of it like entering an icy pool with a weak heart. To jump in when vulnerable could overwhelm and kill. I eased him in and out, a little more each time, ever more accustomed.'

'I worry for him. Will he be the boy we knew? He was a good boy. Will he be anything that he was?'

He knew it! His eyes blinked open and he sat up, startling the three men in the room, the largest jumping with a shout. 'Grakk!' The delight he felt filled his voice and more.

The tribesman stood beside the narrow bed he had been lying upon. Brann threw his arms around him, pulling him tight. Grakk's father stood to one side, bemused, and a diminutive and unhealthily wiry old man with the face he remembered from his haze-filled dreams was at the foot of the cot.

When he let go, the tattooed man was smiling tentatively. 'You know where you are, young Brann? How you got here?'

He frowned. 'I could hardly cross a desert, pass through a hidden door, travel a tunnel dug apparently by dwarves and find a secret city in the heart of a mountain and not notice at least some of it.'

'And before? What of that?'

He shrugged. 'Oh, the fighting pits? Yeah, there was that.' His eyes widened in dismay. 'Oh by the gods!'

Grakk's concern was instant. His hand went reassuringly to Brann's shoulder and his voice was gentle. 'You need to rest.'

Brann shook off his hand. 'We left the Lady there. And Einarr and Konall – they will still be in the citadel, if they still live. We must go back. We must rescue them.' He pushed back the sheet, finding himself naked, and rolled from the bed, casting about for clothing. 'We must leave at once. We can plan on the way.'

The large man coughed pointedly. 'Is he the boy you knew, son?'

Grakk grinned. 'It appears so.'

Brann had found his clothes washed and folded neatly on a stool in the corner and was almost clothed. He paused, a darkness in his eyes. 'And Loku. He must die.'

Grakk looked at his father. 'Perhaps with some differences.'

Brann pulled on his boots and made for the door. He could don his tunic on the way. 'Grakk, hurry up. There is no time to waste.' A thought occurred to him and he popped his head back into the room. 'Apologies, I forget myself. Thank you.' He nodded to the large man and the old one. 'Very much.'

The large one raised his eyebrows at his son.

'Yes,' said Grakk. 'He's back.'

Emerging into the dazzling sunlight, Brann squinted and tripped over a figure sitting outside the doorway. Gerens was on his feet and catching him before he was even halfway to the ground. He looked past Brann at Grakk with a question in his eyes.

'Yes,' said Grakk again. 'He's back.'

The boy stepped back to look into Brann's eyes with his dark stare. 'I can't stop the storms from coming, Chief, but when they do come, I can stand at your side in the wind and the rain, and I will.'

Brann hugged him and, while the boy was stiff as a shield, still he did not resist or push him away. 'I know you will. I have no idea why you will or why you do, but there is no one I would rather have there.'

They sat on a terrace, the setting sun splashing great swathes of crimson across the blue canvas of the sky.

They had not left immediately, not for several days more. It appeared that the strength of Brann's body had been sapped by the healing of his mind to an extent he could not have imagined. Now rest had restored him enough to travel, and guilt had prompted them all to determine that they could not indulge themselves in the tranquillity of the city within the mountain any longer. Hard as it would be to tear themselves away, they would leave on the morrow.

Still, they had this evening and they sat as a group, content in each other's company.

Brann broke the silence. He hadn't wanted to do so, but the thought was in his mind and falling from his lips before he knew it.

'Grakk, I asked you when we arrived, and if we are to leave such a place, you must tell us how you could do so when you were born to this.'

The calm eyes stared from the bald head but they seemed to be looking over time rather than the vista before them.

'Leaving is not a problem when you know you will soon be coming back. Our people frequent the Deadlands. In particular, as adulthood beckons we are expected to roam there, partly to build skills but mainly to perpetuate the myth that our home is in the great sands. Hence our name among the other races: the Tribe of the Desert. When you know that you cannot return for much of a lifetime, though, that is when your heart breaks at the leaving.'

'So you were sent forth?' Cannick asked. 'They asked much of you.'

'With deeds to accomplish?' The excitement in Marlo's eyes betrayed his imagination.

Grakk sighed. 'I was sent away. I was ordered, not asked. And for deeds done, not planned.' He looked around them, his whole demeanour uncomfortable. 'We have shared much together. You have a right to know, and I have the trust in you to tell you, but this goes no further than we seven. It is how it must be.'

His eyes swept around his companions, and were greeted with a nod from each.

He sighed. 'It seems more than a lifetime ago, but when I look at this view I feel like it was only yesterday I was growing up in this place.'

His eyes grew distant. 'To understand what transpired, you must understand this place. To be born here is to be born into a culture like no other, one dedicated to a single purpose: preserving what is here. And what is here is that

360

building yonder.' Their eyes followed his pointing finger to a long low building a quarter of the way around the circumference of the area within the mountain. 'Our House of Treasures.' Sophaya's head jerked to attention. 'Be calm, young lady. Not your kind of treasure, but one more valuable than all the gold in the world. My people are collectors of knowledge. Within that building lies as much of the written learning of this world as a thousand years have permitted us to accumulate, original documents or copies we care not, for it is that which is within them that is of value. Much of what is contained in there is already known, and we merely ensure that it is preserved for future generations; much else is not even known to us, such is the volume of documents held here. But retained they are, for knowledge lost for all time is a tragedy beyond compare to my people. We scour the countries of the world, ever in search of more, and we preserve what we have. Our scribes are true scribes, working from boyhood to dotage in the Halls of the Quill, replacing what is fading, adding what new information is gleaned. Our greatest defence is secrecy. To the world, we are nomads, scraping a life from the desert, our eloquence a quirk of a bygone past and a trait that is as much endearing as it is disarming. This city is a myth, and not one associated with our people in any case. Even those who tell the stories of its existence know not of the true treasure it harbours.'

Cannick cleared his throat. 'If I may ask, what is the point in keeping such a store of knowledge if it is unknown to the world?'

Grakk smiled. 'It is a question debated long and often by our elders, and always they conclude the same. Great knowledge makes for great power, and great power can work for good or for evil, can be misguided or subject to errors of judgement. It might only be abused once, but such is its power that the one occasion could be the end of us all. We have not the right to unleash that possibility. So we merely retain it, nurture it, protect it. We are its custodians until those wise enough to benefit are walking this world.'

'Pardon me for asking, and don't take this as doubting you, but...' Hakon was sounding anything but convinced.

Grakk's eyebrows twitched. 'But?'

He nodded at the building. 'Are you sure that place is big enough for what you describe? You're talking about an awful lot of stuff.'

The tribesman smiled but it was Gerens who spoke. 'The city in the desert? The temple? The chambers within? Do you think maybe...?'

The big boy's face broke into a delighted grin as realisation swept across it. 'You've dug into the mountain.' He looked at Grakk. 'Well, not you, personally, of course. Your people. And long ago.'

Grakk nodded. 'And, in this case, downwards. Ten levels, it has. Room aplenty for all we have and more.'

'Impressive,' Cannick mused.

Marlo's eyes were wide as a thought struck him. 'Did you people create all of this? Was it they who dug out this entire mountain to create this valley? Or was it the people who built the City of Ghosts?'

'Neither, young Marlo, neither. No race of man could create this, only the gods and the world itself. There is fire under the ground, fire hotter than you can imagine, with a heat that can melt rock itself until it runs like water. Some say it is the furnace of the gods, others that it is just the way it is. Either way, it can shape the land and build mountains such as this, for sometimes the fire burns so hot the ground itself cannot hold it and it spews forth, piling high and cooling to form mountains. Some are wide inside such as this, and some have just the narrowest of chimneys; some spit forth still, bubbling and boiling within; others wait generations before surging forth once more; still others are like this, cooling and hardening for evermore.'

Marlo shifted uncomfortably, looking down at the valley floor. 'You are certain it is for evermore? Absolutely certain? It would seem not the safest place to hide your treasure.'

'You do not live in a land without gaining an understanding of how that land works. We have a trade where men and women are taught the secrets of this land. They study the other mountains formed from fire-rock. The very ground for miles is formed from that same rock as well, and they learn to read it all. Most is inhospitable to life but, strangely, where soil is formed, it is more fertile than any other. We learnt to live here long ago, and if it ever shows signs of turning on us, we will know.'

Cannick stood and walked forward to stare across at the House of Treasures. 'Your people place a great burden upon themselves.'

Grakk shrugged. 'From birth, it is all we know. Some are trained to write, some to be custodians of the documents. Some to farm, some to study the land, some to search afar for new knowledge. All are taught to fight, for should our secret be threatened, there should be no means of defending it that we cannot employ. Everything is to preserve the treasure we hold. We see it not as a burden, but a privilege.'

Brann spoke softly. 'Still, though, you say nothing of why you left.'

Grakk's face clouded. 'There was a boy, my age near

enough. He loved knowledge, loved order, loved everything we stood for and strived for. He would read and read, delving in his own moments in the bowels of the House of Treasures. He was destined to be a great custodian. But those times became not enough for him. He started taking documents from that place, into his family's house to read through the night. Always, he would replace them, perfectly preserved, for he loved them, lived for them as if the written sheets were his brothers and sisters, but still he took more. It was only a matter of time before he would be discovered. And so he was. It was late afternoon, still and hot, and he sat to drink on a bench at the side of a path through the city. I also sat there, for my training had but recently finished and I was resting, time on my side, as my mother gave birth to none but me, and died before I was old enough to know her, and my father would be working still at that time of day.' He picked up a fragment of rock, turning it in his fingers as he stared at it. 'I can feel it as if it were playing out here and now. The boy's bag lay between us and a sharp-eyed elder saw the corner of a document protruding from within. That tiny scrap of paper turned our lives to a path never imagined.'

Sophaya shrugged. 'He was not a thief. He was returning it. Why worry?'

Grakk's piercing gaze turned her way. 'The knowledge on the paper is our whole reason for existing, it is everything to us. It must never leave the House of Treasures. To take anything from within its walls is to court the penalty. The penalty is death.'

Marlo was shocked. 'He was put to death? For that?'

'You think that unfair, young Marlo, when he was on his way to return those documents?' The boy nodded hard. 'I also. I did not know the boy well, but I knew him, and it was plain to all he encountered just how much he loved the treasures we kept. He would never see them harmed, or lost. He loved them too much. He would have died for them. And now, ironically, that was exactly what was about to occur. I could not sit there and let it happen.'

Hakon was engrossed in the story. 'So you killed those who discovered them and the pair of you escaped the mountain.'

Grakk smiled. 'Not so dramatic, my Northern friend, and thankfully so. The boy was asked if the bag was his. He said that it was. So I did so also.'

'You what?' Hakon was aghast.

Grakk shrugged. 'If there is one thing my people are, it is considered and logical, and slaves to justice. They could not execute an innocent, and it was clear that the bag could only belong to one person. The boy tried desperately to persuade them that it was he who was guilty, but the more he did so, the more I did as well. As we both claimed to be the guilty one, they could not put us both to death. Instead, we were cast out.'

'That must have been hard,' Brann said quietly, sympathy for the young Grakk welling up in him. 'What did you do?'

The tribesman looked across the valley, as if drinking in what he had been forced to leave. The evening sun gleamed on his scalp. 'Saw the world. I travelled, thinking that if I found some new knowledge of value they may let me back early. I experienced much, learnt much, but nothing of value enough to atone. I found places and people I had never imagined, and word eventually reached me that age had claimed enough of the former Council of Elders for the new regime to hold a different attitude to my punishment. I could return, but as I made my way back, pirates found our ship and I added rowing to my list of skills.'

Marlo was curious. 'And what of the other boy? Did you travel together?'

'At first. But he felt guilt at my punishment, even though it had been my choice to do what I did. Indeed, he had tried his utmost to change my mind. Guilt, as it often does, turned to bitterness. It gnawed at him, draped itself over him, and he grew to resent me as the source. We parted on poor terms.'

'That is unfortunate. Did you ever wonder what became of him?'

'Often. And then we met once more.'

The Sagian boy's face lit up with heightened interest. 'You did? How was he? Where was he? What was his fate?'

A sigh escaped Grakk. 'You know as well as I. He is the Scribe to the Emperor.' His voice became soft. 'His name was Narut-ul-Taripha.'

Images of the aloof slave filled all of their memories in a long silence. Brann wondered what knowledge the Scribe had shared with the Emperor. Or worse, with Loku.

'So,' Brann said, a thought occurring to him, 'will you stay? When we leave in the morning, will you stay or travel with us?'

The solemn man turned and stared long at him, then slowly looked at each in turn. 'A quarter of a century, I was away. A different life is formed in that time, a different man too. I will always be drawn to this place, but I would never settle here; restlessness would always claim me. My place is elsewhere. And, for now, my place is with you. After all,' he looked at Cannick, 'I made a promise to a wise old lady.'

'But you could stay here if you wanted to? They would

let you, wouldn't they?' It felt important to Brann that this was so.

Grakk nodded. 'After all, I did at last bring them something of sufficient interest. Something they felt had a combination of factors that were already worthy of note, and that held the potential for further significance to come.'

'Really? What?'

The piercing eyes locked with his. 'You.'

The sun had set on their conversation, and it rose on their departure.

There was little fuss about their leaving, and little notice taken. Those who focus their life on a duty find most else merely of passing interest.

Brann found an opportunity to take Hakon to one side. 'I want to speak to you about something,' he said, looking up at the broad honest face. Right now, it actually felt like it was the last thing he wanted to do. 'I remember... from before.' Hakon looked enquiringly at him. 'From where I met you...' The bigger boy's eyebrows raised, requesting more. Brann groaned. 'From where I met you and, you know, met you and...'

Hakon guffawed. 'I can't keep it up. I was just enjoying you being Brann again.' He grinned and slapped Brann on the back, almost knocking him from his feet. 'Valdis.'

Brann nodded. 'Your sister,' he said lamely.

'My sister,' confirmed Hakon. 'So?'

Brann could feel the heat in his cheeks. 'Well, you know... Myrana. You must think terribly of me.'

'Brann.' The boy eased his large frame onto a rock to bring his head closer to Brann's height. 'I come from a people hardened by danger from the sea and from each other. It makes us very practical. It is not the first time a young man falls in love, that is important, nor the second third or whatever, but the last, for that is the one he stays with. It may be that life gives us many choices or that the dangers of the waves and the sword reduce a man's or woman's options, but that is just the way it is. You may find someone you fall for more than my sister, but if you return to her, you do so knowing with more certainty that she is the one for you.' His grin returned even wider. 'But if you hurt her, I'll take your head from your shoulders.'

Brann jumped as Cannick laughed right behind him. 'I was worried, big Hakon, that this place was getting to you and turning you all philosophical. But you redeemed yourself at the end.'

Brann stared at the older man. 'How much of that did you hear?'

Cannick's eyes twinkled. 'All of it.' He whistled jauntily as he sauntered on his way.

Brann groaned at more discomfort than he could remember. But when Hakon amiably clipped him on the back of his head, he also felt the relief course through him.

It took moments to gather their possessions, and food and water were brought and received with thanks. Grakk had spoken privately with his father the night before, and though the older man was present when they mounted the camels, a nod was all that either needed to add to what had been said. There was, however, a warmth in the exchange. Brann found himself smiling.

It was hard to turn their backs on the peace of the valley, but Brann knew the truth in Grakk's words. Each morning when he woke, the feeling was stronger that he was waiting – hoping – for something to happen. It was *too* tranquil.

Still, there was also an ache at leaving something so beautiful, and a longing that he would someday return.

The conversation with Grakk from the night before played in his mind. He sighed. As if a prophecy from a Soothsayer, adorable as she may be, was not a burden enough, he now had to shoulder the interest of these secret guardians of knowledge.

But when the door of rock shut silently behind them and they faced down the road towards ul-Detina, the only vision in his head held the faces of Einarr and Konall. And, behind them, Loku.

Prophecies and mysterious tribes could wait. He had business in Sagia.

Chapter 8

Good never comes without bad in its pocket, and never bad without good.

His mother had said that and he had thought of the truth in it more often than any other advice through the years. In planning, reacting, manipulating, redeeming, always it had served as his starting point. Never be complacent, never assume; never panic, never freeze.

Today there was more dry dust in the air than usual, but it was brought because a soothing breeze blew in to where he sat on his balcony. Bad and good.

The soft wind was not the only thing the desert had sent this morning. The boy had returned, entering the city shortly before dawn.

'He is here,' she said. 'In the city.'

'Think I do not know?'

'I assumed so, though your lack of contentment hinted that you may not. It does not please you?'

'It pleases me. But it is done and immediately we must move with the news. And now we must entrust everything

we plan, everything that must be, in the hands of one whose stability may be that of a desert cat.' Good and bad.

'It that is his state, it is one due wholly to the horrors he has endured and the realisation of what he had become. All, I point out, instigated by you.'

He snapped. 'You know it had to be. He had to become what he must be. Man cannot teach that, only life can. I did not make him, I put him where he could learn.'

'He could have been killed. Or worse, destroyed. He may yet be damaged. He has been through a dozen hells and the effect of that will never leave him.'

'I am counting on it.'

'You care not for what he has suffered?' She shook her head. 'I wonder if you are a greater monster than those we seek to oppose.' There was a soft rap at the door, and she moved to answer it.

He waited until she had moved from earshot before he whispered, 'Of course I care.'

****

Brann stood before a door with a grand-looking crest burnt into the wood, feeling far too vulnerable for comfort in the palace corridor.

They had been met outside the house they had left what seemed a lifetime ago by a stout slave who pointed at Brann and beckoned. Marlo had recognised him for who he served and, on that basis, Brann was allowed to accompany the slave alone. Given their destination, the fewer who went, the less was the chance of being noticed.

Brann was certain that Gerens had been close right until they had slipped through a small gate in the outer wall

371

designed for use by those who maintained the sewers of the citadel. With a surety that spoke of the slave's frequent passage by this means, they strode quickly on treacherously slick walkways alongside channels of dark water and through a stench that made Brann's head swim. Such was the length of their journey through intersecting tunnel after intersecting tunnel that they were only partway along their route when the smell was forgotten and his steps became confident. They reached a square shaft just wider than the span of Brann's arms. It extended out of sight directly up, narrow steps winding around the outer edges to leave only a third of its width clear in the centre. They were well up the steps, the bottom and the top both out of sight in what dim light they were afforded, when a shape flicked down past them, followed by two more. Brann flinched away, his shoulder blade bouncing against the wall. The slave's arm steadied him as he threatened to lurch towards the emptiness and follow the shapes to the bottom.

The slave looked at Brann, at the middle of the shaft, and back at Brann, his face impassive. 'Don't ask. Just avoid the centre, to avoid both the drop and what may come from above.' They were the only words he spoke during the entire journey. Brann just nodded in return.

They climbed through what he could only assume, from the height they went, was the central keep, occasionally passing shadows in the wall that proved to be doorways when he almost fell through the first he came across. They neared the top and the slave led him into the doorway there. It bent to the side almost immediately and the stocky man motioned him to wait beside him in the cramped space and to be silent.

A man coughed, hawked and spat. Brann almost shouted in surprise, catching the sound barely in time. The wall in front of them, though stone to the touch, must have been only as thick as the width of a couple of fingers. He heard some shuffling, then silence. A grunt led into three explosive farts. Both of his hands pressed against his mouth, desperately stifling the giggles that threatened to rival the man's wind for ferocity. The slave glared at him. After what seemed eternity, the man gave a sigh of contented relief. Brann squeaked as tears ran down his cheeks.

'Bloody rats,' the voice grumbled. The door banged as the footsteps quickly receded.

The slave waited, listening intently, then slipped a catch and slid a section of the wall to one side. As Brann had guessed, they stepped into a privy and the man went immediately to peer from the door. Satisfied with what he saw or, more particularly, satisfied with seeing nothing but empty passageway, he stepped forward without hesitation and Brann followed with alacrity, almost caught unready by the suddenness of the movement. Half a dozen paces took them to a corner, where they turned, and a dozen more brought them to the door with the grand crest.

The slave rapped softly on the wood and, without a word or even a glance, left Brann alone.

The door opened almost instantly, revealing a lady of great but indeterminate age, her bearing proud and her eyes keen. She ushered him in and stepped out in the same movement, shutting the door behind her as soon as he was inside the room.

He stepped back, feeling the wall behind him as he scanned the room. It was a large chamber, similar in size and shape to the one Myrana had occupied. His heart constricted at the sharp memory of betrayal and the deeper, burning desire for retribution, but just as quickly he pushed the feelings aside. This was a time to be alert, ready.

The room had an old feel. The furnishings held an air of a bygone era, though not a lesser one: they were rich and ornate, and of a quality few could afford. They were not, however, over-numerous. There was only what was necessary, being a large bed, shelves bearing old tomes, no two of which were the same size and shape, and beside them a desk strewn with sheets of parchment, all blank. A huge map was fixed to the wall near the desk and a few small tables stood here and there and a tall-backed easy chair sat before a large fireplace with the tracks in the dust still evident from its partner having been dragged to the balcony where it now sat, facing out to the Deadlands that he had just crossed for a second time. A curtained opening to one side led, he guessed, to a privy; this was the room of someone of far too lofty rank to have to wait in the passageway to empty their bowels like the lesser beings.

And the door which he had entered was the only visible means of exit.

The wide sleeve of a robe extended sidewards from the chair on the balcony and the long fingers of a thin-skinned hand beckoned to him.

He walked across the room, his soft Deruul boots silent on the stone flags of the floor. Shading his eyes against the glare of the sunlight on the balcony, he walked to its edge to allow room to turn and face the chair. An old man slouched in it. Very old: his beard was long grey wisps, as was his hair, his skin was tight across his bones, his frame sagging under the weight of time.

But the eyes: there he possessed fire greater than many a

374

fraction of his age. To be complacent with this man would be a grave mistake.

Those eyes regarded him, and Brann waited in respectful silence. When the voice came, it grated against his throat like rock against rock. 'Know who I am, do you, boy?'

Brann shook his head. 'I recognise you, but do not know who you are. I have seen you sitting to the side of the Emperor.'

The old man spat into the sand that formed a fine cover for the balcony. 'Emperor.' The word was spat as well. 'He is an insult to that word. When you think of those who held that title before him, what they achieved, how they ruled. To use this great empire as a plaything, a means for luxury and lifestyle...' He shook his head and snorted in disgust. 'Were my arm strong enough, I would take his head from its shoulders, and the Empire would be served a favour.' Brann's eyes widened in shock. 'Oh, you think me unwise, uttering such treason in the hearing of another? Think on it, boy: were your presence ever discovered even close to anyone who matters in this place, you would be dead before your lips could ever betray me.'

Brann shrugged. What could he say? The truth in those words was clear. But the words also showed that this man could prove a useful ally.

The eyes looked him up and down. 'I see the grime of the desert still upon you. You did not take time to clean yourself before you came to visit.'

Brann slapped his hands against his tunic and the top of his breeches, dislodging just a small amount of the travel dirt. There was the beginning of anger in his movements, though. 'I apologise. I had no time before your man brought me and I trailed through tunnels of shit to attend you.'

A hint of a smile threatened to twitch the corner of the

man's mouth. 'You misunderstand. I count it a compliment to me that you did not attend to yourself in even the slightest way before you answered my call.' Brann decided against mentioning that he had been given no choice in the matter. 'In some small recompense, can I offer you wine?'

'Water is fine, if you have it.' He was sure he would need his wits as sharp as they could be.

'Of course.' The hand waved to a small table, where a pitcher of water stood alongside two glass goblets, one still half filled. 'If you would excuse the weariness of age, I would ask you to pour for yourself.'

He did so and moved to top up the other glass while he was there. The hand stopped him. 'Thank you, but I have enough in mine for now. But drink, please. You must have a thirst after such a journey.'

Brann's head snapped round. 'What do you know of my journey?'

A small laugh, but humourless. 'Everything.'

His eyes narrowed. 'Who are you?'

'I am Alam-ul-Nazaram-ul-Taraq, though that will mean less than nothing to you. However, the least you deserve is the courtesy of being told my name.'

'The least I deserve? Why would I deserve anything?'

The eyes fixed on him. He waited. A bird of prey keened high above, and the breeze gusted fresh relief and fine sand dust over the balcony. Both of them instinctively covered their drinks with a hand until the soft wind dropped.

'For I put you through much.'

Realisation dawned. 'You are the mysterious benefactor that Grakk and Cannick spoke of?' A nod. 'Then it is I who should show gratitude, not you. You helped our escape, did you not?'

Another nod. 'From the tunnels and from the city. And more, though on a more subtle scale.'

'Then your words confuse me. Why should I deserve more from you? Apart from anything, you helped me from the City Below.'

He took a sip of water. A long look, then: 'But I also put you there.'

Brann's hand dropped to the hilt of his dagger at the words and at the memory of the scene in the Princess's chambers. 'Loku, or whatever you people call him, put me there.'

'How do you think he knew?'

This was very strange. 'You told him?' A slight shrug answered him. 'He works for you?'

He grunted. 'Many undertake work for me, but only a few know that they do. Those who most think they manipulate are themselves the easiest to manipulate, such is their thirst for opportunities and information.'

He felt incredulous. 'You let him put me in the pits?'

'I hoped he would. It was a calculated risk. I felt it likely he would want you to suffer over time rather than have the quick release of death. And he also prefers others to do his work while he is free to watch and continue his other work unhindered. The pits were the perfect solution, and he did not disappoint.'

Brann was thrown by the candour, but aghast also. 'You wanted that? You have no idea of the life I had there. Of what I went through. Of what I had to do. *Of what I became.*'

'I had every idea. That is why I wanted you there. And why I sent the others after you.'

The fury surged through him and emerged in a shout.

'You did that? My friends could have been killed.' The knife was in his hand.

'They lived, did they not? Because of what you had become.'

'You arrogant, callous bastard!' He stepped forward, bare steel catching the sun. His voice was a growl. 'I should cut your throat right now.'

With a suddenness of movement unexpected from his appearance, the old man was on his feet and in front of Brann, his open hand striking hard and fast at the boy's face. Instinct saw his own free hand catch the wrist a finger's width before his cheek. The blade was at the man's throat, drawing a faint line of red on the ancient skin.

'You think I cannot, old man?'

The rasping voice was right in his face, so close he could feel the breath and the punctuating spit that came with it. 'I know you can. Just as I know you will most likely not. You were made by the gods, as all of us are when we are spat into this world. But we are built by life, and what I put into your life has added to what you had already become to create the you who stands now before me. The pits gave us the man who could slice my throat without remorse if that were necessary, and the skills in the fabled city brought back the man able to place thought before action.'

'You found out about the city?' He stepped back in fear of what might be. 'You know the secret?'

'Calm your panic, boy. I knew of that city and what it holds before even your father left his father's balls. It is a secret entrusted to a few who have proved themselves of a sort who would protect it, and who can.'

He sat back down and lifted his water, calmly sipping it. An unease grew within Brann and he scanned the room warily, angry with himself. He should have wondered why the slave had not relieved him of his weapons before leaving him with a defenceless old man. He drew his sword as his eyes flitted over every possibility. No other balcony overlooked this, so archers would not have a shot. The chamber within was light where the sun flowed through the wide opening that connected it with the balcony and no places of concealment were available, not even under the bed, which was high from the floor and open to sight underneath. He strode to the curtained alcove and stood to one side as he used his sword tip to pull the covering aside. It was indeed a privy; an empty privy.

'Had I wanted you dead,' the voice rasped from the chair, 'there were plenty of opportunities without bringing you here to mess up my chamber with your blood. Now settle yourself and ask what you must.'

Brann sheathed his dagger as he moved back onto the balcony and rested half-sitting against the sill, facing the old man. The sword remained in his hand, though, and the anger still burnt hot behind his eyes.

'You play as a god. No man has that right.'

'But some have that duty.'

'Meaning?'

'When you have knowledge that affects many, and the opportunity to act upon it, you have no option but to do so.'

'And that knowledge?'

'Is for me just now. You have other matters to focus on.'

'I do, do I?'

The eyebrows rose. 'I believed you had friends who were detained in this very building. Friends who you would offer the chance to walk out from it. But perhaps I was wrong.'

'It happens you are right. And I will. My preparations have been delayed only by this visit.'

'Your preparations will be for naught. You will all die, and all will fail.' He slammed his empty goblet onto the fine wooden table, threatening to shatter both. 'Think on it, boy,' he snapped. 'This is not an inconsequential thief and peasant Northern boy running away while the Emperor cares less about whether they live or die than he does about the next shit he has. These are two high-ranking hostages, held for reasons of diplomatic strategy and guarded with potential escape in mind and predicted. You need the help of someone with influence within the palace itself. And even you have to admit you are not blessed with alternatives.'

'You.'

'Should I consider it advantageous to my cause.'

'And do you?'

'Fortunately for you, I do.'

'Then let us plan this at once.'

'Let us consider this at once. They are not going anywhere. But you are.'

'Speak without games, old man. A large part of me is still straining to put this sword through your neck.'

'Very well. You will perform a task for me. I have need of it, and I believe you and your companions are capable of carrying it out. Should you do so, I will help you with your two hostage friends.'

Brann stared out over the desert he had travelled, the expanse greater than he could see even from this great height. His thoughts considered the options.

He sighed. Not capitulation, but reluctant acceptance of the facts. He did need this man's assistance. 'Fine. What do you require of us?'

The man stood and shuffled into the room. 'Come. See.'

He shrugged. What did he have to lose by following? If it was a trap after all, it was already sprung and he was in its clutches.

The old man made for the fireplace, his slippered feet kicking motes of dust to dance in the sunlight as he passed. The hearth, of brick and stone, had clean uncomplicated lines that created a simple beauty, an impression enhanced by the skill of the craftsmanship. He stopped to one side of it, reaching to one of the bricks. Curiosity caused interest to nibble at Brann's anger, and he watched as the bony fingers grasped at one of the bricks and slid it free with an ease that had not been suggested by its fit, that had appeared to be as precise and tight as that of the bricks around it.

A small alcove lay behind it, just large enough to hold the box of finely tooled dark wood that he pulled forth with what appeared to be nothing less than reverence. He turned and laid the box on a table and faced Brann across its top, reaching down with both hands to ease open the hinged lid.

Brann gasped. He had never seen its like. If the fireplace had shown beauty in its simplicity, then this was the epitome of that concept. A black dagger lay nestled in velvet of the same colour, the gleam from the blade dull not from lack of care or cleanliness but from an otherworldly quality that almost seemed to absorb the light. Not only light was drawn but, even more so, eyes. He was unable to drag his sight away from it, running his eyes over every clean, perfect line.

The old man slipped the fingers of both hands under the knife and lifted it gently. Brann's eyes followed its every move. 'Take it,' the man said softly.

Brann reached his right hand and wrapped his fingers

around the hilt, the soft leather seeming to melt into his grasp. A gasp escaped him as he lifted it, surprised by the lightness. His other hand felt for the blade, wondering if it was formed from a light wood, but to his touch it seemed far too hard and sharp.

'It is metal.'

The old man read his movements well, but he scarcely noticed. Brann ran his thumb lightly against one edge and jerked it back with a gasp at the blood on his skin, not from pain but surprise that it had cut with such ease.

'It is metal, but no metal that we know. It is harder than steel, yet not brittle. It is lighter than steel, yet stronger. It seems not to lose its edge and it takes much to even scratch it, far less bend or break it. It is the metal of the gods.'

It had to be. 'So how is it here?'

'Many hundreds of years past, more than a thousand, a stone fell from the sky, lighting up the night with the fire of its passage. Where it landed, it blew a great crater from the ground, despite being little more than the size of a sack of grain. You know that spot well, as a matter of fact. It was there that they built the Arena when they were forming a city here.'

'So this is a weapon of the gods?'

He shrugged. 'Indirectly. It is formed from the metal of the gods. This weapon was wrought by man from metal contained within the Star Stone. This is the only item ever wrought from it.'

'How so?'

'None has lived for many generations who could work it. This was made by those who built the wonders of the city between the Deadlands and the Blacklands, and the tunnels beyond. When they passed, the Star Stone came back to we who had settled where it had fallen, but the secrets of their working passed with them.'

Brann turned it over and over in his hands, reluctant to let it go. It was a perfect weapon, with the single purpose of *being* that weapon. Its plain simplicity was at the heart of its beauty, for to adorn it would be to detract from it. 'It is indeed a wonder beyond all wonders.'

The old man held out a hand. With sadness, Brann handed it back, but the man merely lifted the velvet and produced a simple sheath, predictably in black, and slipped the blade into it. 'While you carry out this quest, I shall permit you to carry this so long as you ensure you bring it back safely to me.' Brann reached for it immediately. One wispy grey eyebrow rose. 'That would be your acceptance of your task?'

Brann nodded, and in the space of a few excited breaths, the knife sat on his belt. He told himself that it was because of the lightness that his hand had to keep straying to it to check it was still there.

'So,' he said. 'The task?' Whatever it may be, it had to be carried out so that his friends could be freed.

'I want you to take what's left of the Star Stone to one who will work it.'

'You said that no one can work it.'

'I said that for many generations no one who has lived can work it. Lived, not lives, for there is one now who is reputed to be a smith like no other.'

'Why has he not worked it before?'

'Few know what is within the Star Stone, and just as few know the value of this smith. He has a strangeness about him, a strangeness often found in men and women whose talent is beyond the understanding of all others, and a strangeness that scares many. He was seen as mad, or invaded by a spirit of the underworld, or both, and was chased from town. I had my people save him and enable his escape, but now his strangeness is heightened by the experience and he has little faith in other humans.'

'But he is in your debt.'

'He is. I wish you to take the stone to him, allow him to work with it and, if he finds success, bring me what he has made. He may keep what he does not use, for if he can work it, he will be the only one and it will be of no use to any other. I know him of old. I can trust him and he is far from stupid, no matter what impression he may give. No one else will know of his work, nor will they suspect him, for what apparent madman would be capable? They certainly will not know that he has the remainder of the... material. Unless you or your companions are careless with the truth.'

'I know them. We have been through much.' His voice was cold. 'As I am sure you know.'

The answer was of similar tone. 'I have no option but to trust your judgement on them. However much we may dislike risks, sometimes there is no other way.' He offered his hand. 'Should you do this, I will help you find a route from here for your friends.'

He thought of Einarr and Konall. Even if his friends were unwilling to accompany him, he would go himself. He took the hand, feeling an old strength within the thin skin and bones. 'I will do it.' He cast about for another possible location for a secret alcove where the Star Stone might lay hidden, then cursed his stupidity. If he could spot it, it would not be so secret. 'Where is the stone? Tell me the location of this smith and I will take it and be on my way.'

'It is not so simple as that. It is elsewhere in the keep.

You will have to fetch it, though I suspect you will have to go away and work out how to do so.'

He sighed. He might have known. 'A vault? A treasure room? A display in a throne room? Where?'

The man smiled as he told him. Brann did not.

****

She stepped through the door the instant the boy was out of sight around the corner, as he knew she would. The sound of the bell in the servants' room, the double ring that would summon the stocky slave, was all the sign she needed.

She refilled his goblet from the fresh jug that she had brought with her. 'So, you and he have met. You feel he will be what we hope for him.'

'There is a chance.'

'The two sides of him are finely balanced.'

'They are. But the one that holds the other in check is the one we would wish. He has the speed of the impulse and the capacity to use it. But also the thought to control it. Should he unleash it, however, I would fear to be the one who faces him.'

'Not now, I am sure, though you were a fighter who commanded respect, once.'

He grunted. 'Once. But even then, had I faced him, I would not be here now to tell you about it. I am thankful that he has that control back.'

'So I see.' She wet a small cloth from the water jug and dabbed at the dried blood on his neck. 'You were confident your efforts had succeeded with him. It was a risk meeting him alone with no protection. And with him armed, too.'

He grunted. 'You think he would have needed steel to

385

kill me? Two blades or none or ten, he posed the same risk.'

'You told him you were behind what he endured?'

'I had to. Should he have heard it from another, he would have sought me out and killed me. For him to turn to our cause, he had to hear it from me and accept it.'

'And he did accept it?'

'In part. We can only hope he will do so fully in time.'

Crouching beside him, she laid a hand on his arm. 'Still, you took a terrible risk in telling him this.'

'I knew he would not kill me.'

'Did you really?'

He looked at her.

'No.'

****

'It is *where?*' Hakon knocked his chair over as he leapt to his feet.

Brann sighed. He not even had time to wash and don clean clothing after the slave had brought him back through the sewers and to the streets near to their house. All he could do was grab a chicken leg and a flagon of ale before he had been sat down and question after question came from every angle. He had no option but to quieten them and tell what had happened from the beginning, uninterrupted until Hakon had exploded.

Brann shrugged. 'It had to be in the keep somewhere.'

Grakk leant forward. 'But where in the keep?'

'You remember the entrance hallway? The one with the giant statues? The warrior on the horse and the monster? The warrior's shield?' Every question was greeted with nods from those clustered around him. 'Remember the black stone

386

that was the boss on the shield?'

Hakon threw his hands to his head and groaned, walking in a circle. 'So we are not only going to steal an ancient artefact sent from the gods, but we have to take it from a statue that is a renowned wonder of an entire empire.'

'It is easier than having to break into a guarded vault,' Sophaya suggested helpfully.

Hakon ignored her. 'Then we have to smuggle it out of the city to find a mad smith who many believe is demon-possessed, and give it to him to work on. This "it" being a metal that no one can work, remember. Then if, by some miracle, he can make even a thimble from it, we have to bring this back and only then will the old man deign to help us rescue our friends.' He snorted. 'I say if we are going into the keep anyway, bugger him and his special stone, we might as well just get Einarr and Konall while we are there.'

'Do that,' Cannick said, 'and the old man, whoever he is, is right. We will never see the outside of that building, and we won't be locked up either.'

Grakk came to stand in front of Brann. 'My people have trusted this man for many decades, a necessary trust to receive his protection in helping to keep our truth undiscovered. He proved he was a shield, not a threat. But how do you feel about doing this for him, this man who orchestrated all that you had to face as though you were his puppet and he the master making you dance?'

Brann stared into the fire. 'I hate what he did and I hate him for doing it. Of course I do, and that burns inside me. I'd be a liar and a fool to say it did not. But what is done is done and cannot be otherwise, and now he can help us if we help him. What is in the future for our two friends is worth far more than what is in my past.'

'Good enough for me,' Cannick said as Marlo drew his chair closer, his eyes shining with excitement.

Gerens was leaning against the mantelpiece at the hearth. 'So what do we do, Chief?'

Brann stared at him. 'Actually, I'm not at all sure yet.'

Sophaya stood and stretched. 'In that case,' she said, her voice as languid as her stretch, 'it's just as well that I have an idea.'

Gerens looked around the group. 'Did I ever tell you she was magnificent?'

It was close to a full moon when they huddled against the final wall before the keep, but that was, Sophaya told them, helpful.

While it lit certain areas brightly, it also plunged others into contrasting shadow. In more even light, while there was more darkness overall, guards' eyes became accustomed to it. This night the shadows offered more effective cover. Hakon hadn't been convinced but a glare from Gerens when he had dared to suggest it had cut off any criticism of Sophaya before the sentence was even half complete.

Brann glanced at the others. Only Grakk, Gerens and Sophaya accompanied him, dressed like he was in black tight-fitting clothing, the fittings for their weapons bound in cloth to muffle any noise. Cannick and, especially, Hakon were not built well for quiet and agile sneaking, and Marlo's geographical knowledge only covered the areas outwith the citadel walls and so he was better used in guiding the pair through the darkened streets to the point where the intruders intended to exit the great outer wall.

Brann pulled his light hood over his head in an attempt to merge with the shadow as much as he could and peered around the corner at the main gate. A small postern stood to one side, and the helmets of two sentries could be seen just above the top of the wall, their bored chatter clear in the night air. He nodded to Grakk, who whirled a sling and sent flying a collection of small stones to rattle against the thick wood of the postern door.

The sentries' conversation was cut and two faces peered down. Seeing no one at the door, they shrugged and turned back to lean on the parapet, resuming their chat. Grakk's arm whirled again and another tattoo of pebbles rapped on the door. By the fourth time the sling had struck, one guard was roused enough from the torpor of relentlessly uneventful night duty to grumble his way down to ground level. The door opened and he peered out, a lantern held aloft and curses spilling from his illuminated lips. Spotting nothing, he started to turn back inside just as Grakk sent another consignment of stones to patter against the wall a short distance from the gate.

'There's something there,' his companion called from above, pointing to the noise.

'Think I'm deaf?' He drew his sword and crept along the shadow of the wall, his lantern held before him.

Grakk loosed again, this time targeting a clump of small bushes, bright in the moonlit area. Gratifyingly, it produced movement as well as noise as the shower of rocks struck the leafy branches.

The guard above leant out over the wall, away from them. 'There. You see? The bushes. Move your arse.'

'All right, all right, give me a chance,' the one below grumbled, adding in a lower voice, 'If you weren't twice my size you could have moved your own fat arse down to look for yourself.'

Brann had to stifle a giggle, but Sophaya was watching the guard atop the wall. He had leant at an angle, intent on trying to view the bushes as best he could, and was facing as much away from them as he ever would be.

'Now,' she whispered and set off at a silent lope without waiting to see if any followed. Brann felt Gerens shove him between the shoulder blades and followed as quietly as he could, certain the noise of his heart pounding was loud enough on its own to alert both sentries. Give him six guards with swords drawn any time rather than this sneaking about.

He rethought that image as he neared the door and he realised that they may be about to enter a guard room full of soldiers. Sophaya slipped inside and, welcome party or not, he had no option but to follow.

His sigh at finding an empty room – what must be a staging area for a small group, were the door to be used in wartime – was echoed by the pair who followed. Gerens looked up and Brann followed his gaze. Massive blocks were suspended, ready to be let loose should the doorway ever need to be sealed, and Brann moved nervously from underneath them. Grakk loaded his sling to send forth one final distraction, but Brann scuttled back to stay his arm. The sentries were still in shouted conversation and there was no point in delaying any further. 'Nothing to gain,' he whispered and Grakk nodded, stowing the sling and remaining rocks in a bag at his side as they slipped down a short passage to find a door, its studded wood as thick as the one on the outer side. Silently thanking those who maintained the hinges with a healthy dose of oil, they slipped through and past the stairs that would lead the guard back to the top of the wall once he had given up his search.

Hugging the wall, they crept around the edge of the quiet

courtyard. The sentries had ceased their activity and whinnies from the stables were the only sounds to break the night-time hush. They wore the Deruul desert boots once more, their design perfect for noiseless creeping, and their passage was uneventful, allowing them to make good time. Past the smithy, they reached the armoury and Brann caught at Sophaya's tunic as a thought struck him.

He nodded at the door and breathed in her ear. 'Think you can open that lock?'

Her expression was withering in its disdain and she had the door ajar before he had even noticed her starting work on it. He slipped inside and cast back in his mind to his last visit here, in what seemed almost a different life. He pictured the location of what he sought and was back outside in seconds to face three querulous faces.

He pulled up his sleeves and showed the knives strapped to his forearms, similar to the ones that he had chosen when equipping himself to be Myrana's personal guard. It felt good to take back something from that time, as though they could not strip everything from him. And while he had been through much, he had to admit he preferred his life now with his companions rather than those days of repetition at the beck and call of the girl, even if the nights had held their compensation.

They neared the switchback ramp to the main door and faced a decision: risk the exposure of the direct route up the ramp, or take the longer route internally from ground level. They looked at each other, concern on each face that they had not thought to consider this previously.

Brann weighed it up. To work their way up from the servants' quarters and work areas would keep them from the eyes of the sentries on the walls, but it also took them past a host of sleeping servants, any one of whom could wake as they passed their quarters, or be wandering the corridors to or from a visit to a communal privy. And it would take far longer, and their time was scarce as it was. There was risk of being seen on the ramp, but also risk of being discovered at work in the hallway were they to arrive too late. He nodded. The ramp it was.

The others were waiting for him. Grakk and Gerens had recognised the look on his face and were content to wait a moment for his decision, the grim boy laying a hand on Sophaya's arm in suggestion that she trust Brann also. He pointed to the ramp and they started up without hesitation, laying their feet softly on the wood and their bodies pressed against the cool stone of the keep. Brann found himself wishing he had never thought of the servants' privies.

They had just passed half the distance and were starting to feel their nerves relax when a door slammed below, spilling light and a troop of guards into the courtyard from the barracks that Brann remembered was reserved for the duty soldiers. The four froze, pressing hard against the wall as if wishing they could become part of it. The moon's light shone from the side but was more than enough to show them starkly against the stonework to even the briefest of glances.

The soldiers tramped across the courtyard, splitting partway to find those they would relieve, laughing and grumbling in equal measure. Brann found himself holding his breath, though not with as much effort as it took to hold his bladder. Even trying not to squirm from the effort was a trial.

Brann's eyes widened with realisation. 'We have to move,' he hissed. There was little chance a guard would look up at the ramp – why would they think to? – but when those who had finished their shift started to make their way back, they would be staring directly in the direction of the keep. 'Now. Fast.'

The noise of the guards as they walked would cover the most minimal movement, but no more; the men were aware that were they loud enough to wake those on the top level of the keep, they would be lucky not to lose their heads. Brann moved as quickly as he could while still being quiet, and the others – more adept at this than he – followed closely. The barely resistible urge to break into a sprint assailed him with every step and it seemed an eternity before they reached the massive doors that barred their way. Sophaya scanned them. While the others saw their size, her attention was more specific, spotting a keyhole in the ornate metalwork. A pair of rods appeared in her hands and less than half-a-dozen deft movements later, the massive lock gave the softest of clicks. Gerens pressed his shoulder against the door and eased it open just enough for them to slip through, and Brann helped Grakk to ensure it shut with only the slightest thump as it settled back in place.

'How did you turn a lock so large, so quietly?' he whispered.

'What?' She arched an eyebrow. 'You think I play at this business?'

'And how did you know that those would not be in place?' He indicated two massive beams, almost vertical to one side of the doors now but pivoted at their lower ends and each ready to be dropped by pulleys into six iron holders, two on each door and one to either side. Had they been dropped into place, not even a battering ram would have opened the door.

She smiled sweetly. 'I didn't.'

His jaw dropped. 'We would have been trapped.'

The smile remained. 'With you to thank for it. It was your choice that brought us here.'

The horror was so plain on his face that even Grakk chuckled. 'She toys with you. They are only dropped in times of attack.'

She returned his glare with an even broader smile over her shoulder as she sauntered towards the statues. 'I believe we have too much work to be chatting.'

Gerens watched her walk away. 'Is she not...?'

Brann groaned. 'We know, we know.'

'Magnificent,' Grakk finished drily for him.

Gerens looked at them with approval. 'Indeed.'

The statues seemed even larger in the dim lantern-light. Rearing high, they loomed above them, seeming more living creatures frozen in a moment than artwork in shining stone and precious metal. If they did not overwhelm with awe as the gods in ul-Detina's temple had done, still they commanded respect and wonder in each of the men beneath them.

But not in the one woman.

Sophaya bounded from horse's raised fetlock to stirrup to rider's knee to saddle as if she were climbing a flight of shallow stairs. She looked at the gaping trio beneath her and a forced whisper floated down to them. 'Are you thinking of waiting for others to come along to help us, or do you want to get this done?'

They shook themselves into action. Gerens swung the pack from his back and hurled it to her. Holding on with one hand, she leant out and caught a strap with the other, swinging herself back into the rider's lap in the same movement. She hooked the strap onto the stone hilt of a giant scabbarded sword and, standing on the rider's thigh, she gripped the rim of the shield and rolled round to its front. Bracing one hand against it, she eased a slim dagger around the rim of the oval black rock, an arm's length in height. Every so often, frowning in concentration, she would probe with her fingers at the rock for increased movement until, eventually satisfied, she sheathed the dagger and reached across the rock to wriggle her fingertips under the far edge. With a sharp tug, the rock came away and fell into the crook of her arm.

The three below started breathing again.

She swivelled to rest her back against the shield, allowing her to use both hands to hold out the rock, and checked below that someone was prepared to catch it. Brann stood ready, arms outstretched but, as Sophaya let the rock fall, Gerens shouldered him out of the way and let the rock land in his own arms. He looked at Brann. 'I've seen you catch,' he murmured. Brann couldn't argue.

High above, Sophaya produced a tub and a cloth from her bag and smeared a pale paste in the cavity that had held the rock. She shuffled to retrieve the pack from the sword hilt and returned to the shield, pulling forth a large black oval object and fitting it where the rock had sat, kicking the empty pack down where Grakk caught it and Gerens slipped the rock safely inside. After a few adjustments to angle the oval to resemble the rock as closely as possible – certainly enough to make the difference indiscernible from ground level – she held it in place, her lips moving as she silently counted. A quick attempt to wobble it with her hand proved its security, and without fuss she dropped from one statue body part to another until she was standing beside them.

Brann looked at Gerens. 'I thought you might have been gallant enough to help such a magnificent lady on her last stretch to the floor.'

The boy frowned. 'It would hardly be gallant to insult her magnificent capabilities by interfering with them.'

'And yet you follow me, ready to murder anyone who would even think of doing me harm.'

The dark eyes regarded Brann. 'Indeed.'

'Oh!' The shrill female voice bouncing off the hard surfaces of the hall and ringing with its echo froze their thoughts. Brann looked at Sophaya, as did Gerens and Grakk, but the girl merely looked back at them, the sound as much a mystery to her as it was to them.

'I got such a fright.' The voice was quieter now and with less of an echo they were able to determine the source. A young girl in nightclothes stood on the great staircase. 'I was ever so thirsty and thought I would just go for a drink. I'm sorry if I startled you but I never expected to see someone. Are you cleaning the statue?'

Grakk stepped forward with a disarming smile. 'We are indeed, young lady. These tasks are best completed while those who would admire such wonders are abed. I do hope we have not disturbed your own rest?'

She smiled back. 'Oh no, my chamber is too far away, and I could see when I came down that you were trying very hard to be quiet.'

Grakk bowed slightly. 'We can but do our best, young lady. But please, do not let us keep you from your drink.'

'You are most kind, sir.'

She turned with a swirl of flimsy fabric to angle down the wide steps but, in doing so, her eyes dropped on the weapons hanging from Brann's and Gerens's belts. She looked back at Grakk and, for the first time, noticed the hilts of Grakk's crossed swords protruding above his shoulders. Her hands flew to her mouth and she screamed, turning and bolting back to the stairs, her shouts echoing as she went.

'Attack! Attack! We are under attack! Attack!'

Doors started to bang and drowsy shouts resounded in the hallways above. Brann ran immediately to the main doors and heaved one open, leaving it ajar. The guards on the walls had not heard the noise from within the keep yet, but they soon would. They might not be able to leave their posts, but they would alert those in the barrack house.

Sophaya ran to stop him. 'We can't go that way now.'

'We never could. Hopefully they will think we did when they see this lying open.'

'Not if they see us standing here, they won't,' said Gerens, heading for a door to the side of the hall. They piled through and Grakk shut the door behind them. They stood in a small servants' hallway, stairs heading up and down and a corridor leading towards the back of the keep.

They looked at Brann. 'Down,' he said. 'We need to go down.'

Four flights took them down two floors before Grakk halted them with a hoarse shout and pulled them into a store cupboard. 'Wait. We forgot.' He reached into his own pack and drew out four loose robes in the style worn by the royal servants. More important than the style was the fact that they were large enough to cover not only their dark functional clothing but also their weapons. In a fight, they would be hard now to access, but if they got into a full-blown fight they were as good as caught anyway. Better to pass unnoticed.

Grakk threw his pack in amongst the stores – all that remained within was his sling and a few handfuls of stones, and none of that was needed now. The pack Gerens wore was too bulky so he had to be content with slipping it on over the top of his robe. It would have to do.

They moved down the stairs at a run. They had planned to pass through the levels carefully and quietly, the disguises mostly intended to make their appearance credible should someone stir as they passed a dormitory or should they chance upon a servant with nocturnal duties. As the alarm grew, however, there would be much running and confusion in general, so there was little need for cautious movement now. It would be more out of place to be walking sedately through the mayhem that would surely ensue. They rushed, when the stairs ended taking any corridor until they found more downward steps.

And so it transpired. Bells had started to ring, and men and women in various states of dress spilled from doorways, yawning and questioning. Most moved past them in confusion, seeking guidance on how they were expected to help with whatever the reason was for the commotion, but one man, a shift pulled half on to reveal an overly hirsute torso, stopped in front of Grakk, staring in doubt at the tattooed tribesman. Immediately Grakk grabbed him by the arm. 'What's happening?' he asked anxiously. 'Do you know?' The man made to pull away, but Grakk grabbed his arm tighter. 'Wait, we need to know what to do.'

'Ask the master of your section,' the man growled, his bushy brows lowering as he wrenched his arm free. 'I will not risk any lashes for your panic.' He made off along the corridor, shouldering others out of his path.

They moved in the same direction before branching into

another passage. Gerens looked at his companion. 'That was more successful than the last time. You are improving.'

Grakk grinned. 'It's easier when you merely have to join in with chaos and panic.'

'To be fair,' Sophaya pointed out, 'you were doing well at charming the young girl until she opened her eyes.'

Grakk looked innocent. 'Are you trying to say that I am not always the most charming of men?'

She lightly tapped his cheek in affection. 'I would never dare suggest such a thing, dear Grakky.'

Brann and Gerens looked at each other. 'Grakky?' Brann said.

The man merely shook his bald head. 'There are times when the magnificent is not quite so magnificent.'

A door lay open before them, the courtyard visible beyond. Sophaya gleefully made for it, but Brann shouted to Gerens and the boy caught her by the arm.

'We might not get a chance if we don't go now,' she protested, wriggling futilely in Gerens's grip. 'That area will soon be teeming with soldiers.'

'Possibly with us only halfway across,' said Grakk.

She looked angrily at Gerens. He shrugged. 'I have found it wise to listen to Brann at times like these.'

'Times like these,' she spat. 'This is why I work alone. In and out with not a trace, those are the times I am familiar with.'

Grakk raised his eyebrows. 'All the more reason to listen to others when it is a little noisier, no?'

She shrugged. Brann stepped forward. 'Your plan got us in and gained us the rock, and it worked perfectly, none of us can deny it. But my part was to get us out. It is not transpiring exactly the way I had hoped, but it is still possible.

Confusion suits us more than them at this point. Come.'

He took them away from the door until they found stairs once more heading down. They encountered varying concentrations of servants although, as they descended they did become fewer, unsurprisingly. The first two levels were still relatively dry, though the air was cool, suiting their use as a vast store with anything from food to bed linens carefully arranged in orderly precision in a series of rooms cut from the rock. As they dropped to the next level, the atmosphere became palpably damper and grew even more dismal as they realised they had reached the dungeons. Brann shivered, not from the chill but the sight of the cells hewn from the rock and barred at the front, eerily reminiscent of what had been his home in the City Below. He had the memories of what had transpired there, but only a detached recollection of the person he had been forced to become to endure such a time.

He was snapped back to the present by a large guard who stepped to block their path. He was bareheaded and armoured only in a breastplate, but carried a wicked-looking sword, curved like those that Grakk favoured but with a heavier blade. Once they managed to pull their own weapons from under their robes they would overcome him without difficulty, but in the time it took them to disentangle themselves he would have already cut down at least one of them, and that was one more than they were prepared to accept.

They froze. The guard started to speak but stopped at the sound of a sharp thud. His eyes rolled up and his knees buckled as he dropped to the ground, revealing the stocky slave who had led Brann to the old nobleman. The man held up a short thick club. 'There are some old habits you don't lose,' he said simply. 'Follow.'

He led the way down the passage between the cells, sullen and defeated faces watching them from the compartments.

'Did you know he would be here?' Sophaya whispered.

Brann nodded. 'I asked for it. We need a guide for what comes next. I could get us to the general area of the dungeons from the directions I was given. The next part needs local expertise.'

That local expertise took them to the far end of the passage where their guide lit a small lamp. Gerens put a hand on his arm. 'The two Northern nobles. Are they in these cells?'

The slave shook his head. 'Not that easy, I'm afraid. They are hostages, not prisoners, remember. Their rooms are on the upper floors, in altogether more pleasant circumstances. To place them here would, should they be returned to their people, be almost as much an invitation to war as killing them.'

He stepped into a hole in the floor that gave access to steps cut to wind upon themselves in an oppressively tight coil through the solid rock. They followed, finding the footing treacherous from the moisture that now coated the walls and, occasionally, trickled. An opening the height of an average man was cut immediately at the stairway's base to allow them into a chamber that was a crossroads for four passages. The slave headed into the one to their right and they followed quickly, fearful of being left beyond the lantern's reach. Illuminated by it as they passed each one, the cells in this level lay empty, the bars rusted and the drips of water loud alongside the sound of their footsteps smacking on the wet floor. All but one empty. The final alcove to the left boasted solid bars and, as their light approached, a figure scuttled back from it. A sound of shock burst from

Brann and all four flinched in surprise. It was impossible not to look. What had once been a man and was now just skin, bones, hair and rags, cowered as far back as he could manage, turned away from the light and with both arms shielding his face.

A shudder wracked Brann and he looked at Grakk. 'Had you not come...' He couldn't bring himself to complete it, but the tribesman nodded his understanding.

The slave had not faltered for even a step and blackness claimed the prisoner and his cell once more. It was only a dozen paces more before the man slowed carefully, then stopped. He held the lantern over a circular hole in the floor to reveal a vertical shaft through the rock, iron loops set into one side for hands and feet and a rope hanging beside them.

The lantern's handle had a hook on it, and he used this to hang it on his belt. 'I will light the shaft and you will climb down. At the bottom, place your back against the wall and move to your left to allow room for the others. I will follow the last of you. The rope is to lower anything you cannot carry.'

Grakk's eyes narrowed. 'And how do we know you will not depart with the light as soon as we are down, leaving us blind and with only that wretch we just saw to ask for directions?'

The man shrugged, handed the lantern to Gerens and climbed down into the hole.

Brann followed, the shaft narrow enough for his shoulders to brush each side. He found himself thankful they had not brought Hakon. The depth to the next level was further, and the press of the rock around him made it seem even more so. As much as Gerens tried to bathe him in light, his

402

body blocked most of it from travelling past him and when space opened around him it came as enough of a surprise for him to grasp tightly at the metal rings he had reached, pausing slightly, fearful that disorientation might cause him to fall. Had he lost his grip, he would not have dropped far: the floor was barely a person's height below the ceiling.

His feet found a slick surface and he pressed back and hands against the wall, taking tiny nervous steps. The others followed quickly, the darkness behind the lantern's reach pressing them on. Gerens pulled up the rope and used it to lower his pack to those below before the swinging of the pool of light on the floor of the chamber signalled that he was lowering the lantern and, as it emerged from the hole in the ceiling, their surroundings were revealed. His own approach followed closely.

Brann saw the wisdom of the advice to hug the wall. He had assumed it was to keep them together in the dark and to offer balance without eyes to help them, but the truth was now evident: they stood on a narrow ledge that ran around the circumference of a circular room. Four passages led again from the chamber, as on the level above, possibly to more cells, but this time with a central channel collecting the moisture from the surroundings and letting it stream to this room. The main difference was, however, that the floor of the central room where the corridors met sloped beyond the lip of the ledge to a wide dark hole in the centre. The incline was shallow but perilous, for not only did water stream down its surface but it did so over rock filmed with streaks of a pale-green slime, similar to a secretion Brann had seen on the sea walls of the docks back in Hakon's homeland.

He looked at the slave. 'Which passage?'

The impassive face never twitched. 'None.' Brann's mix

of confusion and suspicion was mirrored in the faces of his companions, and Gerens's hand noticeably stole to his knife. Unperturbed, the man nodded at the centre of the room. 'That is your passage from the citadel.'

They looked at him. 'To where?'

'Few know it, but an underground river flows beneath the keep. It is possibly its greatest defence against siege. There are several wells giving access to it, but not one is of sufficient size for a person to pass through. This is the only access to it.'

Gerens grunted. 'So we just slide down and drop through the hole into only the gods know what?'

'Only if you want to hit the side of the hole and break something. Look at the floor.' He indicated small indentations, vertical at their lower side. 'Turn sideways, use them to brace your feet. Ease your way to the hole. Then drop through into only the gods know what.'

Grakk's voice was less controlled than they had ever heard. 'We will be walking beside this river, or travelling within its waters?'

The slave shrugged. 'There may be a ledge here or there, but most likely you will be in the river, letting its current take you to the sea.'

'Then I have a problem. I cannot swim.'

The others looked at him. Brann was astounded. 'I always assume you can do everything.'

'There is not much call, nor opportunity, for swimming lessons in the desert.'

Gerens was equally surprised. 'You spent how many years at sea without being able to swim?'

Grakk shrugged. 'There is as much chance to learn when you are chained to a bench as there is in the desert.'

404

'So,' Sophaya said, 'that is the why. Now we need the what. That is, the what we do now. Go back up?'

The slave shook his head. 'It was thronged with soldiers when you came down. There will be many times more of them now. The water does not swing swords or shoot arrows.' He produced a length of rope. 'This will keep you together. The task of keeping your friend afloat is yours to achieve.'

He was right, and Grakk nodded. The slave gave them a bag of waxed canvas to protect their weapons as much as they could, and each of them strapped their bag tight to them. They tied themselves close together with the rope, partly to reduce the chance of it snagging on anything as they travelled in the river, but mainly because each of them wanted to be close to Grakk at all times.

'How many have survived this route?' Brann asked the slave.

'As many as have attempted it.'

That was the first encouraging thing he had heard for a while. 'And how many have attempted it?'

'None.'

'Sometimes,' said Gerens, 'I prefer you to not ask questions.'

It was as treacherous to edge their way as a group to the edge of the hole as it had looked, and it took them an eternity and several heart-stopping slips from each of them before they managed to range themselves around the lip of the hole, Brann roped to Grakk, he to Gerens and he to Sophaya. The hole was wide enough to take all of them and, as they paused to gather their resolve, Brann looked back at the slave, impassively standing with the lantern.

'Thank you,' he said. 'I do not know your name.'

'No,' said the slave, crouching to tie the lamp to the end of the rope hanging through the hole to the upper level. 'You do not.' He grasped the iron rings and started to climb.

They looked at each other, all thinking the same thought. If the slave were about to leave or, more to the point, if he were soon to pull the only source of light with him, this was their time to go.

Words were unnecessary. They nodded in unison, took a deep breath, slipped their feet from the footholds and dropped into darkness.

They knew it was coming, but still the shock of hitting the water was like a punch in the gut, and Brann fought the urge to gasp as they plunged under the surface. He kicked upwards and the others must have done the same, for they dragged Grakk upwards in a heartbeat. As soon as Brann felt air on his face, he pulled at the rope, hauling himself to Grakk and grabbing him around the chest from behind.

'Are you all right?' he gasped.

'I am.' But the rigidity of Grakk's entire frame betrayed the lie.

They were already moving with the current and Sophaya and Gerens quickly joined them. They formed a ring, grasping each other's arms and helping Gerens keep his head above the water despite the weight of his pack. While all but Grakk kicked, they also let their legs drift back a little to feel for the sides of the channel and push gently against them to keep from dragging against the rock.

Brann had been worried about the danger of injury from striking uneven protrusions, but his fears were allayed. His feet could feel that the water, in following this course for however many ages, had worn a path almost as smooth as the tunnel they had travelled from ul-Detina. He could feel it winding, sometimes slightly and others in a sharper arc, and narrowing and widening, bringing changes to the speed of the current, but to his surprise they encountered little danger other than that posed by trying to keep above the surface of a river in complete blackness.

The dark had been as oppressive as he would have expected for the first part of their journey, but he found himself adapting, as his other senses filled his attention, trying to read his environment until he realised that he had stopped feeling the lack of light like a clamp around his brain. Grakk, too, seemed to have become more accustomed to it, though in his case he was possibly concentrating more on the sensation of being in the water than on the inability to see. He had certainly relaxed slightly, although the fingers that gripped Brann's left arm still did so with a strength far beyond what was necessary. Brann didn't mind: it reminded him that his friend was still there.

The water was cool, but not cold, not sapping the energy from their muscles as a Northern river would have done. After one swift bend, however, he started to feel a difference. There was a definite drop in the temperature and, as he looked ahead, he felt there was a very slight light creeping into the dark.

He spat out a mouthful of water that had a definite briny tang to it, and Grakk sniffed the air as he caught the same flavour in it. There was no need to tell the other two: their faces were turned expectantly in the same direction. The sense of relief felt by each of them was so strong that it was as if Brann could reach out and touch it as it emanated from the others. They could hear the surf now and, spreading into a line so they could all face it, they began to kick forwards in their eagerness. They were nearing it, and were able to tell that the light came from a large opening, what must be a cave mouth, that was letting in the breaking dawn. After such complete darkness, even the merest light was the most glorious of visions.

Then they saw it. At first it was a smudge against the soft morning light, but before long it resolved itself into a huge grate, metal bars blocking the exit and sweeping despair into their souls.

They had no option but to let the current take them right to the barrier. Fortunately, the channel was at one of its wider and deeper stages so their speed was slow enough to save them from serious injury, although Brann did take a painful rap to the shin.

They looked up. The cave entrance was narrow for its height and tapered to a slender point, the bars stretching to the very top and filling it to its sides with heart-breaking precision. They gripped the metal and stared at the outside world, close enough to reach their arms into it, but only their arms. Gerens shook at the bars, but there was no give; they were solid enough to imprison them. He roared in fury.

'Maybe there is another exit,' Sophaya suggested. 'There could have been a branch of the river that we passed in the dark.'

Grakk stared out at the sea, the rising sun glistening on its gently undulating surface and the swell competing against the flow of the river to push and pull them back and forth against the bars. 'That same darkness would be the reason we would not find it, were we to somehow battle the current to get there. I fear this is the only exit we will find.'

Brann looked at the bars again, willing a weakness to appear: a gap near the cave wall, a broken or loose bar, anything. His eyes roved up one side and down the other and, as they did so, his attention was caught by the rock wall to the side. He gasped as a thought hit him.

Sophaya's eyes narrowed. 'I'm beginning to know that look.'

He grabbed the knife strapped to his left forearm, and lifted the rope. 'Grakk, do you mind...?'

The tribesman nodded at his hands that threatened to become one with the bars, so hard were they gripping them. 'The water is taking me nowhere right now.'

The blade cut the rope quickly and Sophaya raised an eyebrow. 'I thought the recommendation was to bag the blades?'

'I did,' said Brann. 'Mostly.' He shrugged. 'I always like to keep something extra, just in case.'

Sophaya grinned and reached to the back of her neck to draw a slim blade of her own.

Gerens looked from one to the other. 'I may have to rethink the level of protection you two need.' He swung round to face Brann. 'So what are you thinking, Chief? Going to climb to see if any are breakable? If so, you'd be better cutting me loose. You know I am the better climber.'

Brann shook his head. 'Not up.' He pointed at what had caught his attention higher on the wall, a clear line left by the sea. 'It's just a guess, but it bears a look.'

He took a breath and ducked under the surface, using the hated bars to pull himself downwards as quickly as he could manage. The water was clear and the low sun was shining almost directly into the cave mouth, allowing him to see well enough for his squinting eyes to follow the bars ahead of his movement.

His chest constricted in excitement as the view changed. He moved faster as much from eagerness as from the burning desire to breathe. Then he was there, and his hands found what he had so desperately hoped to find: an end to the bars. He kicked back upwards and erupted from the surface, bouncing off a surprised Gerens as he spluttered and sucked air into grateful lungs.

Hanging onto the bars with one hand, he wiped water from his face with the other, and grinned. 'The bars do not go all the way to the bottom. We can pass underneath.'

They howled with joy and relief. 'How did you know?' Sophaya asked.

'I didn't, it was a guess.' He pointed up at the tide mark on the wall. 'That would be the high tide. The encrusted parts of the bars extend only to that height also, reinforcing that theory. It made me think that if the tide went as high as that, it probably wouldn't drop much further than we are just now, or it would be more of a rise and fall than any I ever saw in my time on the ship. I guessed if there was always a significant depth of water here, they might only feel the need to block only what was necessary.'

'And you were right,' the girl smiled. 'Now let's get out of here.'

She produced her knife once more and cut the rope between her and Gerens, while Brann severed the length attaching Grakk to Gerens. As he did so, he could feel the tribesman's body tense almost as much as when they had entered the water.

'I'm sorry, Grakk, this must be a taste of the hells for you.'

The man's voice was quiet. 'The greatest fear of someone who cannot swim is the thought of not being able to make your way to the surface. To take yourself downwards, there-fore...'

410

Brann put a hand on his shoulder. 'I know you can do it. I have seen the strength you have in you.'

A smile came back with the words. 'I must do it. I will do it. I just will not enjoy it overly much.'

Brann couldn't help smiling back. 'We will all go together, but I will stay right behind you. I will be able to see you all of the way.' He spoke to all of them. 'It is far enough down to make you feel that you need to breathe, so the best way is to go fast and get moving upwards as soon as you can.'

'Remember,' Gerens said, 'we most likely have no one chasing us. We have time. If you struggle to get far enough down, just come back up on this side and regain your energy.'

They all nodded at the good sense of it, but Brann could see in all of them that they just wanted out of this place without delay. Gerens and Sophaya looked at each other and ducked down, quickly disappearing. Brann was about to give some further encouragement to Grakk but, before he could start, the man sucked in a giant breath and threw his head below the water, pulling himself down. The boy followed closely, staying to one side to avoid the thrashing legs. Grakk looked back to check Brann was there, a brief look but enough of one to show his eyes wide with terror. The fear worked in his favour as well, though, driving his arms at a frantic rate. Brann had to move quickly to keep up. He saw the shapes of the first two float up on the other side and knew he must be close to the gap and, sure enough, Grakk was pulling himself under the bars, his movements speaking eloquently of his desire to be anywhere but there.

Relief flooded Brann as he saw his friend start to rise to safety but, as he did so, he was dragged back. His hood

411

had snagged on the end of a bar and, as his momentum swung him under the barrier the fabric pulled tight. The surge of the water was not rough, but it was enough to twist him and the grip of the hood became even more secure. He grabbed behind him as his legs swung high and fear swept down through him. His fingers scrabbled frantically, but the water pulled him away from the bars and the hood became taut, caught out of his reach.

The urge to breathe became almost irresistible, and he had to clamp his teeth together to avoid the insane reaction of opening his mouth. He looked despairingly at the brightness of the surface as Grakk, almost there, glanced back. Immediately the man grabbed at the bars to halt his ascent.

A dark look fell over his face and he started pulling himself back down. Brann was shuddering with the effort of not breathing and flailing behind him at the hood. Grakk's hand brushed his arms aside and, with a flick, dislodged the hood. Grabbing each other, they kicked for the air.

Gerens and Sophaya had looked down in time to see Grakk free him and dived to help pull them the last few yards.

Air had never felt so good. Brann coughed and retched, but it was a delight to do so. Grakk was doing the same while the pair hung onto their companions.

'I think,' said Gerens, as he started to steer Brann towards the closest rocks, 'I'll return to being over-protective about you.'

They hauled themselves onto the rocks, uncaring about the scrapes and knocks from the swell of the sea that hit them repeatedly against the rough surface until they were clear of the water. Brann glanced to check that Gerens still had the pack with the Star Stone and marvelled, not for the first time in his life, at the boy's deceptive strength. Then he was content to lie, as the others were, with the sun on his face and the sea breeze brushing over him. When you reduce your life to just dying or not dying, it is astounding how wonderful the most mundane things feel.

It would be good to see the others again. His eyes shot open. 'They won't know!' Three pairs of eyes turned to him. 'Cannick and Hakon. And Marlo.'

'Of course,' Sophaya said. 'They will have waited in the district where they thought we would emerge.'

Brann cursed his mistake. 'When I was told we would escape the keep from below, I assumed it would be through the sewers.' He thought on how their companions would have scoured the most likely areas while instead they had travelled the gods only knew how far from the edge of the city itself.

He pushed himself to his feet. 'We must find them.'

The movement of the others was all the agreement that was needed.

The cliff above them was sheer and unscalable, but enough rocks rose from the sea at its base to allow them passage around the wide cove to the headland. Beyond that was perhaps an easier way away from the coast and there was only one means of finding out. As they scrambled their way, Brann couldn't help but notice it to be the perfect location for the secret river to emerge. Numerous clefts, fissures and caves cut into the cliff, making the cave leading to the river commonplace enough to avoid drawing attention. Further, the bay was littered with rocks that would deter water craft, something that was augmented by the lack of access to and from the land above. There was no reason for anyone to enter this cove, and no chance short of a shipwreck for anyone to find the barred entrance even by accident.

Grakk seemed to have the same thoughts. 'Perhaps they should not have installed the bars. If someone found themselves here, they would seek to leave as we do, not explore caves. That draws attention to it.'

'That is true,' Brann mused. 'But perhaps the thought of leaving open access to this river was more than they could bear. There are many strange remnants of the past and maybe they gambled that someone wrecked here would have more pressing matters on their mind and would dismiss it as unimportant.'

'Perhaps,' Grakk conceded. 'Still, I would rather they had not felt the need to build it.'

Brann smiled. 'I also. And Grakk, thank you. Once again I owe you my life.'

The man leapt over a small gap as they neared the headland. The rocks here were above the tide line and dry enough to give them a confidence in their footing. 'I felt it would have been a terrible waste of time and effort to take you across a desert and back, only to lose you here.'

Brann laughed. 'Maybe, but I will never forget you turning back under the water.'

'Fear not, neither will I.'

Brann's laugh was redoubled.

They worked their way gingerly around the tip of land, the rocks here spray-soaked and slippery. The effort was worth it, though. A portion of the cliff not far ahead had collapsed some time in history and offered a route to the top. They took it.

The area they found themselves in was the last type of landscape Brann expected to see, more akin to his homeland

than the arid baked land around and beyond Sagia. It was
farmland, fertile and green, stretching to the extent of the
view. Not as lush, perhaps, as around his village but then
he expected few places were treated to as much rain as the
plants in his homeland enjoyed. What grew here had a
hardier look to it, which made sense considering that,
however fertile the soil and however much it was watered,
it still had the unrelenting sun pounding down upon it.

But it was green where all before had been brown, and
Brann saw his surprise mirrored on the faces of Gerens and
Sophaya. Not so Grakk, who had torn a strip from the
hem of his tunic and was winding it around a shallow cut
on his left hand. It was more seeping than bleeding, and
the cloth would suffice in the meantime. He glanced at the
countryside. 'Behold the garden of Sagia. We must be west
of the city, for there lie the farmlands that feed it, whereas
the villages that fish are to the east. The city was founded
here more for the great river that runs to a bay not much
further along the coast. It splits though, maybe two days'
ride inland, and the smaller branch heads east; smaller only
by comparison, for itself it is wider than most other rivers
you will see. It runs to another bay, one that has deeper
water for anchorage, one that is a natural harbour. The
city grew from the mouth of that river, but the two arms
of it make a triangle with the coast, and farmers have fed
their water into this land to bring forth all the crops that
a city teeming with people can need. Some of the richest
men in the city are those whose forebears bought the farms
of those around them, or acquired them by less honest
means.'

Gerens looked at Sophaya. 'You did not know of this?'

'Of course I know the Tagorus. It runs right through my

city and feeds the canals, everyone knows the river. But this...' She shrugged. 'I had never left the walls of the city until this man dragged me across a desert. In the poor quarters you are more concerned that there is food on your plate at all than wondering where it came from.' She smiled sweetly. 'And anyway, my crop is reaped in the houses of the rich and from their purses and pockets in the streets.'

Brann turned to Grakk. 'How far are we from reaching those streets?'

Grakk squinted into the distance. 'Maybe a couple of hours, or three.'

'And if this area is so precious to the city, how likely are we to encounter soldiers safeguarding it?'

They looked at one another and crouched to retrieve their weapons from the canvas bags. It had been sensible to keep them compact and strapped tight to them when clambering over rocks that they could have caught upon, but now they all felt much more comfortable with them restored to more familiar, and accessible, places.

They found a dusty track between endless rows of vines and followed Grakk's lead. It didn't take long before the sun finished the job of drying their clothes, a process it had started while they climbed over the rocks but which had been slowed by the occasional spray of sea water. Small tendrils of steam escaped the black material, as if it were smoke and the fabric were about to burst into flame, but the vaporising water had a cooling effect and Brann enjoyed the feeling while it lasted. The sword bumping gently against his leg felt good, too. After their recent experiences, such simple things were the stuff of the heavens.

The beating sun drove their thoughts towards shade, but the idea of lounging under a tree didn't appeal in an area that was regularly patrolled and, in any case, they were urged onwards by the need to find their friends.

In the end, though, it was their friends who found them. Movement in the haze of the heat resolved into a cart drawn by a single horse. As they drew towards the meagre cover of some twisted olive trees, their trunks barely half the width of even Sophaya's torso, and conscious of the suspicious appearance of four people clad identically in tight-fitting black clothes, a shout of delight from the cart stopped them. Marlo stood beside the driver – presumably Cannick, from his build – waving vigorously. The pace of the cart was obviously not enough for another, as Hakon leapt from behind the pair and loped towards his four friends.

Without waiting for words, the boy's large arms enveloped each of them in turn. Brann's ribs creaked under the exuberance of the hug and he feared for Sophaya's slight frame, but still it was a welcome that cheered him to his soul.

Marlo was soon upon them, also, slapping backs and grinning, while Cannick sat quietly on the cart, reins loose in his hands and a smile settled on his face. 'You decided against the direct route from the keep, then.'

Grakk was disentangling himself from Hakon. 'It was cluttered with too many sharp objects.'

Brann's curiosity was cutting through his delight. 'How did you know where to come?'

Cannick lifted a wide-brimmed hat from his close-cropped head and wiped his brow with a scarred forearm. 'The slave who helped you. His master guessed your route would be unknown to us, and sent him to the house with news of the area to head for to look for you.'

Marlo was almost dancing in glee. 'I told you I knew

where to go. I did, did I not?'

Cannick reached down and ruffled his hair, but Sophaya's eyes narrowed. 'How would a city boy like you know these lands?'

The boy winked. 'Some poor children earn a few coins by picking the harvest rather than pockets, you know.'

She smiled innocently and handed him his dagger.

'So,' Hakon said. 'What happened? You must have a story to tell.'

'We can tell it as we travel,' Grakk suggested.

'You got it, though?' Cannick asked.

Grakk patted Gerens's pack, and the veteran nodded, replaced his hat and started to turn the cart.

Cannick was joined by Grakk on the seat and the younger members of the group ranged themselves in the back, leaning against the low sides. Brann, though, lasted only a few moments before he stood, resting his hand on Cannick's broad shoulder for balance as he used the height of the cart to scan the surrounding countryside. 'Soldiers?'

The veteran shook his head. 'Unlikely we will see any until the city gate. All patrols have been recalled to the citadel, and only the basic complements are left at the guard towers around the farmlands.' His face was straight but his voice betrayed his amusement. 'It seems the very keep was breached by raiders and a young noblewoman was left traumatised after being molested most uncouthly.'

Grakk was indignant. 'I was particularly respectful and pleasant.'

Cannick couldn't keep the smile from his face. 'I'm sure you were, my friend. I would expect nothing less. It would be an unjust besmirching of your reputation, if only anyone knew it had been you.'

418

Grakk stared at the road ahead. 'Anonymity is a good friend, on occasion.'

Cannick grunted. 'On many an occasion. You cannot be a target if your enemy knows not of you.'

'So,' Brann said, 'we just ride through the gates?'

Cannick laughed. 'We shall have to be a little more subtle than that, youngster. And especially not into a city panicking about mysterious intruders with you four dressed as if you are trying hard to look like everyone's idea of an assassin.' He jerked his thumb at a sack lying behind the seat. 'You will find that clothing more appropriate.'

Brann pulled out the plain garb of common workmen, and passed it among the other three. Before long they were dressed as were the trio who had met them, and their dark clothing had been buried in a shallow hole scraped from the hard dirt of an olive grove.

They fell into silence and Brann enjoyed the chance to rest his weary limbs. He rested against the side of the cart, the bumping and creaking of the wheels on the baked track a simple pleasure, and drew the black knife, toying with it and marvelling once more at its every facet.

Grakk glanced round to scan the track behind them and caught the movement in Brann's hand. His eyes widened. 'Young man,' he said softly, holding out a hand. 'May I?'

Reluctantly, Brann handed it over, a slight panic clutching his heart as he saw it pass to another. The tribesman turned it slowly in his hands, his eyes drinking in every angle, and grasped the hilt to feel its balance.

'I have heard of such, but never suspected the reality of the craftsmanship. It is truly a wonder.'

The attention of the others had been aroused and there was nothing for it but to allow the weapon to be passed from one to the other, eliciting gasps and murmurs of admiration from each in turn.

Sophaya was the last to hold it. 'When you revealed the task, you omitted to mention you had this.'

'I did not want to boast like a child.'

Sophaya smiled. 'Or perhaps you did not wish to risk it falling into another's possession. You should have trusted me.'

Brann bristled. 'I have trusted you with my life, without which no item has much use to me. We all have, with each other. This was entrusted to me for a short while, and my reasons for saying nothing of it were purely because I thought it unnecessary.'

Gerens laid a hand on his arm. 'Steady, Chief.' He looked at Sophaya. 'Not every situation requires talking.'

She smiled disarmingly. 'I am sorry, Brann. I should not have teased you.' Her wrist flicked and the blade quivered in the wood to the side of Brann's leg. 'It is a beautiful weapon.'

He sighed, the anger drifting from him as the water had earlier from their clothes. 'I will find it a wrench to return it to its owner.' He pulled it from the wood and slipped it back into its sheath.

Noise ahead started to reach them. Raised voices and the clang and rattle of work drifted on the sporadic breeze and grew as the horse pulled them towards it. At first all they could see was the haze of a dust cloud that was raised beyond the fields of wheat they travelled between but, as they drew closer, they could see construction being undertaken on a large scale.

'This, young Brann,' Cannick said over his shoulder, 'is our slightly more subtle route into the city.'

420

They were all standing to gain a better view, and Brann gripped the back of the seat to steady himself against the push of the jostling bodies. 'What do they build?'

'Houses,' Marlo said simply. 'The Emperor has decided to ease some of the worst of the crowding in some areas.'

'Beyond the city walls?'

Sophaya had returned to sit near the back of the cart. 'There are many parts of the city that sit outwith the walls. The fortifications were built a hundred generations ago, or more. The population did not stop growing at their completion.'

Brann frowned. 'Does that not leave them vulnerable in time of war?'

Grakk turned in his seat. 'Do you not remember my lesson in military history when first we walked through the royal floors of the keep?'

Brann closed his eyes. It seemed so long ago. The position of the citadel, the fortifications of the keep, the organisation of the army's millens... His eyes opened. 'They fight in the open. The city walls are not a defence.'

Grakk nodded in approval. 'Indeed, for these walls have been nothing more than a means of monitoring who enters and leaves the city, more for taxation reasons than anything else, although any form of defence becomes a defence should you need it to be so. However, they do indeed prefer to fight their battles on the plains, after the foe has dragged itself across the Deadlands.'

Gerens glanced over his shoulder. 'And if the enemy is uncooperative and chooses to land by ship instead?'

'Remember, this Empire was won by war but maintained by trade. Seaborne trade. Those vessels that survive the warships of the Emperor's fleet will find the warriors they discharge will face the Imperial host before they have even left the clutches of the surf. This is a practical people: they deal in warfare according to what is necessary, and nothing more.'

Brann nodded. 'I can understand that.'

They had reached the edge of the construction and the clamour overwhelmed them. Men were in constant motion, small groups overseen by leaders who ensured they kept to their highly organised tasks. Cannick turned along the edge of the activity for a short distance before finding a small area where several other similar carts were ranged neatly and horses were corralled. A tall man, wearing only an open vest over his broad chest and his long black hair tied behind to swing like the tails of the horses he was tending, noticed their arrival and walked to meet them. He caught the bridle of their horse and stroked its face in affection.

Cannick tossed him a small purse that clinked as it was snatched from the air. 'A bonus, for your future discretion.' The man grinned, waited for them to dismount, and led the horse away.

They bunched as Cannick turned to them with a smile. 'You may have noticed that my clothing is black, while yours is a lovely shade of light brown. You may also notice if you look further at our surroundings that the overseers are wearing black, while the common workers are in the same lovely shade of light brown. You are now Cannick's squad of workers. Come along.'

Without further ado, he turned on his heel and strode purposefully into the maelstrom of activity. They had no option but to follow.

Cannick walked until he saw what he must have sought. Loose stones were piled to twice the height of a man and a team of men, their tunics turned dark by sweat, shovelled them into heavy sacks that were then tied to secure them. A stream of workers fetched the sacks and carried them under the direction of their particular leader, and Cannick loudly indicated that his workers should do the same.

A sack each on their shoulders, Cannick led them on a meandering route that headed for the nearest gate to the city. Only two almost-completed buildings, the wooden scaffolding indicating structures five storeys in height, remained between them and their goal when they were questioned for the first time.

A gaunt Scribe a fraction of Cannick's age halted the veteran warrior with a light rod of office laid across the chest. Cannick looked down at it, then at the man enquiringly.

The Scribe's tone was predictably haughty. 'And why do you take these materials to there?'

Cannick's tone was suitably bored. 'Because Barus told us to.'

The Scribe frowned. 'Which Barus?'

Cannick frowned and squinted at the sky. 'The big bald one.'

The Scribe pulled a sheet from his satchel and examined it. 'I was not aware of a consignment of this sort being necessary at this time.' His words had become unsure and he looked at Cannick, who was unconcerned and watching a mason above them adjust the edge of a block to ensure it sat more snugly in the building's outer wall. 'Big, you say?'

Cannick nodded encouragingly. 'That's the one. You know, the grumpy bastard who broke a labourer's jaw last week,' he added helpfully.

'I do not know this Barus.' He looked at the sacks and back at Cannick. 'But if you are sure it was for here, then you had better make sure you deliver them. For your sake, of course.'

'Of course,' Cannick smiled. 'Come on, lads.'

They wound their way between the workmen and past a young woman who was using a design on a large parchment to instruct several overseers, drawing a complimentary and lingering glance from Hakon. Brann assumed the boy wasn't admiring her technical expertise.

They gained sight of the gate and stopped in their tracks. Grim soldiers thronged about it, questioning all who sought to pass through in either direction, and searching them assiduously.

'Well, that's that, then,' Hakon said, looking pointedly at the Gerens's pack.

Cannick looked embarrassed. 'It wasn't like that when we left the city.'

Grakk dismissed his apology. 'It is what it is. If the rest of the gates are like that, and you would expect they are, then we will have difficulty in reaching the house.'

Marlo's voice piped up. 'Only if we have to reach the house.'

Cannick frowned. 'We must rest and equip ourselves for the next part of the task.'

Marlo smiled. 'Cassian's school has facilities and equipment.' He winked at Cannick. 'And it lies outwith the walls.'

Cannick grinned. 'Young man, I could hug you, would it not arouse suspicion for your overseer to do so.'

Grakk nodded. 'If we are all in agreement, it would seem the best option.' The expressions of his companions confirmed that they were. 'Which way, then, young Marlo?'

The boy stared at the city until he got his bearings. 'Back the way we came just slightly, then angle to follow the line of the wall, keeping the city on your right.'

'Fine, let's go.' Cannick stopped and turned. 'And bring those sacks again. We will attract less attention if we look as if we are engaged in work.'

They groaned but could not argue against the logic.

They worked their way back past the two apartment blocks. The young lady had moved on, to Hakon's clear disappointment, but the Scribe remained where they had last seen him and he stared as they passed.

'Wrong Barus,' Cannick said without missing a stride.

Their approach had been spotted and Salus had opened the gate personally and with a broad smile.

Welcomed with even more enthusiasm by Cassian, washed, rested and fed, their spirits had improved somewhat, and Brann and Marlo strolled quietly through the garden as afternoon started to turn towards evening.

Marlo could never stay quiet for long, though. 'This old man we met in the keep,' he mused. 'Any idea who he is? He has managed to help us with a fair amount of resources.'

'We?'

Marlo shrugged. 'Your description sounds exactly like the man I was sent to whenever a message needed to be passed, and how many old men do you think there are in the keep taking an interest in you? I asked Cassian who he might be, but you know what he's like. Did you get a hint of his standing?'

'I wish I knew. I'd like to know more of him, given he knows so much about us.' He laughed softly. 'Which is a situation that is not too comfortable when people seek my death. If only we knew someone else with contact with the royals.'

It was Marlo's turn to laugh. 'You make us sound like nobles moving in high circles, with many friends at the court of the Emperor.'

'True, true.' He noticed Cassian's burly form leaning into a plant and pulling it close to breath in its aroma. 'But maybe not. Do you remember that our Cassian has a brother who may have connections and sources?'

He approached the elderly man. 'Cassian, I've had a thought.'

The old soldier beamed in delight. 'Well done, my boy! You must be very proud.' He clapped him on the shoulder and ambled up the path. 'Keep up the good work.'

The boys looked at each other for a long moment before the laughter burst from them. 'Well,' Brann conceded, 'at least I was given praise. But I feel that might not be our most productive path to information.'

The pair were still chuckling as they passed the Sleeping House. A small stone flicked off the back of Brann's head and he turned with a yelp of pain as a familiar voice called out a challenge.

'There's enough light for a sparring bout. If you cry like a girl at a tiny stone on the head, I reckon I could take you easy this time.'

Brann grinned, rubbing the back of his head ruefully. 'Cry like you, you mean, Breta?'

She was leaning against the wall, arms folded, but now she stood straight, seeming bigger than ever. 'Oh, so the little flea does want to fight?' She advanced on him.

Brann help up his hands. 'I admit it, I got lucky last time.' She came on, still. 'I'm not here for sparring, Breta, just...'

She was almost upon him and his smile slipped. She lunged at him and he realised too late that she was actually coming for him. The huge arms wrapped around him and drew him into a hug.

'I am glad to see you back, little flea. Only Breta is allowed to beat you, no one else.'

He was finding it hard to breathe and his face was squashed sideways against breasts that were, each one, bigger than his head. He was beginning to wish it had actually been a fight she had wanted. 'Thank you,' he managed to say into her chest, though it was debatable whether any present would be able to tell what the muffled words were. She was satisfied, though, and he was released. Marlo grinned at the sight of him sucking in the warm air of dusk.

'I hear it would take some feat to beat you, right enough.' Mongoose was crouched against the wall, watching with amusement in her eyes as well.

Brann managed a weak smile. 'Not right at this moment, it wouldn't.'

She rose to her feet and paced over, every movement filled with balance and menace, as though she could spring in an instant. 'I also hear you are embarking on a short trip.'

Brann and Marlo looked at her sharply. 'What do you know?' Brann demanded. 'How do you know?'

It was her turn to hold up her hands in supplication. 'Only we two know. Cassian asked us as soon as you arrived to prepare for you what you would need for a short journey. That's the sum of our knowledge. Not where you go, or why, though it might be nice to learn such, were you to have enough sense to take us with you. We are hoping you may benefit from a couple of extra pairs of hands.'

Brann stared in astonishment. 'You want to come with

us? Even though you have no idea where we are going or with what intent?'

Breta shrugged. 'Nothing better to do, to be honest.'

'And,' Mongoose said, 'we have been here many a year, Breta and I. Arrived within a day of each other, we did, and been here ever since. It keeps a roof over our heads and food in our bellies, but after a while, it all gets a bit repetitive. A change would be welcome.'

'And Cassian would let you go?'

She pulled aside the collar of her tunic. 'Do you see a chain here?' She stood on her toes to grab the larger girl's collar. 'Or here. Cassian has a say in whether we are allowed to stay, but not in whether we can leave.'

Brann grinned and bowed extravagantly. 'Then I am delighted to welcome you on board.'

Mongoose looked unsure. 'You can say so? I thought you would discuss it with your companions. You are certain the others will accept us, too?'

'Let's face it,' Marlo grinned, nodding at Breta. 'Would you like to tell her she wasn't welcome?'

Chapter 9

She caught him by surprise, as she often did. His senses were not as acute as once they were, and she had a particular way of moving unnoticed.

Had he heard her approach, he may have quietly closed the narrow wooden box and hidden it by his side in the chair, the shadows cast by the fire hiding it from a casual glance. He cursed his lack of care. The brick lay to one side, exposing the secret of the compartment, and the box lay on his lap for all to see. She knew of it, so no harm was caused, but had another approached, they would have seen all.

It would not have been disastrous; it would not have exposed any plans or even that he planned at all. It was not so much the possible exposure of a secret that he cursed, but more the lack of forethought that had made it possible.

She must have seen it in his face. 'I am old,' he growled. 'I know.'

'You are old, yes, as am I,' the hoarse whisper acknowledged. 'Age brings its own strengths and removes those we previously possessed. When you think, you can draw on a

life of lessons, so it balances the loss of a little alertness. It is no great failing that you heard me not, for I move like a cloud's shadow. It is the way I was taught to walk, and it has never left me.'

His eyes snapped up, new life within. 'You were taught?' At last, a grain of knowledge of her past.

She gave a slight smile. 'It has been a long time, what seems a different life, but yes, I was once an acolyte.'

'An acolyte to whom?'

She just shrugged and walked to place a vase with fresh flowers on a table. He knew from past frustration that there was no point in pressing her.

She was back at his side and lifted the box from his hands as he stared at the dancing flames, her finger stroking at the softness of the velvet interior.

'You worry about its safe return, do you?'

He sighed. 'The truth?'

'Would I ask otherwise?'

It was not easy to say, but the words came nonetheless. 'I have had what was in that box for half a century and a score more years, and was with the boy who now straps it to his belt for less than the time it takes the sun to move a finger's width, and yet I fret more for his safe return than that of the knife.'

She gently shut the box and rubbed at the wood absently with one thumb as she thought on it.

'Sometimes...' She carefully placed the box back in its alcove and slid the brick back in place, taking care to ensure its fit rendered it indiscernible from its immovable neighbours. She stared at the brick, her back to him. 'Sometimes we must turn our eyes and our thoughts from that which we hold dear, and trust to the gods to watch over it. And,

430

more, trust the object of our anxiety to be strong enough to fulfil its purpose.'

He nodded slowly. *'And prepare for their return. For return, they must.'*

****

They travelled on foot, for they had been advised that the terrain would not be amenable to horses or camels, though they did bring a sorrowful-looking mule to carry the bulk of their supplies. It was sure-footed and happy to walk at two-legged pace.

The reason for walking soon became apparent a day from the city. Cassian had directed them inland in a great arc that would take them away from curious eyes that may glance their way from atop the city wall and then eastwards towards the area known as the Plain of the Axeduel, and the reason for the name became as apparent as the need to walk, for both sprang from the same feature. The huge gently sloping slabs of rock underfoot, the smallest the size of an average marketplace in the city, were littered with clefts hacked from the ground when, legend told, two axe-wielding gods had fought a mighty battle. Where the blades had missed the foe and bitten into the rock, the long tapering gullies had been left, some too narrow for anything other than a small animal to enter, others of a size that could accommodate a city warehouse. Where the sweat of the gods had landed, it was said, it had melted the very rock itself, and sure enough, the surface of the slabs was pocked with small holes, from the size of a fist to that of a washing bowl, though Brann thought it was more like great slabs of reddish-brown cheese rather than from sweating gods. Either way, a horse would have snapped an ankle within the first hundred yards.

They were dressed once more as they had been in the desert, and Brann was glad of it. If anything, it was even hotter here, the rock beneath them holding the heat and baking them from below as much as the sun was roasting them from above.

After a further day of walking, they stopped. They had entered the area fully now, and the vastness of their task was apparent. The bare rock stretched to the limit of their vision, and it was impossible to walk more than a hundred paces at a time, and often far less, before it was necessary to pick a path around a crevice. Brann looked around the party; not one of them exuded any sort of confidence and Hakon looked as mournful as the mule.

Cannick scratched his ear. 'They give you any directions from here?'

Brann shook his head. 'I don't think they know themselves. This man took himself here to get away from people, and he seems to have picked the right spot.'

Cannick looked at the three women and Marlo. 'You locals know anything about this area? Where we might start?'

'Don't look at me,' Breta grunted. 'I came off a ship when I was sixteen and went straight into Cassian's compound when my parents and sister managed to shit and spew themselves to death within a week.'

Mongoose shrugged. 'I don't know where I am from. Can't remember much before Cassian's place but streets hard under my arse and a begging bowl in my hand. Cassian's wife even gave me my name. I was twelve, they believed, when they took me in, and as far as I know my name before then was Girl.'

'Doesn't matter where we've been or who we are.' Sophaya walked forward from the group to stare over the landscape. 'No one knows anything about this place. No one from the city comes here. No one in their right mind from anywhere comes here.'

'Which, I guess,' Cannick said, 'is why our mad smith came here.'

Grakk was scanning the area with the tube he had let Sophaya use in ul-Detina. 'There is one advantage in this terrain: should a man build a house between here and the horizon, we would see it.' He snapped the tube shut with an air of finality. 'We do not.'

Brann looked at him. 'If we don't know anything about what is here, then all we can work from is what we do know.' He looked around his companions. 'All we may know is that he is a man and he works metals. At the very least a man needs food, and a smith needs something to burn and metal to work. Do you see a ready supply of any of this around here? Unless he can eat and burn rock, he must be getting provisions from somewhere.'

Grakk smiled, and pointed south. 'The fishing villages. Pine trees were one of the main reasons they settled there, for the trees become their boats. They grow aplenty between the villages and the plain right along this stretch of coast. They have some small areas of crops and livestock, but their diet is, of course, mainly from the sea. From the villages he can source food, wood, clothes, even charcoal. And, though they will have their own, the villages will always need the work a smith can offer with repairs and replacements.'

Brann was satisfied. 'Then I say, in the morning we follow your finger. He will not want to have to carry his supplies

433

overly far. When we encounter a village, we can ask if they know of him.'

A collection of nods and shrugs indicated their acceptance, and the next morning their path turned south. Slowly they made progress, and eventually a smudge on the border of land and sky was revealed by Grakk's looking-tube to be a line of trees.

The tribesman was happy. 'The coast, and the villages, lie to the other side.'

They had not even reached a point from where the trees were defined to the naked eye when Sophaya gave a shout and a point. Their eyes were drawn to another smudge in the distance, but this one was far closer than the horizon and in a single location. And rising a short distance towards the sky.

Grakk's tube was already at his eye. He smiled. 'Smoke.'

They grinned at each other and Hakon whooped and slapped Brann on the back with a force that felt like his eyeballs would be ejected.

They angled their course and headed in as straight a line as the crevices would allow. With every step, though, Brann's nerves grew. What if it was not the right place? Some of the ravines had contained water, springs leaking to the surface, and dry brittle vegetation had fought to emerge as a result. What if some of that had burst aflame from the sun? It was not unknown.

As they closed, his fears were banished. The unmistakable dull ring of metal pounding metal began to reach their ears, and their pace quickened in anticipation, much to the clear annoyance of the mule.

Gerens stopped. 'Do you notice something?'

They clustered beside him, frowning.

Breta sounded impatient. 'I see nothing.'

'Exactly,' said Gerens. 'Where is his house? And his forge?'

A smile spread over Grakk's face. 'He is in a crevice. Thanks be to the gods that a smith makes smoke, else we might never have found his lair.'

They hurried towards the grey plume, becoming aware that it emanated from one of the larger openings, a gully around three times the length of a ship and twice the width at its top in the centre, narrowing to maybe a third of that at the floor level. It maintained its width for most of its length, tapering sharply to a blunt point at either end. Most significantly, a small brook, the gurgling water sparkling in the light from the high sun, ran through a gently winding groove it had cut in the floor over the gods only knew how many thousands of years, disappearing through a crack in the rock at the near end and running from a pool at the other, into which, Brann presumed, it arrived through an equivalent opening from its underground course.

The stream ran directly through structures that had been created near to the pool by fixing two wooden roofs from one side to the other. The building closest to the pond had walls enclosing it. The other comprised merely the roof itself and was the forge, a fact evinced by equipment therein which could be seen under the angle of the roof.

It would have been an idyllic scene; idyllic to a deaf man. The sound of the hammering was accompanied by a relentless stream of curses and invective that was so varied and inventive that some of it seemed new to Cannick and all of it was impressing Hakon.

Brann moved to the lip of the gulley and cupped his hands about his mouth. 'Hello!' he called, hoping it would carry above the sounds of the forge. 'I seek...' He searched in his head for the name told to him. 'I seek the smith, Tarkanan Dar Tenaat.'

The hammering stopped.

'Piss off!'

The hammering restarted.

Brann tried again.

'I bear a gift for you.'

This time the hammering didn't even stop. 'What gift would I need? I have all I require. Why have you not yet pissed off?'

'It is a gift from Alam-ul-Nazaram-ul-Taraq.' There was a stirring behind him from his colleagues, but his attention was on the scene below.

'Why would I want anything that decrepit old bastard has to give? You have one last chance to piss off before I come up there myself and stick this poker right up your arse. And it is glowing hot, by the way.'

Brann took a breath. He would soon have to march down there regardless. 'It is a gift that fell from the sky many lifetimes ago.'

The hammering stopped in an instant and a small wiry man emerged from the cover of the roof. It was hard to tell if he was dark from natural skin colour or from the forge, and he wore only breeches and a leather apron that extended to his knees. His head swivelled until he found Brann. 'You took this long to tell me that? What are you waiting for?' He pointed to slightly further along the side Brann stood at. 'There. Bring your friends if you like.'

'Decent of him,' Hakon murmured.

A shallow path had been cut into the wall of the crevice and the party wound its way down. The hammering had started again and they waited short of the forge, the mule taking advantage of the cool water running beside them.

A burst of steam filled the forge and the man emerged. 'Tricky moment. Joining two pieces. Got to do it at exactly the moment the iron is hot enough.' He looked at Brann. 'This gift from the sky?'

Brann nodded and turned to the mule, which ignored him as he pulled a hessian bag from the load on its back. It was heavier than he had anticipated and his appreciation of Gerens's strength was heightened at the thought that the boy had borne it from the citadel through the journey they had taken, and without fuss or complaint. He made to hand it to the smith, but the man waved him away and gestured at a rough table sitting just outside the forge. As Brann sat it there, the man removed his apron and took a rag from the back of his breeches, wetting it and using it to wipe grime from his face and hands. The skin beneath was as dark in colour as the material he would be asked to work with.

He flashed a grin at the boy that came and went in the time of a blink and strode to the table. Drawing open the top of the bag, the smith reverently removed the Star Stone. He turned it over in every direction, before lifting it high and squinting at it against the sunlight.

Eventually, he nodded. 'It is what you say.' He laid it down gently and extended his arm, placing his palm over Brann's heart. 'I am Tarkanan.' Brann felt it would be inappropriate to suggest that there were not many other contenders for that identity in the immediate area. 'And you are?'

The hand was still on his chest, so he copied the gesture as he spoke his name.

The man frowned as he dropped his arm. 'Not the most

common name in this part of the world. A Brann fought in the Arena, then the Rat Runs, and lived.' He raised his eyebrows. Brann nodded. 'That makes sense.'

'You heard out here?'

'I heard in the village where I barter for food.'

Brann indicated the Star Stone. 'Can you work it?'

'How would I know? I haven't tried.'

'Will you try?'

'What smith would let the chance pass? Or fail to devote their life to trying?'

Brann smiled. 'That sounds dedicated enough, sir.'

'I will start in the morning.' He pointed at Hakon and Breta. 'I will need him. And her. I lack muscle.'

'I don't think that will be a problem. But will you not have to extract the metal from the rock? I have no knowledge of the process, but it would seem lengthy to me.'

The smith frowned. 'Extract?'

Brann pointed. 'From the Star Stone.'

The man was bemused. 'You are as ignorant as the primitives who named it. This is not rock with metal through it. This is the metal, nothing more. The gods did not hide their gift, but gave it to us in its glory that we may try to prove our worth by solving the mystery of working it.'

Brann looked at the artefact with even more respect.

'Sir?' It was Marlo. Brann noticed the way that everyone was more respectful to someone reputed to be mad. If you did not know what the person would do next, he supposed, it was well to try to keep them happy. 'I also have something for you.' He handed Tarkanan a small parchment, folded, tied and sealed with blue wax. He looked at the others and shrugged. 'I was only asked to deliver it. I have no idea as to its contents.'

'Neither should you, too,' the man continued. 'Now, you may make your camp by the pool. Do not drink the water downstream from the forge, as you know not what is in it. And do not piss in it upstream of my house, as I want to know what is in it. Any questions?'

Hakon spoke up. 'I have one, sir.'

The smith looked at him. 'Yes?'

'In your homeland, do you greet women in the same fashion as you greeted Brann?'

Cannick rolled his eyes and Grakk said, 'Ignore him, please. He is a barbarian in spirit.'

Tarkanan, however, was impassive. 'Indeed we do.'

Hakon grinned, but Breta turned to him. 'Try it and you lose your hand.'

The campfire was welcome in the chill night air. With no clouds to blanket the heat, it disappeared into the sky as soon as the sun dropped below the horizon. Brann wondered if the people here even knew what a cloud looked like. Well, inland anyway; he had seen a few over the sea.

'It's a fair-sized house,' Hakon mused. 'You would think we could fit in there in some fashion.'

Mongoose looked up. 'It is his right to reserve his privacy. We showed up out of the blue. And if we had ventured into this land with no means of camping overnight, we would probably not have made it this far.' Mongoose and Breta had been easing their way into a company who had already been through much together, and their reluctance to join freely in conversation was a symptom of that. However, the smaller gladiator's strong sense of propriety had already started to show on occasion and, this time, it had forced her tongue.

Grakk shared her view. 'She is correct.' His eyes slid to Brann. 'You mentioned a name when you shouted to the smith.'

'Tarkanan Dar Tenaat? That's the smith himself.'

'We are aware of that. The other one.'

'Oh, Alam-ul-Nazaram-ul-Taraq. I'm actually quite surprised I managed to remember that.'

'Several of us are wondering why you hadn't thought to mention it before.'

Brann shrugged. 'You know him?'

'Know of him. You don't perhaps recall having seen him sitting to the side of the Emperor at the Throne Room in the Sky?'

'Of course. I thought he was an old retainer, perhaps, or a senior official. Maybe even a beloved former servant.'

'He did indeed serve the Empire.' The tribesman's eyes rose to meet his. 'As Emperor.'

Brann didn't know what to say. Grakk looked at Marlo. 'You did not know either, though you met with him when bearing messages?'

Marlo was pale. 'I had never seen him or his image when he was in power, and he stepped aside when I was a young boy. I am still struggling to believe I was in the presence of Alam the Magnificent.'

Breta grunted. 'And probably soiling your breeches since he was also known as Alam the Merciless.'

'There is that, too,' the boy conceded, his smile noticeably absent.

'So now we know who our benefactor is,' Brann said. 'But what good does that do, other than impress us and cause Marlo to lose control of his bowels? Another holds power now, and he is just an old man.'

'He is indeed an old man,' Grakk said quietly, 'but until Alam loses his wits or dies, he will never be *just* an old man. Alam ruled with the ruthlessness of an assassin and the tactical cunning of a general. His Empire grew and was ordered: every dominion knew its place and its place was in thrall to Sagia. He looked outwards, but fought his battles in the corridors and shadows of the court to enable him to do so. The current regime looks inwards, at the life the dominions can bring to the palace, and looks less at the far reaches of the Empire.'

Cannick grunted and spat into the fire. 'Always a mistake. When you walk with your hounds, you talk to them and they keep to your heels; trust them to control themselves and they will run and chase and play and fight, and you have a task near impossible restoring order. So it is with empires.'

Grakk stared into the night. 'Indeed. When Kalos was crowned, it was widely said that Alam had stepped aside because his mind had wandered, and that was certainly the public image we saw at the court. If, as it now seems, that is not so, then not only was he was forced aside, but he has the capacity to plot his revenge.'

Gerens spoke. 'And a man such as that will achieve it.'

'And he continues to plot, from the look of the message young Marlo delivered,' Grakk said. 'Blue wax is used by royalty alone.'

'But do you not think,' Marlo's smile had returned, 'it is good that a man such as he is helping us? That is a kindness, no?'

Brann, however, was starting to feel uneasy about such help. 'A man such as he does not help from kindness. He has a use for us, there is nothing more certain. And his plan,

441

whatever it may be, is more important to him than we are.'

Grakk shook his head. 'If you think how he has helped us, what he has done, it is not us he has a use for, young Brann.' His gaze locked on the boy's eyes. 'It is you.'

Brann's unease redoubled. He did not sleep that night.

Brann took the final watch and let Mongoose return early to sleep. If he could not sleep, someone else may as well do so.

The whirling thoughts that had kept him from slumber refused to leave him. Savage images from the pits swirled into the pain of Myrana's betrayal; rage at Loku's ability to scheme freely and smugly swam into fear for Einarr and Konall; pictures of mysterious riders and reported atrocities from his homeland drifted into fear for his village; the memory of his brother's dead weight in his arms became the sight of his father casting him out.

As the first ray of dawn slipped over the lip of the gulley and touched the tears on his face, he saw the door of the house open and the smith stride towards them.

There was no preamble. 'I need my helpers. Now.'

And so each day began. No other was permitted into the forge, and Hakon and Breta would only return with hunger, fatigue and mumblings of bellows and hammering and shovelling charcoal and fetching water and endless endless trials with small sample blocks of the metal from fragments that the smith had been able to prise from one side of it.

A week passed before Tarkanan even spoke to anyone other than the pair who helped him, and that was to drop a small purse of coins among them and instruct that they hitch their mule to a cart he had in a nearby sloping gulley and fetch from the nearest village more charcoal and enough

stone to double the size of his fire oven. The cart proved
to be a hand cart, but they were able to devise straps to
affix the mule and all but Brann and Grakk walked with
it. Brann had asked the tribesman to help him practise his
swordwork; it had been too long since he had swung a
blade, but first he set off on the run he forced his legs to
complete every morning. The day did not feel begun without
it. Grakk accompanied him, at an easy lope that it seemed
he could maintain indefinitely.

They were permitted into the forge to help rebuild the
fire oven to take more charcoal and become a dome, with
thick walls and a small opening to insert the objects being
worked, a chimney and the forge's two great bellows fixed
in place to either side. A larger opening sealed by a remov-
able stone allowed access at the back to more easily insert
charcoal at the start of the process, although any additional
fuel that was required during the process would have to be
added through the small aperture at the front. The heat that
was generated through the design and the effort of Hakon
and Breta at the bellows was somehow funnelled back into
the oven's core to redouble the burning and was greater
than Brann could imagine possible, as if the sun itself had
been hauled to earth and imprisoned within the structure;
how the smith could endure working in the path of its blast
was beyond belief.

It was on the second day after the great oven had been
completed that the howl of joy was heard. The idle group
were on their feet within a heartbeat and were greeted with
the sight of the smith capering in glee, while the pair at the
bellows stood with their hands on their knees, their faces
scarlet and their breathing ragged.

Tarkanan pointed to the anvil. Lying between a pair of

tongs and a heavy hammer was a black disc, the size of a large coin.

'Is that it?' Marlo felt compelled to ask. 'I don't mean to be rude, but I was expecting something a bit more impressive for Brann to take to a former Emperor.'

The smith's expression was withering. 'Stupid boy. That is not the creation. That is the creation made possible.'

'You will not believe,' Hakon panted, 'how many different ways and combinations of ways he has tried. This is the first time it has worked. He has broken two hammers and nearly killed Breta with a rebounding blow, without changing the shape of any small block even the slightest.'

Breta nodded. 'It is true,' was all she managed to say.

Tarkanan grinned. 'It only needs to work once. So the method is known.' He pulled forth parchments. 'A little bit of this process, a little bit of that.' He swept his hand across the front of a shelf of jars of liquids and powders. 'A little of this, a little of that, but nothing of that. And definitely not that. And heat. Much heat. And water. In this order, then that order, and now we have the little of this and that and the order in our heads, no?' Breta and Hakon looked at him blankly. 'No? Well, probably not. But that is for the best. In mine, there it is, and from there we will work it.' He waved his arms as if driving hens. 'Now, out, all of you.' He turned to the large pair. 'Not my helpers,' bringing a groan from them. He pointed at Brann. 'And not you.'

Puzzled, Brann waited and was pulled over to a workbench strewn with tools and receptacles, and among them he saw the message Marlo had brought lying open. Following his eyes, Tarkanan grabbed it and tossed it among the hot coals, where it vanished in a bright flame. 'Always good to tidy up,' the smith said brightly, ignoring Brann's pointed look at the general clutter of the place.

The wiry man held out a hand. 'I believe you bear an example of the metal worked?' When Brann hesitated, he flicked his fingers impatiently. 'Come on, come on. The message mentioned it. I must follow the style as I work. You need not fear, I shall return it when my work is finished, as must you.'

Brann drew the dagger with his left hand to offer it hilt first. As Tarkanan grasped it, though, he twisted his wrist and an edge ran across the flesh at the base of the boy's thumb, parting the skin as if it were a razor across taut silk.

Brann gasped and withdrew his hand with a jerk.

'Oh my, what have I done?' The smith grabbed his arm and pulled him to the bench. 'You cannot bleed on my floor. Here.' He pulled across a wooden bowl and held Brann's hand over it. 'That's better. You will be fine. I will attend to this for you.' He gave the hand a reassuring squeeze, which only increased the rate the blood dripped into the bowl, tutted and fetched an almost clean rag, which he tied around the hand. At least the application of the makeshift bandage was well done: it was sufficiently tight and well-enough applied that the shallow cut was closed and the bleeding slowed.

The man looked pleased with his work, despite the fact that he had caused the problem, and gave the hand a pat of satisfaction. 'Good, good. Now, you strike with your right, yes?'

Brann shrugged, his mood soured. 'I can fight fairly equally with either, or at least normally I can when I am not carrying a wound. But, yes, my right is naturally stronger.'

The smith beamed. 'Splendid.' He handed Brann a small hammer that proved heavier than it looked. 'Come, observe.' He stopped to look at Hakon and Breta. 'Helpers, the bellows, if you please.' They set to work with long-suffering expressions, sweat soon glistening in the light, but Tarkanan flew into a rage. 'Like before, like before,' he screeched. 'You know what is needed. Do not destroy the process.' Hakon's back was to Brann but he guessed he bore the same murderous look as Breta did. Still, the pair redoubled their efforts, shoulders heaving and grunts growing. The small man turned to Brann, a beatific smile on his face and his voice as soft as the occasional breeze that drifted through the forge. 'We need the heat, you see, we need the heat.'

He picked up the small black disc he had shown to the group, and tossed it to Brann. He almost dropped it but managed to grasp it at the third attempt. It was as light as paper and around twice as thick as an average coin. None of this was a surprise and when the smith held out his hand, Brann tossed the disc back. The man caught it deftly and, in the same movement, inserted it into the grip of a long set of narrow-ended tongs. He turned it on its edge and placed it on the anvil, a heavy block with a hexagonal top. 'Now hit it.' He nodded at the disc. 'With your hammer,' he added helpfully.

Before Brann could do so, however, he held up a hand to stop him and moved to examine the oven. Satisfied, he lifted a chunk of the black metal, this one half the size of a fist, and took it to two bowls of paste standing alone on a table, one of the concoctions yellow and thick, the other off-white, almost grey, and closer to a liquid. He hung the grey over a small brazier where it soon began to bubble and, humming happily to himself, used a small flat piece of wood to smear the yellow gloop over the metal lump.

'Believe it or not,' Hakon grunted, each word coming with a single heave of the bellows, 'one of the ingredients was his piss, though surprisingly not in the yellow one.'

'It does have most remarkable properties.' Tarkanan's voice was almost sing-song in his rapture at this work. 'But you should devote your energy to your effort, hairy boy.'

The hairy boy found the strength for two more words, neither of them complimentary.

The smith stood to one side of the oven and used a hook on the end of a wooden handle to swing open a hinged stone that served as a door over the front opening, the blast causing a wave of heat to wash over Brann even though he stood at an acute angle from the source. A heavy outsized mitt on his hand, Tarkanan used a heavy-duty pair of tongs to place the smeared metal inside the oven, then flicked the door shut.

He retrieved his slim tongs and held the disc in place, edge up, and gave Brann a nod.

The boy struck and the disc was knocked flat, the tongs twisting from Tarkanan's hand. Without a word, the smith picked them up and reset the disc, which was undented and with not even the hint of a bend. Brann frowned. He would have to concentrate better to achieve a straighter hit if he were to make any sort of impression.

He swung directly down and caught the disc perfectly on its top edge. The hammer rebounded violently and his wrist was jarred, but the disc remained as it was. He had the technique now, and increased the power, two, three, four times. He stopped, not as a result of success but because of the stinging sweat seeping into his eyes.

'May I?' Tarkanan asked. He produced a small square of soft cotton, ironically cleaner than the fabric he had used to bind the wound, and wiped Brann's brow free of sweat. He wrung out the cloth over the bowl that already held the boy's blood, and dropped the cloth on the bench. His head tilted to one side, he counted with deliberate slowness on his fingers. When he reached six, he wheeled around.

'You may stop now,' he said brightly to the pair at the bellows, who slumped to their backs, their chests heaving. Seemingly oblivious to the heat, he reached in with the heavy tongs and transferred the lump to the anvil. It had turned a slightly lighter hue, a dark grey, but that was the only discernible difference other than the power of the heat that emanated from it. Tarkanan used a set of tongs, petite compared with even the smaller ones he had already used but not in any way delicate, to dip the metal into the bowl of grey paste, producing a sudden small cloud of steam, and returned to the anvil.

'Now you hit it again.'

Brann did so, and was astounded to find there was give in the block. He hit again, and again, squashing it slightly. He looked at the smith in surprise. He had known there must be a difference produced by the process – the flattened disc he had been shown was proof of that – but the marked nature of the difference from unyielding to malleable was astonishing.

'Here, here.' The small man was impatiently holding out a hand. Brann gave him the hammer and his hand moved automatically to spin it in a whirl as his arm swung to start working at the metal. His arms were less than half the thickness of Brann's, but the metal moved and shaped quickly, far faster than the boy would have believed possible from his own efforts. Like swordwork, he supposed, technique was the key. Like everything, really.

'You see?' The pride and delight were in equal measure in the smith's tone. 'We can do this.' The tongs twisted and swivelled beneath the hammer blows, and the block was flattened and shaped long and broad. 'And this.' He turned and folded it and hammered it once more into a single piece, metal melding as one as if he were a baker working dough. The metal absorbed the paste with each folding until there was no more sign of it, but still the smith worked. 'And over and over we do it, then heat again and again and make double then a single piece over and over each time.' He smiled. 'And that way, we have a sword.' He glanced at Brann and the boy's astonishment must have been plain. 'You are surprised at the work in a sword?'

'I am astounded at the skill you are showing right now.'

The man snorted. 'This? This is the work of an apprentice. My genius will come later.' He walked to where the stream ran through the forge and dipped the metal block into it. Once the steam had stopped rising, he returned to the anvil. Not one of his hammer blows made even the slightest impression. He grinned at Brann.

He turned to Breta and Hakon. 'You, my helpers, may go and rest now. We work the large block tomorrow, and I must prepare sufficient of the unguents for that.'

Brann was unsure whether to follow them. 'Tarkanan? Should I...?'

The smith was already selecting powders and potions from the shelf. He placed them on the table and lifted the bowl of grey paste. He waved his hand dismissively. 'Yes, yes, you go too. I will see you again once the work is done. Oh, wait.'

He walked over, the bowl still in his hand. 'You know the strangest thing? There is no odour once this has been absorbed by the metal but, by contrast, smell this now.'

He thrust the bowl under Brann's nose, the fumes burning his nostrils and catching at this throat. His eyes streamed and Tarkanan used another small cotton cloth to wipe the boy's eyes.

'My apologies, but this is most fortunate,' he said brightly, moving to the workbench at the back of the forge and carefully squeezing the moisture from the cloth into the same bowl as he had used before. He held the bowl aloft. 'Behold! Blood, sweat and tears, the final essential in the forging of a magnificent weapon.'

'I don't think that's quite what is meant by that phrase.'

The smith stirred the mixture in his bowl and sat it beside the two lotions. 'It is precisely what I mean by it.'

It took almost a month before they saw Tarkanan again. Sheets had been hung around the forge to mask the interior, and only Breta and Hakon would emerge before dark, leaner every day despite the feeding of a hunger that necessitated several extra trips to the village for additional food. There would always be a task that would keep the smith at work beyond the hours of his helpers. When pressed for news, all that either of them could offer was 'We worked the bellows, we hammered the large hammer, we held the tongs, we fuelled the oven.' Then they would wash off the grime, eat and sleep.

On the twenty-eighth day, the covers came down. There was no shout of joy from within, no congratulation of each other by the three inside, no triumphant laughter. Just the lowering of the covers.

The group by the pool looked at each other, unaccustomed to the absence of activity's clamour. They rose and, hesitantly lest they should not be doing so, edged towards the forge. But no rebuke came their way, no order to step back.

Hakon and Breta sat back-to-back on the floor beside the anvil, with identical expressions as they stared blankly. Tarkanan stood before the long worktable, his back to them. The table appeared to have been cleared, but as he heard their approach he stepped to one side, still staring at the table.

The long black knife, what Brann thought of as 'his' knife, lay in the centre, its point towards them. Crossed over and with the dagger on top, were a sword and axe, the blade of each slightly broader and thicker than normal and of the same black metal and the same long elegant simplicity of design as the knife. Even the hilt of the sword and the handle of the axe had been bound in identical fashion to that of the dagger.

All were mesmerised, but Brann was utterly transfixed. He had to force his feet forward, unable to take his eyes from them. 'Thank you,' he whispered. 'Thank you for letting us witness such as this.'

'Thank you,' the smith said, 'for giving me the opportunity to do so.' He looked at Brann. 'You may see how they feel, should you wish.'

Brann lifted the knife and placed it back in the sheath where his fingers had felt at the emptiness night after night. Slowly wrapping his fingers around the haft of the axe, he lifted it and weighed it in his hand, trying it in his right, then his left. It felt equally good in either, the balance and movement completely natural. He lifted the sword in his right hand and the two felt perfect as a pair. He placed the axe on the table and the sword felt just as good on its own. If anything, it felt better, but then a sword always was his weapon of choice, should the choice be possible.

'I made the blades with more size to them than is usual,' Tarkanan said. 'Such is the lightness of the metal, I had to give the weapons some weight in that way. Still, they should move quicker than others even of a smaller size.'

Brann breathed out slowly. 'They are beautiful.'

'They should be. I broke two grinding stones before I devised how to put an edge on them. And almost broke your two companions in the forging.'

'You are the master of your craft, without a doubt.'

The small man frowned. 'Of course I am. Else you would not be here.'

The others were gathering closer. Brann passed the axe to Gerens and the sword to Cannick, the latter sighting down the long groove of the fuller on one side then the other with a whistle of appreciation. 'Perfect,' he murmured. 'Just perfect.' He passed it to Grakk, who stared at it for a long time before nodding.

Few words were spoken as the weapons were passed around the group; none seemed sufficient. The appreciation of work-manship unforeseen was clear, however. They made their way back to the table and Tarkanan laid out a leather sheet that he carefully wrapped around the weapons and tied securely in place. The bundle fitted in a long hessian bag with a strap to sling it over a shoulder, and he laid it on the table.

'In the morning, you will collect this and leave. I have completed my work. You must complete your task. You must return this package to its owner.'

Brann lay wakened for much of that night but when dawn shone into his eyes, he realised that sleep must have claimed him at some point. He rose and washed at the pool, realising that the others were doing the same. Quietly, they packed their camp. Tarkanan was waiting at the forge, the bundle in his arms. He passed it to Brann, who hung it over his shoulder, and the small smith gestured into the dim shadow of the forge. 'Come,' he said. 'All of you.'

He led them to the same table where the weapons had been displayed, where now a soft cloth was folded over. When they had all gathered, he spread out the cloth to reveal twelve identical brooches, each one in the shape of a thin circle around exact replicas of the weapons he had forged and the knife Brann had brought, and arranged in the same crossed fashion as Tarkanan had first displayed the real versions. The sword and axe were the length of a finger, and all was crafted from the black star metal.

'We were all here when this metal was worked, and we should all have a token of that. One each, please take.' He took one himself and pinned it to his leather apron. 'I wear it as decoration, but you foreigners may find practical uses, such as cloaks or such things that you wear.'

Grakk smiled. 'They will be perfect on cloaks. They *are* perfect. Our gratitude is incalculable.'

The small man's brows furrowed. 'Your gratitude is unfounded. I do what I do, and I have done what has been done.' He gestured at the table, where the final two brooches lay. 'These are for those who sent you on this task, who made it begin.'

Brann frowned. 'Those? He was one.'

Tarkanan placed the brooches in Brann's hand. 'You will deliver them both with the bundle on your back. He will know for whom the other one is intended. And tell him that the weapons were forged as he had asked.'

Brann nodded. It was a simple enough instruction. Understanding why was not necessary, or important compared with what lay ahead.

He placed his hand on the smith's chest, over his heart. 'I agreed to this task in exchange for help we will receive for our friends. But had I known what I would witness here, I would have walked to the end of the world for it in exchange for nothing more than the chance to be a part of it.'

Tarkanan placed his own hand over Brann's heart. 'Then that is exactly why you were the person to come here.' He smiled. 'Carry them well, Brann of the Arena and the Rat Runs. Carry them well.'

It was nightfall on the second day when they slipped through the gate of Cassian's compound.

A guard ushered them quietly to the Big House, where Salus met them in the hallway. 'Cassian sends his apologies, but he is abed. However, on learning of your approach, he ordered the baths made available to you and food prepared.'

Gratitude and relief spread in equal measure across their faces. The big fighter looked at Brann. 'Not you, I am afraid, youngster.' He glanced at the shadows to one side of the hall.

The stocky slave stepped into view. He said nothing, but no instructions were needed. With a sigh, Brann dumped his travel pack on the floor and slung the long package back over his shoulder. 'May as well get it over with, I suppose. The sooner that is done, the sooner we can start planning to help...' He remembered the slave, standing quietly. 'To help our friends.' There were few people Brann now trusted, and despite his help before, the slave was still not one of them. Nor his master.

Brann made for the door without waiting for the slave,

but Salus stopped him. 'You may be best using the side door. To come out of here and walk towards the city may be a little too obvious.'

Brann looked at him. 'The side door?'

'On your morning run, did you ever happen to notice a tree with white blossom and branches that hung wide and long to the ground?'

Brann nodded. He had never seen its like before, so when he was looking for sights of interest to take his mind from his laboured legs and chest, it had caught his attention every day.

'Behind that. Beyond the wall, a track leads between the rear of two deserted farmsteads and then through the dwellings. At the other side of them you will be close to the gate.'

Brann nodded his thanks and walked out, the slave hurrying to catch up. He was not in the mood for niceties and the slave had not proved the talkative type in any case.

He pushed through the branches of the tree to find the door, a low thick affair, where Salus had said. A latch opened it from the inner side, and when he swung it inwards on silent hinges he saw the hole for a key on the other. It swung shut behind them, flush with the wall and painted the same white so as to be indistinguishable from the stonework, especially in just the light cast by the moon and stars.

They stumbled along the rutted track and entered the settlement, a haphazardly arranged collection of low buildings at complete odds with the precise order of the city itself. They wound their way through, theirs steps lit by the light from windows and the occasional open door. Those still about the streets seemed either ignorant or uncaring of the fact that the pair walking the lanes were not fellow residents.

It was with sudden surprise that they found themselves

about to step into the open, the moonlight shining on a stretch of open ground before the looming black of the city walls. The slave held Brann back and produced a length of rough rope, looping it loosely several times around the boy's wrists. 'Hold it with your hands and they will never know it is not tied.' He gestured to Brann's belt, sword, knife and the black dagger hanging from it. 'May I?'

Brann bristled. This he did not like.

'I would hardly bring a captive and not have relieved him of his weapons. I will return them as soon as we are past the gate. You have a better idea?'

He didn't, so he unbuckled the belt and handed it over. He did, after all, still have the two knives strapped to his forearms, which would be a start until he could acquire whatever else would be needed. The man pulled up Brann's hood and, in his travelling garb, he looked nothing more than a Deruul captive.

The slave led him by the loose ends of the rope towards the gate. If anything, the guards seemed even more bored than the first time he had passed through this gate when he was being delivered to Cassian's care, but then this was the time for night duty. One lazily dropped a spear to hold it across their path.

'And your reason to be coming in at this time?'

The slave grunted, his tone as bored as the demeanour of the guards. 'Took me this long to find the hovel where his captors were keeping him. Just as well he was stupid enough to get caught almost immediately or I could have been setting out even later. Buggers wanted to prattle on, too, about how well they had done. Always the way when you just want to give them their paltry reward and be on your way.'

The other guard grinned and stepped into their path.

'And what about our reward for letting you past at this time of night?'

The slave showed him a badge bearing a crest. 'You'll need to ask he who is dispensing the coin.'

The man coloured and stepped aside. 'It was only a jest. I thought your master was a merchant, not...'

'Well you know now,' the slave said shortly, brushing past them.

As soon as they were around the first corner, the man pulled the rope from Brann's wrists and Brann pushed back his hood, buckling on his belt as soon as the slave handed it over. 'Was that not a bit risky, showing those men the insignia of the royal you serve?'

'It would have been, had I not showed them the insignia of a royal I do not serve,' the slave said. This time it was Brann's turn to catch him up as he headed off without warning.

They entered the sewers at a different point from the previous time, one that was closer to the citadel thanks to the area of the city they had been in, and before long they were circling their way up the shaft towards the privy. The slave was more hurried this time, his steps chopped and quick and his head down in determination.

From a man so normally calm and certain in his assurance, it sat strangely upon him and Brann's curiosity was aroused. 'I take it your master is eager for our arrival, given your haste.'

The reply was panted. 'My master is not the issue. The haste is of my desire, and would be yours also were you to know what we would seek to avoid.'

Having been born in a valley surrounded by hills, slopes did not trouble Brann, and his voice was enjoyably more even than that of the slave. 'Enlighten me.'

'The privies, on whichever level they are sited, are arranged at intervals around the circle so that no one is directly above another. Therefore whatever drops does so unimpeded.'

'Good system.'

'But not infallible. There is always some residue that is not so accurately aimed.'

'So?' He wasn't sure where this was headed, but he was beginning to feel uneasy.

'So all of the water that is raised to the top levels for washing of people or places or whatever use it is put to, once it has been used, it is collected in a vat as wide as this shaft. Balanced on a pivot directly above this shaft. And once each night...'

Brann now knew why the slave had felt nervous. '... it is released.'

'Indeed. And should we be on these steps when that happens...'

'We will be in the shit. Not pleasant.'

'We will be too dead to care how pleasant it may be.'

Realisation dawned. 'Which is why it is a safe route for you to travel undiscovered.'

The man grunted through his laboured breathing. 'Though usually I try to travel it after the daily deluge.'

'I'm guessing from the tone of this and the speed of your steps that today's daily deluge hasn't deluged.'

'Correct.'

He needed no further encouragement. They redoubled their pace, every step fraught with apprehension but slick also with treacherous damp. The entry to the privy they sought seemed an eternity away, but reach it they did. The slave paused to listen intently at the secret panel, though Brann felt he'd rather just burst through and damn the consequences. He was still looking upwards, straining his ears for sounds above as much as the slave was for sounds beyond the wall, when the slave opened the section of wall and slipped through. Before Brann could follow, the door to the corridor was flung open, pressing the slave against the far wall of the small room, and a burly guard burst in, already unlacing his breeches. He stared at the slave, astounded that such as he would dare to use a privy as though he were a free man, and with a growl he grabbed at the slave's tunic to drag him out. His fingers failed to find a grip, though, and as his hand slipped he swung round to face directly the open section of wall and Brann stepping through, black-bladed knife in hand.

The dagger drove point-first and hilt-deep into the man's throat, piercing as if through silk. Brann stepped forward with it, clamping his free hand over the guard's mouth, feeling it sucked close in the same way that the knife was held tight as the chest tried to suck in breath to scream. Dark blood seeped between his fingers and the eyes above his hand opened wide first in shock and then wider in horror, before the light in them faded and, with a shudder, the body sagged. Brann wiped his hand on the man's tunic and eased him through the opening, letting him drop head-first and pulling the dagger free as the body slipped from sight to avoid any tell-tale spatter of blood on their clothes or within the privy. They waited in silence until there was a faint splash of corpse into water.

'Neatly done,' the slave said, leaning against the now-shut door to the corridor.

Brann shrugged, and closed the secret panel. 'Had to be.'

'I doubt it would have been done so neatly before the Rat Runs.'

'I reckon so.' Another shrug. 'Everything leaves some mark on you that cannot be erased. What is, is.'

'That's the truth.'

There was a massive rushing of water behind the wall and the pair looked at each other.

'Fortunate,' said Brann.

'And now also helpful, considering what will be washed away from below.'

'Indeed.'

The passage outside was clear, and they crept swiftly to the chambers that were becoming familiar. The slave knocked softly and they entered without waiting for a reply.

The grey old man looked up from his chair by the fire. It was angled differently from last time, Brann noticed, allowing sight of the door. He glanced at the blade in Brann's hand. 'Trouble?'

'Dealt with,' said the slave. Alam, the former Emperor of ul-Taratac, nodded.

'Do you have a rag?' Brann said. 'I should wipe this clean before returning it.'

'You should.' The wispy grey-white hair stirred as he nodded at the table to the side of the chairs. Beside a decanter of water and a spare goblet lay a linen napkin, folded neatly. It was of the finest quality, but the finest linen counted for far less than the finest blade. Brann meticulously, almost reverently, wiped all traces of the blood from the knife and set the napkin back down. Alam pointed at the fire, and Brann threw the napkin instead onto the small flames, fuelling them higher for a short while.

'Not easy to explain the blood to a servant,' the dusty voice rasped.

The old man looked at him closely, then glanced at the slave. 'Any consequences of dealing with it?'

The man was as impassive as ever. 'Only a missing guard.

460

I will leave a mostly empty wine skin behind a statue near to where he was stationed. Hopefully that will suggest an explanation for his leaving his post, and then not wanting to be found when they look for him.'

Brann's eyes narrowed. 'How do you know where his post was?'

'It will be the one without a guard.'

He nodded. It was a fair point.

The old voice whispered, 'Best to go now then?'

The slave was already leaving as they heard him say, 'Indeed.'

The old man looked at Brann in silence, his eyes never straying to the package on his back though he must have noticed it the moment they had come through the door.

Brann stared back. 'You never told me you were once Emperor.'

'I told you my name. The title is what I was. The name is what I am now.'

'And what would you be? Emperor once more?'

'What I want is not your concern, boy. You should be concerned with what you want.'

'I am. I brought what you wanted.'

He swung the narrow hessian bag from his back and walked to the desk, drawing the long bundle from it and laying it on top of the assorted papers to untie it and carefully roll the leather aside. As the old man stood, Brann laid out the sword and axe as Tarkanan had done, and put the knife in its place where the weapons crossed.

For a long while the man stared, pulling at his long beard, the crackle of the fire the only sound. Eventually: 'They are a wonder.'

He picked up the sword, testing it with movements that

spoke of a fond affinity for such a weapon. 'This is more than a wonder. It is beyond belief.'

Watching him weigh the weapon and sample its swing, a thought occurred to Brann. 'He has made one mistake, however.'

A sharp look. 'How so?'

'Your people favour a blade with a curve, and one cutting edge. This is straight, with two.'

'Indeed we do, and indeed it is. Curious. But that is what he has done, and that is the way it is.' He replaced it gently. 'He will be well rewarded.'

'I had thought possession of the remainder of the Star Stone was reward enough.'

'To him, maybe. But I value his work more highly than he does. To him, it is what he does. I marvel at flying, but a hawk just does it, for it is its nature. But I see him for what he is: the only one with the power to do what he does. As I see in one other. I will reward him in the form that best enhances his talent, as I will with the other.' He sat in his chair by the fireplace. 'So. Your confined companions.'

At last. 'My confined companions. And your promised help.'

'Indeed. My word has always been kept, and I have no reason to do otherwise now. Return tomorrow, at the time of the evening meal when all others are busy tending to their stomachs. My man will fetch you as normal. I will think on it in the morning.'

Brann felt his anger rise. '*You will think on it tomorrow?* I did what you asked. We risked our lives for you. Yet you have not even thought to consider it before now?'

The eyes blazed and the voice was harsh. 'Watch your tongue, boy, before I have it cut from your head. You presume much, to think to tell me how I should act. You are fortunate to have my assistance at all.'

Brann stared at him, his head throbbing with fury. But the fate of his friends was worth more than venting his anger. He said nothing, other than, 'Where is your slave?'

The former Emperor walked to a cord that hung from the ceiling beside the bed. He pulled it, and said, 'Right outside my door.'

Brann turned and left.

When he stepped back into Alam's dusty chamber the next day, he was surprised to see a lady standing on the balcony beside the former Emperor. A slave in appearance, but the same weight of years, the same proud demeanour and, as they turned to regard him, the same calculating eyes.

'Save me, there are two of you,' he groaned. 'A sister?'

'Oh, gods, no,' the pair said simultaneously. The woman spoke as softly as the man beside her, but hoarser, drier, as if the sand-suffused wind of the desert had a voice. There was not the same cruel harshness about her, though she gave Brann the impression that to underestimate her would be just as much a peril as to oppose the man.

She glanced at the man from the corner of her eye. 'Is he always as rude as this?'

The whisper replied. 'A consequence of his experiences, I presume.'

She nodded. 'No doubt it is, and something you would know much about. What is your excuse for the same fault?'

'Having to put up with you.'

'I was not present at your birth. You are carnaptious by nature, to your bones. The boy is plainly brought to it by you.'

'Enough, crone!'

She smiled calmly, and winked at Brann. 'And so my case is proven.'

Brann was enjoying this. He smiled back. 'I apologise for my discourtesy towards you, my lady. I do not know you and you deserved respect in that circumstance.' He bowed in what he hoped was an appropriate manner and took her hand, laying a light kiss on the thin skin, feeling a tingle course through him at the contact. 'I am Brann, a miller's son, from what you know as The Green Islands.'

She looked at him, a long, cool look. 'You are precisely that and so much more than that, Brann of The Green Islands.' She gave a chuckling curtsey. 'I am Cirtequine.' She turned to the old man. 'Despite your relative ages, I believe you could learn much from this boy about how to treat a lady.'

Alam had dropped heavily into his seat, however, staring at her, eyes wide, mouth working soundlessly. At last words emerged. 'And so the veil is lifted. I knew your eyes. But I knew not from where the memory came.' He sighed. 'How could I not see? How could I not deduce it?'

There was a kindness in her voice, but an authority also. 'Because it was not the time. And because I willed it so.'

He had recovered his composure. 'No more secrets.'

She made a show of toying with the idea. 'That works both ways.'

Brann interrupted. 'That works three ways.' He looked at Alam, once Emperor of much of the known world. 'An old girlfriend?'

The old man almost spat. 'It only works so far in your direction, boy.'

The lady put her hand on Brann's arm and the same faint

sensation ran through him at her touch. 'In the terms of you young people, it was more a one-night stand.' Brann spluttered almost as much as former Emperor Alam. 'But not in the sense you young ones would mean it. Further than that is a truth for another time.' She looked pointedly at the man.

He nodded. 'There are other truths you should know now.'

A knock rapped at the door.

They looked at each other in surprise. The sound had been sharp, authoritative. Not the knock of a slave.

Alam's head snapped to Brann and the boy moved at once for the privy, but the old man's hiss stopped him. 'Under the bed. Now.'

Brann looked at him. 'You are joking. That is where illicit lovers hide. It is the most obvious place.'

The knock came again, and a glare from the former Emperor showed clearly his feelings at not being obeyed in the instant. 'And that is why it is the perfect place. Just who would suspect me of having an affair? Why would anyone look anywhere? They might, however, visit the privy.'

He had to acknowledge the logic and dropped to his stomach, sliding under the bed just as the woman, head bowed in subservience, opened the door.

Boot heels rang across the floor as the visitor strode into the room, clearly having ignored the slave who had opened the door. Whatever her actual identity, she was clearly adept enough at passing as a slave to be accepted as such.

The footsteps moved with purpose towards the desk, where Alam must still be, and came into Brann's view. Expensive boots, a man's boots. Familiar boots.

Loku spoke, and Brann's fingers curled around the hilt of his knife. He held his breath as he fought to keep himself from hurtling from under the bed. 'Your Imperial Highness.'

The whispered voice replied, 'Taraloku-Bana. To what do I owe the pleasure of this visit?'

'I would draw upon the vast knowledge of your past, if I may, Highness.'

'Really? And what would I know that is a mystery to His Imperial Majesty's Source of Information?'

'Your grandson, His Imperial Majesty, has a niece. She is fond of you.'

'I am aware of this.' The former Emperor's slippered feet moved into and out of Brann's view, the noise of the shuffling steps receding towards the fireplace. 'You will not mind if I rest tired legs for the remainder of our conversation?'

'Of course not, Highness.'

The man breathed a sigh as the chair gave off the sound of a frail old body being lowered into it, dropping wearily the last part of the way. 'You are kind. Now, we were talking about?'

'Your dear niece.'

'Yes, yes. Of course.'

'There was a boy.'

'Ah, yes. I heard word of a scandal. Remind me of the outcome, if you will, Taraloku-Bana.' The change in the old man's tone was fascinating. To listen to him, he was just that: an old man. Vague of thought, unsure and harmless.

'He was supposed to die, broken in misery, as befits one who besmirched the name of the royal house and the honour of one of its number.' Hatred forced out every word.

'Oh.' Alam sounded bewildered. 'Supposed to? It did not transpire, then? How so?'

'He had help. His former companions conspire against us. Three times he should have died.'

'*Should have*, my good man? He still lives?'

'I fear so. I now believe he was the assassin in the Northern delegation, intended for our Emperor.'

'Really? A mere boy?'

'I suspect they were relying on the benefits brought by surprise.'

The old man mused on this audibly. 'You have thought it through well, Taraloku-Bana. It is fortunate for us all that you are capable of seeing through all surprises.' Brann almost giggled. 'But did you not wish to ask me something?'

'Indeed, Highness. I believe your niece is fond of visiting you.'

'That she is, though what pleasure she derives from an old man such as I is beyond me. Still, it brings me pleasure.'

'I also believe that she retains a measure of fondness for the boy, misguided as it may be.' Brann sucked in his breath as his chest constricted sharply.

'Oh, surely not. Unfathomable even more than misguided, I would say, given that some say he treated her badly.'

Loku's voice had an edge to it, as his impatience grew. 'Indeed, Highness. Extremely badly. But I wondered if, in any of her conversations with you, she might have mentioned if a boy had attempted to be in communication with her?'

'Oh, a boy, yes.'

The eagerness in Loku's tone was instant. 'Really? She has talked of him?'

'Oh, many times. It is really very sweet. A young man from one of the Eastern families. She really is terribly smitten.'

'Oh.' Disappointment now. 'I see. There were whispers that he had returned to the city, but all that there is to draw him here is her welcome. If her attentions are turned to another, I can only assume that he has fled. He will be headed north, and I must pursue him. I will not take such designs on His Imperial Majesty's life lightly, and will attend to this dog myself. The Northern ship has been seized, but no doubt they will have laid their hands on a smaller boat to slip away. I shall follow in a faster vessel and should I not overhaul them at sea, I shall hunt him down like the rabid cur that he has proved to be.'

'Excellently deduced, Taraloku-Bana. I see why you have risen so high. I wish you the favour of the gods in your endeavours.'

'I thank you for your time, Highness. Now, however, I shall make my preparations for my journey with haste. I bid you a good evening.'

'A good evening to you also, Taraloku-Bana, and many thanks for your visit. It was most pleasant.'

The boots clicked across the tiles and the door shut. Brann slid from his hiding place.

'Well,' Alam said, his normal demeanour returned. 'That was informative.'

Brann nodded. 'We know that he is chasing me north.'

The look was withering. 'Fool. We know he is heading north. You are merely his excuse to his masters here. He will be heading north to further his designs.'

Brann frowned. 'I am quite sure he wants to kill me.'

The old man snorted. 'I am certain he wants to kill you. But his personal pleasure is subservient to the wishes of his masters in this scheme he follows and enacts. Killing you would be a bonus he would indulge in if, and only if, it did not interfere with his duty.'

The lady walked quietly over and poured water for three, setting one on the small table beside Alam's seat and giving another to Brann. 'There is more, young man, and it is more you may not like.' She paused and looked at the man in the chair, who nodded. 'The hunter must become the hunted.'

Brann smiled, but he felt no humour. 'Why would I not like that? You think that the chance to send that man to the hell he deserves would not appeal to me?'

A groan escaped the old man. 'Obedience and wit, that is all I ask from those who serve me. You do not serve, so I cannot command, but only persuade, bargain and explain. The wit, though, I need from you, else you are useless.' He leant forward intently. 'Think on it, boy: were you to kill him, he would be gone but the problem would not. You think he has engineered all of this alone? Devising a conspiracy to topple one order while roving bands unleash atrocities in a country that lies a sea away? With who-knows-what happening in the lands you sailed past on your journey here? While he also runs the largest spy network in the known world? You must think he has abilities akin to those of a god.'

Cirtequine moved to Brann and laid a hand on his shoulder. Her voice was earnest. 'We believe there is a group of men such as Taraloku-Bana. He is at least one level, maybe several, from the one who controls it all, who plots it, who moves the pieces as on a gaming board. That one is the one we need. Should you meet him, you are welcome to bring death his way, unless you find there is knowledge we would have from him.'

He looked from one old face to the other. 'So you need me to follow Loku and find who he works for. And who they work for. And who *they* work for until I find the master of them all?'

They nodded.

469

'Why me?'

Alam rose and shuffled to the fire, picking up the poker to prod absently at the glowing logs and raise sparks to dance in the rising heat. 'Because we are about twenty years too old for that sort of thing.' She coughed and raised an eyebrow. 'Maybe more than twenty. But it leaves it to you, in any case.'

There was humour behind Brann's smile this time. 'I meant that you have many you could call upon. Why choose me?'

The man straightened, the poker still in his hand. 'One of my greatest strengths in gaining and keeping power was in reading the use of people. I would not send a hunting hound to carry a man across a desert when I had a camel saddled and ready, but nor would I ask the camel to seek prey in the sky when I had a hawk on my wrist. You have the incentive, your companions have the knowledge of the lands and you all despise the man you seek.' He paused, and looked at Cirtequine. 'And then there is…'

Brann's eyes narrowed. 'There is what?'

Alam stared into the deep red between the logs. 'There is a prophecy.'

'You know of that? How can that be?'

The man's head snapped up sharply. '*You* know of it?'

'It may be,' the lady's voice whispered, 'that you both know of words different.'

Brann closed his eyes. He could hear the voice of another old lady, this one in the dim bowels of a ship, as if he were beside her now.

'Paths you will travel, in many a realm,
You'll be blind to the journey, trust to Fate at the helm,

> *But you'll know you are standing in Destiny's hall*
>   *When heroes and kings come to call.'*

He opened his eyes. Both were staring at him, the man with heightened interest, the woman intently.

'From whom did you hear these words?'

'From a lady older than you, in a ship on the sea.' His voice was soft, tender. 'All she did was touch my tear.'

She smiled gently. 'We all have our ways.' She looked at Brann. 'I would like to have met this lady.'

He shrugged. 'You still could. She is in the house we lived in, down in the city.'

A small intake of breath was all the emotion she showed, then her calm descended once more. 'That is of interest.' She looked at Alam. 'It is only polite that you reciprocate.'

The former Emperor looked at her, stared at her, the firelight dancing on his face as he drew himself straight, his eyes those of the man he once had been. His voice was measured.

> *'One will come*
> *Thought nothing by all,*
> *A seed there will be*
> *In a breast thought so small.*
> *From one who is nothing,*
> *Greatness will spring,*
> *Of the deeds of that one*
> *Great songs will they sing.*
> *But the seed must be nurtured*
> *And the shoot must be fed,*
> *For the flower to blossom,*
> *For the man to be bred.*

And nations will stand
Or nations will fall,
When heroes and kings
On the One come to call,
On one they once thought
So small.'

The lady's lips moved soundlessly with each word. Brann said softly, 'You have heard this before?'

The old man spoke. 'She told me it.' He stared at the woman. 'Did you not?'

She smiled softly. 'I did, you know. Many years before you were born, young one.'

Alam shuffled to a bowl of dried fruit on a table near to his desk. 'So now we know.' He looked at Brann. 'Fate can carry a heavy weight. Think you that you can bear it, boy?'

Brann shrugged. 'A man told me I should think not of the entirety of the journey, but only as far as I can see at the time.'

The former Emperor grunted. 'A fine strategy if you are incapable of forward planning.'

Brann stared defiantly. 'You can plan according to what you know and what you need. To look further takes attention from what is necessary.'

'If your capacity to look both near and far is limited. The right action for now may place you in a worse position later.'

Her hoarse voice cut across them. 'You are both correct.' She stepped to the fire, breathing in the heat. 'There is a third prophecy,' she said at last.

They stared at her. Brann started to speak, but the old man raised a hand to stop him.

She breathed slow and deep, her eyes distant. When she at last spoke, her voice was low, their concentration grasped by every word.

> *'Three seeds planted, but grow intertwined,*
> *They spring forth as two stems, though not two of a kind.*
> *Each brings strength to the other, adds power to the one,*
> *Threads twisted together when their fate has been spun.*
> *And evil will grow, as a cloud it will spread,*
> *Death its desire, world enveloped in dread.*
> *. Despair o'er nations and empires will fall*
> *And heroes and kings will send out their call.*
> *Their only hope is that Hope births a son:*
> *Three seeds in two souls become one.'*

The heat of the fire warmed their faces as a cool breeze slipped from the balcony to prickle the back of their necks. Brann and Alam stared at each other. The boy broke the silence.

'It seems we are linked.'

The old eyes bore into him, and there was a strength in the whisper. 'It seems we are.'

Brann frowned. 'Three seeds?'

'Three prophecies. This third one links not only us to each other, but also itself to the other two. The woman is right: thought needs strength to act, might needs design to guide it.' He turned to the lady. 'These words: they were uttered by whom?'

She shrugged. 'I know not.'

'Then how do you know them?' His patience, ever thin, was starting to wear.

'They are written. Cut from stone, deep in a cave. My mistress showed me, as her mistress showed her, as her mistress showed her.'

'Written by your order, then?'

She smiled. 'Written before my order was ever an order. Written by those who came before, who crafted the gods in the black rock, who worked the Star Stone, who walked these lands in the world before ours.'

'And you saw these words before you uttered those of your own to me?'

The head shook slightly. 'When you came to me, that one time, I held office, but not yet the highest office. Only on that final ascension are the most secret of secrets passed on, this among them.'

Brann was puzzled. 'So there are three prophecies, from three people who never knew of the other words, years and centuries apart, yet they all share words and speak of the same thing?' He looked at the lady, the fire still burning bright to silhouette her. 'How can this be so?'

Her smile was gentle. 'Destiny has no regard for time or circumstance. Destiny is and will be.'

'So we must win, for it is foretold?'

Alam was terse, his desire to move beyond explanation to consideration of action filling his voice with tension. 'Think again on the words. The outcome is not foretold. They only set the pieces in their places on the board. They tell of a time, so we may be ready for that time when it arises.'

Her tone was the antidote to his. 'It seems that time is now.' She looked at both of them. 'And it seems that you two have some work to do.'

Brann felt an unease growing. 'I don't care if there are a

hundred prophecies. I will not leave here without Einarr and Konall.'

The man who had once ruled the Sagian Empire sighed. 'We may be bound by the prophecies uttered by others, and we may be compelled by fate, but I am also beholden to my own words. I have made a life where it was known across nations that once I had spoken, I would be true to my word, sometimes to the delight of those the words concerned, and sometimes to their horror and fear. I am not about to change that now. My assistance was offered and will not be withdrawn.' He turned to Cirtequine. 'If you would arrange food and inform my man that the meeting we spoke of should be arranged, we will set to thinking. We have plans to lay.'

The faintest of glows on the horizon heralded the lightening of the sky that in turn spoke of the sun's impending appearance. Brann dropped into one of the chairs beside the fireplace, the logs now reduced to smouldering embers. He prodded at them absently with the poker to stir the last of the heat from them, grunting in satisfaction at the sprouting of a single yellow flame, then sat back to run his fingers through his hair.

'I believe we have a plan that may work.'

'We have a strategy.' Former Emperor Alam stacked sheets bearing lists and diagrams. 'A plan is a precise set of instructions. A strategy is a set of plans, a collection of scenarios that all contribute to the one goal. The greatest importance is whether the goal can still be achieved should any scenario change or fail completely.'

Brann smiled. He had been astounded at the capacity of a man of those years to remain awake at all through the night, never mind show a sharpness of mind and attention to detail that even now continued. A vibrant alertness had coursed through the elderly frame from the first instant of the process. They had discussed, suggested, asked and argued their way through the night but the purpose had been achieved. 'Is that the accepted military definition of plans and strategies?'

The old man didn't look up as he sorted through the pile, separating the occasional sheet. 'It is my definition. Bugger the rest of them.'

'You don't rate the great military minds of history and their teachings?'

'Their theories worked for them. And their teachings, those I was schooled in as a child, served their purpose to give me the ability to command and learn what worked for me.' The cold eyes were raised to Brann's. 'I have had rather more years of experience than of childhood learning.'

'You should write a mighty tome of your accumulated wisdom.'

'Hah! So others do not have to think for themselves, as I have done? Learning to think for yourself is the greatest lesson you can be taught. What is right for me may not be right for others; may not be right for the world they live in. And in any case, why would I wish to spend my final years scratching my thoughts in ink when I could instead be using those thoughts to live?'

He moved towards the vacant seat, the pile of parchment in a hand almost as dry as the paper, presumably to read through it once more as they sat. He passed on to the hearth, however, and tossed the pile onto the embers. Brann leapt to his feet, aghast.

'What are you doing?'

'These?' Alam poked to stir the flames that caught at, and were fuelled by, the paper. 'These ordered our thoughts when we planned, calculating what would work and what would not. What you need as it unfolds is within your head. If you need to read it as you go from stage to stage for an undertaking such as this, then the prophecy spoke of someone else.' He nodded at the table. 'That is all we need.'

Brann stretched weary shoulders as he walked to the desk. Just three papers remained from the host they had filled in their deliberations. Three lists, and he spread them to glance at them: those they would contact and brief; materials to be gathered; and the shift rotas of the citadel guards and of the three millens that currently shared the defence of the city.

He nodded in understanding. 'And,' he looked at the fire, 'the less that remains written, the less that can be found by those we would rather not find it.'

'Precisely.'

Cirtequine quietly picked up a plate of crumbs from the desk to take to a tray of used crockery. She paused at the feel of Brann's hand on her arm. 'Thank you,' he said. 'It has been a long night for you with little to do but wait on us. You were made for more than that.'

'I was made to contribute where I can,' she smiled. 'I have had more chance to contribute ere now, and I will have again. I thank you for bringing some excitement into my later years,' she winked, 'though I apologise for bringing you into contact with this ill-mannered lout.'

Former Emperor Alam grunted. 'I'll manage. But your apology is acknowledged.'

Brann laughed as the lady whispered to him, 'I believe he is serious.'

'So,' said the old man. 'We are done. Leave me so I can sleep and remind the dullards who inhabit this building that I am a decrepit wits-wandered old man.'

'One more thing,' Brann said. He reached into a pouch at his waist and pulled forth the two remaining brooches of star metal that Tarkanan had given him. He pressed them into the palm of the man. 'All who were with the smith were given these. He gave me these for you.'

Alam held one brooch in front of him and studied it in the firelight, wonder plain on his face. 'Such craftsmanship is beyond even what we have seen already. The man is blessed.'

'He said you would know who should wear the second one,' Brann said.

The man nodded. 'A day ago I may not have been certain. Today I know.' He held out his hand, palm up, the years causing the slight tremble. His voice was as cold as ever as he looked at the woman. 'You may still be an old crone, but my blind old eyes now see the old crone you are.'

She softly lifted the brooch from his hand. 'All my life I have waited for such a compliment. You have a way with words all of your own. I shall have to wear it hidden, but I shall wear it to remind me of you as much as of the task in which we have immersed ourselves, and the impossible that can become possible.'

Brann smiled. 'I think I should take my leave.'

The old man looked into the fire and waved his hand dismissively at a chest at the foot of the bed. 'Take your things and go.'

Brann frowned. 'My things?'

'Of course. Why would I wish them cluttering up my chambers? Hurry yourself, I am tired.'

478

Brann opened the chest in confusion. Within lay a coarse dark blanket wrapped to form a long bundle. His chest constricted as he laid it on the bed to open it out. Three weapons lay within, finely tooled leather scabbards holding a sword and a long knife, and a leather strap around the handle of an axe to allow it to be hung on a belt, with a hood that slipped over the head that, he was sure, would be designed to be removed in an instant. None of the blades was visible but he knew the black metal that formed them. He stared at them, barely able to breathe.

The old man's voice was irritable. 'Are you going to hurry up? I have had a long night and need to rest.'

Brann found his voice. 'You would give these to me?'

A snort of impatience. 'If I am to entrust an incompetent such as you with a responsibility of the scale we face, I would feel better if you are as well equipped to kill the people who matter as you can be.' He rose and moved to his bed without looking over. 'Besides, what use are they to old arms such as these? And what a crime it would be to hide them away.'

Brann felt the excitement unleashed within him and his fingers could not move fast enough to fasten the three weapons to his belt. He noticed a strap on each that helped to retain it in its holder, as masterfully crafted as the rest of the leatherwork.

'These are unusually sized weapons,' he said. 'How did you manage so quickly to have this leatherwork crafted to fit their shape?'

The old man stopped and frowned, as if in confusion. 'You doubt the resources of one who once ruled this Empire?'

Brann smiled. 'Of course not. I cannot find the words to adequately thank you.'

'Then do not. I'd rather you leave me alone and let me sleep, for you are irritating me now. Both of you.'

Brann made for the door. 'And boy?' He turned back. 'Stay alive, will you? It would help.'

'I'll do my best.' The lady balanced the tray with one hand and opened the door with the other. She made a slow turn to reach to close it behind her, casually scanning the corridor for curious eyes, even at this time of the morning, before nodding to Brann. He slipped out to find Alam's stocky slave awaiting him.

Without a word, they entered the shaft through the privy and wound their way down the wet staircase. At the bottom, as they stepped onto the now familiar walkway beside the channel of darkly flowing water, the slave turned to face him, a warning hand held up.

Brann stopped, straining his ears for the source of danger, but hearing only the drips and the running water, and the occasional scurrying of the rats.

Strong hands gripped his arms and pinned them, as the slave stepped forward and pulled a black hood down over his head. He had no option but to go where he was directed.

Chapter 10

She paused at the doorway. It had been many years since she had felt nervous. Four seasons had turned since she had started dealing with the man who was once feared beyond the Empire, but nerves had never afflicted her. Concern, worry for others, even anger, but never nerves.

She was nervous now.

Her stomach knotted, a sensation from her teenage years, and she was surprised she could remember that distance into the past. During that long night of planning, the boy, Brann, had taught her the knock, the set rhythm that would gain her entry, but still she hesitated.

What would she find? Who would she find? Would the person within the body be the one she had known?

She scolded herself and rapped at the door. It almost immediately opened slightly, its movement limited by a heavy chain, to reveal... no one. Movement caught her eye and she noticed a pair of eyes staring at her from a mirror held on a stick from one side of the doorway. As the eyes focused on her, they crinkled in what could only be a smile and the door closed, the sound of a chain being released rattled loudly, and the door was flung wide, a very large boy with shaggy hair and an infectious grin filling the space.

'You must be the lady the old man's slave told us about.'

She smiled awkwardly. 'I must be.'

He stepped aside. 'Then please come in off the street.'

She did so. It was a large room, with an assortment of characters in a variety of activities, or in no activity. She looked at the large boy. 'I was told that a certain lady could be found here.'

A man broad of shoulder, grey of close-cropped hair and creased of face stepped forward. 'Indeed she is. Please, come with me.'

He offered his arm with courtesy and with appreciation she took it, allowing him to lead her up the staircase. 'It is not often such a gesture is made to a slave,' she said.

'That is true. But I do not believe you to truly be a slave,' he said.

'That is true. But I do not believe it would have made a difference,' she said.

'That also is true.'

The stairs stopped at a corridor and, partway along it, they reached a doorway. The man tapped softly and, at a faint voice, pushed open the door. He nodded, and stepped back.

She hesitated, the feelings she had felt outside the building returning tenfold. It was so improbable. The likelihood was so small. It could be anyone.

She stepped in and her breath sucked into her chest in a small cry.

She dropped to her knees before the figure in the chair, taking one of her hands in both of hers. Her voice, normally *a hoarse whisper, was choked even more with emotion.*

'Mother.'

She had thought the lady slept, but she now saw that the dark eyes regarded her calmly, love washing from them in a gentle stare. 'My girl.'

She stroked the hand. 'I did not dare to believe it was you. But I hoped. But there had been so many false hopes in the past.'

The ancient face smiled. 'I have waited for this day, so I have. I knew it would come, but I did not know when. No, I did not know when.'

A smile in return. 'Of course you knew. I wish I had that power.'

'You do. You took a different path, so you did.'

'I left you.'

'I wanted you to, so I did. You had the opportunity I never had, but always dreamt of. For you not to take it, for us both to have missed it, my heart would have cracked.'

'I thought you would always be there. Every visit, I thought you would be there. But then you were not.'

The lady in the chair sighed, and the familiar silver trinkets chimed against each other at the slight movement of her head. 'You will have noticed over the years, my daughter, that the ways of men do not always allow the paths of women to be what we would wish.'

She felt the anger rise, as it had done so often over the years, the decades. 'I heard there were raiders.'

'At first, there were. And then worse, so there was. But my skill was my safeguard: they dared not risk harming what I could offer. No, they could not dare it. Then the boy Einarr took the ship that was my latest home, and the gods repaid my suffering with the chance to help good people.'

483

She felt her eyebrows rise. 'They did good? Who in this world does all good?'

'They did good things and they did bad, but always from trying to be right. A good heart requires a strong arm, or it fast stops beating, so it does, it fast stops beating.' A hand reached out and she felt the back of the fingers stroke down her cheek. For a moment, she was a child once more. 'What happened to your voice, girl? Once you sang so sweetly.'

'The smoke, the incense, the vapours. There is not a flue in the caves, and it takes its toll over time. I have not sung in many a year.'

'A shame, so it is, a shame. Still, you had that life. You learnt the true depth of your gift. It warms my soul that one of our family has done so. It does indeed.'

'Three of our family.'

A frown. 'How so?' Her whole body had stiffened upright in interest.

'I have a daughter. I have two, in fact, and one now serves in my place. The other is happy in a far land, in a different life but just as happy. The one with the gift had a son, and before he died on the Emperor's border, he had a daughter. She now studies with the Order herself.'

Her mother sank back against the cushions in her chair. 'Your presence would have been kindness enough, daughter, but your news adds jewels to gold.' She paused. 'Though tell me this: you say you did not believe it could be me. So what led you to step this way on this occasion?'

She could not help but smile. Her mother's mind was as sharp as ever. 'This time? I felt it as soon as the boy mentioned you.'

'Ah, the boy. The boy is a child of fate, so he is. A child of fate.'

'*I fear we place too much on his shoulders.*'

Now it was the older lady's hands who took hers. 'My child, you have held the highest office in your Order, the most revered of its kind in the known world. Yet have you learnt nothing? Not you, nor I, nor any fallen Emperor can place destiny on the shoulders of another. It was there from the moment he was born, as was yours from the instant I saw your face. It is just that the gods do not permit us to know unless the time is right, unless the world is in need of what we can give.'

She looked at her mother. 'It seems that time is now.'

Her mother smiled that same gentle smile that had made her feel safe so many times before. 'Then we should trust in fate, and labour in its cause.'

****

Brann started as the hood was pulled from his head, and blinked in the sunlight. He stood, his hands tied behind him, in a ruined building, walls several storeys high bounding an empty shell.

A man and a woman less than a decade older than he stood before him, male and female versions of the same person. Both studied him with the same appraising expression, heads tilted to the side, one to the left and the other to the right.

They were dressed similarly also: practical but well-cut clothing, grey with black detail on the man, and black with grey detail on the woman. A shortsword hung on the woman's right hip and the man's left, and hair the deep red of the setting sun was cut short on the man and long and tied back on the woman. Her features, the same high cheekbones and full lips, were slightly softer but her eyes, like his, were anything but soft.

He waited for them to talk. It hadn't been he who had engineered this meeting.

The woman spoke first. It was a cool voice, measured and controlled. 'We have a mutual friend.'

It was then that Alam's words to Cirtequine came back to him. *Inform my man that the meeting we spoke of should be arranged.* It appeared that it had indeed been arranged.

'I wouldn't call him a friend.' No more than the hand was called a friend by the sword, or by the hammer, or by the stick that scraped shit from the boot.

The man laughed. His manner was more languid than his sister's controlled tension, and his voice proved to match his demeanour. 'Nor I, Brann of the Arena, nor I. Let us say that we and you have a working relationship with a person unnamed. And now we have been asked to extend this relationship to you to aid with a certain enterprise you have in mind.'

Brann shrugged. 'It is hard to work at anything with your hands tied behind you.'

The man smiled his easy smile, though it barely reached his eyes. 'I apologise, but your reputation for killing people with some ease has preceded you. We could not take any chances with your possible reaction on the hood being removed.'

'I will not kill you unless my life is threatened.'

The woman nodded. Brann heard movement behind him and metal brushed cold against his skin as his bonds were slashed. He flexed and rubbed the circulation back into his wrists before his hands dropped automatically to check his sword, axe and knife on his belt and the knives on his forearms. He didn't need to draw attention to the blade in one boot and the one under his tunic behind his neck; he could feel both pressing against him. At his movement, there was the sound of weapons being drawn all around him, but he kept his eyes on the pair facing him.

The man held up a hand of restraint. 'Relax, my friends. It is clear our new friend merely feels more comfortable knowing the tools of his trade are with him.'

Brann heard his voice emerge harsh. 'My friends are among those who I know, not those I do not.'

'A sensible approach, my young acquaintance. Do you at least know who we might be?'

Brann shrugged. 'I know what you are.'

The woman's voice was cold. Not unpleasant, just matter-of-fact. 'And what might that be?'

'I have a friend who leads her life on the side of society that the laws seek to control, but do not. I can recognise gang leaders when I see them.'

The man feigned outrage. 'Gang leaders?'

'Oh, you are perfectly legal then?'

The man feigned horror. 'Now you really do seek to insult us.' He sighed theatrically. 'There are gang leaders, then there are those who lead them. And those who lead them, and those who lead them, and so on and so forth. And then there are us.'

'So you control the criminals of Sagia.'

The woman sighed. 'It is a large city. It is administrated in quarters.'

'So you control a quarter of the criminals of Sagia.'

'A quarter of the city, not the people. Some work independently of us, it is their choice. So long as they do not interfere in our work, they are welcome to do so.'

'So you control the criminal activity in a quarter of Sagia.'

The blond man beamed at his sister. 'You see, he has got it!'

He still felt grumpy. 'So why am I here?'

The man raised his eyes in anguish to where the roof should have been. 'Or perhaps not.'

She looked at him still coolly, and spoke the same. 'We were asked to help.'

'Why would you?'

'More than one reason, but one is that it suits us. When eyes are turned one way, they are not turned another.'

The man grinned. 'We like it when we know which way eyes are turned. And which way they are not.'

'So what can you do?'

'We can create impressions. We can create disruption, confusion, alarm.'

'How can this be achieved?'

She was as matter-of-fact as she would have been giving him a list for the market. 'A deception and a decoy.' Her brother's eyes flicked briefly to a figure standing to one side, almost in the shadows, his wrists bound and head bowed almost enough to conceal the swelling and fresh blood on his face. Something familiar about him nagged briefly at Brann until he realised that the man had the same build and height as he, and while his features were different, his skin was pale. The woman continued. 'The details you can leave to us.'

He was happy to do so. 'Do you know where? And when?'

She almost smiled. 'We will when you tell us.'

So he told them.

She nodded. 'We can do that.'

488

Brann smiled, though there was as much warmth in his eyes as in hers. 'Then we can work together.'

'You met with The Triplets?' Sophaya was astounded.

Brann frowned. 'There were two of them, not three.'

She sliced a knife casually through an apple, reclining on the high windowsill where he had first seen her what seemed a century ago. 'No one ever sees the third, Abraxas. He is the organiser, the one who is aware of everything, remembers everything, plans everything. He is their brain, but it is said that he is scared of his own shadow and is uncomfortable in the presence of anyone but his brother and sister. Few meet the two, and fewer still do so with life still in them at the end of the meeting. Dareia and Phrixos do not normally meet with anyone other than their own lieutenants or the other three Shadowlords, unless it is to deal with treachery amongst their own. They take betrayal badly, and personally.'

'I guess I was fortunate.' He was still surly after being dragged from his meeting hooded once more, but he chided himself. It had not been of her doing.

'I guess you were considered important,' she said. 'Though you will be fortunate to escape without a broken nose if you adopt that tone with me again.' She flicked her knife to send a chunk of apple bouncing from his head.

He smiled. 'Apologies, Sophaya. You did not deserve it. I don't like being under someone else's control like that.'

'No one does.' She arched her back and dropped from the sill, more like a cat than ever. 'But your apology has saved your nose.'

Cannick was stomping down the stairs with Hakon in tow, their arms cradling an impressive collection of weapons.

'Oh, you're back,' he said simply. 'When do we move?' The steel was dumped on the table with an ear-ringing clatter.

'Tonight.' Brann slumped in a chair, weariness catching up on him. 'Sundown. What of the arrangements here? Our Lady?'

Cannick smiled. 'She will be safe. She had somewhat of a reunion. She will take residence for the time being with her daughter.'

So his suspicions had been true. He was glad. 'And the delivery has been made?'

The grey head nodded at a pile of guards' armour heaped in the corner of the room. 'While you were visiting the less reputable elements of society. You are certain the blue plumes are correct?'

Brann nodded. 'I have seen the rotation schedule. The Fourth Millen has responsibility for the citadel this week.'

Hakon looked doubtful. 'The right armour or not, some of us will never pass for locals.'

'You need not worry on that score, friend Hakon,' Marlo said brightly. 'The Imperial Host is well named, for its numbers seem countless. It can only be so if it draws from the full extent of the Empire, and the Empire is a large place of many people. People with greatly differing appearances.'

Breta strolled across the room, steaming leg of chicken in hand, and sat beside Brann. 'So that is settled. The clothes are right. Now tell us how we will spend our night.' He looked at her in surprise, and she raised her eyebrows in return. 'What? Did you expect us to miss out on this excitement? Last time you just took us into the desert and I was left labouring in a forge with a lazy oaf.'

'Hoi!' Hakon objected. 'I wasn't lazy.'

She ignored him and offered Mongoose a bite from her

chicken as the smaller girl perched on the bench beside her. 'We are hardly likely to wander off just when it starts to get interesting.'

Brann nodded, pleased. Two more swords at their disposal, especially when they were carried by hands as adept as these two pit fighters, would be more than welcome.

'So,' Grakk said, uncoiling from his seat by the fire with sinuous ease and looking Brann over, 'you should tell us what is expected and get some sleep. You need to be at your best, as we all do.'

So he did, and he did.

They moved through the city as the sun slipped from sight. The streets were quiet but not deserted, and they drew little more than a cursory glance at most from those they passed. It was not unusual to see a squad of soldiers leading a couple of captives of some sort.

Cannick took the lead, the bearing of the old warrior lending itself to the image of the sergeant in charge of the troop. Grakk, Sophaya and Mongoose had their hands bound before them and were led by a rope around their necks by Brann. Gerens and Hakon on one side, and Breta (a man to any watching, in her armour and the helm with the grill across the mouth and nose, leaving only her eyes visible) and Marlo on the other escorted the captives. Brann had left his new weapons at the house in favour of a sword, long knife and shield matching those of the others and in keeping with the standard issue of the Imperial Host, though it had been a wrench to do so.

It was close to the end of the guard shift as they approached the first citadel gate, and the slouch to the guards' demeanour lent strength to their hope that food, rest and diversion would be foremost on their minds.

Grakk coughed and Cannick halted the group to let him speak, ostensibly examining the security of the captives' bonds. The tribesman's voice was a murmur, but they had packed close enough to hear him. 'Remember, they may be bored, they may be hungry, they may be tired, but they are also soldiers of the Imperial Host. Duty is all and standards are there to be kept, so they will always be attentive. Do not be complacent and play your part without laxity. Especially you who are soldiers: carry yourself as such.'

Brann felt his stomach lurch. He had not been any less nervous when he had walked into the Arena for the first time. If anything, this was worse, for on that occasion his faith in Grakk's ability had meant it was only his own life that he saw hanging in the balance.

With an unintelligible bark of command, Cannick led them forward. As expected, the guards dropped spear points and raised shields at their approach. 'Your business?' the burlier of the two asked.

Cannick curled a lip in disdain. 'Baby-sitting. Taking these slaves to be held for the Prince's decision on their fate for stealing from him.'

'Which prince?' The younger guard was slimmer, taller and more curious.

Cannick grinned. 'If I say they picked the worst one to do it to, who would you think?'

A sharp laugh greeted that. 'Not Kadmos? Those three had better enjoy the feeling of the chain around their necks before the executioner's garrotte is added to it.' He looked at the trio, who were doing their best to look dejected. 'At least you should be given a royal send-off. I hear the Prince is partial to wielding the wire himself.'

'So I have heard. It should be quite the spectacle.' Cannick smiled and nodded in thanks as the spears parted to allow them passage, and he stepped forward with purpose. The others followed, but Brann's stomach knotted even further. Where was the shout? They needed it now, or at least soon. Very soon. The within-twenty-paces sort of soon.

The shout came before they had even cleared the archway, to his relief.

'Alarm! Alarm! To arms! To arms!'

The clamour on top of the walls was soon matched below. A tall guard with haughty bearing, his deportment and insignia that of an officer, strode from the guard house set immediately inside the wall. He looked at Cannick. 'You. What are you waiting for? Take your men to their post. Immediately.'

Grakk stumbled into Cannick. 'Captain,' he muttered.

The veteran roughly pushed his captive back in annoyance. 'At once, captain. As soon as I deliver these captives.'

'Fool!' the officer snapped. 'Do you not hear the alarm? Leave them here. The guard house has a cell. You can return for them later.'

The fear in Cannick's face was plain. 'Captain, these slaves are for Prince Kadmos. He has plans for them. My orders are to take them directly to him.'

This time the captain roared. 'Your orders are for peacetime, soldier, and when we know we have peace you can fulfil them. For now, your duty is to your commanding officer and to the expectations he has that you will be where you are supposed to be. Leave them with me or, by the gods, I'll garrotte you myself.'

Cannick was clearly distressed, but had no option but to nod obedience. The guards took the ropes from Brann and

493

bundled their three bound 'captives' into the guard house. Cannick looked at his remaining companions and forced himself to remain in character. 'Right, you cretins, you heard the captain. With me.'

He set off at a trot into the area beyond the wall, the four behind following in tight pairs into a scene of bustling commotion. Torches flared in every part, bringing light to the night, and soldiers spilled from every crevice of the citadel like ants from a poked nest. Ordered and drilled as they may have been, still the sudden call to action could not help but produce a milling of bodies that baffled the eye. While each man or squad moved with a definite purpose of their own, the overall effect was of whirling confusion. It would be easy for a few people to lose themselves in the mass, so they did.

Cannick looked at Brann. 'What do we do now? We are three light already. And we have an additional task now to free them.'

Brann snapped at him, his tone as much a result of his nerves as anything else. 'What is done is done. We stay with our target. We have no option and to discuss it is to waste the time to be achieving it. Right now, we need a vantage point.'

Cannick nodded. 'At least we know they are safe for the time being.' He led them to steps leading to the top of the wall, and they climbed fast to see the source of the consternation. At the parapet, they stopped, mouths agape in surprise.

A host of campfires flamed in the darkness of the plain as though the stars had fallen from the sky and lay burning where they had landed. Dust that must have been raised by the movement of the horde rose in the light of the fires, and

Cannick grabbed the arm of a passing sentry to ask what he knew.

'An army, crept to the shadow of the walls, sergeant. Three in all: the one you see, one facing the back of the keep, and one mirroring this on the other side. Who'd have thought they could approach unknown?'

'Who indeed?' Cannick kept his grin from his face until the man had hurried on his impatient way.

A deception and a decoy. This would be the first. Brann smiled. 'It seems The Triplets keep to their word.'

Hakon frowned. 'But the dust? There must be thousands of them to raise such a cloud.'

'I saw something similar in the dry lands across this sea, once, when hired as a young warrior to a local lord,' Cannick said. 'He wanted to convince an enemy his numbers were many times the truth. It's amazing the dust cloud a few horses dragging branches and brush can make.' He looked out over the glowing fires and the dust swirling red in the flames. 'Would you bet against it?'

Hakon grinned. 'I would not.'

'That may be so, and it is an admirable effect,' Gerens said, 'but when do we move?'

Brann's eyes had been scanning the scene below them. He pointed to a short column of soldiers moving in the direction of the citadel's interior. 'If they continue their course, as soon as possible. We should descend closer to the next wall and join them if we can.'

The troop was indeed heading their way and they leapt low hedges to latch onto its tail, passing with the men through each of the walls as their commanding officer's cursory words satisfied the guards at each gate. Shortly before the fourth wall, the column wheeled to climb to a broad tower that held at its top a mighty trebuchet, and Brann's group neatly peeled from the rear to angle towards the final gateway. As they approached, Cannick spoke over his shoulder. 'Move fast and purposefully. It's amazing where it will get you.'

They broke into a trot and headed for the gateway, an opening that was more of a tunnel through a wall as thick as a ship is long. At its inner end, a guard sought to grab Cannick. 'Where do you head?' he demanded.

The old warrior shrugged him off. 'Where do you think?' he shouted back, and continued his run without a pause. Before the guard could answer, they were beyond him and a plethora of other matters demanded his attention.

They paused beyond the wall to assess the scene. The well-to-do were streaming from their villas towards the sanctuary of the keep, leading Brann's eyes to the building itself. His gaze followed the switch-back of the ramp to the great doorway and then rose to the terrace, where small figures – the royals – stood, watching the scene unfolding from their lofty perch.

Brann indicated the stream of people converging on the keep like a multicoloured river funnelling into narrow rapids. 'It looks like our progress may be slowed. At least they are heading in our direction.'

He was pleased to discover that his assessment was wrong. The sight of soldiers amongst them lent a reassurance to the panicking throng, an effect that Cannick soon exploited.

'Do not fear, good people, do not fear,' he bellowed, removing his helmet to allow his words to carry better. 'The Imperial Host will ensure your safety. Please make your way to the keep in an orderly fashion.' The people parted before him and appreciative hands clapped them on the back and

arms as they passed. Cannick warmed to his task. 'No need
to hurry, stout walls and brave soldiers will keep all at bay.
The only risk to your safety, my lords and ladies, is through
panic, so keep yourselves calm and safe and trust in your
army. If we could just be permitted to reach the keep
ourselves, we will assist in ensuring your security and wellbeing.'

Light applause broke out among those immediately
around them and a small cheer threatened to break out.
Brann touched Cannick's arm. 'I know you're enjoying this,
but it's time to rein it in. We don't need the attention of
those looking from above turning onto us.'

The veteran warrior grinned and shrugged. 'Spoilsport.'

The effect had already been created, however, and they
had reached the foot of the ramp. They kept to one side
and eased their way up, the back-and-forth nature of the
construction allowing those they approached to see them
coming and be prepared to let them pass.

Breta looked approving. 'This has worked surprisingly
well.'

'This,' Brann said, 'is only the start. Most of our task
lies ahead.' They were approaching the door and Brann
moved close to Hakon. 'Now,' he said quietly, 'would be a
good time for panic.'

'I can do that,' the big boy said brightly. He turned
suddenly and stopped, staring into the darkness beyond the
walls. The fires themselves could not be seen but their glow
crept into the sky above the top of the battlements. When
he shouted, there was alarm in his voice. 'Oh by the gods,
they are coming! They are coming!'

Consternation broke out around them immediately as
Marlo grabbed his arm and added in an exaggerated whisper

loud enough to be heard four rows of people away, 'Quiet, you fool! It'll be bad enough when the people realise they are cannibals!'

That did it. Screams and a surge for the door were enough to spread panic down the ramp and across the area below faster than fire across a sun-baked field of grass. Most couldn't hear the shouts of '*Cannibals!*' and '*Already at the walls!*' but terror and unseen danger are an infectious combination, and a full-scale stampede broke out.

Brann's group were through the door as the first of the crowd started to stumble in behind them.

'Quick, shut the doors before we are overwhelmed,' Cannick shouted to the startled guards as he tripped and knocked to the floor the first one to start to obey. The delay was all it took for the crowd to begin to stream through in earnest and the chance to close the huge doors was lost. Cannick winked at Brann.

The people were milling around the foot of the enormous sculptures and Brann cast an eye at the fake Star Stone on the shield. It was as Sophaya had left it, and he felt a surge of pleasure as his hand dropped to his sword. The people were by now filling the hallway and countless more were running and falling into the building, shouting and crying and screaming as they came. It was pandemonium and the few guards on hand were pressed back as they sought to establish any sort of control.

Gerens looked across the room appraisingly. 'Confusion and hysteria will do our chances no harm at all.'

Brann grinned. 'Exactly.' He looked at Marlo. 'Cannibals?'

The boy smiled sheepishly. 'It did work.'

'It did. Let's go.' He led them up the sweeping staircase and into the start of the royal area of the keep.

Instantly, the atmosphere changed. Bustling activity and hurried movement still engulfed them, but brittle nerves and volatile anxiety were replaced by purposeful haste and determined focus. The end result, to their relief, was similar, however: too many bodies moving in too many directions and all too concerned with their own priorities to pay any attention to, or even notice, the half-dozen soldiers passing through on their own task.

Bran cast his mind back to the directions whispered in that old hoarse voice. 'This way.' They found a further stairway, and climbed quickly, finding that the faster they moved, the less attention they attracted in the current state of alert. They removed their helmets as the confined space and exertion soaked their hair in sweat and streamed it into their eyes.

Hakon noted the narrow, plain design. 'Not quite so grand.'

Brann spoke back over his shoulder. 'Remember the rising passages we walked when we first came here? They ascend too slowly for the duties of servants. These stairs are quicker, and as far as we are concerned more befitting soldiers, although at this time it seems that soldiers are welcome anywhere.'

'Much further?' Breta grunted.

Brann shook his head. 'Three more floors, no more.'

The stairway ended at a simple doorway that took them into a large hall filled with calm aristocrats in groups, sipping cool drinks and taking small pastries from the trays held by slaves who moved serenely among them. It could have been an evening soiree but for the soldiers and serving staff who also moved across the room, their pace hastened by a mission, task or directive driven by the events outside.

499

A line of arched windows opened onto the large terrace they had seen earlier, a vast area of manicured shrubs, fountained ponds and elegant nobles lit by delicately wrought lanterns rather than the crude torches allowed to the areas thronged by the masses. At the far end of the hall, where two pairs of slim pillars fashioned as slender trees framed a doorway to a more elaborate staircase – one more befitting people of rank and privilege – stood a full platoon of two score elite royal guards, ten of them archers, the rest heavily armed infantrymen, and all in armour gleaming with the attention of fanatics. Fronting them was a lean officer, with glowering eyes above a hooked nose and the look of a man eager for someone to challenge his authority. The sort of man who communicated with hard words and harder blows.

Cannick grunted. 'Might be three more floors too far.'

Hakon cocked his head in consideration. 'I reckon we could take them.'

Brann looked at him with a grin that faded as he realised the boy was serious. 'It could draw more attention than we would ideally like, though.'

Hakon frowned. 'True. Pity.'

Brann touched Cannick's arm. 'There.'

The older man followed his gaze to spot Alam's slave waiting quietly to the side of one of the windows to the terrace, and nodded. 'Right, helmets back on and follow me, boys.' He glanced at Breta and winked. 'And girl.' He paused, and looked round the group. 'Remember to carry yourselves like drilled soldiers. That big-nosed bastard over there looks ready to pick a fight with his own shadow.'

He squared his shoulders and raised his chin with an air of assurance and strode across to the window where the slave waited. They followed closely, trying to look like professional soldiers and hoping that those around them had too much on their minds already to look too closely.

The slave said not a word as they stopped beside him. Standing side on to the wall just next to the window, he had a view of the room and the terrace, and he stared straight ahead as though the affairs of royals and soldiers were above him and he merely awaited instructions from any who may have need of him. Where he stood was clever, Brann thought, and not just as a vantage point: few, if any, passed him and so few, if any, would demand his service, catching instead whatever slave was closest to them.

Brann scanned the scene. Apart from the phalanx blocking the stairs, guards could be seen in every direction: at the two wide doorways to the terrace, around the perimeter of the garden area itself and, as would be expected, in close attendance to the Emperor as he stood at one wall, surveying the city beyond and expounding to a coterie of admirers. Despite a military presence greater than the one that normally surrounded Kalos, it was a scene of tranquillity at odds with the chaos only a few floors below. Brann could even feel himself relaxing slightly. Almost.

'So.' Breta broke the silence. 'How do we go to your friends, then? The collection of soldier boys over there would seem to be an unexpected problem.'

Brann and the slave exchanged a look and the slave nodded slightly. 'We have time,' the slave murmured. 'He is not there yet.' Brann had agreed with the old man to share certain crucial aspects of the plan with the others step by step as they became necessary. That way concentration was focused purely on the task in hand, and should any be captured, there was little that could be divulged. Loku may

501

not be in town, but his people still were and they were known to be brutally persuasive.

Brann looked around the group, suddenly feeling the weight of responsibility descending on shoulders that were younger than those of the others, and in two cases considerably so. Marlo, Hakon and Breta were openly expectant, while Cannick waited calmly for instructions, as befitted a veteran of military experience. Gerens alone was not looking at him, his dark eyes flitting around the room. Brann knew well that the boy would have only two things on his mind in a situation such as this: protecting Brann and unquestioningly accepting anything Brann said. He had grown used to it without ever understanding it.

'Those soldiers over there are a problem, but an expected one. It is standard procedure in times of attack. So we do not get to them, we have them brought to us.' Brann grinned at their mystified faces. 'In times of threat to the city, the citadel is sealed, as now. But there is a suite of rooms – self-sufficient with a well, provisions and a source of air, and able to be completely sealed to intruders – in the very heart of this building. It is virtually impregnable, as far from one side as another, and at the base of the building to protect it from missiles from above, but entered only from a stairway that starts halfway to the top, to render access for outsiders as hard as possible. The rock beneath makes it impossible to tunnel to it and should the building be collapsed upon it, it has its own tunnel, formed from a natural fissure and enhanced by engineering long forgotten. It is there that the royal family and any prisoners of great value are protected in times of direct threat to the Emperor's life.'

Gerens turned to him. 'So their escape tunnel is our escape tunnel.' Brann nodded. He should have known that Gerens would see his thoughts first. 'But we would need them to be moved there.'

'We would need,' Cannick said softly, 'cause for them to be moved there.'

'Indeed,' said Brann. 'We would need exactly that.'

He looked at the slave, who was watching the Emperor, who had taken the arm of a tall, slender but remarkably buxom matron in expensive robes of dark and light blue and was walking her along the wall. 'When he reaches the furthest point,' the man said simply.

'Why there?'

'Furthest for help to reach, and furthest to bring him back. The longer it takes, the greater the panic, and while they panic, they have little regard for aught else.'

'Did you know,' Gerens said to the slave, 'that there is a man over there watching you? A slave with long dark hair and a red tunic. Do you know him?'

'Possibly,' said the man, his eyes never leaving the Emperor.

'He has stared at you all the time we have been here. He still does.'

'I hope so. We have a problem if he does not.'

The Emperor and his companion reached the front extreme of the terrace. The slave turned calmly and looked directly at the youth with the red tunic, and nodded once. The lad turned and moved as a soldier ran across the room, his shoulder colliding with him just enough to knock his balance and send him hurtling towards a life-sized statue of a maiden with a basket of polished stone fruit. The body encased in heavy armour was almost airborne as it struck the figure and the statue was knocked flying from its plinth to crash and shatter against the shining tiles of the floor with a sound that could not have been louder or more shocking to the unsuspecting if it had been dropped from the highest storey.

Screams of shock and a scattering of people away from the source of the crashing noise were accompanied by the rattle of armour as spears were lowered and the scrape of swords being drawn. All eyes in the hall and from the terrace turned in that direction. All except those of the slave, who now directed his gaze back out along the line of the building's wall to a small storage alcove from which slipped a cloaked and hooded figure, slightly shorter than average and broad shouldered. The slave nodded confirmation to him and the man slid over the sill of the nearest window into the gardens and moved with little fuss behind the assembled nobles, out of the line of sight of those turned towards the scene of the commotion.

At the sight of the exchange between the slave and the hooded man, Brann beckoned the others closer. 'Listen,' he said quietly. 'Remember we are Imperial soldiers and whatever happens next, we must act as such. When I say, move to those doors over there that lead to the lower level, as if to guard against intruders. When Einarr and Konall are taken to the safe area, the place they call the Sanctuary, we will follow and intercept them when their route is quiet.'

'And should they decide they are not important enough to be taken there?' Cannick asked.

'My well-connected source assures me they are considered as crucial to political strategy. They will be taken.'

Around a score-and-a-half paces from the Emperor the hooded man moved in front of a soldier who was craning his neck in trying to see what the fuss was about and, without a hint of warning, placed both hands on the guard's breastplate, running him backwards and over the wall and grasping the spear from the man's hand as he fell with a scream that turned from shock to horror. The clamour from below attested to the horrified panic caused by the plummeting body and, as those closest turned to discover this latest disturbance, the assailant ran a few paces to launch the spear with a desperate roar at the Emperor.

The spear flew true and fast and the Emperor flinched to the side and flailed an arm in panic, knocking the weapon by nothing more than chance and deflecting it to strike the unsuspecting woman just below her chest with enough force to protrude the length of a forearm from her back and propel her to sit against the parapet. She clutched in disbelief at the wooden shaft extending from her front as her robes turned dark around it and dark-pink froth bubbled from her mouth and nose.

Shock brought a sharp silence for a moment long enough for the Emperor's nonchalant tone to be clearly heard across the terrace: 'Well, that was close.'

The guards, like their ruler, ignored the wide-eyed woman's gurgling and agonised horror and surrounded the Emperor, a group pulling him low between them while the rest turned on the source of the danger. Before the hooded man could draw another breath, arrows transfixed him. Still he stood, swaying, as a huge bearded guard ran at him with a spear, impaling him upwards from his belly and lifting him clean off his feet. As the soldier's arms bulged and the man was flung from the spear and over the wall, the hood fell back to reveal pale Northern skin and a face already bereft of life.

Brann watched from the window with the others. 'And that would be the decoy,' he said softly to himself. The cost was great. But it was paid, and hesitating would not bring back the man.

The officer commanding the soldiers at the staircase, helmet tucked under his arm to allow his orders to be clear, was already directing them at a run to the terrace, danger to the Emperor superseding all other orders. He kept back a small squad and shouted to them to help any other guards on the upper levels to sweep them for any members of the Emperor's family and escort them to the Royal Sanctuary.

'Quick,' Brann said urgently. 'To the door, now.'

As they moved, however, they caught the eye of the hook-nosed officer. 'You men,' he barked. They stopped, and Brann tensed, his left hand finding itself on the hilt of his sword, ready to start the draw for his right. 'Fetch the Northern hostages. Take them to the Sanctuary.'

'Oh,' came Marlo's low but bright voice from within his helm. 'That would be even better, no?'

'Indeed,' Brann smiled as he turned with the others to comply.

The officer turned his back to them to watch with everyone else the main part of his squad racing across the terrace towards the Emperor, and Brann's group moved immediately behind him, heading to the stairs at a hurry that both suited them and was in keeping with their adopted characters. As Hakon passed the man, a huge fist crashed into the side of the officer's unprotected and unsuspecting head. He was already unconscious as he hit the floor and Brann wasn't even sure if his neck remained intact.

A snort emanated from Hakon's helmet. 'Well, you didn't really expect me not to, did you? You have to admit, he had the sort of face that deserved it.'

Brann couldn't argue against it.

Cannick turned and gestured to Alam's slave. 'You,' he shouted. 'Lead us to the room where the hostages are kept.'

The man bowed his head in acquiescence. 'At once, sir.'

He ran to join them and led them rattling up the stairs. This was grander than their last ascent, wider, airier, decorated in style as it switched back and forth to allow royal feet a quicker trip to the terrace area should they so desire. Four levels they climbed until the slave led them onto a landing and turned down a passage. The thumping of boots and faint shouts could be heard from the floor above where the squad sent to fetch any nobles remaining in their chambers were carrying out their duties, but in the corridors of their level the silence hung heavy, broken only by the stomping of their thick soles and the clanking of their armour.

'That man who attacked the Emperor,' Cannick said. 'He had a remarkably similar build to you, young Brann.'

He thought back to the beaten figure he had seen when he had met The Triplets. 'I don't think that was coincidence.'

Hakon spoke up from behind. 'He must have known he was going to his certain death, though. Why would a man do that for us?'

'Not for you,' the slave said. 'For his family. He stole from The Triplets. He was given a choice: be taken to the roof of his home, have his belly sliced and his guts nailed to the roof and be pushed off to hang and die while he watched his family butchered before him in the street below – or do this.'

'That is no choice,' Hakon said, his voice dark.

'Nevertheless,' said Cannick, 'what everyone saw was a man of light complexion and lower-than-average height killed in the process of trying to assassinate the Emperor.

507

As the Emperor himself has publicly stated that he believes at least one of our party came here to kill him, it will be widely believed that the would-be assassin was our Brann.' He glanced at the boy. 'It does no harm in them thinking you dead. And the fear of murderous Northerners in the palace will do no harm to the confusion and panic we hope will aid our endeavours.'

Rounding a corner revealed two guards standing before a heavy wooden door, their eyes tense and anxious through the gaps in their helmets. 'What's happening?' said one, a squat dark-skinned man. 'All we hear are screams and shouts. You are the first we have seen.'

'There has been an attempt on the Emperor's life,' Cannick snapped. 'All of note are to be taken to the Sanctuary at once. We are here for the hostages.'

The man's eyes widened. 'The Emperor? Is he...?'

'He's fine,' Cannick reassured him. 'Not a scratch. But every sword is needed down there. Get yourselves there and help as you are directed.'

The men nodded. 'Of course, Sergeant. Right away.' They turned to hasten down the corridor.

'Eh, lads?' Cannick stopped them. 'The door? The keys?'

'Oh, of course, Sergeant. Sorry.' The squat one pointed to a key on a large ring, hanging from a hook an arm's length to the side of the door. 'Right there, Sergeant.'

Cannick nodded. 'Very good. Now off with you.' They left.

Breta frowned. 'I do not like this. When it is easy, I am uneasy.'

'Embrace it,' Cannick said. 'There will always be the unexpected, good or bad. It is how you take advantage of the good and how you deal with the bad that matters.'

Hakon had grabbed the key and was at the door, his

eagerness causing him to fumble at the lock. Breta snatched the key with a snort of annoyance and had the door open only shortly, Brann guessed, before the large boy would have resorted to crashing bodily through the wood. He did burst through as soon as the key was turned, however, followed closely by the others, leaving the slave at the door to keep watch.

Einarr and Konall had been standing at the window, trying to determine the cause of the uproar outside. They wheeled around at the bodies bursting through the door, instinct moving their hands to reach for non-existent swords.

Einarr's tone was frosty. 'What this time?'

Hakon's armoured bulk raced across the room and enveloped Konall in a massive hug.

The blond boy disentangled himself and pushed the crazy Imperial soldier away. 'What in hell's name are you doing? Are you mad?' If a helmet ever looked crestfallen, this was that moment.

Einarr's eyes narrowed as he looked at the build of the large boy, then at Brann. He frowned. As his gaze fell upon Cannick, the old warrior spoke urgently. 'How fare you? Can you come now? Right now?'

Shock and hope swept across Einarr's face in equal measure. 'Surely it is not,' he whispered. Then tentatively, awkwardly, as if expecting to be embarrassed by a negative answer: 'Cannick?'

The group looked at each other, realising as each saw the others that they had become so accustomed to wearing the helmets that they had forgotten they were hiding their faces. They removed the helms, the Northern three ripping them off while Breta and Marlo, as the unknowns, moved at a more normal speed.

Cannick grinned. 'How are you? In health?'

Einarr nodded. 'We have not been mistreated. A little soft from lack of exercise, but mainly just frustrated, furious and bored, as you would expect. And more than ready to leave this luxury.'

That Einarr and Konall were family was demonstrated in an instant. The elation of the meeting was quickly replaced with practicality.

'What is the plan?' Einarr pulled a hooded cloak around him and threw another to his nephew.

Every head that faced him turned to look at Brann. Einarr groaned. 'I might have known.'

Brann grinned, and told them. As he did so, he gestured to Marlo and the boy unwound a rope from around his slender waist and passed it to him. He affixed it to a heavy statue of a lion by the window and dropped it outside to dangle next to a balcony only one level above the terrace inhabited now by only the body of the Emperor's hapless erstwhile companion, the spear shaft like an empty flagpole. 'It never does any harm to direct attention in a different direction,' he finished.

Moments later they were out of the room and escorting the hostages, rope looped around their wrists in a semblance of being bound. The slave led them a different route from the one they had come. 'We will take stairs that lead closer to the entrance to the Sanctuary. And which will be further from the area they will search should they discover the rope.'

They approached the entrance to the stairwell but as Cannick started through, a rumble of heavy feet gave a moment's notice before soldiers almost collided with him. He stopped and an officer faced him, then strode forward, forcing Cannick and then the rest of his group to back up into the wide corridor. A dozen soldiers followed, forming up behind him with grim efficiency, two of them being archers who moved, one to each side, to train drawn arrows on the group. And behind them all stood Myrana and Persione.

The officer stared at them, then focused his piercing eyes on Cannick, whose own gaze settled on the insignia on the front of his breastplate, the same symbol as they had seen on the officer at the gatehouse.

'Is there a problem, captain?' Cannick said.

'You tell me.' It was a harsh voice: not in itself, but in tone. 'A time of crisis, of danger, yet a squad of Imperial soldiers is running about partly dressed?'

Brann's heart jerked. In their haste, every one of them had forgotten that their helmets were still dangled by their chin straps from their shield hands.

Cannick's expression didn't even flicker. 'I might ask you the same. The Fourth Millen guards the citadel at this time, yet you wear plumes of black and not our blue.'

A smile crossed the officer's face. A cruel smile of triumph. 'And so you are undone.' He looked at Marlo. 'You look local enough to be able to enlighten this fool.'

The boy swallowed, then spoke in a voice broken by despair. 'The black plumes are worn by the personal force of Taraloku-Bana. They enforce the will of the Master of Information,' his voice grew in strength as anger infused it, 'and the black is said to signify the time of day when then do most of their work, though it is said that it better suggests the colour a man's heart must be before he joins their ranks.' He spat savagely on the spotless floor.

The officer looked at him with disdain, before his eyes swept across the rest of the group. They stopped on Brann.

'A familiar face, is it not?' Brann stared back in silence. Without turning, the man raised a hand and flicked a perfunctory finger forward. 'Princess, if you please?'

Head held regally high, Myrana stepped forward. At the sight of her movement, and as he looked on her face, and despite all that was happening around him, Brann could not help but feel his heart beat harder.

The officer waited until she was beside him. He pointed at Brann. 'Would this be the dog who violated you, Princess? The one sent to the pits beneath?'

She stared at Brann, then spoke calmly. 'Similar, but no. Whoever this is, Captain, it is not the one of whom you speak. If it were, I would kill him myself.'

The voice was colder than ever. 'I admire your efforts, Princess, though I do not understand your motives.' She paled slightly, and looked at him, but he never removed his stare from Brann. 'But you need not worry about staining your tender hands with his blood. We shall see to that for you.'

He gestured to the archer to his right. 'Kill him.'

As the bowman adjusted his aim, Brann's knees bent to dive, but his attention was caught by Myrana as she ran at him, screaming and arms outstretched in command to the archer to hold his shot.

The arrow was loosed regardless of her instruction. Her movement carried her into the arrow's path. It struck her under her shoulder blade and at that range the power of the shot saw a third of its length burst from her chest as she fell into Brann's reaching arms, his helmet and spear dropping, forgotten.

In the same instant, uproar blasted across the hallway. Men roared and metal crashed on metal as spears were lowered and the two groups crashed together.

Brann was oblivious. He cradled the girl in his arms and she looked up at him, a smile on her lips.

'I thought I would never see your face again.' She smiled weakly. 'In my chamber... I thought I did right. I thought if I played his game I could find a way to help you. But I failed. I could not find a way. I cannot play their game.' Her voice was a whisper, and she coughed, spraying his face with gentle red drops as he leant closer. 'I failed. Do you forgive me?'

He stroked the hair from her brow. 'There was never anything to forgive. There was nothing to gain and only more pain for both of us, had you acted in any other way.'

She coughed again, and her voice was fainter. 'I thought of you every night and every day since. I want you to know that. You are in my heart.'

'And you in mine.'

She smiled. Her body tensed, then was limp in her arms as his tear dropped on her cheek. He laid her gently on the polished floor and his fingers wrapped around his spear as a coldness settled over him, awakened and familiar.

With a snarl, he rose and surged with savage speed into the chaos of blood and straining and killing. He drove his spear into the side of a man pressed against Gerens and left it there, drawing his sword and hacking it into the side of the neck of another, spraying gore over Breta who had just parried the man's sword.

The captain pushed through to face him, easy confidence in his movement and disdain in his voice. 'Time for a lesson in real fighting, boy.'

Brann's eyes drank in his frame: more than a head taller than his height and with the added reach to match it.

He thrust at Brann's unprotected head, fast but more

testing than expecting to draw blood. Brann stepped into it, deflecting the blade slightly and continuing the movement to smash his own sword, pommel first, over the man's shield and into his eye. The head was knocked back and before the man could even scream, Brann had dragged the edge of his blade across the exposed throat.

He had already turned to seek imminent danger when the body was hitting the floor. His blood-spattered companions, chests heaving and arms hanging, were standing or crouching among figures twisted in the agony and indignity of death. One black-plumed soldier remained, backing from the scene then turning to run for the stairs. 'None can tell,' Cannick yelled but Konall had already ripped a spear from a corpse and he sent it precisely between the man's shoulder blades. Gerens moved to check for life, but straightened with his knife unused.

Emotion returned to Brann in a rush and his knees almost buckled. He felt tears welling in a surge and pushed them back with his remaining strength. Gerens looked across at him in concern and Brann desperately wanted to talk to the boy, but there was not the time. He did walk to Myrana, though. Whatever happened, there would have to be time for that. Oblivious to the violence all around, Persione had walked through the mayhem to the girl and was kneeling, Myrana's head cradled in her lap, stroking the brown hair. She looked up, venom in her eyes.

'I hate you, for taking her from me twice. Once her heart, once her life. I will hate you till I die.'

Gerens stood beside him, his knife still in his hand. 'We cannot leave any to talk.'

She never took her eyes from Brann. 'I will not talk to them.'

Gerens's tone was flat. 'You say that now, but when the fear fades...'

Her eyes did now swivel to Gerens. 'Had I been fearful, would I not have run while you were all occupied? I will not talk for she was not the only one I served.' She looked back at Brann. 'We share a master.'

Brann nodded slowly. That explained much. But, 'He is not my master.'

She shrugged, as if it were of little consequence. 'Whatever you call it, our goals are the same. I shall report to him, and no other. Should you release me now, I shall run screaming appropriately below to alert them to an attack on the soldiers escorting the Princess. I can do so at a time of your suggestion, to gain you time. I need not mention that I recognised any of the attackers. You would be helmeted in any case.'

Cannick walked up behind her, his Imperial shortsword, naked and gore-smeared, in his hand. He looked over her at Brann. 'What do you think?'

Brann stared for a long moment, his mind working. 'It makes sense that she serves... *him*. If he trusts her, she will do as she says. As for the actions she proposes...' He paused, weighing his thoughts. He nodded, assuring himself he had thought it through, and looked at the girl. 'Tell them your party was attacked, but that your escort were guards of the Fourth Millen, and that your attackers were posing as Black Plumes. That will divert them further and if it causes others of these bastards any ill fortune, so much the better. Wait one hundred breaths after we leave, then go, down the steps to the terrace.'

She nodded.

'And...' His voice cracked. 'I am sorry. Truly sorry.'

She shrugged, and stared down at the Princess.

Brann turned back to the scene. His companions were cleaning weapons on the tunics of the dead and disentangling themselves from lifeless limbs. Marlo had a deep gash on his left arm, just above the bicep, and on his left thigh, and Cannick had cut strips from a corpse's tunic to bind the wounds tightly until they could be attended to properly. Breta had bent her sword against a helmet and was selecting a new one and Einarr was sitting, wiping a sword and knife on the tunic of the dead man who lay across his legs, a large pool of blood spreading away from them.

The Northern lord looked up, and pushed the body from his lap. 'We should go.'

Brann nodded. He was uncomfortable already at the delay, but the fact that they were alive and free of capture outweighed it. As Einarr stood, however, his left leg slipped from underneath him and with a scream he fell hard to the floor. Konall was the first to his side, concern clear on his face.

'Uncle, did you slip? The blood?'

It was then that they saw his leg.

A blade had cut clean through his ankle, the foot attached only by the skin that the sword had failed to reach at the far end of its cut. Einarr looked at it in surprise. 'I felt the blow, but thought the flat had hammered it. It felt just like a thump. I never realised...' He stared in shocked confusion.

Marlo retched, but Cannick was moving immediately, a strip of tunic still in his hand from tending the boy. He tied it tightly around the leg.

'That will slow the blood until it can be treated as it truly requires.'

He turned his attention to the foot. 'Let me see.' On his last word, and without warning, his knife sliced the small stretch of skin and the foot fell clear. Einarr's back arched and a groan of pain ground through clenched teeth.

Cannick grimaced. 'Apologies, old friend. It could not be saved, and I thought it better to spare you the thought of what was to come.'

Einarr smiled weakly. 'I know.'

Cannick was as practical as ever. Gerens had been sent into the nearest chamber to find a sheet, and he was binding it to two spears to form a rough stretcher. He looked up at Breta, who was hovering over him. 'Fetch belts from the dead. We will bind him to this, at his knees, waist and chest. You and Hakon have stairs to carry him down, and it would be best if he doesn't fall off.'

Cannick finished binding Einarr's ankle as best he could. 'He needs proper treatment in the near future. The very near future.'

There was a croak of a voice from the side of the wide passage and Gerens shouted, 'Chief. Another one.'

Alam's slave sat propped against the wall. Brann was first at him, and saw a knife embedded through his ribs, his hand pressed to his chest around the wound and his face pale. The man cleared his throat to try again to speak and spat blood onto the floor. 'There is a surgeon assigned to the Sanctuary. He will have the tools and skills you need.' Each word seemed an effort, but his determination to speak them was clear in every one.

Brann nodded. 'We will have you and Einarr with him immediately.'

The man shook his head. 'Not I.' He flicked his eyes down at the knife in his chest. 'My time is done. I will last until the girl brings help, so I may confirm her story, but I will manage no more. My apologies.'

Brann glanced at Cannick, who nodded his agreement with the man's diagnosis, though it did not take much expertise to do so once the knife had been seen. Brann felt the emotion rise once more. 'I will ensure he knows what you have done.'

A hint of a smile twitched at the corner of the man's mouth. 'He will know. I always serve his will.' He grimaced. 'Descend three levels, turn right into the passage, then left into one that will take you to the centre of the keep. All it leads to is a square portal that will be sealed by a stone slab lowered from the inside. Pray that it has not been dropped before you reach it. When you find the surgeon you will find the entrance to the escape tunnel, for it is behind a hinged set of shelves at the rear of his chamber.'

Brann smiled and gripped his arm. 'Thank you. For everything.'

He started to rise, but the man grasped his arm in return to stop him. 'Tychon.' Brann looked at him. 'You once wondered about my name. It is Tychon.'

Brann smiled. 'Thank you, Tychon.'

The hand released him. 'Now go. Should you die by tarrying here too long, I will not have completed my task.'

Brann nodded and rose. Einarr was strapped to the stretcher and the rest had readied themselves, this time remembering their helmets.

Gerens held up a hand. 'Wait.' He dipped his fingers in the pool of blood where Einarr had sat and, one by one, flicked and smeared it on their helms. 'Had we been wearing our helmets, the blood would have struck them and not our faces.' He finished by running his bloodied hand across his own.

Breta grunted. 'Had we been wearing our helmets, this

fight might never have happened, nor the aftermath.'

Brann knew it was a fact that would haunt him without end.

With a final nod to Tychon and a lingering stare at Myrana as Persione pointedly declined to look up, he followed Cannick into the stairwell. They worked their way down the steps, Breta at the rear of the stretcher with her hands at her waist and Hakon at the front with it on his shoulders to keep it as flat as they could manage. Marlo limped quickly and without complaint.

They reached the level they sought and hurried down the passageways. All was quiet: there had been ample time for the majority of the royal family to have reached the haven. A single pair of guards stood at the portal, staring at the blood-sprayed party who approached with a stretcher.

Cannick snapped at them. 'This man requires urgent attention. We are to take him to the royal surgeon at once.' One look at the missing foot and the guards needed no further explanation.

'Down the stairs, Sergeant, and at the bottom turn right. The left would take you to the Sanctuary proper. The surgeon is there, and will be ready as all he has had to occupy him until now has been hysterical women.'

Cannick nodded his thanks and led them through the door to wide and shallow steps that turned sharply to the right after a short flight. Footsteps sounded behind them and Brann waited until the stretcher had rounded the corner before running back to the top. He saw four soldiers approaching the door. One of them told the sentries they had been sent to help where they could.

Brann cut in. 'Good. You can watch this door. My sergeant says that you two,' he looked at the original guards, 'are to accompany us to guide us to the surgeon. Time grows short for the patient and he wants to ensure we are there as soon as we can be.'

The guard who had spoken before cocked his head with a frown. 'The directions were not complicated.'

Brann shrugged. 'I know. But, believe me, now is not the best time to disobey an order after what we've been through.'

The guard looked at his companion. The other man said, 'Why not? The door is doubly guarded with these ones now.'

They followed Brann at a run down the square spiral of the stairway, passing occasional soldiers and slaves as they went and catching Brann's group as they reached the foot of the steps. A surreptitiously raised hand signalled to them not to query the presence of the two soldiers.

'To the right,' the first one said. 'As I told you before.'

Cannick nodded. 'Good. Lead us.' As they walked, he continued conversationally. 'We were worried you would have sealed the entrance before we managed to reach it.'

The man shook his head. 'It will not be shut until it is certain it is needed. The Emperor is not convinced there is any more danger, and is not enamoured of the thought of the time it takes to raise the slab again once it has been closed. There will be two blasts of a horn from either within or without to signal danger, and we answer with a single one and drop the slab.' He looked them over. 'Had they known of the bother you have had, they might have considered doing it already. Was it much?'

Cannick grunted. 'Amateurs, that was all. I gave my report upstairs and the captain was satisfied.'

The man accepted that, obviously convinced that the quality of the Imperial soldiers would be superior to any others they would encounter.

They reached an open door and marched in without any preamble. A slightly built balding man in a simple deep-red tunic and with a thin scar down one cheek looked up.

'A patient sir,' the guard said. 'Lost a foot.'

The surgeon wasted no time. 'On the table.' He washed his hands in a basin to one side of the room, and called, 'Gnaeus!'

A bulky slave pulled aside a curtain to emerge from a second room. 'Master?' As he spoke, however, he saw Einarr on the table, and assessed the situation in an instant. The surgeon nodded briefly as the slave started to stoke a brazier and pull an assortment of shining implements from a set of drawers.

The two guards turned to go but Brann nudged Cannick and gave a slight shake of the head. 'No, wait here,' the old warrior barked, removing his helmet and wiping the sweat from his forehead. The query from both men died in its beginnings as Cannick glared at the hint of an order being questioned. 'You may remove your helmets. It is hot in here and we will hear any danger approach.' He looked round at his companions. 'All of you.'

Breta moved behind the two men, out of their line of sight, before exposing her face. If the surgeon and his slave thought anything amiss about a female soldier, they did not say. A squad of soldiers adorned with fresh blood was an intimidating sight, and in any case they had pressing work to attend to.

And it was attended to surprisingly quickly. The medical pair were clearly skilled and well practised in working together, and after a broad flat metal tool had been heated in the brazier and used to seal the end of his leg – causing Einarr to almost bite through the wooden peg placed between his teeth in his attempts not to scream – the stump was tended with deftness and assurance, an ointment was prepared and applied, and the leg was bound in fresh bandages. The slave ran eyes narrowed in appraisal over Einarr and disappeared into the side room, reappearing with two simply made but finely crafted crutches. He placed the first under the man's armpit to find it was almost a perfect fit, but was not satisfied and tried the other. Happier, he left it lying beside Einarr on the stretcher and took the other back to the store.

'Good,' the surgeon said. 'The crutch will help, but for now he will be light-headed after all he has endured and you must carry him some more. Other than that, he should be fine, though if his leg shows any signs of infection, you must seek the help of a healer as soon as you see it.'

The surgeon gestured to Marlo. 'I notice your wounds also. I will treat them.' In moments the two gashes had been inspected, washed, sewn and freshly bandaged.

Cannick had watched the treatment of both patients with close interest and moved forward to bow slightly in appreciation. 'A most impressive display of skill. And swiftly done, also.'

The man turned to wash his hands. 'My education was beside a battlefield. You learn there to be effective as quickly as possible and move on to the next.'

Cannick said, 'I have been on many a battlefield, but have seen few with your skill. It is appreciated, sir.'

The surgeon looked into the old warrior's eyes. 'I believe you have. Your appreciation is valued.'

Cannick looked pointedly at Brann and raised his eyebrows. Gerens and Breta were behind the two guards and Brann caught their eyes, resting his hand on his knife hilt and flicking his eyes at the pair of soldiers. They moved up behind the unsuspecting guards, their own knives in hand. At the last moment, Brann realised he should have been more specific. 'Alive!' he shouted.

The guards started and reached for their swords but found a blade at each of their throats. Brann's party had their weapons drawn and the slave shrank back in horror. The surgeon remained calm and watched them, and Brann faced him. 'Apologies. After the assistance you have given, you do not deserve this. But it is necessary.'

The man remained impassive. 'Unless you kill me, I have endured worse.'

'You will not be killed.' He turned to the guards. 'Nor will you, unless you resist.' He sighed. 'There has been enough death already today for there to be any more if it is not necessary.' Hakon and Breta were relieving the pair of their weapons, and Brann added, 'We also require their armour, and tunics. Or, at least, our hostages require them.'

The men were quickly stripped, much to the amusement of Breta. Konall was soon dressed as a soldier of the Empire and Cannick and Marlo helped Einarr to do likewise.

Brann said, 'The four of them, in the other room, bound, gagged and blindfolded.' He looked at Gerens. 'And alive.'

The boy's dark stare returned the look. 'You sure, Chief?'

Brann nodded, and that was all the confirmation the boy needed. As soon as the curtain was drawn again, Brann's eyes found the shelving at the back of the room. There was no catch and all it took was to pull one side towards him for the structure to swing easily on its hinges. A well-crafted passage, smooth of floor, sloped down into darkness and a collection of lanterns lay to one side. Brann nodded. It would do.

The others were readying themselves to enter it but Brann shook his head and gestured for silence. He picked up a bowl the slave had used to catch the last of Einarr's bleeding and flicked a little over Einarr and Konall as Gerens had done with the rest of them, then walked into the passage to flick the bowl hard, casting the remainder of the blood in a trail as far down the floor as he could manage. He left the shelf-door lying wide open.

He pointed to the door back the way they had come and they followed him out. Once the door to the surgeon's room was shut, he spoke as he kept walking. 'Change of plan.'

'Change of plan?' Hakon was aghast. 'Our way out of here was right there in front of us.'

'Every plan plans for failure at any stage,' Cannick said. 'I am sure young Brann has a reason. And an alternative.'

Brann nodded. 'It was when we were coming down the stairs with Hakon and Breta carrying the stretcher. I thought that we have no idea of the form the tunnel will take. It may be a perfect passage for all of its route, or it may not. I did not want to take the chance that we may not be able to take Einarr through it.'

Hakon nodded slowly. 'I can see that.'

Cannick halted the group. 'So what now?'

'Some will think the hostages left by the rope from their room. Others will have seen them come in here, but none will have seen them leave. Their only other way out will be the escape passage, which emerges near the docks.' He grinned. 'The docks are therefore cut off from us as they will swarm there with their soldiers, but the deception does allow us an alternative. We walk out of the front door of this damned citadel.'

Which they did.

As soldiers and slaves and the noble and wealthy of Sagia ran and shouted and carried and fetched and drank and cried and passed rumours and sought news, no one spared a second thought for one more troop of guards passing among them. Three great gates they passed through with no sign of an obstacle or challenge. Until they reached the fourth.

They saw the problem as soon as the gate was in view from the torchlight around it. A huge wooden problem. A portcullis.

They stopped before it, their hearts sinking. Two guards walked from the gatehouse and looked over the party with interest. There was no point in even reaching for their weapons: they would overcome the pair with ease, but to attack Imperial guards at any time, let alone during the alert of an imminent attack, would find them overwhelmed themselves from all quarters in seconds.

The guards stared at them for a long moment before one walked to Brann and, with the tip of his sword, lifted one short sleeve of his tunic higher up his arm to reveal his Dragon tattoo.

A tinny laugh came from within his helmet and he and the other soldier lifted off their helms. Grakk and Mongoose stood grinning before them.

Laughing, the group embraced as Sophaya, her uniform a little large for her, sauntered from the gatehouse, much to Gerens's obvious relief.

'How?' said Cannick.

Brann smiled. 'It always helps to have something in reserve. I was worried that we may not make it to the Sanctuary, so thought we might need to have help waiting at this gate.'

Grakk clapped Sophaya on the back. 'Our young friend here has a rather impressive way with locks, so we vacated our cell once the commotion reached a crescendo. The guards became somewhat indisposed, so we kindly finished their shift for them.'

Brann looked at the portcullis. 'What about this, though? I had planned for you to be here to ease our passage past the guards, but I had not anticipated this.'

'Worry not,' Grakk said. 'The engineering is a wonder to behold. One person may turn the wheel to raise the gate high enough to grant passage in mere moments. Mongoose, my friend. If you would?'

The girl disappeared through the doorway and almost instantly the wooden structure, each squared beam the thickness of a ship's mast, started rising.

'The gearing is a work of mechanical genius,' Grakk enthused, 'but I fear we do not have the time available for me to show you.'

Gerens grabbed Brann's arm. 'Indeed we do not.' He wheeled him around.

Around two score Imperial guards were running directly towards them, shouts of triumph carrying in the air as they spotted the group and attracting the attention of others.

Quickly they slipped under the portcullis, its looming weight palpable above them, but Brann was worried. 'We cannot outrun them with the stretcher.'

'True,' Sophaya said, before ducking back through the gateway. Sword in hand, she ran into the gatehouse and a second later the portcullis crashed to the ground with a force that left their ears ringing.

'She cut the rope,' Gerens said in horror.

'She has bought us the opportunity to get clear of them.

But only if we move now before they repair it.'

'In any case,' Brann laid a reassuring hand on Gerens's shoulder, 'high as these walls may be, I suspect she may reach the house before us.'

She did.

Brann steadied the horse beneath him, watching the dawn rise behind the capital city of the Empire. The others were quiet on their own mounts, each with their own thoughts on the events at the Emperor's palace.

Cannick cantered towards them with Breta and Mongoose in tow, completing their party. Brann was glad the two fighters had elected to travel with them; after what they had been through, it would have been hard to leave them behind, and he was sure that every sword would be vital, although Breta looked as if it would be a while before she felt comfortable on the horse that was currently bouncing her about as if she were a doll strapped to its back. At the thought of a sword, his hands dropped to his own weapons, strapped back on to his waist the instant he had entered the house. He smiled.

'All good?' he said to Cannick as the veteran reined up beside them.

The man nodded and tossed him a bundle. Brann's eyes widened as he opened up heavy black material, a neatly stitched repair near the hem. 'My father's cloak.'

Cannick smiled. 'We grabbed what we could when we fled the ship, and fortunately for you we found that among among what we had salvaged. It wasn't much use in this climate, but I knew you were partial to it and, in any case, you'll thank me for it when we reach the Northern weather.'

Brann smiled. 'I thank you for it now.' His horse whinnied and he stroked its neck comfortingly. 'What news?'

'Threefold,' Cannick said. 'Einarr has safely taken up residence with Our Lady and her daughter. He will convalesce there much more successfully than he would with us. Secondly, the Lady Cirtequine passed a report from a certain former Emperor that his own sources of information tell him of a man asking questions in several locations of your South Island about a former mill boy from the North.'

'Loku?'

The grey head shook. 'One of his men, most likely, who hasn't had the message yet that you travelled to Sagia. I expect there are others seeking you in Einarr's land also. You should take care when we return to your rain-soaked islands.'

Brann shrugged. He could expect nothing less and, given what Alam had told him, it would certainly get worse. 'And the third?'

'The reason I know it is not Loku seeking you there is that the Lady also passed the information that the man may be a dangerous plotter of evil, but he has the maritime knowledge of the Deruul. He has been delayed by the storms that plague the south coast of the continent at this time of year, and it will be some time before he can reach the point where he can turn north. Should we work it cleverly with horse and then boat, we could arrive at your islands close on his tail.'

'In that case,' smiled Brann, 'now would be a good time to start.' Clenching his fingers around his father's cloak, he touched his heels to his horse and started it forward.

He headed home.

****

They stood on his balcony. They could not see the rising sun around the corner of the building, but they could see its glow as it lightened the sky.

'It seems,' he said, 'that there was no enemy at the walls. It seems there were an army's campfires, but no army.'

'And so,' she said, 'the royal elite can return to their lives as normal. It did make for an eventful night, apparently.'

'So I hear.'

They stood in silence.

'It would have been nice, however,' he said, 'if even one of them had enquired after my welfare on our return to our chambers. It seems I am not high on their priorities. I am an insufficient asset or threat.'

She stared over the desert, and her voice was that of the sand. 'Fools.'

He smiled. A cold smile, but a smile still. 'I thank the gods that they are.'

Epilogue

The storyteller smiled. 'And so tonight's story draws to a close.'

A murmur ran around the crowd. The villagers had proven a receptive audience, and so they should, given where he was. And now they wanted more.

Which was always the perfect time to take his leave.

He swept into a low bow. 'I have more years behind me than in front, good people, and those years require me to rest. But if you permit my return on the morrow, I shall conclude our tale, for it is a tale of three parts. You have heard our hero born and you have heard him grow.

'Meet with me again to hear him rise.'

Acknowledgements

It is often said that a second book is harder than the first, but I found the opposite to be true. Hero Born was my first novel, and as such a leap into the unknown: the unknown of whether I could even write enough for a full-length book, never mind the mechanics of actually how to put the story together properly. So I launched myself into it, feeling my way and, much as Brann does in his fights, just did what felt right.

When, therefore, I sat down with this one, I had the benefit of the experience of writing Hero Born and the advantage of the lessons I had learnt from the writing process and from expert editors. And I already knew the characters and the world – it was like stepping back into a familiar place after an absence and meeting old friends who had changed not one bit since I had last seen them. So the writing flowed comparatively more easily for me this time.

But, despite this, it is safe to say that nothing would have been possible, were it not for the inspiration, expertise, support, help and advice of those near and far who had an impact beyond their awareness.

My wife, Valerie, who is my confidence and my reality check, my rock and my refuge; and my family, Martyn, Johnny, Melissa, Nicky, Adam and Nathan, who continue to inspire me, encourage me, make me laugh and fill me with wonder.

My parents, Ian and Diane, and my brother, Gordon, whose enthusiasm for my books remains unbounded, unchecked and energising; and my parents-in-law, Frank and Nan, whose relationship with me matters more to me than they can know.

To my first-two-chapter-testers, Melissa and Claire, whose approval and enthusiasm helps fire me on though the rest of the writing.

And, of course, to those professionals who made it all possible: Rachel Winterbottom, who edited with keen perception, deft skill and an unexpectedly-deep feel for the story and characters; Simon Fox, who copyedited with such an astounding eye for detail; Ben Gardiner whose evocative cover design was so perfect at the first attempt; Anne-Janine Nugent, whose publicity photos somehow manage to make me appear vaguely natural; Lily Cooper, who endures my naive questions and replies with relentless cheer; all at HarperVoyager whose work goes unseen by me but is no less appreciated for it; and, of course, Natasha Bardon, who oversees all with a touch that is as deft as it is infectiously enthusiastic and who, right back at the start, invested the faith to launch me on this incredible journey.

And all those who read Hero Born and liked it enough to move on to this book. Without you, I would just be a guy who sits in his house and makes up stories. It's an amazing feeling for those stories to move outwith my home, and I thank you for it.

Lightning Source UK Ltd.
Milton Keynes UK
UKHW040821050422
401092UK00002B/449